MARK STEYN

The Prisoner of Windsor

(after Anthony Hope)

ALSO BY MARK STEYN

Broadway Babies Say Goodnight:
Musicals Then and Now
(1997)

~

The Face of the Tiger
And Other Tales from the New War
(2002)

~

Mark Steyn from Head to Toe:
An Anatomical Anthology
(2004)

~

America Alone:
The End of the World as We Know It
(2006)

~

Mark Steyn's American Songbook
Volume I: Words, Music, Song
(2008)

~

A Song for the Season
(2008)

~

Lights Out:
Islam, Free Speech and the Twilight of the West
(2009)

~

After America
(2011)

~

The [Un]documented Mark Steyn
(2014)

MARK STEYN

The Prisoner of Windsor

(after Anthony Hope)

STOCKADE
BOOKS

Copyright © 2023 by Mark Steyn

All rights reserved. No part of this book may be reproduced or transmitted in any form or by any means, electronic or mechanical, including photocopying, recording, or by any information storage and retrieval system now known or to be invented, without permission in writing from the publisher.

This book is a work of fiction. Names, characters, places and incidents are either a product of the author's imagination or are used fictitiously. Any resemblance to actual people living or dead, events or locales is entirely coincidental.

Published in the United States by
Stockade Books
PO Box 30
Woodsville, New Hampshire 03785

Printed and bound in the Province of Québec (Canada)

ISBN 978-0-9973879-1-9

First Edition

"The difference between you and Robert," said my sister-in-law, who often (bless her!) speaks on a platform, and oftener still as if she were on one, "is that he recognises the duties of his position, and you see the opportunities of yours."

"To a man of spirit, my dear Rose," I answered, "opportunities are duties."

~Anthony Hope, *The Prisoner of Zenda* (1894)

AUTHOR'S NOTE

I had just read a kind comment from a generous listener who had belatedly discovered my audio serialisation of *The Prisoner of Zenda* – Anthony Hope's bestseller of 1894 - which led to sequels, prequels, stage plays, musical adaptations, film versions, and an entire genre of tales of fictional kingdoms that came to be known as "Ruritanian".

And immediately after that listener's comment I chanced to see a BBC news bulletin reporting on something or other in the weirdly deserted London of the Covid years, followed by a story on the Polish election. And it occurred to me, not for the first time, that life in most Eastern European capitals looked more normal than life in most Western European capitals. It is one of the odder twists of fate that, having had the lousiest twentieth century one could imagine, the far side of the Iron Curtain seems to be navigating the currents of the twenty-first rather better than the west. And so, with Sir Anthony's Ruritania still floating around the back of my mind, I wondered if today a Ruritanian wouldn't find life in London at least as fantastical as Hope's Rudolf Rassendyll found life in Strelsau.

So herewith a sequel to *The Prisoner of Zenda* set in today's England - and not just a sequel, but an inversion. Hope's romance of 1894 spawned an entire atlas of barely credible kingdoms, into which literary tradition the contemporary UK fits just fine. You don't need to have read *Zenda* to get this caper - although, if you haven't heard my serialisation, you're more than welcome to check it out. Still, I think most listeners are familiar with the basic conceit: an English gentleman visiting Ruritania is called upon to stand-in for his lookalike, the King, at his coronation. When I describe this latter-day rendering as an inversion, I mean that in this instance a Ruritanian from the House of Elphberg is called upon to return the favour and stand in for an Englishman in London.

Sir Anthony wrote two other books set in Ruritania – the famous sequel *Rupert of Hentzau* and the rather obscure prequel *The Heart of Princess Osra*. What follows draws from and alludes to all three.

New Hampshire
March 2023

I
Sport Royal

Chapter One
The Elphbergs
— with a word on the Rassendylls

"I WONDER WHEN IN the world you're going to do anything, Rudolf?" said my brother's fiancé.

Big Sig Nados, the betrothed in question, needs no introduction, being Ruritania's biggest media mogul of all time. Previously he was Europe's smallest pop star, so that is quite an improvement. In the privatisation era — or, as most of us think of it, the civil war - he bought for a very low price the remains of a state TV studio accidentally bombed by Bill Clinton. In Ruritanian terms, he had done very well, and not for the first time he was wondering when I was going to do anything at all.

"My dear Siggy," I answered, scraping off the apricot-and-sour-milk sauce the waiter had very liberally poured over my cabbage rolls and goat-stuffed potato dumplings. "Why in the world should I do anything? I have my EU-mandated welfare benefits and no talent for the drug-running, sex-slaving, money-laundering and bio-warfare that Ruritania's transnational masters have helped make our most lucrative industries."

I gave a stage sigh, and may even have pouted. Just to be clear, Sig's the gay guy, not me. But I have a modest and reflexive gift for mimicry (what little income I earn derives from it), and, not for the first time when talking to my brother's beau, my rhetorical style had become insufferably theatrical. Misreading my pout, the waiter, wandering past with a huge skillet, slapped over my defenceless dumplings a fresh slick of apricot-and-sour-milk.

We were in Sig's restaurant, of course. A great promoter of traditional Ruritanian cuisine, he had published the first post-Communist celebrity cookbook, by a homosexual soldier he marketed as "The Gay Hussar". The restaurant had borne the same name, although latterly had been discreetly re-christened "The New Hussar".

"You are an Elphberg!" intoned Sig, dramatically. "An Elphberg who does nothing?"

"In the damning words of Comrade Bauer, First Secretary of the First Congress of the First Soviet of the First People's Republic of Ruritania, my family spent hundreds of years as parasites doing nothing except living off the proletarian masses. We weren't raised to 'do' things, and it generally didn't work out well when we tried to."

I could see I was annoying my dinner companion, which was not my intention. I am the rightful King of Ruritania, and so my brother is heir to the throne. A throne that no longer exists, of course. But Big Sig was inordinately proud of his catch. As he put it, how many queens have their very own prince? My sibling didn't care for being a novelty collectible. Content to be plain old "Harry Elphberg", he resisted Siggy's entreaties to swank around as "His Royal Highness The Duke of Strelsau". There's nothing so silly as a royal house without a home, is there?

Papa was the last king. The last real king. For about twenty minutes at the end of the Second World War. Not yet out of short trousers when my grandfather was prevailed upon to abdicate, Henry the *Knabenkönig* was propped up on the throne in order to be a "unifying figure". He succeeded brilliantly. In no time at all, the whole of Ruritania was unified in its general assessment of his reign as total crap. So the Commies moved in, and the Elphbergs moved out. And we didn't move back until some years after the Iron Curtain collapsed, when my brother decided – in response to a dare from a classmate in Switzerland (an Italian prince who now runs a pizza van in Florida) – that we should return in triumph to say, "See? We told you so."

We made contact with Ruritania's monarchist movement (two nonagenarian spinsters sharing a flat on the old Königstrasse) and then the war broke out. And, by the time the "international community" took over, anybody of influence was too busy kissing up to the Yanks, the Krauts, the Brits, the Frogs, the Russkies, the Saudis, the UN, EU, Nato, the Organisation of Islamic Cooperation, the Arab League and the World Wildlife Fund (the last was something to do with environmental damage from carpet bombing) - and nobody had time to bother with us.

Until, that is, Big Sig's eyes met Harry's one morning at the McDonald's on the corner of Flaviastrasse and the Grand Boulevard.

So the nonagenarian spinsters now had a third monarchist. "Such a waste of your fine red hair and sharp, elegant nose," sighed Siggy.

"I didn't know you liked redheads." I toyed with a cabbage roll on the end of my fork in what I fancied was a teasing manner.

"You're a dying breed. They said on CNN that the last redhead will die out by the end of next century. Or maybe it was this one."

"The Elphbergs will be gone long before then. Harry and I are the last of the line. I am without issue, and you seem to be in no hurry to have children."

"Oh, you're quite wrong there," said Sig. "Harry and I desperately want kids. We've been trying for some time but without success."

"Has it occurred to you that might be because you're both men?"

He gave me a pitying look: The traditional Ruritanian homophobia was regarded as very déclassé since Sir Elton had opened the new rock arena.

Fortunately, my brother returned from the bathroom. Since the abandonment of our dreams of an Elphberg restoration, Harry had done modestly well in the nightclub business. With the help of an investment from a hedge fund managed by Hunter Biden and a pair of identical-twin Kyrgyz oligarchs, he now owned the three most fashionable post-retro clubs in Ruritania – the Big Apple in Strelsau, the Tinseltown in Hofbau, and the Windy City in Hentzau, built in the shell of the ruined cathedral.

"We've been talking about Elphberg red," said Sig. "You know the old saying about Ruritanian royalty…"

I rolled my eyes. "Can't you find him a hobby, Harry?"

Siggy ignored me. "'If he's red, he's right!' That's what they cried from the rooftops when Rudolf V rode through the streets…"

Harry sank into his chair, and dabbed some mustard on his *tarlenwurst*. "Is this the one you do the ads for?"

I affected disdain. "Oh, please! Mine's far more upmarket." And I did the voice: "*Pošhspicĕ – for those who cut the mustard…*" A few heads from adjoining tables turned, startled.

"What a waste of your talents," sniffed Siggy.

"It's a living," I said. "Well, actually, it's not. But it might lead to something. A ketchup ad. Or mayonnaise. Maybe even a low-sodium or non-fat organic condiment. That's where the big euros are."

"What does Jovanka think of that career plan?"

"Who?"

Jovanka and I were no longer together. She's an actress. Well, actually she's a lookalike for an actress. We work for the same celebrity lookalike agency in Modenstein, where I keep a small flat, in defiance of the terms of my EU post-conflict external-zone shelter allowance.

"Ah," deduced Sig. "So no more double dates with me and Harry, and you and Gwyneth Paltrow."

"Angelina Jolie," I corrected him.

You've never booked a lookalike? They're great fun. For a small fee, "Lindsay Lohan" turns up drunk at your wedding and hits on your bridesmaids, or "Mel Gibson" crashes your bar mitzvah and launches into an anti-Semitic rant, or "Miley Cyrus" interrupts your grandparents' golden wedding and twerks in her thong all through their anniversary dance. Me? Oh, I was the lookalike for the host of *Duelling with the Stars*. No, not the camp guy with the loud doublets. I was the other one, the one with the beard, the straight man. Ludwig Antheim. I didn't look that much like him, but I could do the voice brilliantly, and they just needed someone to make up the numbers for the double-act. People loved us. We'd go to weddings, and Miroslav would do round-by-round analysis, and I'd feed him little prompts about the likelihood of the bride receiving satisfaction and where the groom's duelling scar was, and off he'd go.

And so Sig, Harry and I bantered on, through dessert and cognac, about this and that - who would be the new judge on *Ruritania's Got Talent*, which group we'd draw in the Euro championships, all the important stuff. It was, as I look back on it, a magical night. After Big Sig's renovation, the New Hussar was radiant, almost like the glory days of the 'tween-wars monochrome photos lining the wall to the men's room. *Le tout* Strelsau was there – the globalist bigwigs hogging all the best tables and expensing their champagne, and the local purpose-girls hoping to catch their eye and land a ticket out, and beyond them the city's most eminent fixers and dealers, and, at the most prestigious booth, a short chubby man with a girl's name, Lindsey Graham, said to be the most powerful senator in

Washington but dining with a couple of Z-list provincial warlords. Between the tables, impeccably discreet, motored the smartest wait staff in the country, in long black neckties and stiff white aprons.

Lesser eminences came over to pay court to Big Sig – the ad man who did the commercial with the woman in a burqa and the sexy lingerie underneath; a lady who wanted to appear on *Real Housewives of Hentzau*; and the "reformed" Commie apparatchik now working for the EU's High Representative who snidely enquired if we'd been invited to the King of England's coronation...

Yeah, like that's gonna happen.

"But surely," he asked Siggy, "Silver Ship published the Ruritanian edition of King Arthur's book on climate change?"

Silver Ship Editions, named after the old Nados family smithy, was Big Sig's publishing arm and had become, thanks to a cultural heritage grant from the CIA, the leading purveyor of intellectual stimulation in Ruritania.

"We did indeed publish His Royal Highness, as he then was," said Sig. "The book about how we only had two years to save the planet."

"I missed that. When did it come out?"

"Three years ago."

We all laughed heartily. Sig always enjoyed the joke, it being his only consolation from the Arthur deal. My brother enquired why the Commie kingpin wasn't at the fashionable new EU insect restaurant. "I hear the sautéed termites are to die for."

The Euro-bigwig ignored Harry. "Why don't you get that British Prime Minister to do a book?"

"Rassendyll?" scoffed Sig. "Wanker!"

At midnight we said our farewells on the sidewalk. The streetlamps were out, and most of the adjoining businesses had closed, so the windows of the New Hussar appeared to blaze. But outside a fierce wind was howling, and toppled trash cans rattled somewhere down the block. I shivered. The glow of the evening seemed suddenly distant, and we did not linger. Turning up my collar, I kissed my brother on the cheeks. Siggy and I usually opted for the traditional Ruritanian head-bump, but I was in a sentimental mood, so I kissed him too. Turning to go, I stopped and looked back – at Harry and Sig, arm in arm, as they walked into the Lauengramplatz. And then I set off through the crisp night air to my own humble apartment.

The following morning I drove the circuitous route via the only open border post to Modenstein for a lookalike gig. A private party for some government minister. Dobromil, who ran the agency, had bad news. "You're cancelled," he said. "They called and asked for Kamala Harris, but she's doing the wet T-shirt awards, so they went with Dame Judi Dench."

"I've just driven from Strelsau…"

"I'm sorry, Rudy. But no one wants a lookalike of Ludwig Antheim. He's been off the air for a year."

There had been a shake-up at RFM and the new Head of Artisticness thought *Duelling with the Stars* needed to move with the times, and so they had replaced Ludwig with a bisexual supermodel from Moldova who was sleeping with the Minister of Culture. I could have done her voice with a bit of practice, but I looked even less of a lookalike of her than I did of Ludwig Antheim. If only I'd looked like Ryan Gosling or Ed Sheeran. The only thing sadder than being a former Modenstein celebrity is being a former lookalike of a former Modenstein celebrity.

Dobbi was sympathetic. Before starting his own agency, he'd been a Boris Yeltsin lookalike.

"Maybe I could be repositioned as a Mohammed lookalike…"

"They've got enough of those," said Dobbi, with a sour glance at the kebab shop across the street.

He fumbled among the papers on his desk, found a laminated card, and offered it to me. "By way of recompense."

"What's this?"

"A Coronation Diversity Lottery Attendance Permit. From England. They're like gold dust."

"How did you get one then?"

Dobbi reminded me of his TV sketch - when he'd played that Canadian prime minister, the one who likes blacking up. So Dobbi had blacked up and beamed: "Now I'm diverse I can go to the coronation!" And the host had punched in the online application live on air just to extend the joke – and three weeks later the card had arrived in the post.

"Take it back to Strelsau," he said. "You can sell it to a Mohammedan for big euros."

Actually, that wasn't a bad idea. So I was heading back to Strelsau when the radio announced that, due to an alert from the American "Intelligence Community", all land border crossings were closed. On the autobahn, the traffic slowed, and then ground to a halt, right by the Modenstein International Airport exit. On a whim I took it, and drove to the secure lot. I sat there for five minutes before deciding I couldn't face kicking my heels all day waiting for a lookalike booking that would never come. At the entrance to the terminal, the World Health Organisation-mandated Vaxometer was malfunctioning, but, as usual, the guard waved us through. The concourse was its customary forlorn self, but there was a lone plane out – a cut-price German airline, headed for Munich.

I had no particular desire to go to Germany, only a full-on overpowering urge to get the hell out of Modenstein. In Munich I'd hit the bars and then take the train back to Strelsau. Judging from the small throng milling around the counter, the same escape route had occurred to all other would-be high-fliers. Alas for them, there was just one problem, spelled out in blinking letters on the departure board:

All flights EU passports only.

Ah-ha! The advantage of being a dispossessed royal raised in exile! I reached into my pocket and produced the passport of the land of my birth – Spain. An hour later, I was in seat 27C enjoying a Blasebrenner. An hour after that, the pilot announced that, due to a "public health alert", the plane was being diverted to Hamburg. Please see the gate agent for connections.

Hamburg was not so congenial as Munich, and a lot less convenient for the train back to Strelsau. I settled back and fished the in-flight magazine out of the seat pocket. The cover story was about how London would be looking its best for King Arthur's coronation. That's one of the many disadvantages of being a dispossessed royal – continual reminders of what might have been. I flicked through the piece – fawning interviews with the choirmaster of Westminster Abbey, a groom at the Buckingham Palace stables… The build-up had been going on so long it had become more or less a permanent feature on the news.

It was raining in Hamburg as we taxied to the gate. Inside the terminal there were the usual slow-moving queues traditional to societies more advanced than Ruritania and Modenstein, lines of sagging humanity dribbling back and forth across the concourse, while surly guards barked instructions about making sure the QR code was on the left side of the mask for scannable digital-identity confirmation. Thousands of refugees from the Yemeni-Papuan double-mutant slothpox variant awaited reprocessing, dozing across rows of seats with rucksacks piled up all around. Body-armoured police with helmeted dogs were stopping every third or fourth passenger for "additionally enhanced screening". It was a long time since I had been in Germany, and I had forgotten how, the further west you go, the safer and slower everything gets. The departure board offered chaotic, shifting information about delays and cancellations, and in the middle the confident announcement of a lonely on-time flight to London in an hour and a quarter.

It was a combination of factors. The wasted drive from Strelsau, the blown-out booking in Modenstein, the thwarted night in Munich, the Diversity Lottery Coronation Permit in my pocket, and the dismal sense of nothing to go back to except a long, long wait for a lookalike gig as a guy who no longer looked like anyone worth looking like...

Or I could get on a flight to London.

Why not? I've been a "pretender to the throne" since my dad died. It was about time I saw how the real deal went. And it can't be worse than a rain-sodden night in Hamburg. I mentally calculated how much of my mustard money remained on the credit card, and checked in my wallet to see that my "vaccine passport" was up to date. The Ruritanian Health Ministry had run out of the vaccine a year earlier, but had not noticed because low-level officials were still issuing the passports, and in fact charging more to those with a disinclination to being injected, which was now a majority, following the sudden deaths of one-third of our European Cup team. So fake vaxports had now become the latest vital industry to the Ruritanian economy.

Mine declared that I had been boosted only last Tuesday.

Ha! I set off for the ticket counter.

CHAPTER TWO
The Great World City

IT WAS A MAXIM OF my great-uncle, the late Count of Festenburg and quite the bon vivant in his day, that no man should pass through London without spending four-and-twenty hours there. I could barely afford twenty-four hours at London prices, but I thought it time to honour his advice, by putting up at the Great British B&B – possibly not his own preferred accommodations, but all that my meagre budget could aspire to - and with an EU Quarantine Compliance rosette, too!

I confess I broke my quarantine and left my depressing hotel room after twenty minutes. On the streets of Ruritanian cities one will find Ruritanians, plus multiple "refugees" and a few globalist busybodies, and that's about it. On the streets of London are *everybody* – except, oddly, Londoners, at least as I understood them from the historical dramas Siggy imports for his subscription arts channel. Everyone appears to be from somewhere else, even if one cannot always deduce where: Was that a svelte Tongan I brushed into, or a corpulent Pushtun? Presumably, given the first coronation almost within living memory, these were inhabitants from distant parts of the Empire scraping together their savings to spend a few days in the metropolis. I walked down Tottenham Court Road through the great tide of humanity to Cool Britannia in Leicester Square and admired the Coronation mugs and Coronation hats in the window; then, after waiting half-an-hour in vain for a space to open up in the shop, I gave up and had a Coronation cappuccino at the Great British Cuppa, and afterwards dropped by Brit Happens in Piccadilly Circus to browse, again through the window only, the Coronation thongs and Coronation condoms, all of which was followed by a steaming plate of Coronation locusts from the Great British Bugger. It's no New Hussar, that's for sure.

I walked the most famous thoroughfares on earth – Piccadilly, Regent Street – amid the unceasing din of the Great World City. There was apparently a special Coronation vaccine that would protect you for up to six weeks before the big day, but some pedestrians still took the precaution of perambulating in Perspex visors and Coronation face-masks, or novelty face-masks made up to look like split-crotch panties, or social-justice face-masks that said "Brit Spring! Dump the King!" The more anxious pedestrians had faces down in their *handifons*: there was a popular app which informed you whether anyone unvaccinated was within a five-metre radius of you, and which direction to head to in order to restore one's isolation. So half the citizenry moved erratically, zigging and zagging suddenly into one's path and out again, two steps forward, one step back. I preferred to admire the celebrated red double-decker buses as they shuttled slowly between circus and square, their sides emblazoned with huge Coronation greetings from diverse groupings of loyal subjects:

Congratulations to HM The King from Pensioners Against Racism.

...from Patience: The NHS Waiting List Administrators' Union.

...from the Greater London Suicide Support Alliance.

Speaking of which, the Great British B&B had given me a voucher granting priority access to a pub in Mayfair called the George & Dragon. I had been expecting an ancient English hostelry, but it looked less authentic than the bad fake British theme-pub with the plastic beams at Strelsau Airport. Nevertheless, after donning a complimentary if complex mask-cum-personalised straw that made everyone look like an anteater, I was invited to partake of the latest fashionable cocktail, a "Suicide Belt".

"What is it?" I asked.

The barman laughed. "It's the dog's bollocks, that's what it is, bruv."

That brought back painful memories of a rough night in Hofbau. I wouldn't have thought it met UK food safety codes. But when in Rome and all that...

"Cheers!"

I was woken by children's voices, and opened my bleary eyes to find myself outside and contemplating a procession of girls and boys in English school uniform being led across the grass. In the distance, a handful of young tykes kicked a ball around a muddy patch of turf. On the path, half-a-dozen mummies stood some distance apart and idly rocked their baby buggies while yelling pleasantries. Sprawled on a bench, I became aware of an unpleasant whiff from a stain on my shirt. I also felt lighter. And then I remembered that after the second Suicide Belt I'd started talking to a girl who was with a workers' collective that was organising a "people's coronation", and, even though a "people's coronation" aroused in me about as much enthusiasm as Comrade Bauer's "people's republic", I'd had a third Suicide Belt and her sweater seemed to be getting tighter, and she said she didn't mind gingers, even bearded ones. And, just as I was thinking I needn't have bothered with a room at the Great British B&B, while I was getting a fourth Suicide Belt there was a virus raid and everybody suddenly moved very far apart. By the time I returned to the table, a friend of the girl in the tight sweater had taken my place on the banquette, and I found myself down at the end wedged up with a friend of the friend. And after the fifth Suicide Belt two friends of friends of friends of hers had very kindly accompanied me as I staggered from the pub over to Hyde Park and had helpfully suggested that they take my wallet and mobile and credit cards into their safekeeping in case there were any footpads about.

"Enjoying the view are we, sir?"

I craned my neck to find a police constable standing behind the park bench. Thank goodness. I had always heard great things about the British "bobbies", so unarmed and friendly. Bobbies on bicycles, two by two. I was aware that I couldn't really sit up straight, or talk without slurring my words, but I told him that I had had all my valuables stolen and I liked his bobby helmet.

"Do you always pick this bench, sir? In front of where the young lads like to run around?"

I said I had never been here before in my life, but had just flown in from Hamburg.

"From Europe? Grooming expedition, is it?" And he stared thoughtfully at the boys kicking a ball around. "You are aware that your trouser pockets are turned inside out, are you, sir?"

I looked down. They were indeed. I remembered my friends of friends of friends – Afrim and Bujar, I think they said – had done that when they removed my money and my mobile. For safekeeping.

"Nice game of pocket billiards while you watch the young 'uns, is that the idea?"

He pointed to a sign that said this area of the park was reserved for those participating in an exercise session. "I think we all know what you've been exercising, sir," he said.

The constable was very polite. I daresay he would have liked to have helped me report my burglary, but he was from the Royal Parks Childwatch Community Predator Response Unit's Rainbow Dance Team, on his way back from Coronation rehearsal, and it wasn't his department. He asked me for ID, and, when I repeated that it had just been stolen, he took me to the station.

The interrogation went on for some while. So it was late by the time I got back to the Great British B&B, and my small, narrow room with the barred window and the psychedelic wallpaper in purple and yellow spirals. The threadbare eiderdown sank in the middle of the bed as if the Invisible Man were taking a nap. I lay down in the indentation and joined him.

The bed screeched. I sank deeper into the thin mattress, and turned on my side. Another screech. My big toe felt the coil of a spring poking through. I carefully moved it. *Screech.* I lay perfectly still staring at the only picture in the room, a small framed print of the late Princess Fiona and the late Michael Jackson dancing together in heaven. I had not known she could moonwalk. Then I pulled myself up – *screech* - and sat on the edge of the bed – *screech* - with my knees brushing the wardrobe. An awkward position in which to ponder what I was doing here. Why would an uncrowned monarch attend another fellow's coronation? *Screech.* And then get mugged. *Screech.* And then get taken to the police station as a suspected paedophile. *Screech screech screech.*

In the entire history of monarchy, had that ever happened before?

A dispossessed king gets robbed on the eve of the other king's coronation. So now he's not just dispossessed, he's penniless, too.

What was I going to do? I settled back on my non-king-sized bed – *screech-screech-screech-screech-screech* - and imagined Mitteleuropean railway lines snaking around the ceiling stains and back to Strelsau, to screech to a halt at Flaviaplatz Terminus.

Chapter Three
The Barista of Hofbau

AND SO THE RIGHTFUL King of Ruritania became, like every other Ruritanian male in London, a Ruritanian plumber.

You know about the Ruritanian plumbers? They arrived in Britain after the international "peacekeeping" mission took over in Strelsau and botched partition. Having helped wreck the country, the UK very sportingly said they would be willing to take in those fleeing the west's efforts at Ruritanian nation-building. They assumed my compatriots, having no reputation for any marketable skills, would merely add to the diversity of the welfare rolls, as had the Somalis and Afghans. Instead, within a few months of arrival the Ruritanians had taken over much of the home-improvement business. (We had gotten competent at remodelling after Nato's errant smart-bombs destroyed so much of our cities.)

My own plumbing career began the morning after my robbery. I had gone to bed, as you might imagine, somewhat distraught. When I finally dozed off, it was a very deep sleep, and I dreamed of the coronation. Not in London, but in Strelsau, with me as the king. I had had this dream many times. My sword was in its scabbard, the Red Rose of Ruritania was pinned to my breast, and the gnarled denizens of the Old Town filled the streets to cheer the restoration. On the broad steps of the cathedral, the finest oak doors in Europe opened to receive me, and from within came the mighty chords of the organ playing the coronation anthem. I passed through the nobility and the hussars and pages and up to the great nave where the Cardinal Archbishop and the Chancellor of the Kingdom awaited. The Chancellor knelt before me in flowing robes and lifted his head. And then, in a departure from the usual script, I saw that he was the police officer from London's Royal Parks Childwatch Community Predator Response Unit Rainbow Dance Team and he'd had another complaint about me.

I awoke drenched in sweat and too late for the self-serve buffet breakfast, but the Great British B&B graciously agreed to let me sit in the Hospitable Lounge and make myself an instant coffee. On the television news, a canine puppet was in trouble for something he'd said in his one-dog show live on stage in Leicester. Leicester is in the same county as a backbench Member of Parliament whose manor house had been permanently occupied by gypsies or, as they say in Britain, "travellers". The canine in question, Colin Corgi, came out and quipped that he'd gone back to his dressing room at intermission and found it had been occupied by Rover the Roma. I thought that was pretty funny myself, but Rock Against Romaphobia had filed a complaint under the Race Relations Act.

I trudged upstairs and considered my predicament. The only money I had left was on the nightstand, and I only had that because British coins are lumpy and heavy and odd shapes, so, if you break a five-pound note at the airport and another at Paddington Station, you're already walking with a limp. So I had taken some of my change and put it on the table before I went out yesterday, and I was very happy to see it when I returned to my room penniless. After adding up the "50 pees" and "20 pees" and "two pees", I was delighted to find I had £6.43.

My stomach growled. So I put on my complimentary mask and ambled up the deserted street past greengrocers and newsagents and *handifon* shops and discount electronic outlets and more *handifon* shops, and then finally I saw it:

Omdurman Street Fish Bar

– and, underneath, the words in peeling paint:

Frying Tonight – and Every Night!

I pushed open the dust-clouded glass door and found myself in a dingy room of wooden chairs at small square tables. Above them a strip light flickered fitfully from blotchy red ceiling tiles.

But the counter didn't seem to fit. It looked like a bad Modenstein version of an American fast-food chain – a purple and orange plastic display case in front of an espresso machine. Leaning sideways against the counter was a sign saying "Big Tex Diner".

"Fish'n'chips, please," I requested, tentatively.

"No," declared the proprietor, with an oddly familiar lugubriousness. "The last fish'n'chips was sold on Thursday. We are now Big Tex. I put the sign up later."

"I thought the Cockney working man loved his fish'n'chips."

"He does. But there is only one of him left. And the Romanians and Bangladeshis and Sudanese don't. So I troy something diffuhrunt before I go even broker than I omm. Now we are Big Tex Diner."

I considered the menu.

"One Lone Star Croissant, and a coffee, please."

"You want flavour? Caramel, maple, peppermint, caramel-peppermint…"

"Just coffee. Regular coffee. Black."

"Seex pounds and 37 pee, pliz."

I should have checked the prices.

The guy behind the register was about my age, with dark greasy hair, fleshy lips, black eyes, a nose like a Hofbau dumpling, and a strong whiff of Turkish cigarettes. Notwithstanding the best efforts of his gaudy orange tunic and jaunty purple hat, there is no mistaking the squat stock of the sturdy Ruritanian peasantry. Sad. A woodsman of the Zenda forest reducing to selling caramel-peppermint macchiatos.

"Would I be right," I ventured, "in detecting a slight accent? You're not by any chance …Ruritanian?"

"You taking the peezz?" he answered. "Ovrywon in London Ruritanian." He pointed at the only other customer, also a man with dark greasy hair, black eyes, and a Hofbau dumpling of a nose. It was like a Strakencz High School reunion in here.

The other bloke looked up from his mobile. "Ruritanian? Fonny. You don't look Ruritanian. Maybe it's the beard. You're not a Zendak, are you?" he said suspiciously. "Pipple will think you're Mozzie."

I'd thought my Ludwig Antheim cut was a little neater than that, but maybe it needed a trim.

I sat down at a nearby table. "At last," the hitherto lone customer declaimed to the barista, "I hof someone to social distance from!" – and they both laughed. Then he asked me what I did in London. So I said I was here on holiday.

More laughs. "Otho, we have truly historic first!" exclaimed my fellow patron. "The only Ruritanian to come to England for holiday!"

"I give you complimentary refill!" said the barista. Both men appeared to have difficulty grappling with the concept: A Ruritanian in London for pleasure? If you weren't painting or plumbing or plastering, or whooshing up hazelnut lattes, why would you be here? For my hardworking compatriots, it was good money. And you didn't have to be that hardworking up against the local competition, who were, I was informed, uniformly shoddy, lethargic, unreliable and expensive. "The first woman I worked for," recalled Otho's customer, "told me that English workers never finish any job on time, except when they have sex inside you and then they finish early! Pretty fonny, no?"

"Yeah," said Otho. "Like the Brit birds say: Once you go Ruritanian, you won't be complainian'."

The other man stuck out his hand — but Otho the barista glanced through the door and discreetly shook his head. So I withdrew my own arm. "The name's Ladislas," he said. "But in England everyone calls me Laddie, like in the mags."

"Rudy," I offered. And then, throwing caution to the wind, we did the traditional Ruritanian head-bump. It felt good. Laddie explained that Otho used to work for him but had always dreamed of running his own café. He'd named it the Big Tex because he'd noticed the most popular nightclub in Hofbau was called Tinseltown, and he'd been to one in Strelsau called the Big Apple. Amazing.

Then I tried my croissant.

I like a croissant now and then, I really do — breaking off the tips and then, while just a little butter is melting into the pastry, scooping up the stray flakes and eating them first. But no flakes fell from Otho's "Lone Star Croissant". It was rubbery, with peanut butter and pepperoni in the middle.

I took a second nibble to be polite, and considered my situation. I now had precisely sixpence to my name.

"If you're not finishing..," said Laddie, sliding his hand toward my Lone Star Croissant.

"By all means."

When a man has broken croissant with his fellow, each can be honest with the other. So I took a deep breath and asked Laddie if he had any work.

And that's how I came to meet Lady Belinda Featherly.

"She is a high-class bird," he warned. "So don't try to *bumsen* her. Plenty of other English girls for that. Not like Strelsau. Lady Belinda is on the telly. *Two Oiks and a Toff.* Or *Two Toffs and an Oik.* She is the posh totty. It's crap, but she is almost famous, like a lot of London people. Also she is second banana to a dog."

"What does that mean?" I asked. Sig says the westerners invent these new positions, and we don't get them in Ruritania until years later. So I didn't want to appear unsophisticated if a London girl asked me to do it to her.

"I don't know what it means," said Ladislas. "Somebody said it on the radio this morning."

Laddie had been doing some emergency painting work for her. She had needed the colour in her study changed urgently from Limpid to Ellipsis. There had been an English plumber working there, but a problem had arisen and she had enquired if Laddie knew anyone. "Are you a licensed plumber?" he asked.

"Only in Modenstein," I lied.

He laughed, and went to his van to get me a tool belt and some parts.

The Big Tex fancied itself an "Internet café", which meant it had two grubby computer terminals that, with a swipe of your credit card and an arm and a leg, would connect you to the world via Windows 98. So I persuaded Otho to let me have fifteen minutes on account and wedged myself behind the desktop. The first order of business, my *handifon* being stolen, was to check my email. Aside from my brother inquiring whether I'd seduced any Windsor princesses yet, it was just the usual Viagra spam, virus cures, vaccine cures, and dictators' widows. The relict of the late General Secretary Bauer of the Ruritanian People's Republic had thoughtfully written to advise me that she had 42 million euros retrieved from his personal safe in Zenda Castle and needed to transfer it out of the country immediately.

I Googled the infomercial on do-it-yourself plumbing I'd voiced for Siggy's company after all the Ruritanian plumbers had moved to Britain. For some reason YouTube had marked it as hate speech violating community standards, but I found another video on the same theme and it all seemed simple enough. Laddie returned with a tool belt, and told me I was ill-advised to go on Otho's computer. "It will put gay porn in your QAnon feed," he cautioned.

Otho scoffed. "You wish!"

Laddie instructed me to be at Lady Belinda's address in South Kensington at five o'clock. "She never hears the door bell," he said, "so call her on her mobile when you get there." Halfway there, I remembered that I didn't have a mobile to call her on her mobile on. In the Kingdom of the Mobile, I was the only man without, thanks to those Hyde Park ne'er-do-wells. So I would have to use a famous red telephone box. They were on all the postcards, but not so much in the streets. Some had been converted into defibrillator stations, others into vaccibooths that sprayed the new booster on you and told you your temperature. A few were now works of "art": On top of one phone box, a model of the Great British Lion reclined pawing at a tree branch above; in another, a sooty-faced Dickensian chimney sweep had pushed his brush up through the ceiling. There were a few red boxes without novelty jungle beasts or antiseptic nozzles, but, in accordance with ancient tradition, they functioned mainly as public urinals and bulletin boards for the faded business cards of long-established prostitutes, so long-established indeed that one Russian lady promised her clients "the ultimate Soviet union".

Funny. If there were any Ruritanian prostitutes, they could promise you the ultimate Ruritanian pipe fitting! In between the art phone booths and the defibrillator phone booths and the urinal phone booths, I passed pedestals where the statues had been conveniently removed and the empty plinths converted into mobile chargers. I missed my *handifon*.

But eventually I found a red box with a telephone that actually worked, and so I dialled the almost famous Lady Belinda Featherly.

"Hair-*lair*," said the voice at the other end, which I deduced was either a high-class English "dolly bird"'s way of saying hello, or alternatively the name of an expensive South Kensington *Friseursalon*.

"Lady Belinda? It's Rudy Elphberg."

"Who?"

"Rudy Elphberg."

"I'm sorry, but we don't support Jewish charities."

"No, no," I said. "I'm the Ruritanian plumber. From Laddie. I will be outside your door in two minutes."

"Oh, bliss!"

Lady Belinda's street was not as crowded as the famous shopping thoroughfares: Coming toward me was an elderly couple, but they clutched their visors and crossed the road. It was a very expensive address, I inferred. Fresh white exteriors, all newly painted. You could see your reflection in the gloss of front doors and the polish of brass letterboxes and the gilded trim of ornate lamp-posts. Luxury cars were jammed together along the sidewalk, barely a centimetre apart. All the homes were worth millions of pounds, but, as I proceeded along, they became ever more squeezed together, and many were very peculiar shapes. One was a lock-up garage that had been converted into a "studio residence", with big French windows where the roll-down metal door had been and a "roof terrace" on top. If you sold the Royal Palace in Strelsau with all its gardens, you might be able to afford a concrete storage locker in South Kensington!

Just beyond the garage was a handsome Georgian town house drooping wisteria. I was about to knock when the door opened, and there stood a lithe and leggy figure with hands on hips in clinging Hentzau pants - or Capri pants, as the English say. She had a loose-fitting shirt knotted at the waist, glossy chestnut locks pushed back by a hairband, and honey-gold skin that radiated good health and foreign travel to destinations more desirable than most of her countrymen could now access. "Oh, take that silly mask off," she said. "I'm old enough to remember when the only chap who wore a surgical mask in public was Michael Jackson, and look how that worked out..."

I unlooped my "Laddie's Working" facial covering, much to my relief as it had a faint but persistent smell of cabbage. Lady Belinda seemed about to say something else tart and withering, but instead she froze, open-mouthed.

"Hello," I offered.

Her ladyship recoiled, and cocked her head. "Who *are* you?" she said accusingly.

"I'm Rudy. Rudy Elphberg. The Ruritanian plumber."

"The Ruritanian plumber? Why, I'm agog!"

"It suits you," I said, and made a note to remember the expression.

"No, I mean, it's extraordinary. You're the spitting…"

"No, you're the spitting!" I chortled, and flashed my best smile. There was far more English in England than I had expected.

She waved me inside, and I trotted behind her clacking heels down the marbled floor of a narrow hall lined with landscapes of the rustic England I had yet to visit. Like her street, she exuded a glossy style and meticulous upkeep. "I'm just back from my trainer," she said.

"What is he training you for?" I asked, to be polite.

"The 2,000 guineas at Newmarket, I think." She had a wry smile, twinkly almond eyes, and lips that appeared to have been sculpted into a permanent semi-amused expression. "Sorry about all the calling-first nonsense. We converted the attic for my office and I can't hear the bell for toffee. This way!" She led me up the stairs. "In this street, you can only go up or down: lofts and basements. You should see what they've done at that ghastly garage conversion. It's like Tora Bora down there. So we've got floors galore with only one room apiece. Up and down, up and down, all day long," she said. We set off up another flight of stairs. "We really should put a lift in, but then there'd be no room for any rooms." At the next landing she showed me into a petite but handsomely appointed study with a mahogany desk, an intricate Persian carpet, and nineteenth-century seascapes too big for the space, plus one nude on a sofa, done like a bad Modigliani.

"That's me, if you're wondering," said Lady Belinda. "Birthday present for George yonks back. God knows what I was thinking. Fortunately, Dirk was hopeless at faces, and gave me knockers that could stop a train, so no one can tell it's yours truly. George is frightfully loyal to it, if you're thinking of making an offer."

I gathered George was the husband and this was his study.

"He flies back late tonight, and this is the problem." She opened a narrow door to the side of his desk. "*Voilà!* The loo *de monsieur.*"

It was a small room with a sink and toilet, but the floorboards to the side of the cistern had been removed and in the hole there was a piece of pipe missing and a kitchen pan positioned uncertainly on top of the insulation with some faintly discoloured liquid in it.

"All my fault," she said. "I'm doing a piece for the *Telegraph* on how the whole Ruritanian-plumber craze is overblown, and in fact the good old British plumber is much better and very reasonably priced.

THE PRISONER OF WINDSOR

No offence." She contemplated the gap where the pipe should have been. "Not sure I really believe that, but it's contrarian, isn't it? So I hired an English plumber to test my theory. Reg. Can't go wrong with a Reg, can you? But at four o'clock on the Friday he downed tools and left. Said he'd be back on Tuesday – it was Spring Bank Holiday weekend, and he had an emergency job in Marbella. And I said, 'But there's just one piece of pipe left to do. Couldn't you stay an extra half-hour and put it in?' And he said he couldn't, he had a plane to catch. And, of course, come Tuesday not a Reg in sight. And now I can't get hold of him, and George will go ballistic if it's like this when he gets back. He can't stand it when I use the house for my *Telegraph* experiments." She clutched my arm, and leaned in close, nose to nose. "Could you be an angel?"

I said I could.

"Oh, bliss! I have the most gruesome dinner guests coming tonight. George was supposed to be back in time, but he's let me down as usual. He should be an English plumber."

I got to work. Reg had left the missing pieces piled in the corner. White pipe, an elbow to the main exterior pipe, and two floorboards. I examined Laddie's tool belt. It had everything I needed - except one small thing: pipe cement – to glue the new bit to the old. But where would I find it in this part of South Kensington? I had seen brasseries and boutiques and real estate agents and *handifon* shops. But no hardware stores. So I went back into George's study. On the credenza behind his desk he had a model ship. In the third drawer down, I found a tube of Organic Superglue.

Taking the Superglue into the super loo I got to work. Compared to getting robbed and being investigated by the dancers of the Royal Parks paedophile police, it was very relaxing. Time passed.

"Belinda! You in here?" I looked over my shoulder to find a dishevelled man with a chaotic mop of blond hair and a crumpled pinstripe suit had entered the study. "Can never remember which floor the so-called reception rooms are on in this bloody house. Highest drawing room in South Ken."

He glanced down at me on my knees in front of the toilet. "You're new in town, aren't you?"

"How can you tell?" I instinctively reached over to the sink for my mask, and fingered it nervously.

"That awful beard," he said. "I got rid of the face fungus when I was kicked out of Honkers. The English are notoriously pogonophobic."

"Pardon?"

"Beard haters. You can't be homophobic or Islamophobic or Europhobic, so they were forced back on pogonophobia. The last acceptable hatred. Except for Muslim beards. Or a teeny-weeny gay one. But then, between the Mohammedans and the pillow-biters, there was a lot of hirsuteness about. So the pogonophobia declined, except as a sub-phobia of gingerphobia. If you're a bearded ginger, you're buggerooed every which way. Pogonogingerphobia everywhere you turn. I'd buy a razor if I were you. Unless you're gay or Muslim. Are you? Harder to spot than it used to be." He reached over George's desk, opened a tin of Quality Street toffees sitting on the blotter, and popped one in his mouth.

"Rupert!" Lady Belinda floated in, having changed for dinner. It was a simple blue number, but the sleeves were different on each arm, and the blue was an alluringly deep eggshell that you wanted to dive in, and the neckline was low with a rope of pearls resting on her breasts.

Her guest flopped down in George's chair. "Give me five mins, Blinnders, old girl. My poor ticker can't take another seven flights of stairs."

Lady Belinda perched on the side of the desk, and her dress slid up her thigh. For a moment, I felt dizzy – the dangers of plumbing on an empty stomach. "I see you've met my Ruritanian super-plumber." I hammered the first floorboard back into place. "I say," she marvelled. "You're cracking on, aren't you? Not like Reg."

Rupert rummaged in the Quality Street tin, produced a gilded delicacy and peered at it suspiciously. "The toffee penny is going the way of the real one," he said. "Smaller every year." He wiped a chocolate smear from his lip, and stood up. "Right! That's enough dawdling at base camp. Bring the oxygen, and let's head for the summit, Sherpa Featherly. We'll leave the bearded yeti to guard the bog." Lady Belinda followed, and the blue of her dress shimmered on the curve of her hips.

I worked on, finished up, and cleaned around the work area. Ladislas had said that was what he'd noticed about British workers:

They never swept up at the end of the day; they would leave black thumb prints on the rim of the toilet, that sort of thing. So I wiped down the boards and the cistern, and I sneaked her husband's tube of Organic Superglue back into the drawer.

Then, following the chink of glasses and the burble of cocktail chatter, I climbed the stairs. Everyone was talking very loudly, their Prada and Dolce & Gabbana face masks unlooped and dangling. Through the hubbub and the crush, I heard Lady Belinda yelling, "That mutt is indestructible", and suddenly there was Rupert's beaming ruddy mask-less face, inches from mine. "It's your hairy ginger, Blinnders," he announced. "Come and have a drink."

Thanks to Rupert, all conversation ceased, and a pathway cleared to the centre. With as much dignity as I could muster, I said, "I have finished my work on your loo, Lady Belinda."

"See?" she informed the room at large. "Didn't I tell you he was marvellous?"

They all smiled at me, as if at a child.

"Well, thanks awf'lly. Renata will show you out."

I stood there awkwardly.

It was Rupert who broke the silence. "If I know our Ruritanian friends, I think he wants his dosh. A few groats for quaffing and wenching, eh?"

"Oh, I am a billy," said Belinda.

We headed down to the ground floor, and behind us, instantly, the burble resumed. Lady Belinda disappeared into a room off the hall and emerged with a handful of banknotes. *Yes!* She opened the front door, and I stepped out into a cool London evening.

"Thanks again, Mister Ruritanian Life-Saver."

"Rudy Elphberg," I said.

"I remember your name," she replied. "I'm good at that." She leaned in close again, and her perfume was all around. "But you are a life-saver."

"Well, goodbye," I said.

She had already lost interest and was returning to her guests.

Chapter Four
Concerning the colour of men's hair

HAVING INTRUDED on Lady Belinda's cocktails, I was in the mood for some convivial social interaction of my own. In the Great British B&B telly lounge the only company was a buxom lady dressed several decades too young for her years and her two daughters, both approaching middle age but favouring the garb of teenagers. They were loud and raucous, and enjoying a programme about an East Anglia sperm-donor clinic specialising in seed from celebrity lookalikes – so you could design your baby to resemble Russell Brand, or Jamie Topham, or someone from Radiohead. I cursed my luck. The chances of any viewers wanting their child to look like a former co-host of Modenstein's formerly top-rated *Duelling with the Stars* were slim.

Afterwards the BBC announced, "And now a statement from the Prime Minister." My telly lounge companions jeered "Leave it aht!" and "Wanker!" and set to chattering among themselves. An unctuous man, like an aristocrat straining to play a regular bloke, blinked into the autocue and began to read:

> *Good evening. As Britons prepare to celebrate the bright dawn of a new Arthurian era, three recent events have cast a pall over this time of joy and celebration. And I would be remiss in my duties as our new king's first...*

And so I got my first view of the Right Honourable Robert Rassendyll – whose face I had known my entire life. Watching the Prime Minister on TV was like looking in the mirror – if I'd had a magical fairy mirror that instantly puts you in a suit and tie.

The younger of the two daughters shot a glance my way. "You should go in for that celebrity sperm thing," she said. "'Cept for the beard, you look more like Rassendyll than that Justin Bieber lookalike looked like Bieb."

She was a cheerful curvaceous wench whose bosom wobbled when she laughed. And so it wobbled away as the Prime Minister twittered on about sharing the concerns of those camped out at Westminster Abbey about rising inequality, about venal men – "and it's usually men," he added - who make little contribution, yet seem to enjoy all the spoils.

> *...chose to commit ourselves to a life of public service have little sympathy for those who chose the path of private greed. Before the police made their regrettable intervention, I, like many of your fellow Britons, found myself watching the so-called people's coronation and wondering, 'Why, oh, why can't we incorporate some of these ideas in the real coronation?' I say to the leaders of this movement that I am ready to meet with you in Downing...*

"When's *Outed, Innit?* coming on?" asked the mother.

"Soon as 'e's finished nattering," said the older daughter.

Her sister nudged me in the ribs. "Prefer this Rassendyll 'ere. The strong, silent type."

On TV, the Prime Minister was announcing the appointment of a retired judge to head a Royal Commission to investigate systemic disinformation spread by fake news sites.

"Rassendyll's like you - red as a fox," the younger daughter said to me. "But not so hairy..." She tossed her head at her sister's reproving face. The Prime Minister had moved on to something about how the government and "our European friends and partners" were about to start negotiations about bringing an end to negotiations, if I heard correctly. Rassendyll smiled, and then adopted a furrowed brow. A boy had brought something called a "Coronation Teasmade" to school, only to have it mistaken for a bomb by his teacher, who was now being prosecuted for Islamophobia. The girls' mother looked from Rassendyll to me. "Gingers were bad luck in my day," muttered the old lady. "Trouble."

> *...in a very real sense an alarm clock for Britain...*

Rassendyll furrowed his brow again and clamped his fist on the desk.

My cheery damsel tossed her head and snuggled in closer to me. "I like a man 'oo's trouble." She giggled, and her bosom wobbled.

The Prime Minister cleared his throat, and moved on to "the tragic events in Sudan", which were something to do with an English novelist's book-signing. He'd accidentally autographed a Koran that some fan had put down on the table while fishing out his copy of the novel. The poor bestselling author had made things worse by offering to cross his own name out and write in "Mohammed":

Let me say straightaway that I am...

There was another wobble from milady's bosom.

...passionately...

Wobble.

...one hundred per cent...

Wobble.

...committed to free speech. I live it, breathe it, I would die for it. But there is a balance we need to strike, between freedom and responsibility. The freedom to speak goes hand in hand with the responsibility not to speak — when to do so would outrage our friends and...

"Maybe they've cancelled *Outed, Innit?*" said the old lady.

...gratuitously inflammatory. This is nothing to do with Islam. For example, people are certainly free to dispute the scientific consensus on climate...

"Nah, it's comin'. 'Old yer 'orse."

...loftiest ideals no favours when we defend the right to be insensitive...

"Maybe yer right. Maybe this is instead of *Outed, Innit?*"

...strengthen protections for minorities, and to that end I'll be inviting Sir Mohammed...

On screen, Rassendyll concluded by boldly declaring that there was no right to shout "Fire!" in a crowded theatre.

"I didn't fink they 'ad crowded theatres anymore," said the older daughter.

"Bet it's that one where we saw the hypnotist from *X Factor*. That place was a deathtrap. D'you see 'ow many were in the Ladies? Ignoring all the rectangles…"

The Prime Minister signed off, and we settled in for *Outed, Innit?*, a reality show in which a notoriously heterosexual Brit has to spend a week as a gay man.

"I bid you good night, ladies," said I upon its conclusion. "And thank you for your pleasant conversation."

With a slight bow I turned to the door. The younger daughter ran to follow, and I let her precede me up the stairs. "There's no pleasing Mam when it comes to gingers," she apologised, accompanied by her idea of a coquettish glance. "But I like yours - Rassendyll red. Long as it's a natural red, if you get what I mean."

"You're very sweet," said I, flipping the wall light and waiting for its spectral glow, "considering colour in a man is a matter of no more moment than that!" I snapped my fingers theatrically and gave her a chaste peck on the cheek.

"You talk funny. You're not gay or nuffink, are you?"

As I was shortly to discover, colour is sometimes of considerable moment to a man.

CHAPTER FIVE

Sport of Kings

THE FOLLOWING MORNING, back at the Big Tex Diner, I paid Ladislas his commission, returned the tool belt, and raised the possibility of more work. Unfortunately, he was in a bad mood. His application for a Minority Business Diversity Development Grant had been rejected because "Ruritanian" was not a recognized "ethnic or sexual identity". The latter rankled especially. He complained bitterly until interrupted by his *handifon*. Lady Belinda urgently needed to speak to her Ruritanian super-plumber.

"This is Rudy..."

"I know," she interrupted, "Mister Ruritanian Life-Saver. Are you free today?"

"Let me consult my diary," I replied, and noisily thumbed a flyer from Camden Borough Council explaining the revised pictograms for variant-compliant recycling bins. "I have a big job in Easterly Kensington, but perhaps it will not take too long."

"I've got the most frightful emergency," she said. "Gents' loo at my tennis club. Royal Chewton."

"Is Royal Chewton near your home in Southern Kensington?"

"No, darling. Halfway down the M4. It's real tennis. Do you play real tennis in Ruritania?"

"I play real good tennis," said I.

She shrieked with laughter. "So can you? Save our gents? I'm tearing my hair. Our usual plumbers are at the new prison, reorienting all the loos that face Mecca. Typical Derek Detchard cock-up."

I did not follow all of this, but I said that, sadly, I had no car. She assured me that her assistant and her nephew would be driving down to Somerset, and could give me a lift.

Well, I needed the money, and the motor journey with British people would help get my English back in shape. I liked Laddie and Otho, but, if I spent much more time at the Big Tex, I'd be talking like them, the *wonkers*. Ha.

So I said yes – and twenty minutes later I climbed into the back of a small car behind a young couple I recognised from Lady Belinda's party: one of those English chappies with the careless floppy hair and natural confidence of his class, and at the steering wheel a glossy-haired dark-eyed girl in a distractingly tight mauve T-shirt and tan culottes. The latter's hand waved over the seat. "I'm Belinda's PA. Osra. And he's the nephew, Lord Hugh Culverhouse. But you can call him Lord Hugh." And they both giggled.

"Osra? Are you Ruritanian?"

"I'm British," she said firmly. "I was born in Zenda. My dad died in the civil war, and my mum married my stepdad."

"I'm sorry to hear that."

"Not as sorry as I am," said Lord Hugh. They tittered conspiratorially.

"Is your stepdad Ruritanian?"

"He's Albanian," she said.

"Oh. Interesting."

"That's not the word I'd use," said Lord Hugh. And they giggled again.

I didn't know they had Zendaks in London. There were no Muslims in Strelsau until after the First World War when, courtesy of the Versailles Treaty, in the heady rush of so-called Greater Ruritania, we gobbled up a bit more of the adjoining Habsburg and Ottoman real estate than we could handle. In turn, the Nazis and the Soviets gobbled up the choicer bits from us a few years later. The old Zendaks and Ruritanians had got along fine: Lapsed Catholics and lapsed Muslims, they married each other's sisters and drank each other's health. Then the war came, and the Saudis and Iranians started throwing the cash around and competing as to who could build the bigger mosques. I still remember the first time I heard, in a Hentzau café, one fellow say to another, "*Salaam Aleichem*". Where had that come from? Then came the Pentagon's latest Arabian fiasco, and the German and Austrian governments closed their borders to "refugees" - and by the time Ruritania's transnational administrators thought to do the same a multitude of implacable young men were occupying every town from Zenda to Hofbau. Hence all the beards.

We headed west, where the roads widened and the handsome architecture yielded to modern office blocks and shopping centres with rain-streaked concrete walkways. "Those Coronation decorations are

31

pretty nice," I said. They loomed every few metres. Tall poles topped by attractive gold crowns.

"Security cameras," replied Osra. "To celebrate the new reign, they commissioned state-of-the-art CCTV in the shape of the Tudor Crown. See the jewelled cross pattée surmounting the arches?"

"Wow. You know your crowns."

"Belinda did a feature for *Sorted!* Inside the cross is a laser thermometer, and a wireless radio transmitter linking each camera to central control."

"They like them so much," said Lord Hugh, "they advertise them." He pointed to the posters on alternate street lamps: "Easy Lie the Heads Watched by the Crown." Underneath the slogan was a little anthropomorphised Tudor Crown shining its spotlight on some barefaced blackguard as loyal law-abiding subjects in Union Jack face masks looked on: "Have A Safe Coronation! from Hammersmith & Fulham Council."

"The new bollards," said Osra, "can detect whether you're carrying liquid nitrogen or fertiliser." She pointed to a row of waist-high black metal posts lining the pavement. "Lot of false positives, though."

"Do a lot of Londoners walk around with fertiliser?" I asked, wondering if my English was a little rusty. As to the watched heads, they were tricky to watch: The streets were crowded here, and there were more women in hijabs than in Zenda, although on closer inspection half of them turned out to be sullen teenage boys in hooded sweatshirts with thin furtive eyes peering out from above their masks.

"Big day tomorrow," I offered. "The Coronation and all."

"What are you on about?" said Hugh. "That's not for a month."

I pulled out my Coronation Diversity Lottery Attendance Permit, which stated clearly "5th June", and passed it to Osra.

She snorted. "That has to be one of the worse fakes I've seen. Everyone knows it's 5th July."

"Birthday of the NHS," added Lord Hugh. "What other day would you schedule a coronation for?"

I slumped back in my seat. I'd come to England for nothing: Even if I could afford to hang around at the Great British B&B, I had a fake permit that wouldn't get me anywhere near the celebrations. I'd never see King Arthur.

We drove on in silence awhile, and then, just to break it, I said: "So we're going to a tennis club?"

Lord Hugh corrected me. "A *real* tennis club."

I had no idea what he was talking about.

"Every year," said Osra, "when they can't think of anything else for Belinda to do, some or other BBC producer says, 'I know, let's do a feature on real tennis!' And because they're all on three-month contracts so the Beeb doesn't have to put them on the pension plan, nobody remembers that she did it the previous summer. But the real tennis people do. So when Royal Chewton asked if she'd be on the events committee, she felt she had to say yes."

"Sport of kings," chipped in Lord Hugh. "Henry VIII played it."

Sport of kings. No wonder I knew nothing about it.

"Belinda seemed to think you were an old hand," said Osra. "I'm hopeless. Makes a change to have someone who knows a railroad from a giraffe."

On the radio a reporter was talking about Brussels' proposed treaty amendment on diluting the amendment on qualified recognition. So Osra switched stations to a discussion of famous farts. The runner-up on last night's *Asbo Zombies* had apparently "backfired" live on telly. The country was in the grip of an outbreak of celebrity flatulence. "'Oo would you like to see – or 'ear – farting in public? Text us now at…"

I had been raised to admire the English as a reserved and genteel people. Back home, Big Sig imported British costume dramas and dubbed them into badly-synced Ruritanian, with an introduction to explain how upmarket it all was, delivered by a fruity old Strelsau thespian in a smoking jacket and cravat best known for starring in the Communists' favourite operetta, *The Countess of the Collective Farm*.

"This is the BBC?" I marvelled. "The equivalent of the RFR?"

"Oh, you Ruritanians," said Osra. "So prudish."

We were in "the country" soon enough, where there seemed to be rather more cars but all doing 120 clicks per hour down a winding lane wide enough for about one-and-three-quarter Rurikompakts. Ten kilometres beyond the village of Chewton Magna, a long, high, immaculately manicured privet hedge loomed, through a discreet opening in which the car suddenly lurched left onto a gravel drive: "The Royal Chewton Tennis Club." I looked across the manicured lawns in all directions. "Pardon my asking," I said, "but where are the courts?"

"Oh, that's very funny," drawled Lord Hugh.

In the lobby, Lady Belinda was hobnobbing with hobnobbers. Not a mask in sight. Some were hearty rural types, others of a more metropolitan mien. The latter she greeted with kisses on cheeks: Mwa-*mwa!* - a sound I will always associate with Belinda, although I was surprised it was permitted. I watched her for a moment, until she spotted me, and an expression of joy lit her face. "Here he is! My Ruritanian super-plumber!"

She led me out of reception and down corridors lined with sepia portraits of long-ago champions. "What do you think of Hugh and Osra?" she asked. "He's *so* in love with her. Best thing that could happen to the Culverhouse gene pool, believe me. Can't go wrong with a bit of Ruritanian in you."

"As the Bishop of Hofbau said to the Slovak actress!" I quipped. But she didn't seem to appreciate the old line, so I added: "Your nephew says he wants to work for an NGO in Ruritania."

"Marvellous, isn't it? You send us all your plumbers and carpenters, and we send you all our useless do-gooders. NGOs are the new imperialists. Out with the ostrich feathers and sola topees, in with the Chevy Suburbans and a Biden Foundation coronadiarrhea grant."

We had reached the door of the gentlemen's changing room. "This is as far as I go," she declared. "Can't abide wrinkly old willies this early in the day. You'll see the problem. We have a distinguished personage coming, and we need it dealt with super-pronto."

I entered the changing room, handsome and well-appointed, save for the faint tell-tale whiff of sock. The gentlemen's toilets were on the far side. A shallow pool of discoloured water had spread across the tiled floor. Ten minutes later, I emerged triumphant and announced to Belinda: "You have a leaking flange in the second stall. I will need to get a new one, and a closet bend."

"There's a SuperLoo on the bypass. I'll run you up there. Time is of the essence!"

Lady Belinda was not like Osra and Lord Hugh. In the car, she listened to the classical station. "Mendelssohn's concert overture,"

THE PRISONER OF WINDSOR

announced the host, "Opus 27, *'Meeresstille und glückliche Fahrt'*. *'Fahrt'* is nothing to do with the outbreak of celebrity flatulence reported in *The Daily Express* this morning…"

Lady Belinda guffawed.

SuperLoo was located on a mini-roundabout off a larger roundabout. Inside, more Ruritanian than English was to be heard. Across the south-west of Britain, it seemed that every toilet snake had been downed, except for those wielded by the sons of Festenburg and Hofbau.

Back at Royal Chewton, I set to my labours, scraping off the old wax ring, removing the ancient cracked flange and bend, installing replacements and a piece of connecting pipe, and sitting the toilet on top of it. Beyond the bathroom door, Britain was a land of brutish muggers, dancing coppers and flatulent celebrities but here, among the porcelain and PVC, I found a kind of contentment.

"Why, the devil's in it! Shave him, and he'd be the PM!"

I hadn't heard them come in to the changing room - three fellows, all somewhat advanced in years, standing in the doorway regarding me with much curiosity. One was rather short and very stoutly built, with a big bullet-shaped head, a bristly grey moustache, and small pale-blue eyes, a trifle bloodshot. I set him down as an old soldier, home from a lifetime of service to Queen and country around the world. Next to him stood a taller, languid chap with silvery hair, a merry twinkle in his eyes, and distracting orange furry shoes. The third man I felt I knew from somewhere.

I rose slowly to my feet. The stout fellow approached me.

"He's the height, too!" he murmured, as he surveyed me at my full one metre eighty-eight. Then, with a cavalier doff of his sun visor, he addressed me: "May I ask your name?"

"Have I done something wrong?" I said instinctively, after two days in London. Then I recovered myself. "And anyway who are you?"

The youngest of the trio stepped forward with a pleasant smile. "This," said he, indicating the stout chap, "is Mr Peter Borrodaile, Executive Director, Strategic Communications Unit, for His Majesty The King."

So much for my old-soldier theory.

"And this is Sir Roger Severn-" That would be the orange shoes. "-Lord Privy Seal in His Majesty's Government."

35

Because of my knowledge of the English vernacular, I was momentarily startled. I glanced down at the fresh seam of silicon caulking I'd laid around the base of the toilet, and then back up at Sir Roger. How often do you meet a Lord Privy Seal while you are in the middle of sealing a privy? Lordy lordy.

"And," the youngest of the trio concluded, "I'm the King."

Ah.

Now I knew why Lady Belinda had been willing to pay time-and-a-half for an emergency plumbing job. I'd seen His Majesty in magazines and on the television. But a king is an idea as much as an individual, so, even more than Hollywood stars, he can't help but seem smaller in person. I tried a half-bow and found myself staring at his crotch. His trousers were very creased. "I knew I'd seen your picture somewhere," I said, straightening up. "I am Rudy Elphberg. The Ruritanian plumber," I added.

"Well, Mr Elphberg, you had us awfully confused for a moment," explained Sir Roger. "We mistook you for an entirely different chap."

"Thought Royal Chewton had hired the PM to fix the khazi," said Mr Borrodaile. "Bit of honest labour wouldn't hurt him."

"Elphberg," mused the King. "Any relation to the House of Elphberg?"

"I'm afraid so, Your Majesty."

"Ex-royals," said Peter Borrodaile, brushing a crumb off his moustache. "Bad karma, sir."

The King swatted the thought aside, and a gust of regal cologne wafted across the room. "This thing safe for me to use, Mr Elphberg?"

"This will be the maiden voyage," I said.

He roared with laughter, already unbuttoning his fly. "Like christening the Queen Mary!"

We left him to it, and I went back out to reception to ask if Lady Belinda was around. I needed the cash for the Great British B&B and then a flight out of here. Various committee types were milling about, still excited after seeing the King. These were the British I had heard about and seen on TV shows back home – not people who listen to radio banter about farting in public but people who look at you as if you've done just that. I ignored their stares and pursed lips until milady came charging through the door.

"Super-plumber! Thank goodness you're still here."

"Is it not working?" I said.

"No, it's working brilliantly. I mean, I assume it is. I didn't go in and hold the royal plonker. That's Peter Borrodaile's job." She lowered her voice. "But here's the thing, Rudy. His tennis date's late, and he wants a match with you. He knows you play and all that. But apparently you're a Ruritanian prince as well as a Ruritanian plumber."

"King, actually. But I make more money plumbing."

"Will you do it, Rudy?" she said, squeezing my hand. "I've had the most brilliant idea." She explained that her radio producers had not warmed to her suggestions for a real tennis feature "pegged" to the Coronation. "But thanks to you I've got one they'll die for. Oh, say you'll do it!"

So I did it. She ordered one of the snooty types infesting the lobby to find me some tennis whites, and then shoved me back into the changing room, where I was greeted by His Majesty The King's hairy bottom bent over the bench. I tried to do that English public-school thing where you're all cool about being naked with strangers. But it felt a bit odd when one of the strangers was the King of England and the other two chaps gave the distinct impression they wanted to see whether the rest of my body parts matched the Prime Minister's.

We headed toward the court. Lady Belinda looked very fetching in her little tennis outfit with her long, glowingly tanned legs. But she seemed more fawning than she had been hitherto: the difference between a real king and a pretender. "His Majesty," she cooed, "is a great promoter of real tennis – or, as we prefer to call it, tennis. He sponsored a pro-am charity tournament."

"Who won?"

"A former Spice Girl," Mr Borrodaile replied. "Or was it a Nolan Sister? Lovely day. Rather thought we'd get more coverage."

He held the door for me and I found myself in an enclosed court. Ah, right. It's an indoor sport. No wonder Lord Hugh was *toterkörpen* in the car park. There was a net dividing the court in two, which seemed straightforward enough. Then I cased the rest of the joint. Couldn't make head or tail of it. It seemed a little larger than a regular tennis court, with high black walls all around, but a roofed shed running along one side and both ends. Someone said something about the "penthouse", but they looked more like hovels to me. On the lone shedless wall, there was a big crown halfway down and a strange buttress obtruding a little beyond that. Viewed from head on, the opposite side with its long low-sloping roof looked rather like a mediaeval street scene, a row of cramped house fronts for the townsfolk with the flying buttress representing the local castle and the galleries as the cowsheds – like the Königstrasse in the 1600s, in the gloomy painting that hung in Mama's sitting room. There were netted windows in assorted sizes everywhere you looked. The King strolled up one end, and I noticed Sir Roger settling himself behind, in another bunker with a large opening maybe seven metres wide.

"Mr Borrodaile has kindly agreed to be marker," pronounced His Majesty, and the Executive Director of the King's Strategic Communications Unit dutifully took up position. I'm not one to complain, but the net sagged by perhaps half a metre in the middle. Crouched at one end, Belinda pressed the record button and prepared to give it her most sparkling colour commentary. "Real tennis," she said breathily into her microphone. "The sport of kings - and ex-kings. Of kings soon to be crowned - and kings never to be crowned. Of kings who bestride the world – and kings whose footfall will ne'er be heard again."

I think this is what the English call "laying it on a bit thick". "His Majesty King Arthur I versus His Non-Majesty King Rudolf… Rudy, what's your numeral?"

"Seventh," I said. Sometimes it surprised me I remembered.

The king about to be crowned held up his racket. It was bent, I noticed for the first time. I looked down at the one in my hand. Nor did it seem quite symmetrical. The small head appeared to be leaning off to one side. It was wooden, with what felt to my inexpert touch like extremely tight strings. "Rough or smooth?" he asked.

"Um. Rough?"

His Majesty twirled his racket. It fell to the ground with smooth side uppermost. He gave a wry smile, picked it up, and then declaimed:

If in my weake conceit, (for selfe disport),

THE PRISONER OF WINDSOR

The world I sample to a Tennis-court,
Where fate and fortune daily meet to play,
I doe conceive, I doe not much misse-say.
   All manner chance are Rackets, wherewithall
They bandie men like balls, from wall to wall...

He raised his racket, and bandied the ball over the net.

Chapter Six
Into the Hazard

I WHACKED IT BACK down the centre. Not so hard to pick up, this "real tennis". He returned it, forcefully, and my backhand sent it spinning to the side with the wall. Oh, well. It bounced back on to the court, and he gave it a theatrical flick into the bunker just off to my right. It hit a bell, which rang around the room and gave me a hell of a start, but seemed to delight everyone else. "Oh, well done, sir," said Mr Borrodaile. And Lady Belinda. And Sir Roger.

What was all that about?

Thus began the knock-up. I've always believed that, if a thing is worth doing, it's worth doing badly. But "real tennis" is no game for bluffers. The hand-sewn balls are smaller and heavier than in non-real tennis, and not exactly round. They bounce a little better than the average Hofbau potato, but they spin in interesting ways, which His Majesty seemed to know and I didn't. After another half-dozen shots whose resolution I failed to understand, the King decided he was sufficiently warmed up. So he swept up a ball, raised his bat, and yelled: "T'nay!"

"Pardon me?"

He dropped the ball. "Good God, man! T'nay! Tennis! Take heed!"

Belinda was explaining into her microphone: "The word 'tennis' comes from the French – '*tenez*', meaning 'take heed'. It's the traditional warning from the server to the receiver – that's you, Rudy," she added.

"Everybody knows that," snapped the King. He picked up the ball, smiled slyly, and said, more softly: "T'nay..."

This time there was no dramatic racquet hoist. Instead, the King served underarm, but without slicing the ball. It landed on the shed roof to my right and dropped off in the corner by the back wall.

"Oh, poop!" squealed Lady Belinda.

I suppose, after all the flatulence on the BBC, I shouldn't have been surprised. Even so, given the royal presence, her scatological outburst seemed inappropriate, notwithstanding the awfulness of the serve.

"Indeed," said Roger Severn. "Not often we get a perfect poop on the very first ball."

I didn't think the shot was that awful, but it's all about bodily functions with the English, isn't it? It was only when Borrodaile declared "Fifteen-love" that I realised the King had won the first point.

He served again. This time, the ball arched high up through the air in slow motion. It landed on the sloping roof of the bunkers, bounced once, twice, thrice, and then fell off the eave heading toward me. Judging from His Majesty's smugness, whacking the thing off the side roof is not only permitted but a stroke of genius. So I figured I was supposed to return the ball. I got to it but in tennis-type tennis they don't train you to play shots that bounce off the parking attendant's hut, and my attempted volley skimmed the net, wobbled along it for twenty centimetres, and then dropped back on my side.

"Thirty-love," said Borrodaile.

On the next serve, the ball bounced off the roof, then high off the side wall, and halfway up the back wall, whence it hit a stunned me smack on the nose. It bounced off the floor, and then again. But I was mad, and swung at the ball, just getting to it.

"Piquet!" cheered Lady Belinda.

"Forty-love," said Borrodaile. "Chase the door."

I was about to say, "What the hell are you on about?" But clearly it was a technical term. Something to do with something. I tried to give the air of someone who's entirely nonchalant at having pulled off a door-chase, or been on the receiving end of one, as the case may be.

His Majesty took the first set to cries of "Magnificent giraffe!" Peter Borrodaile emerged from the gallery with a bottle of water, two glasses, and a hand towel for King Arthur.

I started the second set walloping the ball out of sheer frustration with as much force as I could muster. It flew past His Majesty and hit a little grille at the back that I'd assumed was either a ventilation shaft or where the cashier collected membership dues. A cowbell rang.

"Good shot," cried Belinda.

41

Must remember to hit the ventilation shaft more often. I stopped thinking of this thing as a tennis match, and more like trying to play racquets on a mini-golf course inside a giant pinball machine.

"Do you know your Shakespeare, Mr Elphberg?" cried the King, as we switched positions.

"Oh, I did my share in school," I said, breezily.

"Then you'll recall Henry V's speech on being the recipient of a joke gift of tennis balls from the Dauphin of France:

When we have matched our rackets to these balls,
We will in France, by God's grace, play a set
Shall strike his father's crown into the hazard.

The "hazard" is what these real tennis types call the non-serving end of the court – ie, my corner. My father's crown was struck into the hazard long ago.

But I was getting a feel for it now, and we had our first real rally, until my royal opponent brought it to an end. "A splendid turn by the Pretender," Lady Belinda was telling her microphone, "but the true King won the chase."

"Try a railroad," urged Sir Roger Severn.

I had no idea what that meant, and I fumbled my serve, so the ball spun limply over the net. But the King charged too fast, and thwacked it with his full force. It ricocheted every which way, like cartoon bullets. Lady Belinda squealed and ducked. When it was over, Borrodaile pronounced: "Game to Mr Elphberg."

In "lawn tennis", as I was beginning to think of it, everyone serves from more or less the same place. In this sport, the King never served from the same position twice. He stood here, he stood there, he stood near, he stood far, he stood *katzenecke* to where he'd stood before. I would not have been surprised to see him standing with his back to me. So, unlike your average Grand Slam champion, he had no such thing as "his" serve. He followed the high arched roof-bouncer of his previous point with a kind of boomerang. Forty-love. My hand was sticky. "The Pretender wipes his dethroned palm on his dispossessed shorts," Belinda informed her recording device. The King tossed the ball casually up in the air and let it fall, until it was at about calf height, and then he hit it underarm with incredible spin. It danced across the penthouse – bouncing once, twice, thrice, and then dropping from roof to floor. "Mine!" I thought, and lunged. I lost my balance, and my flailing racquet found nothing but air. "Game to His Majesty."

"Lovely caterpillar, sir," purred Belinda.

But I was beginning to figure things out. Unlike Wimbledon, you could only serve from one end. So the object was to gain the serving side. And you could only do that through "chases" …I think. Also, the scoring, which had initially appeared to proceed in the usual 15-30-40 tennis manner, is complicated by the fact that the chases cause points to be held in abeyance. Like a dukedom.

Got that? Simple enough? Try picking it up while the King of England's firing his poop at you. It occurred to me that I had spent far too much of life bluffing my way through. I resolved, upon returning home, to get on top of this bloody game, and become Ruritania's Number One real tennis player. Not sure if Ruritania had a Number Two real tennis player, so I might have to find a Slovene or a Montenegrin to make up the numbers. But a fellow has to start somewhere.

The King took the second set. I decided to revise my earlier judgment: It was more like playing chess with a tennis racquet on a mini-golf course in a giant pinball machine. With a commanding lead, he was back to declaiming: "We are merely the stars' tennis balls, struck and bandied which way please them."

Yeah, whatever. I remembered the first ball, His Majesty's famous poop, and sought to replicate it. Instead, it bounced off the roof into the back of the court and hit the grille. More cowbell! I felt like I'd just pulled off a hole in one.

I took the third set 6-3. Calm, calm, I told myself. I'd pretended to be a real real tennis player. I could easily pass myself off as a real real good real tennis player if I just kept my nerve. The calmer calmer calmer calmer calmer chameleon, that was me. In regular tennis, good shots will win the day. Real tennis is craftier. It's not just about thwacking the thing back. If you can slyly place the ball in a corner of the court just out of reach and get the second bounce as near to the back wall as possible, you can deprive the guy of his serve. "Mr Elphberg takes the fourth set six games to five," announced Borrodaile.

I didn't quite believe it. "Don't you need to win by at least two games?" I asked Lady Belinda.

"That's tennis tennis," she hissed back. "Not real tennis, you jammiest of dodgers."

The final set opened badly for me. Stuck down the hazard end, I brooded on how to lay a chase. The opportunity came with a misfired railroad which His Majesty undoubtedly expected me to thump through the dedans. (I was beginning to "dig the lingo", as the Scots say.) Instead, I gave the ball the lightest nudge but just enough spin to throw him off.

His Majesty was breathing hard. But so was I. He won four games in a row. Two sets all, five games to one in the final set.

But not for long. He missed an easy volley. 5-2. He lost his concentration, and his service. 5-3. He started playing too defensively, trying to sit on his lead. 5-4. And we were tied. Yes! I could do this! One more game, and let the record show Ruritania 1, England zip.

The King served. "Chase the door!" yelped Belinda. Point by point, we slogged on. When we'd started, he was a stick figure on a play set. Now he seemed a giant, vivid and defined, as everything beyond him - the dedans, the tambour, the penthouse and all the other court furniture - faded to a blur. "Advantage Mr Elphberg," pronounced Borrodaile. I heard His Majesty curse, and wondered if Lady Belinda had caught it on tape. But he clawed back the score, and laid another chase. The final chase.

The Windsors are great survivors, aren't they? Ask the Habsburgs and Romanovs and all the rest of us. Ask the prime ministers who've nibbled away at their perks and privileges without ever getting anywhere near to dislodging them. I watched the King coolly weigh the ball in his left hand. And then he served. It wasn't quite a giraffe and it wasn't quite a caterpillar. It skimmed the edge of the penthouse twice, and started to fall. I watched it as if in slow motion, not trusting myself to volley. It bounced off the back wall, and I got to it.

Straight into the net.

"Game, set and match to His Majesty The King."

"The Pretender fails to take the crown," added Lady Belinda.

Story of my life.

THE PRISONER OF WINDSOR

As we left the court, a tall fellow in tennis kit and reflector shades came sauntering toward us, accompanied by a rather gauche manservant. From his oleaginous mien, trim beard, and bronzed arms, hirsute and sinewy, I assumed he was a Mediterranean playboy of some kind. He hailed the King. "Arthur!"

His Majesty bristled, but faintly.

"Sir," he added.

Was he a Greek prince? The Windsors are said to favour them above other ex-royals.

"Ghazi!" cried the King. "You're late, as always. Who's your friend?"

Ghazi explained that he was a graduate of the DRI – the De-Radicalisation Initiative – who was undergoing career retraining as a royal tennis umpire.

"Hmm," said His Majesty without interest. "Well, I had to make do with a stand-in."

The princely reflector shades stared at me coldly, and then spotted Belinda. "My sweetest," he oozed, mwa-mwa-ing both cheeks. "You look ravishing as ever." He cast a second dismissive glance my way. "I'm sure you made an admirable stand-in," he said, and headed out to the court. "Regards to George, Belinda."

"I look forward to a rematch," murmured the King. "Work on that serve, and you'd be a pretty decent player." He shook my hand briskly, and left me with a whiff of sweet cologne and royal sweat.

Chapter Seven
A merry evening with a distant relative

BY THE TIME I WAS back in my plumbing gear, my real tennis match was already beginning to feel unreal. Had it really happened? Had I, the unreal king, just played real tennis with the real one?

In the corridor from the changing rooms, Belinda was delighted. "That was *mah*-vellous!" she squealed. "*Bliss!* I'd like to see that bitch cancel my contract now." I noticed she only used bad language when speaking of her BBC colleagues. "I have got the perfect Coronation feature!" she yelped. "The real king up against a fake king. *Yesssss!*" She thumped the wall in exultation.

"I'm not a fake king."

She did her leaning-in-too-close thing, and her scent swirled around me as we returned to reception. "Oh, darling plumber man, you know what I mean. I always have the most rotten luck, and yet today I didn't. Just think: If Royal Chewton's useless English plumbers hadn't been reorienting the Mohammedan prison loos, I wouldn't have called you. And, if I hadn't called you, we wouldn't have had an understudy on hand when Prince Ghazi arrived late. And, if you hadn't been a Ruritanian royal, the King wouldn't have been tickled enough to want you as a stand-in."

She ceased her effusions to shoot me a look of pity. "Sorry Ghazi went all gentlemen-and-players on you. I'm not like that, am I? I was a waitress, you know. Well, for three weeks in Windsor one summer. Had a pash on a boy there."

I'm not the type to go *yesssss!* and thump the wall, but I was also in a celebratory mood. "I don't mean to be forward," I said, "but…"

"Yes, yes. Your money." And she fished around in her handbag.

"Not that," I said, "I was going to ask if you'd like to have a drink… Maybe there's a pub…"

She stopped counting banknotes, and looked me in the eye. For once, she was keeping her distance. "That's very sweet of you.

You're a lifesaver plumber, and I'm sure you'd have made a wonderful king. But I don't think so."

And she turned and left.

I wasn't trying to pick her up. She's not my type – all that gentlemen-and-players stuff, whatever that means. I just didn't want my big day to end. I'd spent it with a fellow king, a foreign prince, a "lord privy seal", and miscellaneous courtiers and aristocrats. I had had, in other words, what would have been a routine day for the King of Ruritania had Comrade Bauer not staged his People's Revolution. And the fact that, even after I'd played five sets with the King at his personal request, everyone at Royal Chewton Tennis Club marked me out as an obvious loser not worth getting to know only underlined the sad truth of my life – that this day would never come again.

Gentlemen and players. Even the receptionist spotted me for a "duffer" who'd never be back. It's disheartening. Especially if you're a king. I had an urge to yell, "Don't you know my grandfather never drew his own curtains?"

Outside, the sky had turned an eerie yellowy-grey and begun a gusty and erratic downpour. The rain of an English windstorm isn't heavy – it sort of flaps at you from every angle and won't go away, like hawkers in a Zenda bazaar. But it is very chill. My bones felt damper already. And then I remembered: Lord Hugh and Osra had gone to his ancestral estates for the weekend, and Lady Belinda was supposed to be driving me back to London. Unfortunately, she was already motoring through the gates. I sprinted across the puddled car park, but she was turning, and on the road, and accelerating up the hill.

So I stood there getting wet and shivery for a bit, and then I squelched back across the gravel to the clubhouse to see if they might let me back in - just to use the payphone, if they had one, to call and find out where the nearest bus-stop was, if there was one. Halfway across the parking lot, I spotted someone under the veranda - that Lord Privy Seal, the orange-shoes guy, clutching a brown paper bag to his chest. He was looking up at the clouds and preparing to make a dash for it with only a copy of *Country Life* to hold over his hat.

"Mr Elphberg!" he beamed. "Congratulations on a splendid match! Hard-fought, and thrilling to watch. Going back in for another?"

"I'm going nowhere," I replied, bitterly. He was under the roof, but I remained in the rain, declining to set foot on the veranda steps. I know my place.

"In that case," he said, "perhaps I could offer you a spot of dinner? The car's just this way."

"Are you sure that's wise? Lady Belinda didn't want to be seen having a drink with a mere plumber."

"Well, I'm known across the land for my common touch." He looked at the water pouring off my head. "Tell you what – I've got a hat, so you take my *Country Life*." And off we trotted.

Sir Roger opened the passenger door and asked me to hold the brown paper bag. "Guard it with your life!"

It was a modest vehicle with squeaky wipers and a struggling demister. He peered grimly through the fogged glass as we pulled out of the tennis club. "So," he said, "you are a Ruritanian king and a Ruritanian plumber! One just the day job and one what you really want to do?"

The famous British sense of humour: all very pointed, isn't it?

"Delightful to be in the company of a Ruritanian from the good old days," he continued. "The House of Elphberg. Queen Flavia."

"You must be the only man in England who's even heard of Queen Flavia."

"Have you made a lot of friends here?"

I shook my head. "The only non-plumber I know is Lady Belinda Featherly. And I barely know her."

"To barely know her is to know her well," he said, as if it was a quotation I should recognise. "Strelsau is a beautiful city."

"In 1938 maybe. Today it boasts Europe's finest collection of rubble."

The rain drizzled, the clouds darkened, and Sir Roger wiped a small hole in his fogged-up windscreen. "Do you mind if I put on the news? I have to go on LBC, and I don't want to be blindsided by any breaking 'extremism incident'…"

He reached for the radio, and the car veered halfway into the adjoining lane of the "dual carriageway". The supermarket lorry honked, and I had an alarmingly close close-up of its full-length advertisement showing a raven-tressed dolly bird with an unfeasibly long tongue fellating a "sausage roll".

He switched on just as Lady Belinda drawled "Hair-*lair!*", which made me jump. It was a trailer for her live Coronation special, co-hosted by Colin Corgi. They promised "lamppost to lamppost" coverage.

"I'd rather watch *Asbo Zombies*," I said, sourly. The trailer ended, and the news began:

> ...*remarks made by Colin Corgi about the Roma and Travelling communities, the popular BBC children's personality has come in for further criticism, this time about his role at the Coronation, from the chair of the Supreme Islamic Council of England and Wales...*

Sir Roger raised an eyebrow.

> ...*Sir Mohammed Almasri has expressed concerns that the BBC's Coronation coverage will not be embracing of all communities. 'This dog was recently used to promote the Department of Health's free contraceptives...'*

There was a soundbite of Colin Corgi selling "Coronation condoms": "Want to give it free reign? Make sure you wear a crown ...you lucky dog!"

> ...*grossly offensive to many of us who do not think our wives and daughters should be presented as loose women who are, in the Prime Minister's phrase, 'gagging for it'. Muslims in Britain pay for the BBC in just the same way as everybody else, so it is a waste of valuable resources to make programming that excludes...*

"Poor Belinda!" sighed Roger Severn. "I can't see the PM going to bat for her unfortunate co-presenter." He switched the radio off. "First they came for the cartoon pigs, and I did not speak out because I'm not an animated character in any sense. Then they came for the anthropomorphised canine puppets, and I did not speak out because I'm not a cuddly stuffed animal – and, if I am, I'm more of an Eeyore..."

I gathered that the breaking news was in some sense bad for Lady Belinda. *Good!* I wanted to say something witty, but all I could think of was "Colin Corgi's a dog, but karma's a bitch." The almost famous "presenter" and columnist who wouldn't be caught dead drinking with a plumber! Well, who's sobbing into her slivovitz now?

"Don't diminish your fine profession," said Sir Roger. "You can't get a plumber on a weekend, but you could get any number of laid-off *Telegraph* columnists and out-of-work telly presenters."

Funnily enough, as soon as the storm clouds gathered for Colin Corgi and Lady Belinda, the ones outside the car window cleared up and the sun came out. It was a glorious late afternoon when we pulled up at the Lord Privy Seal's mediaeval manor house with tall chimneys, and lead-mullioned oriel windows set in gable dormers jutting out over elaborate corbels. (I had done the Modenstein voiceover for a Swedish architecture documentary, so I know my corbels.)

Sir Roger gestured apologetically. "The moat is dry, alas. An estate agent for one of these Russian oligarch chappies offered me an absurd sum of money for the house. A moat was the Number One non-negotiable on his list of features."

"He wanted to play the English squire," I chuckled.

"Just being practical. A moat is one of the most effective defences against car bombs."

He ushered me to the terrace behind the house, and indicated a seat at a wrought-iron table. Moments later, he returned with a pitcher of what looked like heavy morning urine with leaves floating on top.

"Pimm's?"

He filled the glasses without waiting for a reply. I took a sip and began to enjoy myself. A bee buzzed around a huge rhododendron bush. I could hear the snip of garden shears from somewhere out of sight. The sun was starting to sink over distant fields. I could get used to this Pimm drink.

"England at twilight," Sir Roger exhaled contentedly. He refilled my glass, and inhaled deeply of the evening air, perfumed with the scent of fresh-cut hay. "I've always thought I was blessed with a perfect ha-ha."

I sighed silently. I'd been right all along. The "randy bugger" was "pitching the woo" at me, but he was going to do it with a lot of English-schoolboy naughty-talk. "What was that?" I asked, casually.

THE PRISONER OF WINDSOR

"My ha-ha." He looked at me. "Oh, my mistake. You wouldn't have them in Strelsau. It's an old English landscaping trick. A kind of trench at the end of the lawn to stop the livestock wandering in. It means you can dispense with any unsightly fence and enjoy a long-range view. Mine's very good, don't you think? See those hedgerows all that way over at the far side of the field? They date from the thirteenth century."

"Has this been the family home all that time?"

He giggled. "Oh, no, Mr Elphberg. I'm a frightful parvenu. Can't you tell?"

The sound of birdsong drifted over the lawn. "Do you know your Browning?" he asked.

"It's a gun, isn't it?"

"It's also a man called Robert." He said softly:

The lark's on the wing;
The snail's on the thorn;
God's in His heaven—
All's right with the world!

I looked at him blankly.

"Not a lot right with the world, is there?" he asked. "And yet..." He stared into the distance. "...out here the sun rises and sets on ancient hedgerows and thatched cottages as it has for centuries. The lark's on the wing, the snail's on the thorn, God's in His heaven, and the paralytic yobs and poxy trollops and incendiary imams and grooming gangs are somewhere far beyond the horizon and always will be."

He swung around. "Ah, but it's a small island, isn't it? Shall we go in?" And he led me through the French doors into a handsome dining room of dark wood and burgundy-damasked walls hung with tasteful landscapes. A spry manservant with sunken cheeks and plastered-down hair waited on us over a gleamingly polished table. "Joseph's been with me for years," said Severn. "Topping fellow."

"I don't think I've ever been served by a butler," I remarked. Which is a sad observation for a king. I looked down at my placemat, which showed a hunting scene – "The Meet at Titcomb".

"Oh, I wouldn't call Joseph a butler. My household is far too lowly. He's more of a gentleman's gentleman."

I had no idea what that meant, but he didn't seem to notice. "Chin-chin!" he offered, raising his claret. "To Ruritania!"

Joseph returned and set down two plates of pinkish beef slices spread like a fan. "Hungry?" asked Severn.

"Oh, I play a good knife and fork," I replied jauntily, trying not to give off the air of a man who hasn't had a real meal since he landed. Tastier than locusts from the Great British Bugger.

"Did you know," said Severn, "there are now more butlers in London than at any time since Queen Victoria died?"

"Didn't you say British aristocrats are all 'poor as church mice'?"

"They are. It's the Russians and Arabs who need the butlers. The rest of us make do with a general factotum. Horseradish?" he asked. "Or would you prefer mustard?"

"I do the voiceover for a mustard commercial," I said, seeking to impress him.

"Really? So you're an actor?"

"I wouldn't call it acting. I mainly work for a lookalike agency in Modenstein. That's why I need the beard."

"Modenstein," repeated Severn, thoughtfully. "I don't believe the United Kingdom has diplomatic relations with Modenstein, do we?"

I didn't like to tell him that, after what the do-gooder globalists had done to Ruritania, that's what I liked about it. The great thing about a breakaway republic is that nobody recognises it. "Modenstein," I explained, "only has diplomatic relations with Abkhazia, Nagorno-Karabakh, South Ossetia and Transnistria."

"Dear me," murmured Severn. "You'll have me reaching for my atlas."

"You probably think of us as Milfs."

"I wouldn't say that," said Sir Roger.

"All five breakaway republics came together to form the Mutual Independence and Liberation Federation."

"Ah. MILF. Must look out for the summit briefing paper."

Joseph returned with a fantastical dessert. "Spotted dick, sir?" he asked.

THE PRISONER OF WINDSOR

"I have not yet spotted Prince Dick," I said. "Just King Arthur."

Severn chuckled. "Spotted Dick is something you eat."

Oh, now I got it. "That's what she said, innit?" I bellowed heartily. I was beginning to get the measure of British social banter – penises, flatulence, fellatio, punctuated occasionally by an observation about the weather. I was about to do an old Hofbau joke about sodomising a donkey when Sir Roger wiped away a custard smear and said, "Tell me, Mr Elphberg, I believe your mother, the Queen Dowager, is still alive?"

"After the fashion. She has Alzheimer's."

"Tough on everyone."

"She went to live with her sister, who married a sheep farmer in New Zealand. Then she moved into a home. The nurses are Indonesians on short-term contracts so they never get to know her. I suppose when an old lady in the lounge starts going on about having tea with the Führer at Berchtesgaden it's not surprising they take that as evidence of descent into total dementia. In fact, it's one of the few things she can still reliably recall. She was a little girl and her dad was Ruritania's special emissary during 'negotiations' about joining the Axis. And she remembers a lot – not the Axis, but the tea, and Herr Hitler's exquisite table manners."

"As one would." He put down his wine glass. "I wonder what happens when a society loses its memory?" He motioned to Joseph. "Does it also descend into dementia?"

It wasn't clear whether he wanted an answer to that one, so I let it go.

And on we talked in a desultory fashion until halfway through the spotted dick, when the gentleman's gentleman reappeared. "The Prime Minister is here, Sir Roger," he murmured softly.

I dropped my spoon, and old Severn winked as a ringing voice sounded from the hall:

"Roger, Roger! Where are you, man?"

And then he was in the room. I knew who he was – the star of last night's telly address to the nation: The Rt Hon Robert Rassendyll, formerly the 16th Earl of Burlesdon, Privy Counsellor, Member of Parliament for South Burlesdon and the Clewes, Prime Minister and First Lord of the Treasury.

He had no idea who I was. And, seeing me sitting across from Severn, he drew back, like a vampire recoiling from a mirror – or, in this case, a startled vampire glimpsing for the first time his reflection. Save the hair on my face and a manner of conscious dignity which many years of climbing in and out of ministerial limousines had given him, save also that he lacked perhaps a centimetre of my height - no, less than that, but still something - Robert Rassendyll might have been Rudolf Elphberg, and I Mr Rassendyll.

I rose, and for an instant we stood motionless, looking at one another. "What is this, Roger?" the Prime Minister said quietly. "What's going on?" He fixed me in the eye. "And who the fuck are you?"

"In happier circumstances," replied Severn, enjoying himself, "he would have been His Majesty King Rudolf VII of Ruritania, and you would have just caused a major diplomatic incident. 'Who the fuck are you?' What way is that to greet your cousin?"

"His cousin?" I said. "What are you on about?"

The Prime Minister's suspicion vanished. "Well, I never. Cousin Rudolf! After all these years!" He smiled, and poured himself a glass of wine. "I knew the story as a boy, but didn't quite believe it." He circled around me, peering closely. "I asked my grandmother if we were related to the Royal Family, and she said no, but we were related to *a* royal family." Falling into a chair, Rassendyll stretched out his legs. "If memory serves, it was in the year 1733…"

"George II sitting then on the throne, peace reigning for the moment, and the King and the Prince of Wales being not yet at loggerheads," added Sir Roger.

"That's enough footnotes," said Rassendyll. "Anyway, in 1733 there came on a visit to the English Court a certain prince, afterwards known to history as Rudolf III of Ruritania. The prince was a tall, handsome young fellow, marked by a somewhat unusually long, sharp and straight nose, and a mass of dark-red hair - the nose and hair which I gather have stamped the Elphbergs for centuries. He stayed some months in England, but left rather under a cloud. For he fought a duel with an Englishman, the husband of a very beautiful wife. And in that duel Prince Rudolf received a severe wound, and was adroitly smuggled off by the Ruritanian ambassador, who had found him rather a handful. The nobleman was not wounded. But the morning being raw, he contracted a severe chill, and died some six months after. He had not found time to adjust his relations with his wife - who, after another two months, bore an heir to the title and estates of Burlesdon. This lady was the Countess Amelia, whose picture still hangs in the great gallery there. Her husband was James, fifth Earl of Burlesdon and Knight of the Garter. As for Prince Rudolf, he went back to Ruritania and ascended the throne, whereon his progeny sat until, ah, comparatively recently, as you well know." The Prime Minister nodded in my direction. "But, if you walk through the picture galleries at Burlesdon, among the 200 portraits or so of the years since 1733, you will find some twenty-to-twenty-five, including that of the sixth earl, distinguished by long, sharp, straight noses and a quantity of dark-red hair; these two dozen or so have also blue eyes, whereas among the Rassendylls dark eyes are the commoner."

Long, sharp, straight noses and a quantity of dark-red hair. He had just described both the man he was looking at, and the man the man he was looking at was looking back at.

"So we are both descendants of Rudolf III, aren't we?" continued the Prime Minister. "Which, come to think of it, makes me and not you the rightful King of Ruritania. After all, Countess Amelia bore Prince Rudolf's heir long before your great-great-great-whatever-grandmother did."

"I hope you didn't your renounce your earldom for a throne in Ruritania," I said.

"That's something to think about, Roger, isn't it?"

"Pre-Brexit, you wanted to be the first executive president of the European Union," replied Severn.

"His Apostolic Majesty The All-New Holy Roman Emperor," said Rassendyll. "That'll do me. In the meantime, here we are, a king and an earl, reduced by this democratic age to plain old misters. As we say in Britain, cheers, mate!" He raised his glass. "What do they say in Zenda?"

I clinked my glass against his. "In Zenda the *flüchen* closed all the bars."

Rassendyll laughed. "We'll twin it with Luton." He finished off the bottle and called for another. "What's your poison, doppelgänger?"

"Oh, I'll drink anything," I said.

"Don't poison the doppelgänger," advised Severn, uncorking the claret. "You might need him one day. Like Saddam Hussein."

"I thought Saddam's lookalikes were mostly for the C-list mistresses he couldn't be bothered bedding himself. Whereas I, in line with my modern hands-on approach to government, make a point of personally bonking all my mistresses." He tasted the wine, as if Sir Roger were a sommelier, and then waved at him to pour a full glass. "Ahhhh." He drained it in a gulp. "Fill 'er up, Rog." He drained the second. "By God, doppelgänger, I could use you in Downing Street. Send you over to the Commons when that fulminating Orangeman demands to know when I'm going to stand up to the Muzzies."

"And when are you going to stand up to the Muzzies?" asked Severn, settling back in his seat.

"Oh, Roger," he groaned. "Colin Corgi and some Koran-autographing Hampstead luvvie are not the gates of Vienna."

"Is 'Orangeman' another name for 'ginger'?" I asked.

Rassendyll gave a girlish titter. "I wish. Since I became PM, gingerphobia's on the rampage. Like ancient Egypt, when Set, the red-haired god of storms, darkness and chaos, afflicted the land with earthquakes, and the people sacrificed redheads to appease his rage. Now Rassendyll, the red-haired god of globalist vassalage, afflicts the land with regulations and unaffordable housing and ever longer hospital waiting lists, and the people beat up gingers."

I couldn't think of anything to say to that, so Severn leapt in to change the subject. "How did the meeting with Sir Mohammed go?"

"Very well. Most of his demands were for things we're planning to introduce anyway."

"*In vino veritas*," murmured Severn.

Rassendyll ignored him. "I owe everything to Roger," he told me. "I was president of the party's youth group at Oxford and he came to give a speech."

"You were the warm-up act, and I was impressed by your introductory remarks." Severn refilled his glass.

"And that's how it all started. I'd be nothing without Roger. Well, I'd be an earl, but you know what I mean. Maggie Thatcher used to say every prime minister should have a Willie…"

THE PRISONER OF WINDSOR

Sir Roger chipped in to explain that "Willie" was her deputy, William Whitelaw, and also a vernacular synonym for the male reproductive organ.

"Every prime minister should have a Willie," repeated Rassendyll. He lifted his glass to Severn. "I say every prime minister needs a bloody good Roger."

We bantered on through several swift refills. Rassendyll had seemed exhausted when he arrived, but the tipsiness revived him. He slid into the seat next to me, and snapped his fingers for more claret. "I'm just a regular bloke, doppelgänger," he said, putting his arm round me. He pronounced it "*bleauk*". The wine seemed to be affecting his accent.

"I thought you were a sixteenth earl."

"*Exactement*," he said. "And if a sixteenth earl can pass himself off as a regular bleauk, anybody can."

I was growing sleepy and worried I might be on the brink of another Suicide Belt scenario. But Rassendyll and Severn seemed less larcenous than my previous drinking companions. And then Joseph the gentleman's gentleman reappeared and set before the Prime Minister a fanciful pseudo-flagon in faux-antique glass. It gave the air of having lain so long in some darkened wine cellar that it seemed to blink in the candlelight.

Sir Roger rose from his seat. "Prime Minister," he began, with exaggerated theatricality, "His Majesty commanded me upon your next visit to my humble abode to set this wine before you when the Prime Minister was weary of all other wines, and pray the PM to drink, for the love that he bears his brother."

"My brother?"

"Yes, Prime Minister," said Severn. "This wine is the first biodynamic vintage to be produced at the King's organic vineyards under the supervision of your brother's Organic Vintners Cooperative. His Majesty entrusted it to me, and our fine Ruritanian friend here took personal charge of it all the way home."

"Well done, cousin Rudolf!" enthused Rassendyll. "And well done, brother Michael! Out with the cork, Joseph. Did he think I'd flinch from his bottle?"

The ersatz flagon was, in fact, a screwtop, and, after a deft twist of the cap, the gentleman's gentleman filled Rassendyll's glass. The

Prime Minister tasted it. Then, with a solemnity born of the hour and his own condition, he looked round on us: "Cousin Rudolf, everything is yours to the half of Burlesdon. But ask me not for a single drop of this divine bottle, which I will drink to the health of our soon-to-be-crowned King – and of that sly knave, my brother Mike."

And Rassendyll seized the bottle and turned it over his mouth, devoured it in one, and then flung it toward the fireplace. Fortunately, it landed in a recycling bin.

"Don't worry," said Severn's servant, hastening to retrieve it, "I'll put it in the right one."

"Well done, that man!" cried Sir Roger. "You can retire for the night, Joseph. I'll see our guests out."

Severn shot Rassendyll an amused glance. He yawned. And, from our more mundane vintages, Sir Roger and I drank pleasant dreams to the Prime Minister.

Chapter Eight
A close shave

WHETHER I HAD SLEPT a year or a minute I hadn't a clue. I awoke with a start and a shiver; my face, hair and clothes dripped water, and opposite stood Sir Roger Severn, a grimace on his face, a bucket in his hand, and the caps of those damned furry orange shoes of his blazing like jack o'lanterns. I blinked at the room. On the far end of the table sat a chap about my age, pale as a ghost, black as a crow under the eyes, and wearing a mauve suit whose dangling trouser legs did nothing for my hangover.

I shook the excess water off, and leapt to my feet in anger.

"That's not funny!"

"Dearie me, plumber, we've no time for quarrelling. Nothing else would rouse you. It's 3am."

I tried to focus. Severn seemed unusually urgent.

"I'll thank you, Sir Roger – " I began again, hot in spirit while bloody freezing in body.

"Mr Elphberg," interrupted the younger fellow.

I swung around. "And who's this?"

"Fritz," said Sir Roger, "is a Member of the European Parliament. For a wide tranche of the Tyrol."

"You can Google me," added Fritz, offended. Then he pointed to the floor.

The Prime Minister of the United Kingdom lay full length at my feet. His face was red as his hair, and he breathed heavily. Sir Roger, the disrespectful old dog, kicked him sharply. He didn't stir.

I knelt down and felt for his pulse.

"Drugged?" I whispered.

"You're quick," replied Severn.

"Who did it?"

Sir Roger roared with laughter. "He did it!"

I must have looked entirely uncomprehending because Fritz heaved himself off the table and uttered two words:

"Bad cocaine."

The cold water had seeped through my clothes and was chilling my bones. "The Prime Minister," I said slowly, "does cocaine?"

"Come now," scoffed Sir Roger. "London is the cocaine capital of Europe, according to both our outraged mid-market tabloids and our proudly patriotic downmarket tabloids. It would be statistically improbable for the habit to find no takers at the highest levels of government. And when one has a prime minister with so many glittering celebrity friends…" His hands turned palms up in what seemed an oddly choreographed gesture.

"During the leadership election," added Fritz, "they were all claiming to have 'experimented with drugs'."

"One-upmanship," said Severn. "A bit of pot at uni, an opium pipe at an Afghan wedding, a little light opioid addiction during a secondment to Wisconsin, a meth lab *après-ski* in Vermont, sharing needles during a Sydney climate-change bushfire demo… Nobody wants to come across like Alec Home or Harold Macmillan."

I looked down at Rassendyll, sprawled across the carpet.

"Robert partook as a student at Oxford," continued Sir Roger, "He resumed the habit at a party thrown by one of his telly chums. Said it helped relieve the stress of Number Ten - and his marriage." He pursed his lips like Miroslav does after a bad flunge on *Duelling with the Stars*. "I didn't approve. But I'm square. Not part of the United Kinkdom set. I don't fly my Union Freak Flag."

I knelt down by Rassendyll and listened again to the slow, heavy breathing. "Is the ambulance coming?"

"If we do that," said Severn, "we'll destroy the Prime Minister, the government, the party – and possibly the country, too."

"But you just said everybody does cocaine…"

"The PM isn't a weather girl on the telly or an ex-footballer!" he roared. "What's sauce for the celebrity airhead goose is not yet sauce for the King's prime gander."

"But he could die!"

"Mr Elphberg," said Fritz, leaning back against the table and crossing his legs, "before my election, I was a doctor in Graz. I have seen many cases of contaminated drugs. Heroin laced with anthrax."

"Anthrax?"

"After examination of Mr Rassendyll," he continued, "I conclude that his cocaine was adulterated with atropine, a tropane alkaloid extracted from belladonna or mandrake. We have had several instances in Austria. It can cause ventricular fibrillation, loss of balance, amnesia, disorientation, and in extreme cases coma."

I'm just a layman, but "coma" sounded pretty serious to me. Not to Fritz, though. "I do not believe the Prime Minister's life is in any danger," he concluded airily.

"So you're a doctor in Graz," I said, "and a Member of the European Parliament." I peered at him. "Any other strings to your g'dulka? What's going on?"

Roger Severn chuckled as he lit his pipe and puffed hard. "Are you suggesting Fritz and I spiked the Prime Minister's 'snow'? His 'blow'? His 'charlie'? His 'nose candy'? His 'booger sugar'?"

Eventually my host wearied of his *Thesaurus for Drug Fiends* routine. "I'm afraid Robert Rassendyll doesn't need any help from me to screw up his life, his career and his country." Severn leaned back in his chair. "The Prime Minister's 'bad trip' puts us in a quandary. He has a vitally important ceremonial parade to attend tomorrow. He cannot postpone it for a photo-op in Emergency Ward Ten, followed by a state visit to the Stables celebrity dry-out programme and a heartwarming appearance with Piers Morgan." He grimaced in distaste. "So we have a problem."

For a second he fell quiet. And then, knitting his unusually expressive brows, Severn took his pipe from his mouth and remarked casually: "You saw Rassendyll's address to the nation last night?"

"Bits," I replied. "I was a little distracted."

Fritz provided a helpful précis. "There'll always be an England. Not."

"As a man grows old, Mr Elphberg, he believes in Fate. Fate sent you here. Fate sends you now to Downing Street."

"I don't understand," I said.

There was a long silence before Sir Roger resumed. "There are two stories they tell of the Elphbergs and the Rassendylls. The first you heard earlier - King Rudolf III and Countess Amelia. The second circulates among an even smaller band and took place a century-and-a-half later. An Englishman came to Ruritania on the eve of the coronation of Rudolf V, and did your kingdom some signal service. His name was Mr Rassendyll, brother of the then Lord Burlesdon. Mr

Rassendyll was the spitting image of the then King Rudolf, just as you are the spitting image of the present Mr Rassendyll."

Ah, the spitting. Lady Belinda on her doorstep. She had seen it, too.

And Severn proceeded to relate an amazing tale – of an Englishman who took the role of a Ruritanian king at his own coronation. "There are those," he concluded, "who insinuate that Mr Rassendyll, and not King Rudolf V, may have been your great-great-grandfather – a quid pro quo for the Countess Amelia."

Sir Roger paused and took a long, unhurried puff of his pipe. "An Englishman played the King in Ruritania's hour of need. Now a Ruritanian must play a prime minister. In England's hour of need."

It took a moment for what he was proposing to sink in.

"You're mad!" I said.

He stood up, and walked around the slumbering Rassendyll, prodding him with his marmalade footwear, as if searching for something. A spine perhaps. "This is an Englishman?" he asked, and then answered his own question: "This is an Englishman." He sat down again, with a weary sigh. "And so the fate of England rests on a Ruritanian plumber."

"Why should I care about England?"

"Because sooner or later you'll care about something," snapped Fritz, whirling round from the French windows. "So you might as well start now."

"Because you've launched your little game? Mister I-Just-Happened-to-Be-Passing-the-Prime-Minister's-Comatose-Body-and-I'm-an-Expert-in-Badly-Cut-Cocaine?"

"You little twerp!" He caught himself.

"What do you want with me?"

"You look the part," said Severn, "once we get rid of that beard. Tomorrow morning, you will wake up in Downing Street. Your car will take you to Portland Place, where you will march in a parade to Trafalgar Square."

"Trafalgar Square? You want me to play Rassendyll in full view of London?"

"It's a big parade. Lots of floats, some very eye-catching. You don't have to say anything. You don't have to be that good. It's little more than a grand national photo-op." He paused to relight his pipe. "Think of it as a long mustard ad."

I stood up. "Thanks for a livelier evening than I expected, Sir Roger, but I'm pretty tuckered out after five sets with the King and all things consi…"

And then I sat down again. Because I'd reminded myself of the tennis. In a movie, the underdog would have won that last point, and the match. But in life, as usual, I hadn't. I wanted another shot.

"You want me to impersonate Rob Rassendyll," I said. "But I'm Ruritanian. I can't do the accent."

"Actually, your English sounds too plummy," responded Sir Roger, mimicking me. "Rassendyll is like most of the aristocracy these days, determinedly downwardly mobile. He affects what they call 'estuary English'. But he doesn't do it very well. So you not doing him very well will sound to the casual ear as if his feeble pandering is getting even worse."

"How will it sound to the uncasual ear?"

He shrugged. "It's a big parade. Not a lot of talking. My scheme is a risk. A risk of disaster against the certainty of disaster, if this wretch -" He kicked Rassendyll again. "- has to be de-coked in full view of the world's media. A risk against a certainty. I'll take those odds."

"If he's such a wretch, why not let him be exposed as a cocaine addict and chased from office?"

"Because the alternatives are even worse," hissed Fritz.

"So why do you think this sad husk of a country is worth saving? Or that you can save it?"

"I don't know that I can," replied Sir Roger. "And you're right - this England probably isn't worth saving. But suppose we pull it off, plumber boy! Good God, we'll have something to look back on. I'll be a geriatric bore at my fourteenth-century manor house, and you'll be a leathery old Modenstein turkey hunter, or whatever voiceover artistes do in retirement. But in our hearts will beat a great adventure. We can say we gave it our best. We played the game – and, by God, we lived, man! We *lived!*"

He looked at me triumphantly, and pretty obviously expected me to chip in.

"Spiffing," I said, thinking myself into the part. "Abso-bally-lutely!"

Even as he'd been perorating, I knew what my answer would be. Why wouldn't I say yes? What reason would I have for saying no? "I'm sorry, I have to return to Modenstein for a pressing engagement as a sacked straight man's lookalike." I would never be king in Strelsau but I could be prime minister in London – for a day. Why not?

"So what's the parade?" I asked.

"It's the Pride Parade."

"Because everyone has so much pride in Britain on the eve of a new reign?"

Fritz tittered. "It's the annual LGBTQ parade," said Severn. "There are a few other letters after the Q. More each year, but I wouldn't worry about them."

I looked blank.

"Gays!" he exploded. "Hang it, man! Homosexuals! You must have them in Ruritania…"

I didn't like to tell him that, what with recent demographic changes, gays didn't do a lot of parading in Ruritania. I'd been expecting a pre-Coronation march, perhaps with HRH Prince Richard, Duke of Albany, and the Bengal Lancers. "Why is a gay parade a matter of vital national importance?" I asked.

Severn proceeded to explain that it was all the fault of Justin Trudeau in Canada. Shortly after becoming prime minister, he'd taken the critical decision to be the first head of government to march in a Pride parade – and thereby raised the stakes for everybody else. "I'm old enough to remember when a PM wouldn't have been caught dead marching with a lot of prancing buggers. But times change. Your predecessor but two started the tradition of sending a video greeting, congratulating the LGBTQQ2SEtc community on how far it had come. But young Monsieur Trudeau really put us under the gun. And that was before the whole Tranny-Get-Your-Gun business blew up in Robert's face. We've been debating it in Cabinet for months. Should we give in to pressure and send the Prime Minister? Or hold the line and send one of our several gay and lesbian ministers? Or would that look too obvious? Eventually the spinmeisters decided there was more upside in getting Robert to march and making a big ballyhoo of it all.

THE PRISONER OF WINDSOR

So we can't let the team down now. Big Gay will come down on us like a ton of gay bricks if we have to announce he's 'indisposed'…"

To be honest, I'd have preferred subbing at a coronation, or maybe a state banquet or a Nato summit.

Severn detected my reluctance. "You're comfortable around homosexuals, are you? You don't recoil if they get too close or anything like that? I gather the gaydar gets a bit twitchy east of the Landstrasse. Can't afford anything like that on live telly."

I couldn't really see what the big deal was, but it would give Big Sig a laugh when I got home. "This is your idea," I said. "So presumably you have a razor."

Fritz carefully removed the ring from the Prime Minister's finger, placed it on mine, and then began undressing Rassendyll. Sir Roger returned a minute later with an electric beard trimmer, a wet razor, and a tube of shaving cream. Truefitt & Hill.

"A close shave," he said. "Like all the best adventures."

He opened a side door in the panelling to reveal a small windowless water closet with worn wainscoting, and some framed nineteenth-century cartoons of plump top-hatted Englishmen in Paris with can-can dancers. I stepped inside, turned on the hissing taps, plugged in the beard trimmer, and contemplated in the mirror, for one last time, the hirsute visage of an obscure unwanted Ruritanian royal.

Ten minutes later, the smooth and fragrant face of the Prime Minister of the United Kingdom was staring back at me.

Chapter Nine
Bottom warming

THE DINING ROOM door opened, and the PM and his host the Lord Privy Seal emerged bantering jocularly.

"Love to stay, Roger," said I, "but…"

I was stumped. If I really would have loved to stay, then why couldn't I? 5am cabinet meeting? Breakfast delegation of trans activists? Official release hour of the new variant?

"Alas, *tempus fugit*," purred Sir Roger, smoothly filling the yawning gap. "Busy day tomorrow."

The "protection officer" was already on his feet.

"Indeed," I said. "And I'm sure…"

I looked blankly at the officer. What was his name again? This was more difficult than it looked.

"…I'm sure Sanjay is anxious to get back to his…"

God, did Sanjay have a wife and kids to get back to? Or did he live a solitary life unloved except by his parakeet?

"…get back to his, er, loved ones."

Officer Sanjay stood blank and mute. Why didn't he say something? Nudge the banter along instead of leaving me to do all the work.

I was to learn very quickly that world leaders move from one stilted and sputtering non-conversation to the next. Everyone seems to think it's your job to advance the pleasantries. Tires a fellow out. Especially after five sets of real tennis and excessive claret consumption and dragging comatose prime ministers from the dining room to the wine cellar.

"Nothing like loved ones to get back to, is there?" I asked, without much hope of getting an answer.

"You're burbling, Robert," chuckled Sir Roger. "If I were you, I'd have a well-deserved nap on the ride back to town."

I took that as an order.

The night air hit me harder than Severn's bucket of cold water. It wasn't a parlour game in an English country house anymore. I was in Rob Rassendyll's kingdom and I'd usurped his throne. A few metres ahead, "my" driver, Vic, held the door of the prime ministerial Jaguar. It felt like marching to the scaffold. Everything was louder: the crunch of my feet on the gravel, the faint roar from the motorway somewhere beyond Sir Roger's perfect ha-ha and thirteenth-century hedgerows.

Even at that hour, the car journey seemed to take forever. I closed my eyes, pretended to sleep, and thought about Roger Severn's instructions. It was ridiculous to be impersonating the British prime minister. But then my so-called normal life - the rightful King of Ruritania living in a one-room flat – was ridiculous anyway, so I figured I was pretty much born to it. I struggled to remember all Severn had told me, and made a great show of pretending to rouse myself from my slumbers as we passed Buckingham Palace, went down the Mall, and turned into Whitehall. The Downing Street gates opened, and the Jaguar cruised through and came to a halt at Number Ten. "'Ere we are, sir," said Vic.

I stepped out, and stood before the famous black door with the stark brass "10" lit by a single lamp above. It was one of those very English jests the rest of us don't quite get: The most powerful man in the land living in an upmarket terrace house, "Number Ten", with a letter box in the front door, for the postman to slide through the phone bill, and only the words inscribed thereon ("First Lord of the Treasury") and the lion's-head knocker and the crown surmounting the lantern to suggest that behind the façade beats the iron heart of British power. In the cold night air my alcohol-fuelled exhilaration shrivelled and I knew I was too foreign to pull this off. I would have fled if I'd known how or where. Instead, the famous door opened and, as Walpole and Wellington, Gladstone and Disraeli, Churchill and Thatcher, Blair and ...well, whoever it was after that... as all had done before me, I put my foot on the great white flagstone and stepped across the threshold. Then I tripped and fell over – which, on reflection, Walpole, Wellington et al probably hadn't done.

I lay sprawled on the black-and-white checkerboard marble like a toppled chess piece. "All right, Prime Minister?" said the doorkeeper, helping me to my feet.

"Thanks awfully," I mumbled. "Long night." And, anxious not to prolong it, I tried to remember the directions Severn had given me.

It was difficult. Number Ten looks like an unassuming London home from the outside, and then that bloody door opens and a vast maze of corridors and connecting rooms and multiple staircases spreads out before you. Severn had done his best to keep me on the straight and narrow with very precise directions. I would see on the right of the entrance hall a handsome marble fireplace – that's the one that visiting world leaders get photographed in front of. In the corner was the porter's chair, a wacky hooded Chippendale contraption that, according to Sir Roger, used to be outside on the pavement for the policeman to sit in. There was a drawer underneath to put hot coals in and keep your bottom warm. My bottom was quite warm enough, thank you. As I attempted to slouch past, all I could hear was the deafening ticking of an impossibly loud case-clock booming out the hour of my doom. Two old-time gentlemen gazed down from the wall – former prime ministers, I'd hazard. They eyed me with obvious scepticism. Thank God it was the middle of the night and the place was, doorman aside, deserted.

Beyond the hall stretched endless acres of carpet leading who knows where. I headed for the famous staircase, lined with engravings of my many predecessors. I couldn't examine them too closely, of course – you don't want to appear too obviously a tourist when you infiltrate a big-time head-of-government job – but Lord North, Pitt the Younger, Earl Grey, Viscount Palmerston and the rest of the gang went dancing by like chorus girls on the old SFR *Socialist Variety Hour*. I wobbled at the small halfway landing, and steadied myself on the mahogany handrail. Severn had explained that my bedroom was at the top of another, more ordinary staircase. We'd discussed its whereabouts in some depth, but somewhere in my tipsy haze I'd lost the relevant info. I opened a door onto a high-ceilinged drawing room with chandeliers and heavy oil paintings hanging from picture rails. Didn't have that lived-in look. Onward. There was a large anteroom with drab carpet and wood panelled walls, and in the corner, tucked out of sight, the opening to a small enclosed stairway. I trudged up, and found myself in a poky London flat.

God bless the Brits, I thought. Housing their head of government in an attic. Now where was my room? I didn't want to start my premiership by climbing into bed with the upstairs maid, assuming I had one. But there was no sign of a maid, and not much of an upstairs. The first door I opened had a double bed in it. Good enough.

Big day tomorrow. Off to the Pride Parade to save England! Hey, why not?

I remembered Sir Roger's instructions and tottered off to slumberland. But not before gazing out the window at the glittering city beyond. London at night. Humanity in all its variety was out there under the rooftops. Young lovers were smooching, young cokeheads were hoovering their nose charlie blow sugar, Eurobankers were checking the Hong Kong markets, Asian storekeepers were rising from their beds above the corner shop, bored businessmen were paying off their escorts, transitioning schoolgirls were chugging down their puberty blockers, Albanian migrants were ordering complimentary room service in five-star hotels, Ruritanian plumbers were staring at the ceiling after second bananas with Essex girls...

And I was their prime minister.

II
A servant of the public

CHAPTER TEN

The adventures of an understudy

P RIME MINISTER... Prime Minister... Prime Minister... The words seemed to be oozing through my brain like southern Hentzau's famous pomegranate brandy, sweet and viscose. What a glorious dream!

And then I realised it wasn't a dream. I opened my bleary eyes and through the haze of a full furred-tongue hangover became aware that I was playing to a full house.

"Wakey-wakey, Prime Minister," said a weaselly fellow with narrow eyes, a large veiny nose and toilet-brush hair. "The 7.45 waits for no man."

"Euuurrrgh," I croaked, taking in the crowd gathered down the end of the bed. The morning sun glinting off the *bogbürste* bloke's cufflink obliged me to squint, but I seemed to discern in total two males, one female; two pinstripes, one houndstooth; three different facial hues – black, white, something in between – but the curtains were partially drawn and they moved around and seemed to change colours.

"Tea, Prime Minister," said the lady *d'un certain âge*. She was black, I think, with glossy ringlet hair in a striking up-do. High, sculpted cheekbones, with a hint of authority. The houndstooth suit accentuated the figure, teacup in one hand, the other clutching a pile of papers nestling just under the assertive swell of her ebony bosom... *God, forget that. Focus, Elphberg.* Who was she again? She deposited the cup on the nightstand. Brisk. Touch of the blue pantyhose, is that the English expression?

"Great." *Remember the accent, remember the accent.* "Greeaaaaat." *Whoa, too much drawl: rein in the accent.* I raised myself up and took a gulp. Eeugh, it was a sickly sweet tisane.

"Hoo aboot breakfurrst in bed, ye wee capper?" offered a man of South Asian extraction with impossibly good Bollywood looks and a pronounced Scottish burr. "I' woo' sehv taem. We need tae start o' th' doot."

I lowered my eyes to his chest in hopes there might be scrolling subtitles.

"It was your idea," said the black *blauerstrumpf*. "Said it was important to get all our ducks in a row. Make sure we're all singing from the same hymnal."

I stared at her open-mouthed. Hard to handle all this vernacular first thing.

"Personally, I was looking forward to a meeting-free weekend. But you texted on the way to Roger Severn's to put it back. Unless it was another mobile prank from the reptiles at *The Sun*."

For want of anything useful to contribute, I remained slack-jawed. Sir Roger had said nothing about meetings in Downing Street. It struck me this might be a good time to claim there'd been a terrible mix-up, and I was really a Ruritanian plumber who'd lost his bearings on the way back from the pub. But instead I sank back on the pillows, and dribbled, "Ducking reptiles from the same hymnal? Excellent."

"Looks like ye ha' a roof nicht, PM," said the Bollywood Scotsman, peering intently. "Ye face i' deathly pale, well peely wally."

That's because it had been under a thick forest of facial hair until the small hours. "Give me ten minutes," I said, "and I'll be fighting fit." *Good. Confident command of vernacular English.* "Ready to face the day. Shipshape and Bristol fashion."

"Shipshape and Bristol fashion?" repeated the weaselly one. "Ten minutes." And they shuffled reluctantly from the room.

I should have seen this coming when Sir Roger was spinning me his ripping yarns from Rudolf V's coronation, but isn't this just typical? You agree to fill in for some chap at a quickie parade to Trafalgar Square, and it sounds a piece of cake, and next thing you know you're expected to take over a working prime ministership. And the critical difference between mega-important people and everybody else is that the bigshots are never alone. It had required enormous strength of will merely to deflect that trio from accompanying me into the shower. I turned my pallid face up to the thin spray and tried to scald a bit of colour into it while I pondered the lie of the land. She didn't miss much, that …what was her name again? Dame Millie Trehearne, Chief of Staff, that was it. And the Highland Hindu was Angus Bannerman, Director of Communications and Strategy. The bog-brushed weasel was Rory Vane, Senior Policy Advisor to Rob Rassendyll.

I switched on the radio hoping for something jolly from Stormzy or Nigel and the Reverts. Instead there was breaking news about a fertiliser explosion in Geneva. Someone had driven a lorry at full speed through a sidewalk café. There were unconfirmed reports, said the news reader, that the driver had been heard to yell "Allahu Akbar!" before the vehicle burst into flames. But on the other hand his Facebook page showed a picture of him visiting Florida nine years ago, so he may well have links to the American alt-right. Or he could be a populist farmer objecting to having to convert to locust production. An expert said this showed why we needed to invest more in hybrids and electric cars.

The room was curiously devoid of human personality. On the desk there was a framed photograph of a woman of approximately Rassendyll's age. His "missus", presumably. But it gave the air of having no particular connection to him – as if it was the generic smiling-relative snapshot that comes when you buy the photo frame.

Still, he had a well-stocked wardrobe. Have you ever acted? The drama-school classes go on about motivation, but I would say sixty per cent of it's the costume. Clothes makyth the man, or a plausible simulacrum thereof. I'd felt like a fake naked under the sheets with the entourage hectoring me. But a freshly starched shirt, cufflinks, dark blue tie and suit had a transformative effect: I looked in the mirror and suddenly felt like a million euros. Every centimetre a prime minister. I tried out a couple of useful lines: "Why don't you handle that one, Sir Roger?" At the dresser, they worked great.

So I exited the bedroom with a confident stride, and found myself in a very crowded non-socially-distant sitting room. People were either sprawled or perched - everywhere. The sprawlers took the well-stuffed armchairs and a pair of floral-print sofas. The perchers perched on chair arms and squeezed into awkward window seats. Whether perched or sprawled, they were all staring at me, aghast.

"Oh, my God!" cried Rory Vane. "*Quel horreur!*"

"The Geneva attack? I know, I just heard about it."

"Wha' iss she wurrin'?" said Angus, the Bollywood bloke.

Rory stood up. "Let's not go rogue on the big day, okay?" He took me by the elbow, marched me back into the bedroom, and pointed at an Ottoman: "Every item as agreed." On top was a pile of neatly folded clothes I'd failed to spot. "So whip off your kit," said Rory, already sliding off my jacket, "and don't come back until you're in the approved gear."

Six minutes later, after something of a struggle, I returned to the 7.45 clad in a tight T-shirt and even tighter trousers that, as well as being canary yellow, clung somewhat painfully. Everyone applauded.

"That's more like it," said Rory. "Wait till Justin Trudeau sees this."

"Eminently shaggable," piped up a young lad scrunched on the radiator. "Sorry," he mumbled, blushing.

"Love the T-shirt," a girl in a boxy suit perching next to him agreed in a cut-glass accent. It was black with a bright orange slogan: *Nobody knows I'm gay.*

"But I'm not gay," I said. And then it occurred to me that Sir Roger had briefed me rather hurriedly, and who knows what he'd forgotten to mention. "Am I?"

"Honestly, PM," groaned Dame Millie. "Please cut out these Roger Severn benders. We've been through that." And she "reminded" me that it was, because I'm not gay, that "Nobody knows I'm gay" was a pitch-perfect line. It signalled to gays that I was at ease with being thought gay. But because I was so obviously heterosexual (at this Rory Vane sniggered) it was non-threatening to my homophobic Brexit base.

"The focus groups loved it, didn't they, Angus?"

"Och, tha dood," agreed Angus. "Fae be'er tha' Option B." Option B, it seemed, was a T-shirt with the slogan *Nobody knows I have a vagina*, which sixty-seven per cent of the focus group thought was "edgier" but forty-three per cent assumed was literally true. "Bu' we dinna focus-grupp ye trews," he added, "an' they shoo off ye wee bonnie bahoochie well byoo'fly."

Dame Millie beckoned me to sit, patting the cushion between her and Rory. I sank into the flowery sofa, and kept sinking. I thought it would swallow me and ma wee bonnie bahoochie, but eventually it stopped. The sofa had only two cushions, which meant I was sitting on the seams. I'm not one to grumble, really I'm not, but in buttock-hugging pants tufted piping was the last thing I needed after two hours' sleep.

"Th' PM had a wee dram orr twae yestreen," explained Angus to the perchers.

"We have good news and bad news," said Rory.

"About Geneva?" I asked, anxious to get on to the terror attack.

But Angus was passing around spreadsheets. The bad news was that Rassendyll's approval rating had fallen to twenty-two per cent. The good news was that the early polling showed a clear majority thought "my" remarks would defuse both the autographed-Koran crisis and the genetic-defects crisis.

"How can they possibly know that?" I said.

"Och, it's th' noo taechnology," replied Angus. "Pur barry. Wurr peggin' oot a coffer tae Panopticon, bu' iss woorth every plack an' farden. Ye can really drill doon intae th' metrics."

"No, I meant, how can anyone know whether my speech will defuse the genetic-defects crisis?" The perchers stared at me uncomprehendingly. "I mean, until it does defuse it, how can anyone know that it's going to?"

Angus gave me a faintly condescending look. "Iss the same as th' polling on th' NHS reforms. Th' anticipation o' success prefigures th' perception o' success."

"Which in turn may prefigure actual success," said Rory. "Who knows?" And everyone laughed.

I thought I should do something to prefigure the perception of me as prime ministerial, so I said: "What about this attack in Geneva?" It didn't sound quite right coming from a chap in bright yellow trousers, but I gave it my best. "Pretty grisly."

Rory gave an exasperated sigh. "We all know the drill. No formal statement unless the death toll hits double figures and there's at least one British national. Imogen?"

The perching girl in the boxy suit who'd admired my T-shirt thumbed her *handifon*. "Eight. So far no Brit fatalities, just one wounded Bermudian on his way to open a bank account. There seems to be some confusion as to whether the hashtag should be #JeSuisGeneva or #JeSuisGenève. Lots of people don't seem to know what the latter is, and can't do the accent on their phones."

"Any preference, PM?" asked Rory.

I thought I should try to sound assertive. "Do we *have* to have a hashtag?"

There was an embarrassing silence.

"Anything else?"

The lad on the radiator who'd found me eminently shaggable said: "External Zone (Qualified Recognition) Harmonisation Directive Modification Order…"

"Zzzz. Growing so sleepy..," droned Rory, and pretended to keel over.

"One other thing to keep an eye on, Prime Minister," said Imogen. "The British Council building in Jalalabad has been set alight."

Dame Millie yawned. "Any particular reason?"

"Do they get the overnights in Jalalabad?" I asked Angus.

Rory got to his feet, and contemplated me as if I were a small child. "I think we're done, PM. And we don't want to keep Cabinet waiting, do we?"

Cabinet? Then who the hell were this crowd?

"Cabine' on a braw bricht Saturday morni'," said Angus. "Shoos hoo awfy impurrtant thuss busnaess is."

Righty-ho. Emergency Cabinet for the terror attack. As we descended the famous Downing Street staircase, foxy women in business suits emerged from who knows where and hovered at my elbow with manila folders.

"Belgian excess mortality you wanted, PM. Love the T-shirt."

Belgian excess mortality: always good to have that. I nodded prime-ministerially, and took the stairs with a renewed, albeit trouser-constrained, spring in my gait. Then I spotted, waiting at the foot, a secretary. Or maybe she was Chancellor of the Exchequer. Who knew? And it occurred to me to wonder whether, gait-wise, Rob Rassendyll was the springy type. I slowed and took the remaining steps cautiously, trying to remember how the PM had walked into Severn's dining room. As I reached the bottom, I brayed, "Morning, Alison!"

"Brenda," she said. "But I'll take the compliment. Alison's at least fifteen years younger."

I laughed awkwardly. "Late night, I gather," she continued briskly, giving my trousers the once over. "Most men your age couldn't carry off canary yellow, Prime Minister. Most men any age really."

THE PRISONER OF WINDSOR

I stood frozen, as I hadn't a clue in what direction I was supposed to be heading. "Come on," she chided, taking my elbow. And I followed her into a room of florid wallpaper with little to relieve it except, glowering down, a portrait of Winston Churchill in wartime-resilience mode. I bet he'd never had to wear a "Nobody knows I'm gay" T-shirt.

Brenda and Alison held open the double doors, and I entered the Cabinet Room of 10 Downing Street. Across the threshold, framed by a pair of classical columns, was a long table, shaped like a very large coffin lid, at which sat a couple of dozen men and women in assorted sizes, colours, and degrees of unattractiveness. I moved to the far side of the right-hand pillar and headed toward them.

"Taking the long way round, Prime Minister?" sniffed a chap who turned out to be the Secretary of State for Northern Ireland. I saw what he meant. Across the other side of the table was an empty mahogany chair, set at an angle. The only one with arms. In front of the marble fireplace. With the clock on the mantle. Underneath the only portrait in the room – of some obviously prime ministerial fellow. Whole set-up had Numero Uno *Oberboss* written all over, and I'd missed it.

Great start.

"Always good to see things from a different perspective," I said, trotting to the far end of the table and heading back down the correct side. There were a few forced, insincere laughs. I slid into the prime ministerial chair, stared at the handsome silver candlestick and put my elbows on the brown baize.

"Baize": there's a word I hadn't used in a while.

Have you ever found yourself chairing a cabinet meeting of a country you don't live in and whose senior government figures are entirely unknown to you? If so, you'll appreciate my predicament. I looked around. Pasty white blokes. A large woman with a heavy moustache. Black guy with a dangling earing. Mousy Asian gal on the verge of tears. An old queen in a two-tone shirt. A trimly bearded Muslim dripping more bling than a pimp. It was like the world's worst Benetton ad.

But no sign of Roger Severn.

How's a cabinet meeting supposed to start? My eyes fell on the leather blotter and the cream paper headed "Cabinet Room, First

Lord" but otherwise blank. No help there. I took a sip of water, toyed with a decorative silver box filled with pencils, and examined the bottom of the candlestick. After that, I was all out of delaying tactics.

"Bad news from Geneva," I said. It occurred to me that using people's titles might obscure the awkward fact that I had no idea of their names. "Why don't you go first, Foreign Secretary?" I suggested toward my right.

From my left came a voice. "Just the usual excitable Mohammedan," said the Foreign Secretary, as I swivelled hastily and found myself looking straight into the eyes of that chap who ate all the toffees in Lady Belinda's husband's study – what was his name? Rupert?

"Unless it's a non-organic farmer," he added. "Heidi's grandfather after he's reverted."

From opposite, a shaven-headed man who looked like a Belarusian bouncer at my brother's nightclub interrupted. "Of more concern to our allies is the smelly snowflakes putting a spanner in Evensong at Westminster Abbey this close to the big day. As usual, the Yanks have their knickers in a twist. Scared of a bunch of fifth-year uni wankers up their own jaxies."

I was evidently expected to offer some penetrating insight here. Not sure I had one to hand. Fortunately, I remembered something from the "7.45". "What about this torching of the British Council in Jalalabad? Any details on that, Foreign Secretary?"

He brushed it aside. "Oh, you know. The natives are restless. When aren't they?"

A woman in a hijab scowled across the table at him. "A protest against Colin Corgi?"

"Buggered if I know," responded the Foreign Secretary. "Could be that this was more of your time-honoured, traditional, bog-standard British Council-torching. Reports indicate they burned an effigy of Theresa May."

I was just wondering where one would get an effigy of Theresa May in Jalalabad, when the doors swung open and there was Sir Roger Severn. "Sorry I'm late," he said. "Bit of a whoopsy round Paddington. Coronation road-improvement. Should be finished in time for the Silver Jubilee."

"You know everyone here, of course," I offered.

"I'm afraid to say I do," he drawled, sliding into the seat next to a tweedy baroness. Of course, he knew everyone here. Just as I was supposed to know everyone here. It's a very strange feeling when everyone in the room knows you but you don't know anyone. Sort of how a king must feel opening a shopping mall.

"The Foreign Secretary was just saying that an effigy of Theresa May was burned in Jalalabad..."

"Yeah, well," responded the nightclub bouncer, "can we leave that for Thursday? I don't want to waste the weekend on our branch office in Hoogivsastan. Can we get to the main order of business?"

"You mean the terror attack?"

"I mean this buggering parade. For the record, I object to that T-shirt. The slogan's obviously designed to make you look like you're only wearing a shirt saying you're gay because you're not - which raises the suspicion that you are and the slogan's a flimsy and unconvincing way to disguise that."

I tried to recall Dame Millie's rationale.

"We've been around this every which way," said a black woman across the table with visible impatience. "The trans thing – what was that slogan again?"

"'Nobody knows I have a vagina,'" said Rupert. "Edgy. But not sure the PM could carry it off. I could, of course."

"Whereas the gay thing is, like, last year's edgy," said the black woman. "And last year's edgy is the place to be – is that the idea?"

"I still don't know why we didn't send *you*," the Foreign Secretary answered her.

"I'm not a professional lesbian," she said, "any more than I'm a professional Negress."

"Yes, but your saying 'I'm not a professional lesbian' every five minutes is becoming a kind of professional lesbianism in itself, isn't it?" boomed an extremely loud woman with spectacular blonde hair, shoulder pads and intimidating cleavage.

"It's a question of diplomatic calibration," said Rupert. "Like the appropriate level of royal duchess to attend a dictator's funeral."

"That's why we have to send someone who's heterosexual," insisted the non-professional lesbian.

"Yes, but not over-assertively heterosexual..." said the lady in the hijab, glancing at the shaven-headed heavy. "...because then it looks as if we're insecure."

"But not insufficiently heterosexual..." He glanced at the bloke with the earring. "...because then the hacks will speculate on whether he's a closet case."

And round and round we went. I stared at a rather dull landscape on the wall opposite and wondered when we'd be getting on to terrorism or something.

But we didn't, and at last it was over. Severn tapped me ever so lightly on the elbow and gave what I think was meant to be an encouraging smile. Presumably he was feeling bad that the dummy he'd persuaded to fill in for one minor photo-op had wound up having to chair a Cabinet meeting. "Best of British, old thing," he murmured as we strolled out to the prime-ministerial Jaguar. And with that I was Sir Rogerless, flying solo.

Chapter Eleven
On the march

EXCEPT I WASN'T. There was a lady on the opposite seat with her back to me, staring out the window. When the door closed, she turned around. It was the woman from the photograph in Rassendyll's bedroom. That's to say, Mrs Rassendyll. His wife. *My* wife.

The car was much larger than Sir Roger's, but for some reason we seemed closer than we ought to be, even with a chunky arm rest between us. Where Lady Belinda expended some care in her appearance, this one seemed to have given up. Her ash blonde hair was a mess and her make-up was applied erratically across a pallid face. The shoulder of her blouse had slipped and a sliver of bra strap was visible.

And yet she was beautiful. Fragile and careworn and beautiful. Her thin translucent hands lay folded on her lap. There was not a flicker of interest in her grey eyes.

"Robert," she said, without moving her lips.

"Darling," I replied, in the absence of anything more specific. Severn had dumped a tonne of names in my head, and I didn't think it would be a smart move to do the Brenda-Alison routine with my beloved spouse. Then again, her grey-eyed death stare wasn't exactly functioning as an *aide memoire*. Mandy? Cindy? Oh, forget it. I leaned forward to kiss her, but she turned away and I wound up mwa-mwa-ing her hair, which smelt of cheap hotel shampoo.

"'Darling'?" she repeated accusingly. "'Darling'? Trying to think yourself into the part, are you?" The Prime Minister's wife expelled a long, weary sigh. "Neither of us are good enough actors to keep up this charade." She stared bleakly out the window.

I was trying to think of something to break the ice, when my door opened and Angus Bannerman said, "Coo' ye lift oop th' wee armrust an' shuft oover?"

"No," I protested. "I had to sit on the middle of the sofa."

"Well, yee're tha wun who cuh th' boodget fo' th' second moh'ur. And ai'm wurrin' ma best suit, no' wee trews wi' nae crease."

I shifted over. Mrs Rassendyll inclined her head and appraised my T-shirt. "Nobody knows you're gay," she intoned, expressionless.

The chill in the car was making my nipples erect. I was feeling less prime ministerial every second.

"Good of ye' tae do this, Mrs Rrrrrrr," said Angus. Evidently, at the last minute, it had been decided that it would look better if, instead of going alone to the gay parade in a gay T-shirt, I were to be accompanied by my wife. Gay-friendly, but not too non-heterosexual: that was the particular sweet spot they were aiming for.

"Good to have you marching alongside," I said.

She snorted. "You're all wet there. No beards allowed in the parade, are there, Angus?"

I was tired and almost said, "They made me shave off mine last night." Instead, I deduced that she would be attending but not actually participating, just standing off to one side and waving. More fine calibration: I was meant to appear understatedly heterosexual, but not ostentatiously non-gay. Angus had numbers showing that focus-groups would be fine with a homosexual prime minister as long as it wasn't me: Rassendyll had come top in a poll of "Which Prime Minister would make the Worst Gay?", just ahead of the Earl of Rosebery.

"Are you hoping for a prize with that costume?" Wendy asked. "A week in Mykonos? Let's get this over with."

And the chauffeur took that as a cue to drive off.

Wendy. That was it. Wendy Rassendyll.

Squeezed on the back seat between Wendy and Angus, I could feel myself sweating, so I grabbed a bottle of Black Country spring water from the seat pocket and tried to chug calmly.

"Hurr'rr th' wee sleekit grupps ye need tae giv a waed burrrth tae." Angus handed me a sheet of impenetrable acronyms and started to test me: "QUIA?"

My mind was a blank.

"Och, tha's easy. Queers Against Israeli Apartheid. Hoo aboot BDS?"

"Bull Dykes for Sharia?"

"Bisexual Divestment Strategies. Och, and dinna go noor EUTOPIA..."

They were the Eurosexual Tops Interchange Association.

"I had no idea there was so much politics in sex."

Angus looked at me as if I'd just landed from Hofbau. "What's this word mean?" I asked, pointing at a particularly lavish acronym.

THE PRISONER OF WINDSOR

"Och, ye can jabber away to them to ye heart's content. Wurr vairy keen tae encourage them." This was the Transgender And Queer Islamic Youth Association, or TAQIYA, and apparently Mr Rassendyll was all in favour of them.

It was a short drive through the expensive part of London to the parade's starting point. Wendy rose from the car to be escorted to the reviewing stand, and with her departure the tension dissipated. I adjusted my T-shirt and checked that my *hochzeitausrüstung* was snug in my excruciatingly tight yellow trousers, and then, with Angus close behind, I stepped out and into the assembled ranks of Portland Place. A gay group of high dignitaries awaited me, meticulously viro-sprayed by a Scotland Yard public-health team. At the head of the group was a tall old woman, covered with medals, and of military bearing. She was the first transgender field marshal in the British Army – which was widely considered to be one of Rassendyll's bolder innovations, even if it did cost Nato the Mali campaign. She waved cheerily to socially distant rows of soldiers, with weapons drawn, lining both sides of the street and the rooftops. Alongside the field marshal stood Canada's first two-spirited High Commissioner to the United Kingdom in his/her ceremonial headdress, and the first non-binary head of the Royal College of Doctors, who spent alternate days working as the first non-binary head of the Royal College of Nurses. No one betrayed the least suspicion of my imposture, and I felt the agitated beating of my heart subside.

Presently we formed into procession. Big Sig would have appreciated all the corporate sponsorship – *The Daily Telegraph*, HSBC, Guinness, British Airways, the Church of England, the BBC. The European Union had sent a float of lesbian bureaucrats from Strasbourg to what they called the "External Zone (Qualified Recognition) Pride Parade" offering qualified greetings. The head of the World Health Organisation, a former Sudanese warlord, strolled over, clapped his arm on my shoulder, and said cheerily that if I'd had the monkeypox booster I no longer needed to wear a condom. There were helpful young men everywhere, and everyone seemed to like my T-shirt, although the Sudanese warlord declined my offer to get one for him. I was making small talk with the parents of some transitioning schoolgirls proudly waving self-affirming pictures showing the scars of their removed breasts, but Angus shooed me away and escorted me to my allotted place. I was amazed to see I was sharing a float with Miley Cyrus! This would be something to tell Harry and Siggy back in Strelsau, eh?

Miley looked very perky in shorts and a skimpy little top that showed off her tattoos. She regarded me warily, so I hastened to reassure her. "I've been a big fan of yours since *Hannah Montana*," I said, clasping her hand.

She replied, "I'm Justin Bieber, you blind fuck."

I stepped back in amazement: "Why, so you are! You've shaved off the moustache. Lot of that about." Still, he made a way better Miley than the one we have back at the lookalike agency. On the other hand, Dobromil discovered that if you put a stick-on moustache on her she made quite a convincing Justin Bieber. It didn't seem the time to explain to Justin that, when I confused him with Miley, I was in fact confusing him with a bad lookalike of Miley...

Then he turned his other cheek. "I'm the one who's still got the facial twitch," he said. And I tried not to stare as his left cheek and eyeball danced frenziedly up and down, a side-effect of the Pfizer Pfacial defroster he'd taken for the paralysis on his right cheek.

We started to ride down Portland Place, past the BBC's headquarters and All Souls Church, and down toward the expensive emporia of Regent Street. I had tried to get myself up to speed on London's demography. We were in the West End, which was gay, while the East End was Muslim. Many Muslims crossed each day to work in the gay end, but few gays ventured into the Muslim end. It was a bit like the social divisions at Rudolf V's coronation, when the New Town was for the King, but the Old Town for Black Michael.

Gay or Muslim, I would have appreciated more of a crowd. But it was the fashion in Britain to hold virtual crowd scenes, where people remained in their homes CyberHooding or UniCrowding themselves in empty rooms cheering the parade from a camp chair set up before a slide of the 1977 Jubilee or the 1953 Coronation. A select number of UK residents had applied through the Immunity Lottery for passes permitting them to attend the event in person. All wore masks either with the rainbow flag or advertising their pronouns, some of which I'd even heard of. And all stood at least five metres apart – every citizen his own one-man throng. In between, armed soldiers and riot police in rainbow helmets enforced the distance rules. London's

THE PRISONER OF WINDSOR

most fashionable milkshake chain, the Shake of Araby, was offering complimentary shakes in the colours of all nine of the LGBTQWERTY parade's official flags: I had a Genderfluid Shake – pink, blue, white, purple and black – or strawberry, lavender, vanilla, blueberry and liquorice. But one marcher complained to me that in the yellow, white, purple and black Non-Binary Shake the black was in the wrong position. I promised to have somebody fired over it. Between milkshake critiques, I passed along, waving this way and that, under a shower of cheers and blessings. That's one advantage of parading with Justin Bieber. Still, I was gratified to see that most people seemed to know who I was. It seems that the doughty British working man, upon glimpsing his prime minister, hails him with a chipper two-fingered gesture. I assumed this was a rearward modification of Churchill's V-for-Victory sign and reciprocated. After a couple of these exchanges, Angus darted out from security and told me that it was "deed droll", and he could understand the temptation, but "perhaps we shoo nae exten' the gree'ing tae uv'rrry citizen this close to the' bae-election."

I was feeling pretty gay myself, in the sense of that classic Ruritanian operetta beloved by my grandmother, *The Gay Margrave*. The truth is I was drunk with excitement. At that moment I believed I actually was the Prime Minister! South of Oxford Circus, the transgender field marshal, swivelling in her saddle, waved her hand, and a phalanx of cuirassiers closed round Justin's and my float, so that the thinly spaced crowd could scarce see us. Behind the glittering store fronts of Liberty and Hamley's lay the wretched lanes and teeming alleys of Soho, filled with a turbulent and hostile populace of gays who worked in bars and media production facilities, and were said to regard me as a "fascist homophobe". This action by the field marshal showed more clearly than words the state of feeling in this part of town. But, if fate had made me a prime minister, the least I could do was play the part handsomely.

"Why this change in our order, Field Marshal?"

"It is more prudent, sir," murmured the much decorated veteran.

"Let those in front ride on till they are fifty metres ahead," said I, indicating the Muslim lads from TAQIYA, who looked none too happy about being put behind a float of gay Haredim. "And those behind wait here till I have walked fifty metres." I waved back at a

87

group of Recovering Misgenderers, who likewise looked none too happy about being put in front of the "Get The L Out" float - a group of transphobic lesbians who regarded Rassendyll's campaign of de-cisgenderisation as a way of reintroducing the phallocracy by the back door. (I think I got that right.) Anyway, I instructed the field marshal: "Make sure that no one is nearer to me. I will have the people see that their prime minister trusts them."

The field marshal hesitated.

"Am I not understood?" said I; and she gave the orders. I began to walk alone down Regent Street. From the lucky lottery-winning parade attendees, there was first a sullen silence, then a mutter of discontent, then a barrage of jeers, impressive from a socially distanced mob five metres apart. I noticed that a lot of the jeering came from many of the riot police, three of whom hurled their rainbow helmets, one of which scuffed my yellow trousers.

Okay, bad move on my part. Enough with walking among my people. I hopped back up on Justin Bieber's float, and the huzzahs resumed. A couple of trans marchers with non-binary-conforming genitalia broached their concerns about recent US airport security changes since male jihadists had started going through in burqas. I promised to take it up at the next G7.

At last we were at Trafalgar Square, under the watchful eye from atop his column of Lord Nelson, the inspirational figure who with his dying breath had had the courage to say, "Kiss me, Hardy!" "Kiss me, Bieber!" I said to Justin, but he didn't seem to get the allusion, and his cheek twitched ever more manically.

Still, the parade went off well enough, I thought. And then right at the end, just as I was dismounting from the float to take a look at the statue of General Napier, a local reporter darted out, shoved a microphone under me, and said, "Enjoy the parade, Prime Minister?"

"Absolutely. A ripsnorting jamboree. Went off like clockwork." I felt myself floundering. "I like to think of myself as a sociable justice warrior," I added.

The reporter asked if I had a reaction to breaking news about the ECHR ruling.

"ECHR?" I skimmed my prime-ministerial mental rolodex and came up empty. Executive Committee for Homosexual Relations?

But the newsman was explaining, for the benefit of his audience, that the European Court of Human Rights had just issued its long-awaited ruling in the class-action suit brought by London lawyers on behalf of people with second homes in France.

"Indeed," said I, hoping for a bit more info.

"Yes," he replied, finger pressed to his earpiece. "The Court has struck down the referendum, and banned future referenda in the External Zone on the grounds that, by definition, a referendum discriminates against a minority. What's your reaction, Prime Minister?"

I was about to answer, when I noticed that Angus had moved behind the news chap and was frantically waving at me. Obviously, he wanted me to wave to the crowd. I hadn't done it for a couple of minutes, and perhaps everyone was thinking I was being a bit homophobic. So I waved jauntily.

"You surely have some comment?" said the reporter.

Oh, yes. The ECHR ruling.

"So the ECHR have banned referenda..." I began.

"Yes. On the grounds that referenda by definition discriminate against an identifiable minority – the losing side."

Angus was still flapping his hands behind the guy, so I waved at a passing intersexual. And then I answered.

"Well, before we ban referenda, I'm in favour of holding a referendum on whether to ban referenda. And, if the British people vote to keep referenda, then we can have a referendum on whether to pull out of the European Court."

Behind the reporter, Angus stopped waving. He looked a little pale, I thought.

Chapter Twelve
Pride comes before a fall

Back in Downing Street, I limped up the stairs and, after some effort, managed to extricate myself from T-shirt and trousers and return my sorely squeezed body to the world-statesman get-up I'd originally picked out. Number Ten was all but deserted and, with Britain's shortest prime ministership drawing to a close, I had an urge to linger. Prior to yours truly, the last mere mortal to reside here was a tradesman called Mr Chicken, who'd moved out about the time Countess Amelia was doing the horizontal gavotte with Prince Rudolf at Burlesdon. Afterwards George II had the place remodelled for Robert Walpole, the first Prime Minister. And so Mr Chicken was the last tradesman to live here until a certain Ruritanian plumber showed up three centuries later.

My musings were interrupted by Brenda. "The Lord Privy Seal is here, Prime Minister."

I could see he was pleased. "What a day for you to remember!" he cried. "Caught a few moments on the box. Absolutely tip-top – and a winning choice of T-shirt!" He took out his pipe. "Good of them to put you next to one of the more fetching rent-boys."

"That was Justin Bieber," I felt obliged to point out.

"I don't need his name," Sir Roger said sharply. "Far too old for that sort of thing. But gad, man!" He clapped me on the back. "Makes me wish I could be PM for a day myself!"

"I'm glad you liked it, but I can't say it was my bag. When you were spinning all those heroic tales about the last big Elphberg-Rassendyll swap, it had a certain dash and glamour, an esprit, an *élan*, a *je ne sais quoi*... I think I would have been rather good dressed up to the nines and swanking down the aisle at a coronation. But just walking about in a silly T-shirt and scrotum-throttling tights for hours... it's not the same."

"Different times, my friend. Different times. But, like that long-ago Mr Rassendyll, you did a small kingdom a great service today." He patted me with genuine affection. "Ready to start?"

THE PRISONER OF WINDSOR

I took one last wistful glance at the famous door knocker of Number Ten, and settled into the back seat of the limo. The old boy lit his pipe.

Our driver coughed. "I'm afraid all government vehicles are non-smoking, Sir Roger."

"I'm not a government vehicle, am I?" said Severn. And he puffed away, merry and chatty as London and the countryside rolled past, until we turned into his drive and the wheels crunched the gravel – a quintessentially English sound, as I think of it.

All was still. No-one came to meet us at the door. Something seemed …off. But Sanjay was behind us, so I held my tongue until Sir Roger and I were safely alone in his study. The heavy oak door to the wine-cellar was shut. It looked in all respects as it had in the early hours that morning.

And then Severn's face turned pale, and he pointed at the floor. A dark red stain had seeped an inch out from under the door, and dried there.

Sir Roger sank back against his desk. I tried the handle. It was locked. I pushed against it. "Call wossname, your gentleman's gentleman," I urged.

"Joseph's afternoon off," he said. "Takes his mum to bingo every Saturday."

"Then I'll get Sanjay."

"Don't you dare!" He opened a desk drawer and produced a gun – and a silencer.

"Sir Roger, don't," I blurted, falling back against a table lamp. "I did everything you asked…"

He switched on the radio full-blast and, as the Song of the Volga Boatmen filled the room, blew off the lock. The door swung partially open and then stopped. The inch of blood that had spread out underneath it was now the edge of a dark pool.

Severn paled. I was petrified, but the old man had no fear for himself, only to what lay ahead of us in the cellar. He flicked the switch, but no light came. So he took a silver candlestick from the sideboard, dipped it into his pipe and, as the hot wax dripped on his hand, inched around the lake of blood, a dark ominous contrast with the whitewashed floor. In the candlelight, I saw why the door would move no further: a shoe with a dull brown stain on it. There was a draught in the passageway and the candle flickered.

"Sorry about that," said a voice behind us.

We spun around, Severn already aiming his pistol. But it was Fritz, standing by the study door and wearing one shoe.

He turned down the radio. "Don't worry, Roger," he said. "It's not the good stuff. Just the second bottle of Mike Rassendyll's organic wine... I knocked it over moving the Prime Minister upstairs. Then I slipped in it, lost my shoe, fell back against the wall and broke the light bulb. I was just coming down to clear it up before you got back. Rassendyll came round a couple of hours ago, and, once Joseph had left for the day, I thought it better to get him to bed than have him recuperate in a well-stocked wine cellar."

"Good man!" agreed Severn. Fritz retrieved his wine-sodden shoe and we went upstairs to find the Prime Minister dozing in a guest bedroom. He looked very contented sprawled under a faded eiderdown.

"I told him what had happened," said Fritz, glancing at me.

"And how did he take it?" asked Severn.

"He said you're a – quote – 'fucking genius'."

"We'll see about that," muttered Sir Roger. "Let's have a pot of tea, and with a bit of luck Joseph will have put out some bath buns."

The Prime Minister woke up an hour later. Severn and Fritz entered first, and explained that I was here. He shouted to come in, and I entered the room to find Rob Rassendyll upright in bed, beaming.

"The man who saved the day!" He motioned me to sit on his counterpane.

"It was nothing," I said. "And I got to meet Justin Bieber."

"My God, it's like looking at my own reflection! Without that tatty old beard, you're almost as dashing as me." He reached up and touched my cheek, tenderly. "I owe you big time, doppelgänger. I don't know where this cunning old bugger dug you up -" He put an affectionate arm around Sir Roger. "- but you saved my premiership today."

"I watched a bit of it on the telly," said Severn. "He looked an absolute corker."

THE PRISONER OF WINDSOR

"That's a good idea," enthused the PM. "Where've you hidden the TV?"

"There's one downstairs. But first we have to get Mr Elphberg out of your suit and, with Sanjay lurking in the hall, I'll spirit him down the backstairs."

It was depressing to climb back into my Rudy-the-loser garb. The cheap Chinese polo shirt scratched and my RuriMart chinos were well past their best-by date, if they'd ever had one. But Rassendyll was so delighted by Sir Roger's ingenious scheme he didn't notice my glumness. Fifteen minutes later, we were all in Severn's sitting room watching the rerun of the parade on LGBBC.

"Oh, look at that T-shirt!" Rassendyll pealed with delight, as I rounded the bend in Regent Street and wiggled about with a transgender samba dancer. "I say, you've really got the rhythm. I can't get the hang of that Latin bollocks at all." He turned to Severn. "Roger, any chance we could get this fine fellow to do all my photo-ops?"

But the next bit was all about that TAQIYA group claiming progress in plans to introduce gay marriage in Waziristan with every top entitled to four bottoms, and I could see Rassendyll getting restless. He glanced at Severn's handsome mantle clock. "Roger, stick it on the news. I'm gagging to see what that wanker Chief Political Correspondent makes of 'my' triumph." He made extravagant air quotes, and nodded deferentially toward me.

Severn switched channels. His clock must have been a little slow, for the news was already underway:

...plunged Europe into crisis.

Sir Roger furrowed his brows. On screen, there was footage of important-looking persons going into grand buildings with French or German flags fluttering above the doors. Then there were some clips of European news readers, helpfully subtitled. From Brussels:

Tonight: Europe on the Brink. Rassendyll reneges – and blows up the EU.

From Paris:

Britain Shatters Europe: Live coverage, including President de Mauban on 'the bitter contemptible non-entity in Downing Street'.

I glanced nervously at the Prime Minister. The colour had drained from his cheeks.

From Berlin:

Breaking News: The End of Europe – and Bye-Bye Britain. Investors brace for a collapsed pound when markets open on Monday…

I was mystified by all this, but fortunately that "wanker Chief Political Correspondent" Rassendyll had mentioned came on to explain that the crisis began when a local reporter from Queer FM at the Pride Parade had asked me about the European court decision banning referenda on the grounds that, by definition, a referendum discriminates against a minority. And then it showed me in my "Nobody knows I'm gay" T-shirt saying that maybe we should have a referendum on whether to ban referenda. And, if the people vote to keep referenda, then we can have a referendum on whether to pull out of the European Court. I thought that was pretty funny myself, but I could see that Justin Bieber, standing alongside of me, wasn't laughing, although maybe he was still mad about all that Miley Cyrus business.

I never heard what came next because at that point the Rt Hon Robert Rassendyll hurled Severn's cake stand at the television, and my face and Justin's were suddenly dripping with sticky buns and clotted cream and thick-cut marmalade. The next thing I knew the Prime Minister was on his feet, raging at Sir Roger. "You've ruined me, you daft old queen!"

"Steady on," I said. "That's a bit homophobic."

He spun round and towered over me. "You shut the fuck up! Look at that." He waved at the screen. "Even Miley Fuckin' Cyrus knows this isn't funny!"

Sir Roger eyed the door nervously, expecting at any moment Sanjay to shoot his way into the room to rescue his PM. Bring it on, I thought. What an ingrate cokehead.

Rassendyll grabbed Severn's remote and switched to Sky News, which had a graphic showing Europe shattering into a thousand pieces and disappearing into a black void. "I doubt it will be that lively," said Sir Roger, keeping his cool. "Who knows? Might even work out for the best. Nothing else has."

"It's worked for me," fumed Rassendyll. "I'm prime minister."

"Well, it hasn't worked for the country," said Severn, coldly, "and you might give a thought to that once in a while."

I had no idea what all the fuss was about, but Sir Roger's calm only intensified Rassendyll's fury. He hurled the remote, which just missed my head and instead cracked a decorative vase on the side table. "I could have you arrested," he told me. "Impersonation is a criminal offence, and nobody's going to care about a washed-up ex-royal from a no-name basket-case operetta craphole."

"It's not a no-name craphole," Fritz protested.

Rassendyll was momentarily stunned by someone rising to the defence of Ruritania, but quickly recovered. "Nobody even knows where the fuck it is!" He stomped over to an antique globe next to the bookcase, and stabbed randomly at Mitteleuropa. "C'mon then, where is it? Some people think Ruritania's in the Balkans, some in Bohemia, some in the Baltic. And if you ask them to put their finger on the map they just take a random guess and hit…" He looked down and peered at the ancient curlicued font: "…Slovenia. No, wait, Slavonia." His eyes narrowed. "Slovakia." He gave the globe an almighty spin, and then threw it at the TV. A splinter ran down the top of my on-screen head, disappeared into the clotted cream, and came out halfway down my T-shirt.

"That's enough!" snapped Sir Roger. "If it weren't for this gentleman here, you would stand revealed to the world as a pathetic figure so in thrall to his addictions that he lacks sufficient self-control to 'stay clean' before a vital national occasion."

But Rassendyll heard none of it. "You duplicitous fruit!" he roared. "Put a Ruritanian in the Pride Parade! What the fuck were you thinking?"

There was a knock from the hall. "Everything awwight, sir?"

The prospect of his security firing through the door seemed to calm Rassendyll. "Quite alright, Sanjay," he called. "I'll be out in a moment."

He paced the room, seething more quietly. "Months of strategy and calculation – vapourised by a dickhead. Where the fuck are the damage-control tossers when you need them?" He paused at the window, and put his hand on the sill to steady himself, staring across the lawn to Severn's ha-ha. "I can do this," he said softly. "I'm the most dazzling political player of my generation. I can get out of any fix." He spun around, glaring at Sir Roger. "Maybe," he said, tentatively, "maybe I can pass this off as an obvious charity skit... for BBC *Children in Need*... It's as unfunny as all those Red Nose sketches... Yeah..."

He stroked his chin and no longer acknowledged our presence. "Yeah, that might do it..." He yanked open the door, and walked out into the hall.

A few seconds later we heard the prime ministerial Jaguar roar into life and head to Downing Street.

Chapter Thirteen
A mini-bar and a king-size bed

I WAS STUNNED. NOTHING I'd ever done in my entire life had ever mattered. Yet my participation in a Pride parade was evidently the biggest thing to hit the Continent since Bomber Harris. You never can tell, eh?

"I apologise for Robert," said Roger Severn. "There's no justification for his behaviour."

"But what's he so upset about?"

Sir Roger sighed, and re-lit his pipe. Fritz picked up the beautiful antique globe and set it upright. It had come off its axis. "*That's* where Ruritania is," he said, emphatically. But I noticed he'd put his finger down on Modenstein. He carried the battered globe back to its original spot. "Robert Rassendyll is upset by what you said. Because the world thinks it's what *he* said."

"Yes, but why is he upset?"

"Brexit," replied Fritz.

That one I knew about, vaguely: The British people had voted to leave the European Union. In a referendum.

"No significant party supported Brexit," Fritz continued. "Not the Tories, Liberals, Labour, Scottish Nationalists, not Sinn Féin… And yet the people voted for it."

"There's an old West End saying," remarked Severn, puffing his pipe. "Nobody likes it but the public. That's how it was with leaving the EU: all the people who matter wanted to stay; only the voters wanted to go."

"So much for the multi-party system," sneered Fritz.

"Oh, we still have a functioning two-party system," chuckled Sir Roger, "once you accept that one party is the establishment and the others are the people – and the people always lose."

"Except with Brexit they didn't," said Fritz. "And we wouldn't want that to become a habit, would we?"

They explained that a group of expensive London lawyers had rustled up a lawsuit on behalf of Britons who owned holiday homes in France. This, of course, had nothing very much to do with Brexit: all kinds of people own Continental property, whether or not they're citizens of the EU. Nevertheless, the lawyers' argument was that referenda are inherently discriminatory – in that they discriminate against the minority: the losing side.

The logic of that gave me a bit of a headache, but it had prevailed in court, and the judges had decreed that referenda had no place in the new Europe. And it seems all the EU bigwigs had been covertly in support of the suit.

"Rassendyll, too," said Fritz. "Also covertly."

"But wasn't he in favour of Brexit?"

"Publicly," said Severn. "That was just a bit of opportunism on his part. He wasn't really in favour of it. But it stood him in good stead when his predecessor ran into trouble. She'd been opposed to Brexit, but not very loudly. That was just a bit of opportunism on her part. But it stood her in good stead when her predecessor ran into trouble. He'd been…"

Now my headache was really back. Fortunately, Fritz cut to the chase.

"The point is that the entire Eurocracy was relying on this court decision to kill the referendum business once and for all. And then you go and wreck it all by saying you're going to hold a referendum on whether we should hold referenda."

"It was just a throwaway line," I said, feebly.

"Well, you've thrown away the entire EU," observed Severn. He tilted his head and took a puff of his pipe. "Rather brilliant, actually."

But I was in a sour mood. "I think I'd like to go now, Sir Roger. Is there a bus stop nearby?"

"Oh, Fritz will drive you back," he said, airily. "Least we could do. Sorry it all went pear-shaped. But, aside from blowing up Europe, you were absolutely tremendous."

Fritz's Europarliamentary electric vehicle was a bit of a comedown after the Jag. He set off down Severn's drive, and some sort of *sprachig-sprechen* station came on. No guesses as to what they were talking about. Fritz hit the button and smooth jazz filled the car. Somehow its unruffled bloody smoothness picked and scratched at me, and by the third insipid sax instrumental I was in an even worse mood. "I have no desire to spend another night in this country," I announced.

"Too late for the Strelsau flight," Fritz said. "And I can't see the King of Ruritania on the night bus with the backpackers and jihad boys."

"I can. When's it leave?"

Fritz snorted. I said nothing.

"You're serious? Well, they all go from Victoria Coach Station. We had a Europol briefing about it." He punched it into his GPS.

We fell into silence, and eventually, after the usual street closures "Due to Coronation Maintenance", my chauffeur pulled up at a semi-deserted station drop-off. After the cool breeze of Roger Severn's graveled drive, Victoria Station was almost sultry, the air heavy with the smells of the city at night – junk food and drains, marijuana and *stinktier*.

"I entered the address wrong," said Fritz. "This is Victoria train station. The buses are round the corner."

"Doesn't matter," I muttered.

But he was pointing excitedly at a trestle table on which a wizened Londoner was setting out piles of newspapers. "The man who sells the first editions! I had no idea they still did that. Tomorrow's newspapers today! You should get something to read on the bus."

"I intend to go straight to sleep."

He laughed. "You're on every front page! Wouldn't you like a full set? A souvenir of your exploits? Come on, my treat."

I can't say the thought didn't appeal. If it was true that I'd single-handedly nuked the EU, it would be nice to have a commemorative keepsake mounted and framed in my Modenstein flat. A talking point, in the unlikely event I ever have a girl round.

We strolled across the pavement to the newsstand, Fritz slipped me a tenner, and I waited behind an old lady. "*Express*, luv? There you go, dahlin'. Fanks." I glimpsed the front page:

Rassendyll: Let the People Speak!

The first editions were spread out on a trestle table. *The Sunday Telegraph*: "Europe in Turmoil as Prime Minister Stands with Voters." *The Sunday Times*: "Rassendyll's Referendum Pledge Plunges Continent into Crisis." *The Mail on Sunday*: "PM Shafts Europe." *The Observer*: "The Pride…and the Shame." *The Sunday Sun*: "Gay Day Cock-Up."

"I'll have one of each, please."

The vendor still had his head down over the table display. "'Arf a mo, guv." He scooped them up, doing the math as he went: "£15.70." And up he looked to receive the cash. "Lor' luvaduck!" he wheezed.

I handed over Fritz's twenty-pound note. The man shyly offered the change, and then added, "I just wanna say what you said was right on. Let's have a referendum on whether to have referendums." He drew back. "Sorry, sir. Didn' mean to breeve on you."

"No worries," I said, trying to remember the slumming-earl voice. "Means a lot." I turned away, and saw the same moment of recognition on faces all around. Just beyond them, Fritz was en route to rescue me. And then he paused.

"Good on yer, mate!" yelled somebody. "Agreed with every word."

"Yeah," said his girlfriend. "Makes you proud to be British."

"Who do they think they are? Banning referendums?" piped up another lad.

They were moving in on me, focusing their cellphone cameras, all social distancing forgotten. "Thanks. Thanks awfully." I smiled and waved, and hoped, after my showstopping "Nobody knows I'm gay" T-shirt, that they didn't mind my discount RuriMart garb.

"Good for you, Prime Minister," said a tarty bird, nuzzling her spectacular and extensively tattooed cleavage my way. "I don't see why we always have to be ashamed jus 'cuz we're English."

"Indeed," I said.

A stooped and very old man tugged my sleeve. He had rheumy eyes and waxy skin. "I jes' wantuh say," he said, through chipped, nicotine-stained teeth, "I was in the war and I thought we wuz fighting for king and country. But we won the war, and I don't see why we should lose our country just 'cuz all these European troublemakers and their London political friends want to take it away from us." He glanced around furtively, as if he'd gone too far. "I jus' try to keep quiet now, wivvowt gettin' into trouble. But what you said today was the troof."

THE PRISONER OF WINDSOR

Filthy and malodorous and potentially infectious as he was, I hugged him to my chest and said, "It *is* your country. And no one's going to take it away from you, not while I'm prime minister."

The small crowd bloke into applause, and there was the flash of mobiles, and then a puzzled looking Fritz led me away. From beyond my circle of admirers, someone shouted, "Wanker!"; and another, "Racist wanker!" I waved cheerily.

"That was a well improvised encore!" said Fritz.

"Yeah, well, I thought I'd stick it to that bastard Rassendyll one last time. They're right: He is a wanker."

We walked round the corner and up Buckingham Palace Road to Victoria Coach Station. Outside the terminus, five brightly lit Eurobuses were waiting to disgorge their bedraggled passengers – from Prague, Bucharest, Istanbul, Alma Ata… The coach station was an art deco structure built for a London long vanished, and through its doors poured the new London – Slavs, Kazakhs, Nigerians, Arabs, blinking and bewildered, dragging their belongings onto the pavement and off to a new life in the great world city.

"You're the only one going the other way," observed Fritz.

"Suits me," I said. Halfway to the ticket counter, I reached into my pocket - and stopped dead. No passport. To get out of this dump, I'd have to go to the embassy, report it stolen, and get another.

Fritz eyed the *Telegraph*, *Express* et al tucked under my arm. "At least you have enough newspapers to sleep under." But I wasn't in the mood for jokes, and he could see that. "I have a junior suite at the Elgin," he said. "It's a very nice hotel. Saudi-owned. Only the best. You can take the sofa."

I wanted to say no. But I'd had barely two hours of fitful napping in Downing Street the night before, and a junior suite at the Elgin was not without appeal.

He was right. It was a very nice hotel, from what I could see walking hurriedly through the lobby with my head down and Fritz's shades on. Safely in his suite, I sat on the sofa and he opened up the mini-bar and set out some drinks and a forty-euro bar of Toblerone. We wolfed it down and I was still hungry, so he ordered some *saumon tartare* and *boeuf Bourguinon*. When it arrived, he suggested I duck into the bathroom, lest room service spread rumours that the "Nobody knows I'm gay" T-shirt was true. So I stood next to the luxury walk-in shower, heard the waiter put down the plates, and then take his leave:

"Goodnight, Mr Tarlenheim."

I opened the bathroom door. "You're *that* Fritz? Fritz von Tarlenheim?"

He smiled. "I thought you'd forgotten. I came to your coronation, and we built a Lego castle afterwards."

"And now Fritz von Tarlenheim is a Member of the European Parliament?"

"An Austrian member," he said. "And it's Fritz Tarlenheim. I don't have a lot of use for the 'von', since the Tarlenheim estates were confiscated by the Communists, bombed by the rebels, and then requisitioned by the 'refugees'." He snapped off a piece of Toblerone. "It was easier when we were children. When you knocked down my Lego Zenda, we built another. We had a lot of fun on your Coronation Day."

My Coronation Day: I hadn't thought about it in years. I was a small boy in Spain. A lot of dodgy coves from Central Europe had fled to Franco's redoubt after the war, but the Elphbergs were left mostly to themselves, ignored by all except the Tarlenheims and a few other exiles from the royal court who'd washed up in Madrid.

And then, when I was eight, Papa was hit by a bus.

On reflection, that was an appropriately and literally pedestrian end to the Ruritanian monarchy, and we should have left it at that. Instead, we had a "coronation" just to keep the expats happy. Mama got me out of bed early that morning. "You're to be crowned to-day, Rudolf," she said. "You must be a good boy. And then you'll be a good king."

"I'll be a great king, Mummy," said I, and she laughed.

We took a taxi to the Puerta del Sol, where a function room at the Grand Hotel de Paris had been booked for the "coronation", our apartment being too small. The Grand Hotel's smallest function room, by contrast, was far too large for the Tarlenheims and Bernensteins plus a few others who'd given service to the Elphbergs over the years – oh, and the society diarist of *El País*, whose column the following day played it for laughs. It was the first time I'd ever worn a sword and I held it up for everyone to see, and they chuckled and patted my head. And then the Count of Tarlenheim, Fritz's grandfather and president of the Ruritanian National Assembly in Exile, placed the crown upon me. I remember liking it, and turning round to wink at Harry. But Mama was frowning, so I tried to listen to the Count. He was a very old man with zany white hair sticking out at odd angles, and I found him hard to follow. He said that, even though we were physically in Spain, this ceremony confirmed me as the sovereign ruler of Ruritania. And at the end he leaned down and told me in a low but penetrating rumble that God was the only power above me, and I had no lord except the king of kings. Then he laid his hand on my head – they'd taken the crown off because it was so heavy, and it didn't really fit – and whispered, "Turn around, boy." So I did, and there was my mother, and she knelt and kissed my hand, and I saw Harry trying not to laugh. And the Count roused himself and cried in a quavery voice, "Rudolfus Rex!" Then someone pressed the button on the cassette machine, and everyone stood stiffly for a tinny recording of the national anthem, which was just about audible in the back of the room, but not so much in the front, where it was drowned out by David Soul singing "Don't Give Up on Us, Baby" from the adjoining Cougar Night disco.

And then Harry, Fritz and I got to play with the Lego set, while the grown-ups got stuck into the slivovitz.

On the way home through the streets of Madrid, we passed the statue of King Carlos III and I asked Mummy to have one put up for me, outside the apartment. She promised to do so. Later, when I refused to go to bed because I had no power above me but God, she docked my pocket money.

And that was my "Coronation Day". At the end of term, Mama announced we were moving to Switzerland, and we never saw the Tarlenheims or any of the other Ruritanian courtiers again.

"You would have been a good king," said Fritz. "You will always be my king." And then in a fit of bibulous generosity he added: "So you have the king-size bed, and I'll take the sofa."

Chapter Fourteen

The chair

I SLEPT BETTER AT the Elgin than I'd slept at either the Great British B&B or 10 Downing Street. But, after wrecking the EU, I felt bad rooming with a Euro-MP, and the following lunchtime I returned to my *Flohgrube* round the back of Euston. Fritz had offered to vouch for me at the Spanish Embassy, so on Monday morning we set off for Chesham Place to apply for my replacement passport. There was a long line made longer by the mandatory vaxpass inspection: In the general panic caused by my referendum remarks, many wealthy Londoners were so desperate that they were no longer waiting for their French passports to come through but had been reduced to applying for Spanish ones. As always, the process was slow and bureaucratic and degrading. There was a problem with the computer, possibly due to Russian hackers or Macedonian bots. I had been robbed, so I had no ID whatsoever, and it didn't help when Fritz said he could corroborate my identity and that I was the rightful King of Ruritania. The lady behind the desk thanked him but said it didn't solve the problem. "I don't personally know you," she said, and she leaned back in her chair and cocked her head. "And honestly, if I had to say you were anyone, I'd say you were the British Prime Minister." (My beard was a stubbly two-day growth, but I had not yet fully deRassendylled.)

"I can see why you'd want to flee the country," she added, "but you need a better disguise." So I was advised to come back tomorrow, when the Russian bots might have relented, and hopefully she would be able to tell me whether I was Rudy Elphberg.

On the pavement outside, Fritz said, "You know the story of when your grandfather arrived in Spain? He went to open a bank account, and they asked for proof of identity. He had no passport, because as the King he didn't need one. So he was without 'picture ID'. The bank teller said in that case he couldn't permit him to open a bank account. Your grandfather thumbed through his wallet while the clerk sneered, 'Surely you have a driving license? Or a library card?' The King pulled out an old 100-krone note and passed it under the

104

grille. 'Are you trying to bribe me?' said the teller. "That's me on the money," replied your grandfather. 'That's my proof of identity.'"

I'd forgotten the story. I'd forgotten all the stories.

"Maybe you should go back to being Rob Rassendyll," said Fritz. "It seems to be easier."

His kindness and generosity only underlined my sense of failure. He loaned me some more money, to my shame, and then I invented a meeting I had to go to. I set off across Belgrave Square and past some of the world's most expensive real estate and realised I was at the back of Buckingham Palace. Over the wall were its famous gardens. So I turned left and hugged the royal perimeter round to the front – to the open parkland, and the isolated knots of tourists from around the world who'd won the Coronalottery, the special Coronation competition. The Mall, the handsome red-tarmac thoroughfare that links the palace with Trafalgar Square, was lined with flags of many nations, so I tried to spot the hideous swatch that represents the post-Communist Republic of Ruritania. But I gradually surmised that these were not flags of "foreign" countries, but only those of the "Commonwealth", the strange post-imperial family to which the old Queen had been so attached.

It's a queer business, monarchy. You'd think it would be relatively suited to small states – like, say, Ruritania. But in Strelsau and Lisbon and Bucharest the thrones had tumbled. The House of Windsor had globalised its brand and somehow survived. Ruritanians had no wish for a Ruritanian monarch, but in the Pacific the Papuans and Tuvaluans were happy to be subjects of an English king who, I'd wager, couldn't find them on a map. As for the rest of the planet, the foreign camera crews filling the Mall – CNN, NBC, TF1, Xinhua News Network – testified that the Windsors were *the* royals, royals for the planet, the last royals standing. In the end, there will be only five kings – the four in a pack of cards, and the King of England. Was it King Farouk who had said that? I wondered if his son or grandson was, like me, somewhere among the tourists, anonymous in Chinese-made jeans and T-shirt.

I walked across St James's Park, trying not to think of that wanker Rassendyll off to my left in Downing Street. It wasn't exactly warm, but it was a cloudless day and the few girls were, below their masks, in sleeveless tops and bare-legged – at least until we approached

Westminster Abbey and the protesters, among whom a dingier aesthetic prevailed. The Abbey was where King Arthur was to be crowned on July 5th - the anniversary of the founding of the National Health Service. I had expected it to dominate the scene, the way the cathedral at Strelsau did before its spires were blown up. But the famous church seemed hemmed in by the factories of political life. It's the Houses of Parliament that seize the eye, and the Abbey merely fills in the periphery. A large non-virodistant demonstration was camped outside: The After-Life Movement. A nice girl called Roslyn, a pale blonde who had very stylishly threaded her nose ring through her face mask, handed me a leaflet: The After-Life Movement was only ten euros to join – they didn't accept pounds sterling because that was the currency of slave-trading and white supremacism. Unfortunately for Roslyn, pounds was all I had. "Is it about the afterlife?" I asked. "Heaven? The angelic host?" She explained that no, it was a movement for human extinction because only after human life had ended could the planet recover from the environmental devastation man had inflicted upon it. "I've had my tubes tied," she said, with a come-hither look. "I can't face the thought of bringing a child into this world. And, for every one unborn British baby with an irresponsible First World carbon footprint, a Somali mother can have ten kids. Are you doing anything tonight?"

"Why? Would you like to see a movie?" I asked.

"We're having a meeting," she said. "We're suing the Church of England for hate speech because 'Go forth and multiply' is a specific actionable threat of violence against the planet."

I politely demurred, took my place in line for the Abbey, and passed through its portals onto the hallowed ground where Albion's kings had been crowned for a millennium.

Inside, you're almost buried by the weight of history. There are statues everywhere, and not in the least bit socially distanced – and all standing upright and undefaced; it was the biggest crowd I had seen since landing in England: Pitt the Elder; Lord Canning; an American Indian lady with a large beaver honouring a former Lieutenant-Governor of Quebec. It was like an upmarket version of *Celebrity Squat*: Take every British historical figure, put them in poorly heated public housing, and see who survives. I thought the clutter might thin out once you penetrate the interior, but it never does: Gladstone, Disraeli,

THE PRISONER OF WINDSOR

Palmerston, all the prime ministers you've heard of, and a lot you haven't, like Spencer Perceval. There are doctors, organists, astronomers, naval officers, bacteriologists; an Elizabethan giantess called Long Meg; a grisly lance-wielding skeleton of Death emerging from the underworld to claim the life of Lady Elizabeth Nightingale while her distraught husband attempts in vain to ward him off; even a former ambassador to Ruritania (Lord Topham, a forebear of Jamie Topham, the pop star who twerked Ed Sheeran at the Brit Awards). It's as if someone had decided to store a ton of old stuff in a church while they raised the funds to build a museum. It's all a bit haphazard, and also very dark, illuminated by red-shaded table lamps that conjure an eternal sepulchral twilight in which the ghosts of England flicker. Between you and me, Ruritania's Hall of National Heroes is a bit short of material, but at Westminster Abbey they're crowding in on you from all sides: Look! There's the memorial to Winston Churchill! And there's Tennyson and Kipling and Charles Darwin and William Wilberforce...

I rounded a corner and, without warning, there it was: St Edward's chair, named for King Edward the Confessor; the Coronation Chair. Viewed from behind a floor-to-ceiling sheet of reinforced glass, it was not terribly impressive in itself, ground and battered, with its gilt faded and its elaborate animal carvings worn away. And, in a building in which a thousand years' worth of monarchs had been crowned since 1066, it was a mere seven centuries old, commissioned by Edward I in the year 1300. But, from the golden lions added as feet in 1727 to the graffiti carved in the wood by Westminster schoolboys across the ages, it embodied a continuity unknown to my own land. An irrelevant kingdom occupying part of an island off the north-west coast of the European periphery had become the greatest empire ever known. But they kept the same old chair. Beyond these walls, everything was utterly transformed. But not the Coronation chair. And for a moment I was lost in Britannia's memories, and mourned for what mine might have been.

Chapter Fifteen
Invitation to the ball

TWO DAYS LATER, I was still waiting for a replacement passport, and back at the Big Tex sipping a single espresso very slowly while Otho complained loudly about so-called regulars who take three hours to consume one beverage item. Laddie was nowhere in sight, so a revival of my plumbing career seemed unlikely. Besides, I owed said employment entirely to the patronage of Lady Belinda Featherly, who was now as reviled an Islamophobe as her canine partner Colin Corgi. Someone had posted to YouTube an ancient video of her doing a "Does my bomb look big in this?" burqa gag on a Channel 4 alternative-comedy show circa 2005. She was under pressure to wear a hijab on the BBC's annual Full Coverage Day, when all its female presenters exercised their right to host their shows in hijabs and niqabs.

Otho's phone rang. And, to my surprise, it was Sir Roger Severn, calling to invite me to dinner again.

I was reluctant, but broke. So a free meal was not to be disdained.

It was lamb cutlets, followed by summer pudding. I savoured the taste, and admired the hunting scene above the fireplace, and over the sideboard the recumbent Burmese girl beckoning an unseen admirer toward a temple. "I thought all England would be like this," I said, sadly. "But you're the only real Englishman I know."

"Dearie me," he chuckled, "were you taken in by my languid drawl and the club tie and the knighthood? Dear boy, I'm an immigrant, indeed a refugee, like so many these days. Alas, I am one of those immigrants who loves England so much that it makes him paradoxically unEnglish. At least to any true Englishman."

"You're an immigrant?"

He puffed his pipe and exhaled the smoke in a long, perfect Z shape. "My name is Sapt."

He paused theatrically, and then sighed. "I see it means nothing to you. Ah, well. When the Communists took over Ruritania, they arrested my father..."

"You're Ruritanian?"

"I was born in Zenda. In the castle. My father served your father, as my grandfather served your grandfather, and as Sapts have served the House of Elphberg for generations." He rose from his chair and retrieved from a side-table a display case with a small faded ribbon and discoloured badge: the Red Rose of Ruritania.

"As you might surmise, our prospects were not good under the new regime. So after his arrest my father smuggled a note to my mother, urging us to flee. Eight months later, we disembarked at Dover. Three weeks after that, my mother was a cleaner in Croydon. A year later, we heard via a cousin that my father had died in prison. He had been, as they say, questioned to death. My mother saved enough money to train as a nurse in the new National Heath Service, and got a job in Hereford. On the journey from London she decided to anglicise the family name. You know your Ruritanian, don't you, Your Majesty? 'Sapt' means 'week' or 'seven'. She toyed with renaming herself Mrs Week, but we had to change trains at Gloucester and we missed our connection and had time to kill. So we went for a walk and looked at the River Severn, and my mother decided that henceforth she would be Mrs Severn. And thus Roger Severn. What could be more English? I used to think I would be raised to the peerage as the Marquess of Severn. But I don't think there'll be an England for me to be a lord in, if that ex-earl keeps things up."

"You mean all that referendum scheming?" I asked. The Ruritanian talk depressed me.

He brushed that aside. "Oh, Robert played a canny hand, persuading the Cabinet's big beasts this was the quickest route to regain control of the narrative."

"The big beasts?" said I.

"The big beasts are a lot smaller than they were in my day," muttered Sir Roger.

"They're for him body and soul, I take it."

"Not a bit of it. They'd all cut his throat for a point or two in their approval ratings. But he's had a good run playing them off against each other."

Severn smiled, but was interrupted by Joseph, announcing, as he had on that first evening, "The Prime Minister".

I started, and a piece of summer pudding fell down my shirt front. I was pulling it off my button, and rubbing the stain into the polyester as Rassendyll entered. Heartier than the last time I saw him.

He extended his hand, once a standard greeting but now reserved only for those whom one would trust with one's life. And yet, despite the honour he did me, I shrank back.

"Oh, come on, doppelgänger," he began. I retreated further, hard up against the sideboard. He withdrew his hand, and his arms hung slack at his sides. "Look, I apologise," he said. "I was wrong to throw the globe at you. And the clotted cream. You're a marvel, really you are. Have you seen my internals?"

"I've no desire to see your internals," I said, coldly. "You English think you can defuse every situation with pathetic *Doppelhorns*."

But he was jabbering excitedly about how, ever since my referendum "gaffe", his numbers had rocketed. The referendum-about-referenda move had stunned his Cabinet rivals, who were all now furious with him. "The polls are amazing: it's a winner everywhere," he gushed. "Well, everywhere except London... But the Midlands, Wales, Northern England, Northern Ireland... The party's even looking electorally viable in Scotland for the first time in two generations." He beamed. "You don't have any more genius ideas, do you?"

I was silent. Rassendyll grabbed a box of Sir Roger's cigars from a sideboard, and offered me one.

I thought back to that reporter's question. "I just said what I believed," I said sullenly.

"What a notion!" cooed Sir Roger. "Although maybe we should focus-group it first..."

Rassendyll ignored the sarcasm. "For the first time in years," he said, "I've got the Big Mo."

"Mohammed?"

"*Momentum!* I don't want to lose it again. You should have seen the look on Rupert Henley's face!"

"Foreign Secretary," explained Sir Roger.

"We were at school together."

"Etonian bluffer," observed Severn. "But he makes a lot of noise in the Westminster village."

"Marjorie's furious, of course..."

"Craftstone," said Sir Roger. "Britain's first black lesbian Defence Secretary."

"She takes it very seriously," cautioned Rassendyll. "As for Yazmina, as usual I've no idea what's going on under the hijab."

"Baroness al-Ghoti," said Severn. "Britain's first Muslima Lord Chancellor."

"Promoted her just as token Islamototty, but she's awfully brainy. Master's degree in Islamic jurisprudence from some polytechnic in Humberside."

"But she told *The Observer* that she has 'no plans' to introduce it to Britain." Sir Roger did his usual extravagant air quotes. "So that's hunky-dory, isn't it?"

"Humphrey's up to something…"

"Lowe-Graham," said Severn. "Britain's first ascetic celibate gay anti-Semitic Jewish Health Secretary."

"Not anti-Semitic, anti-Zionist."

"Bit of a micro-manager."

"Wants to criminalise lunch at your desk."

"I'm with him there," murmured Sir Roger. "Far prefer a convivial three hours at Wilton's."

"As for Derek…"

"Detchard. Britain's first beery yobbo Chancellor of the Exchequer."

"Hardcore Europhile."

"…ever since he got into a footie riot in Brussels, and the Belgian whose head he cut open took him for a drink afterwards. Who's that leave, Robert?"

"Anna Bloody Bersonin."

"Britain's first potty-mouthed 'cougar' Home Secretary," said Severn. "World's most aggressive moderate."

"This Westminster village," I asked, "it's like the outskirts of Hofbau, is it?"

"Look, seriously," said Rassendyll. "You must have some other ideas…"

It's flattering to be valued by important people, isn't it? It's all about the seduction. I tried to come up with something else. So I said to him why not put in a good word for the British Empire once in a while.

"What?" guffawed Rassendyll.

"I've just been to Westminster Abbey and it's really very impressive what the English and Scots and so on have done around the world. It might cheer people up to hear you say it. Make them feel good about their country — I mean, in a bigger sense than just pop stars and reality-show celebrities... Oh, and while you're at it, why not pull out of this European Insect Summit? Everyone knows that's just globalist rubbish..."

"Steady on," said Rassendyll. He drained another glass of wine, and then looked at me quizzically. "Tell you what, doppelgänger. Seeing as I owe you one, how would you like to come to the pre-Coronation Ball? Windsor Castle. Everyone will be there — Sir Elton, Dame Kylie..."

Severn pursed his lips. "This is reckless, Robert. All it takes is one person..."

"Oh, God, Roger. The Lord Privy Party-Pooper strikes again. How about this? You come to the ball, doppelgänger, but under two conditions: You keep growing back that ratty beard, and you dye your hair some colour other than red..."

I could see Severn was still unhappy, but I confess the prospect of a grand ball at Windsor Castle was not without appeal. So I accepted the Prime Minister's invitation, and spent the journey back to the Great British B&B wondering whether I had enough cash on hand for a bottle of hair dye.

Chapter Sixteen
Happy as a King

AND SO I PAID MY FIRST visit to Windsor Castle. Which is a castle in Windsor - right smack in the middle of town. But you don't realise that when they're driving you in for a royal *Oberschenkelup*. Instead, the car approaches from the other side, turning off a nondescript main road onto a giant walkway advancing dead straight through pristine greenery and flanked by parallel rows of chestnut and plane trees. And suddenly a mile or so directly ahead there's the castle with the famous round tower looming above the gates.

Fritz had kindly agreed to serve as my chauffeur, which spared me the cost of a train ticket. The downside was that he jabbered away comparing King Arthur's real estate to mine. We Elphbergs had had a castle once, and, as the limousines in front slowed to permit their occupants to savour the sight ahead, Fritz recalled the words of Rudolf III:

> *An Elphberg without Zenda would seem like a man robbed of his wife. I should not seem King without it.*

Yeah, thanks for reminding me. Unlike the palace at Strelsau, it belonged to us Elphbergs personally – until Comrade Bauer confiscated it. We were, indeed, a man robbed of his wife, and in this case the wife had all the money. So, unlike other toppled dynasties, the Elphbergs were impoverished in exile. When the Communists fell, we assumed the courts would restore our property. Then the war broke out, and the castle was reduced to a smoking ruin. So we are Elphbergs without Zenda, now and forever.

The car rolled through the gates, into the quadrangle, and came to a halt at the foot of the Grand Staircase. I stepped out to the click of cameras – which promptly stopped clicking, either because I was a nobody whose picture would never make the papers, or because everyone was too stunned by my hair. I had followed the Prime Minister's instructions and procured a bottle of peroxide. But it had come out a strange shade of orange. I smeared in some gel to distract from the colour, but that had only made me look like a punk rocker. So Fritz had kindly offered me his "great-grandfather's favourite monocle". Don't ask me why an important Euro-MP travels abroad with somebody else's monocle, but Fritz does. With the eyeglass in, it was all starting to come together, so I thought I'd top it off with a duelling scar. I know how to do it because they always give one to the runner-up on *Duelling with the Stars*. Then they bring all the runners-up back for the summer play-offs, *Duelling with the Scars*. It ran beautifully down my cheek, disappeared into my face mask, and came out on the other side to run down my neck.

And so accoutred I followed my fellow guests up the grand staircase to a dispossessed king's very first Coronation Ball.

Windsor Castle is a millennium old, give or take, but it doesn't feel it. In my part of Europe, there are "authentic" castles – authentically cold, authentically dank, authentically uncomfortable, mostly rubble. By contrast, Windsor has a theatrical quality – as if a big-budget impresario had decided he needed a lavish stage set of a thousand-year-old castle. On such a stage, one's performance must rise to match the scenery. So everyone was being extravagantly bonhomous - "Elton!" "Nigella!" "Kylie!" – except with me.

We shuffled through to a glittering reception room, with an ornate plaster ceiling and high walls lined with tapestries framed by gilded *boiseries*. Because of concerns over UK security, the senior-most diplomat at the US Embassy permitted by Washington to attend the ball was the Acting Minister Counsellor for Agricultural Affairs. He was the second most obscure person in the room after me, so we found ourselves talking to each other, because nobody else could be bothered. He was from Idaho, and glanced around nervously, as if expecting terrorists to start shooting up the place at any moment. But his wife, a nice lady from somewhere in Minnesota, was enjoying herself. "Isn't it amazing?" she trilled. "I hear there are fourteenth-century timbers in the floor!"

"Is that safe?" said her husband.

"Excellent for termite farming," I quipped, attempting to relate to his agricultural portfolio.

A small, nondescript fellow hovered at my elbow. "Do you know the President of Europe?" asked the United States's Acting

Minister Counsellor to the Court of St James's, inviting him into the conversation. He wore his personal standard as a face mask. I would have thought "President of Europe" was quite an important person, but apparently nobody wanted to talk to him either. Another "President of Europe" came up a moment later, and then a third. The Acting Minister Counsellor for Agricultural Affairs asked if they had business cards, and it seemed that the first was, in fact, the President of the European Council, the second the President of the Council of Europe, and the third was the President of the Commission to the European Council. They wouldn't customarily have troubled themselves with anything so footling as a Coronation Ball, but, after the crisis brought on by my remarks on referenda, the various European presidents had been prevailed upon to wangle a group invite to reassure the world that all was well.

"Pretty bad that European Central Bank of yours going belly up," sympathised the Acting Minister Counsellor. "Tough break."

The trio of European presidents pooh-poohed the thought, and insisted it was a mere hiccup. Two Continental women joined the conversation, and pressed their cards upon us: the President of the European Parliament, and the President of the European Commission. "It's like the quarterly Conference of Presidents of the European Union in here," joked one of them. Three of the others laughed, but the fourth said: "In fact, the President of the Conference of Presidencies of the European Union is over by the fifth Gobelin tapestry talking to a footman."

This was the dullest party I'd ever been to. Elsewhere I could hear laughing and glass-clinking. *A-hur-hur-hur clink! A-hur-hur-hur snort!* I decided it was time to mingle. The non-Europresidential guests were a mix of politicians, royals, aristocrats, and celebrities. You could pretty much tell who was who: The princesses and royal dukes were in ball gowns and dress uniform; the non-military grandees were in white tie; the Commonwealth chappies were in their various exotic equivalents; the male celebrities eschewed evening dress in favour of Nehru jackets or white silk tunics, aiming for the effect of the late Dr Rajendra Pachauri accepting the Nobel Peace Prize on behalf of the Intergovernmental Panel on Climate Change, or alternatively Quincy Jones picking up a lifetime achievement award at the Ruritanian World Cultural Gala; the female celebs looked liked extras in a bad sci-fi movie, kitted out with distracting breast plates and novelty headgear; and half the politicians had shiny, baggy, stained lounge suits because they were too class-conscious to be seen to dress up. Among the more strikingly garbed was the former Kissy-Kissy Akhmatayev, the onetime Kazakh supermodel and now HRH The Duchess of Wokingham, clad in men's white tie and tails but with her dizzying cleavage where the shirt front should have been. The Duchess of Woke was said to be the most socially just member of the Royal Family and had won wide acclaim for her decision to raise His or Her Royal Highness Prince Karen non-gender-specifically. Karen lived with his or her nanny in the gardens of Kensington Palace in a sustainable yurt which, ever since the Duchess had fallen out with the royal servants, was guarded by rotating teams of Kazakh wolves especially flown in from the steppes of Central Asia.

The invitation commanded that "Decorations will be worn": ribbons, medals, stars; the Order of the British Empire, the Royal Victorian Order, the New Zealand Order of Merit. So that I might not appear too bare-breasted, Sir Roger had loaned me his dad's Red Rose of Ruritania. The Duchess of Woke's husband, Prince Bertie, stared at it thoughtfully as he passed. He was wearing a set of tails that matched his wife's, but with his personal standard from Papua New Guinea wrapped around him as a sarong.

I was irked to see Lady Belinda there - and with her nephew, Lord Hugh. She caught my eye across a crowded room, and I looked away. But she came up anyway.

"South Ken's super-plumber!" she beamed. "Don't tell me - the King liked your work on the gents at Chewton so much he booked you to unplug the loo in the Round Tower?" She stepped back and squinted at my duelling scar. "What happened? Glassed by yobbos in Slough?" Her gaze went to my hair. "Ah, the old shampooing-with-Cheesy-Wotsits trick. Never grows old."

"Isn't that the prince who was at our tennis match?" I asked, my monocled eye falling on a charismatic figure holding court at the centre of a very attentive group.

She nodded. "Ghazi."

"How do you know him?"

"Oh, a subsidiary of a subsidiary of a subsidiary of his owns George's bank."

"So Prince Ghazi lives in London?"

"He lives everywhere. A castle in Switzerland, villa on St Bart's, the south of France, Montana. A wife in each, I think." She peered thoughtfully through her champagne flute. "He's a tad smooth for my tastes." Her eyes returned to my spiked hair. "Whereas you're a tad unsmooth, you Ruritanian super-plumber you."

"What's Ghazi got that I haven't?"

"For starters, he has the best jet I've ever been on. He gave me and hubby a ride to a WEF beano in the Gulf. Drove his Rolls right on to the plane. Parked it next to the stable for his camels and the pen for his hawks. Can't get that on KevinAir. So when we landed at his palace he rode straight off the plane with his favourite falcon on his arm."

"You're easily impressed."

"It has this amazing prayer room that automatically rotates," said Lord Hugh, "so that, whether you're over Chile or Mongolia or Wales, you're always facing Mecca."

Two hands grabbed Belinda's breasts from behind. "Wotcha, Toff-Tits! How's Britain's most Islamophobic totty?"

She daintily removed his paws, and introduced us. "I don't believe you've met the Right Honourable Derek Detchard, Chancellor of the Exchequer, incredible as it seems."

"I shouldda been Speaker. *Order!*" He goosed Belinda's left buttock. "*Order!*" He goosed her right. "I'd say they're well in order, darling!" He gave me the once-over. "I get it," he sneered. "It's fancy dress and you've come as an obscure Balkan prince."

"Actually he *is* an obscure Balkan prince," said Belinda. "Do you know my nephew, Hugh Culverhouse? Poor boy's my walker tonight."

"So, Hugh," said Mr Detchard, "what do you do? Apart from the gruelling job of being the son of a marquess, I mean."

I found myself between a Canadian actress who kept trying to bring up her children's book *Roland the Rotten Egg*, whom the fresh eggs eventually learn to embrace for his diversity, and the pop star Brittany Lyon, whose new song "Sex Candy" had already had three million downloads. We were joined by His Royal Highness The Duke of Albany. "Slick Dick" had once been famous for practical jokes that misfired. He had hired an underage prostitute to accompany him to a costume party dressed as Mullah Omar and his child-bride. But that was long ago, and his energetic japery had decayed into a portly listlessness. He asked me if I'd picked out the music for my funeral, which seemed an odd conversational topic. I answered no, not yet, no plans to. He said he'd spent the week working on it, and it had been the most tremendous fun. He was going to have Pachelbel's *Canon* and the theme from *Chariots of Fire*. Brittany suggested "Sex Candy" to cheer everyone up. "Duly noted," said Prince Dick, and we all laughed for a bit longer than was entirely natural.

The King walked past, looking at his most kingish. He wore a dress uniform, which all by itself came with gold braid and red sashes, epaulets and sword. From his left shoulder a row of medals spread halfway across his chest. Underneath was the blue sash of the Most Noble Order of the Garter. Somewhere in the general blur was the medal of …was that the Order of Merit? the Royal Victorian Order? Below the medals were three heavy breast stars: the Most Honourable Order of the Bath, the Most Ancient and Noble Order of the Thistle, and the Most Honourable, Ancient and Noble Order of something else. I don't know how the guy moved under all that stuff. Most of us would be too paralysed by a sense of our own ridiculousness to pull it off. But he seemed to glide in it. He looked less implausible than he did in his tennis whites; he looked like a king.

His Majesty asked Belinda if she would care to dance. I don't think she did care to, but she accepted. I noticed Peter Borrodaile, Executive Director of Strategic Communications, frowning as the King took her hand and the other dancers fell back to make room. His Majesty led, but Belinda danced, beautifully. She seemed to float around the floor, and, as stiff as he was, she made him look good – the dashing young prince he'd never been. The orchestra played Strauss and, for a moment, it was entrancing – royalty and aristocracy waltzing at the centre of whirling courtiers and their ladies, jewels and decorations reflecting back the golden chandeliers descending from the rococo ceiling, dappling and darting across the reds and golds of wall hangings and royal portraiture.

"Last dance for Belinda Featherly," pronounced a voice to my left. It was that loud blonde from Cabinet – what was her name? Anna Bersonin. She cast an eye over the side tables, where portlier nobles and dignitaries drained glasses and gossiped and giggled. Except for the trashier telly stars, it would have looked little different a century ago - or two. Eternal undying England. "Not exactly 'celebrate diversity', is it?"

"Oh, I don't know, Sexy-Arse," said Derek Detchard. "There's your successor-in-waiting, Sir Mohammed al-BuggeredifIknow." He waggled his glass in the direction of a large man decked out like a desert sheikh and making small talk with the wobbling décolletage of a willowy debutante.

Lady Belinda returned, and put her arm in mine. "Walk with me," she said. "Can't stand fighting off randy old ex-cabinet ministers who want a dance so they can press their stiffies into your frock. You won't do that, will you?"

Not a chance, I thought. But she struck me as a bit lonely tonight. So I tagged along as she greeted passing dignitaries and celebs, who were friendly but …distant.

A strange misshapen figure was limping toward us. He had a left arm that hung useless and a dramatically disfigured face topped by hair that only grew, fitfully, on his right side – and all seven strands seemed to stand straight up. Yet that wasn't the most striking thing about him. On the BBC the lady presenters are always going on about "white men", but this was the first truly white man I had ever seen. He had very pale, almost transparent skin, and those seven hairs were albino. With his white tuxedo and shirt, he appeared as a disembodied bowtie floating in the air.

"Hello, Mike!" said Lady Belinda. "Not often we have the pleasure of both the PM and the PM's brother."

The PM's brother? He bristled at that designation, but Belinda didn't seem to notice. "So where have you been hiding all night?"

"Shooting the breeze with Larry Spelunker." His tongue clicked, and his voice was not at all like Rob Rassendyll's. "He's very interested in my proposed external-zone travel-allowance plan."

"Wouldn't work for me," said Belinda. "Not with my frequent-flyer miles."

"We would have exceptions for accredited stakeholders," he assured her. Mike Rassendyll stared curiously at my hair and scar, as I stared at his, and then moved on.

"What happened?" I asked Lady Belinda.

"He was Secretary of State for Climate Change, and they were offering tax credits if you had environmentally-friendly foil insulation installed in your attic. It was supposed to lower the carbon footprint of one's home."

"Did it?"

"If memory serves, 516 homes burned to the ground, thereby lowering their owners' carbon footprints very significantly. So Mike announced that to demonstrate his complete confidence in the technology he would have it installed in his own attic. A week later, the telly people came round to film him showing off his perfectly safe green insulation. The director cried 'Action!', and the current entered his foot, came out through his skull, and the result is the charred ruin you saw before you."

"Why doesn't he talk like the Prime Minister?"

"That was the accident. When he woke up in hospital and tried to ask for a glass of water, it came out in a Black Country accent."

"You mean, like Nigeria?"

Lady Belinda explained that "the Black Country" was an area somewhere near Birmingham that had boomed during the Industrial Revolution and thus had filled with sooty chimneys. "They like pork scratchings," she added helpfully. "Before the accident Mike talked just like Rob. Then he woke up with the vowels of West Bromwich. Freak side-effect. He's seen specialists in Switzerland and California. Gone to speech therapists. Nothing's worked. I found him easier to follow before he got fried."

"God, how awful…"

"Best thing that ever happened to him. He gave up on electoral politics, for which he was entirely unsuited, and whichever ninny was PM back then made him a European Commissioner. They gave him a GCMG as a consolation, so the press started calling him the White Knight, which helped."

"Sir Michael Rassendyll."

"White Mike," said Belinda. "Of course, in Brussels he went native in nothing flat. After Brexit, everyone thought he'd resign, as the UK wasn't supposed to have any more Euro-commissioners. But he was born in Dublin, so the Irish made him *their* commissioner. He's clever like that."

The orchestra was cruising towards the finale of its "Commonwealth medley" when a strange man in blackface and blackchest and blackarms and blacklegs accessorised by a swami's loincloth and turban leapt on stage and began joining in with the Kashmiri Song: "Pale hands I loved beside the Shalimar," he squealed in a thin childlike voice.

"Oh, God, the Canadian PM," said Belinda. "Don't encourage him." But the Pakistani High Commissioner was already denouncing the white man's support for Indian aggression in Kashmir and threatening to withdraw from the Commonwealth before the Loyal Toast. Fortunately, the conductor brought the number to a swift conclusion, and Sir Wilf Large, doyen of gay rockers, began his song about the melting ice caps. The elderly courtiers drifted away from the dance floor, and we found ourselves face to face with Ghazi and the Queen and various lesser eminences. The Saudi prince cut an elegant figure in white tie and exotic decorations, but I couldn't say the same for Her Majesty, sheathed in a shapeless sack apparently designed to blend in with the Gobelins tapestries on the wall. The prince didn't seem to recognise me, and I said not a word as the Queen chattered about a rude TV chef who ran a restaurant in a building Ghazi owned, and everyone tried to help her recall a Hugh Grant movie she'd quite enjoyed. "*Holland Park?*"

"No, the other one." She had a voice that seemed to be located very far back in her throat, and to lose consonants as it advanced to her lips to emerge as a purée of indistinct vowel sounds.

Her Majesty asked Larry Spelunker, the famous BBC presenter of *Kick-Off*, about his support for the European Court decision. "The people express their opinion," he said, most assuredly. "But it's politicians who are charged with turning that opinion into action. So we've now had two votes – two opinions. Opinions are easy – anything can be an opinion; my opinion of your opinion is itself an opinion – or is that just an opinion? But action is hard, it's much more constrained. And that's why we entrust action to our leaders – the experts, if you will. They're the ones who have to reconcile the erratic whimsies of opinion with the much narrower options of action. So it's time for the people to cease voting and let their leaders act. When the people and the people's representatives diverge, it falls to their representatives to choose."

"Oh, *yes!*" agreed the Queen, girlishly.

"When the people and their representatives diverge, surely it is time to choose new representatives," I said, without meaning to. It was my first contribution to the conversation.

Prince Ghazi regarded me inscrutably. For the first time that night, I felt nervous, and out of my depth.

"That'th *wubbith!*" said a voice somewhere below me. I glanced down and there, lost somewhere in the general taffeta, was a small moon-faced girl in a tartan smock accessorised by matching tartan ribbons on her pigtails. "He'th wrong –" She glared accusingly at me. "-and the firtht man ith right!" She pointed at Larry Spelunker.

There was a smattering of applause at this, and the Queen patted the moon-faced girl on her large forehead.

Flavia! Flavia Strofzin! The most famous Ruritanian on earth. She had emerged out of the blasted forests of Zenda about a year ago when she was suspended by her teacher for refusing to write an essay on history and demanding they be taught instead how to save the planet from global warming. It had become fashionable among the transnationalist class to blame the Ruritanian civil war on climate change: the ignorant post-Bauer regime had reacted to the fall of Communism with a programme of excess consumerisation and this had accelerated the strains on the ecosystem leading desperate peoples to start butchering each other.

When the teacher insisted she do the history essay she'd been set, Flavia led a class-wide strike, which became a school-wide strike, and eventually a nationwide school strike, and then a global school strike. Some children had never returned to class: In Somalia all the schools were burned down. In Albania they were looted and became youth branches for the local sex-slavery gangs. In Ukraine most of the schoolgirls were now working as escorts in Paris and London; one was carrying the love-child of the son-in-law of the American vice-president. But Flavia had become a global symbol of the devastation man was wreaking on the environment: afflicted with a severe case of climate-derived rickets, she was short with extremely bowed legs. Yet, wherever she went, everyone loved her. Tonight she was even spindlier than usual, weighed down by more medals than you'd expect on a girl who hadn't finished middle school.

She scowled at me. "What you thed about the will of the people ith wubbith," she repeated.

THE PRISONER OF WINDSOR

Just in case I hadn't got the message, Larry Spelunker reprised Flavia Strofzin's savage verdict on my contribution to the conversation: "'That's rubbish!' Well said, Flavia. Not sure I can improve on that."

"Our young people get it, they really do," gushed an elderly lady, who appeared to be some kind of judge.

I thought it might ease the tension if I changed the subject. I knew they'd given Flavia the Nobel Peace Prize a few months back. But what was the other big medal she was wearing – the one with the crown on it? I leaned down and said: "What a pretty medal! What does it say on it?"

She tilted it upward. "'In action faithful, in honour clear'," she read. "I'm a Companion of Honour, and you're not. Your hair ith giving me a headache."

I hated her. Not because she agreed with the stupid footballer about politicians, and the pandering judge agreed with her, and not just because her (okay, her parents') appropriation of my great-great-grandmother's name had instantly eclipsed perhaps the last affectionate folk-memory of the House of Elphberg, but because, thanks to Flavia Strofzin, I was not even the most prominent Ruritanian at the Windsor Castle ball. And she had more medals than me. I took a step backwards, and then another, and widened the circle of chit-chatters - a second cousin of Winston Churchill; an Eighties rocker; the Governor-General of Antigua and Barbuda. I took another step back, and out, and the circle closed up without me.

A few feet away was Roger Severn, but in the company of my sometime wife Wendy Rassendyll. So I swivelled wallward and pretended to admire a picture. I don't know much about art, and I'm not even terribly sure I know what I like. The Elphbergs had the finest collection of Ruritanian paintings in the world, and my family even managed to take some of them into exile, intending to live off it. But, mysteriously, our Ruritanian old masters lost 98 per cent of their value the moment we crossed the border. That wasn't a problem in Windsor Castle. This particular painting showed a muscular lad, rather dishabille and strumming a lute, with angels on a stone staircase. I peered at the small plate. Jacob's dream, by Ludovico Carracci. Early Baroque bloke.

From behind I heard Severn say, "He's got the magic touch. Who would have thought our Robert would have a week like this last one?"

Mrs Rassendyll let that one go. "Having a good time, Roger?"

"Can't complain," he murmured.

"I can."

"We're all glad you came, Wendy."

I recognised the voice of one of the presidents of Europe - the President of the European Council or the President of the Council of Europe or the President of the European Commission or the President of the European Council of the Commission of Europe. Whichever president he was, he was a Frenchman. I half-turned and saw he was in the company of another French president, who was the President of France. That one I'd heard of. Antoine de Mauban was an exquisitely petite creature and the youngest French head of state since Louis XV ascended the throne at the age of five. At the time of his election he was supposedly dating his Albanian bodyguard Visar, but the relationship ended when he was caught in flagrante with Visar's septuagenarian mother and, as other liaisons emerged, he was revealed to have an almost insatiable appetite for older women, the older the better. In consequence, France had been far less afflicted by the gerontovirus than any other western nation: as it swept across Europe and North America wiping out entire populations of retirement homes, M de Mauban had personally moved hundreds of the most vulnerable old ladies into the Elysée Palace and then scoffed publicly at the fatal incompetence of the American president. He was fiercely committed to the destruction of the United States, ever since he had been arrested on a trip to Washington for transporting a senior across state lines for immoral purposes. The relevant law prohibited transporting a minor across state lines for immoral purposes, but the Ninth Circuit had ruled that this was constitutionally prohibited age discrimination. M de Mauban's English was said by various wizened courtesans from Manhattan to Alice Springs to be fluent and charming, but in public he refused to speak it on principle. "The Anglo-Saxons," he had once explained, "are dedicated to the cretinisation of our civilisation."

Still, the leering creep seemed to like Wendy, as cretinising Anglo-Saxons of a youthful mien go. His eyeballs were level with her breasts, and he stayed there for what seemed an awfully long time, staring straight ahead, as if contemplating with relish their inevitable decay, descent and deflation in the decades ahead. Eventually, Wendy said, "*M le Président?*"

"*Enchanté, madame,*" he replied, kissing her hand and raising his eyes from her bosom. He commiserated with her on the poor weather afflicting *le Royaume Uni* and said he would need to recuperate at his riad in Marrakesh.

"*Votre 'riad'?*" replied Wendy. "*Qu'est-ce que c'est un 'riad'?*"

He leered a little closer, as if about to park his nose between her tits, and told her that a riad is a palatial Moorish residence built around an interior courtyard. He gave a Gallic shrug: What socialist with a few years in public service doesn't have a riad in Marrakesh to show for it?

At the urging of the Euro-president, de Mauban asked Mrs Rassendyll to dance. She smiled sweetly, and then said, "I'm terribly sorry, *M le Président*, but I've promised the next to this gallant gentleman here." And, without so much as a glance, she tapped me on the elbow. De Mauban looked at me in fury, as if ready to add a second duelling scar to my other cheek. But Wendy had already taken my hand and was leading me to the floor.

"Thank you for rescuing me," she said, and then stopped. "Have we met?"

"No," I answered. "I am sure I would remember a lady as radiant as yourself." She still looked sad and careworn, but I meant it, notwithstanding my verbal clumsiness. Wendy was in green silk, off the shoulder and with the dark shadows of the ruching making an almost magical contrast with the pure unblemished alabaster of her skin. It was a delicate, vulnerable radiance, and I was enraptured.

"I'm even more sure I'd remember you," she said, taking in the spiky orange hair, monocle and duelling scar. "I never forget a face. Or a hairstyle. Or a monocle. And yet you seem familiar somehow." She frowned. "You don't have to dance if you'd rather not."

"It would be my pleasure."

"Well, Wilf Large has finished saving the planet, so let's seize our moment before Jamie Topham does his tsunami tshowstopper."

I led her on to the floor. It was a song I vaguely recognised from a *Rod Stewart slays the Standards* CD that Jovanka had given me for my birthday. Not really my *hodensack*. The orchestra played it in strict tempo, and I launched, courtesy of Mama's Swiss dance classes, into my best foxtrot. Slow-slow-quick-quick-slow. Mrs Rassendyll held me tight, so I bent down to meet her cheek, and again inhaled the heady whiff of cheap hotel shampoo. She softly sang into my ear:

> *It seems we stood and talked like this before*
> *We looked at each other in the same way then*
> *But I can't remember where or when...*

She raised her eyes to mine, and they glowed. "It's true." Her voice was husky. "I can't remember where or when." And then she lent her head on my shoulder. She was not wearing, I noticed, the tiara customary for married ladies at such events.

Still, it was strangely intimate to have the Prime Minister's wife cooing love lyrics in my ear unbeknown to the massed ranks of princes, diplomats and other grandees. I knew the next one. So I crooned back as best I could:

> *I'm living in a kind of daydream*
> *As happy as a king...*

They got that right.

The number ended, and I took Mrs Rassendyll's arm as we left the floor. "I hope I wasn't too demure a partner for a raffish squire as stylishly accessorised as yourself," she said.

"What?"

"I said I'm not too demure?"

"Not at all." I gave a short half-bow.

"How gallant!" she said, and kissed me on my unscarred cheek above the mask.

"Thank you."

"My pleasure." This time she kissed the scar. "Demure da merrier.

"Oh, God," she said suddenly. "Peter Bloody Borrodaile. Pretend you haven't seen him." I felt a subtle pressure on my arm, and she steered us away, determinedly, through St George's Hall, through the ballgoers, and to a small, empty polygonal lobby at the far end, with the tongue-like Garter badge inlaid in the stone floor. I recalled that Rudolf V had been made a Knight of the Garter, and wondered if he had stood here.

We were alone. Wendy was staring, puzzled, into my eyes.

I looked up into the roof lantern and the night sky above and noticed a narrow inner balcony running around the top of the octagon. She took my hand and drew me into an adjoining room with a narrow elliptical staircase. I let her go ahead, and watched her fingers dance along the bronze handrail till we came out above the Garter tongue. The stars shone through the roof, and we stood facing each other at the balustrade. The voices from the ball seemed very far away.

"We *have* met," she decided, and she reached up and tenderly touched my duelling scar. I hoped it wouldn't rub off. "You look ridiculous," she said, affectionately, "but you're not, are you? It's the rest of us who are, all carrying on as if we're in a fairytale kingdom off on the fringe of the map, like Montenegro or Ruritania..."

"You are, I think, mistaken," I said. "Ruritania is in the heart of Europe. It is Great Britain that is out on the fringe..."

She peered through my monocle with a quizzical expression. A minute or more ticked by. We stood perfectly still.

"Who are you?" she asked.

"Who am I?" I repeated, in a strange dry voice that seemed not my own. "My name is..."

There was a heavy step from across the octagon, on the other side of the balcony, by the stairs. A man walked out from the shadows of the columns, and a little cry burst from Wendy, as she sprang back. My half-finished sentence died on my lips. And there was Roger Severn, with a stern frown on his face.

"Sorry to interrupt, Wendy," said he, "but the Queen is anxious to retire, and wishes to say good night to you."

I met his eye full and square; and I read in it an angry warning. How long he'd been listening I knew not.

"We mustn't keep Her Majesty waiting," said Wendy, and held out her hand to Severn. A sour, sad smile passed over her face, and they descended the staircase.

The ball was winding down. I threaded my way past the Duchess of Connaught; the publisher of *The Spectator*; a property developer and his actress; a celebrated transgender haute couture model; one of the famous Sweety Brothers, London's most sought-after interior designers...

At the top of the same grand staircase I'd come in by was Lady Belinda. "Had a good time, super-plumber?"

I had, and wished I could have lingered longer on that darkened inner balcony.

"Oh, look," she squealed. "Emergency cabinet meeting!" Down at the foot of the stairs and headed for the door, Robert Rassendyll had been intercepted by a trio of colleagues, whom I recognized as Derek Detchard, Anna Bersonin and Rupert Henley. After some hurried conversation, all four headed off down a lower set of stairs. "That's odd," said Belinda. "Why are they going to the kitchen?"

"How do you know that?"

"I did a feature on the Great Kitchen for *Sorted!* Bastards didn't use it, but that's all that's down there." She leaned against the banister, and shrugged. "Odd place for a meeting. My sub at the *Telegraph* would headline it 'Kitchen Cabinet'."

CHAPTER SEVENTEEN
The greatest Englishman of our time

THE FOLLOWING WEDNESDAY, new passport in hand and sans monocle and duelling scar, I checked out of the Great British B&B and went to the Big Tex to say farewell to my fellow Ruritanians. Ladislas's boys were removing the last vestiges of the "Omdurman Street Fish Bar" signage, while Laddie himself was finishing off a Reverse Cowgirl and listening to his *handi*. "You're in luck," he said. "Here comes London's most prestigious plumber right now, Lord Seal." Roger Severn was requesting an urgent meeting with me in Fritz's room at the Elgin Hotel. Immediately.

By the time I arrived, he'd already cracked open the minibar Toblerone. "Two hours ago," he announced, "I attended the Cabinet European Relations committee. That's me, and the Prime Minister, plus Rupert Henley, Derek Detchard and Anna Bersonin. I arrived to find three of the four round the table – but no Robert. At which point Rupert announced that he would be chairing the meeting because the PM is in a 'private hospital' – due to his 'health issues'."

"What health issues?" Fritz demanded.

"Quite. Anna responded that, within the space of a few days, Robert had called for a referendum on whether we should have referenda, and appeared to suggest that mass vaccination was leading to excess mortality and collapsed birth rates, and then said that on balance the British Empire was a good thing, and it might be time to cut funding for wind farms."

I blushed.

"Anna Bersonin pointed out that there was a new paper in *Nature* by Dr Mann showing that these are all symptoms of Corona syndrome."

"Hang on," I said. "Don't you mean Coronavirus?"

Severn explained that it had been discovered about the same time as the last Coronavirus and accidentally been given a similar name, but it was a separate condition – prevalent among white males given to dogmatic pronouncements deriving from their unshakeable belief in their eternal right to exercise power over others. Hence the

129

name – "corona", as in the Latin for "crown", as in thinking you were a king by divine right. A short-lived populist deputy prime minister in an Italian coalition government had died of it just last month. "According to Anna, they could have Robert sectioned under the Mental Health Act, but coming this close to his magnificent performance at the Pride Parade –" The Lord Privy Seal nodded in my direction. "– they're worried it might put a crimp in the trans outreach."

I broke off a chunk of the Toblerone. "I'm sorry to hear the Prime Minister is unwell," I replied.

Sir Roger leapt to his feet. "He's not *unwell!*" he bellowed. "Thinking the British Empire wasn't so bad and that wind farms are a waste of time aren't medical conditions! And, if they were, there'd be a two-year waiting list like everything else in the NHS."

Fritz was quicker than I. "You mean…"

"Robert's being held against his will somewhere!"

Clumsily, I snapped the Toblerone in two, and half of it fell to the carpet.

"They'd be brazen enough to do that?" asked Fritz.

"I understand from Brenda that he wasn't at Number Ten on Monday or Tuesday," said Severn. "He hasn't been in contact since the ball at Windsor."

I thought back to the closing moments of that grand evening. "In that case, Sir Roger, I may have been the last person to have seen the Prime Minister." I told them about my view from the top of the stairs – and of Rassendyll being intercepted by his friends. "And then they all walked down to the next level. The basement, if that's the word."

"There's nothing down there except the kitchen!" responded Severn. "And who were these friends of his?"

I checked them off on my fingers. "Mr Henley. Ms Bersonin. Mr Detchard."

Sir Roger uttered an oath, and his glass slipped from his fingers. "The Prime Minister," he said, "is being held prisoner at Windsor Castle!"

We all fell silent as we digested the implications.

"We should call 112 or whatever the number is here," I suggested.

"You think," said Roger Severn, "the Windsor bobbies will be agreeable to raiding the King's castle?"

"You're a cabinet minister. You can get through to MI5, MI6, MI37½. Rouse every agent!" implored Fritz.

Severn picked up his pipe and lit it carefully.

"Rassendyll could be murdered while we sit here!" I cried.

Sir Roger smoked on in silence.

"Come on!" I urged.

He stood up. "You have another suit, I take it," he said to Tarlenheim. The latter returned a moment later with the purple get-up I'd first seen him in. Severn pursed his lips and then dispatched Fritz to procure something off the peg. He instructed me to trim my returning beard and wash out the remnants of the peroxide.

"What for?" I demanded.

He drew his pipe, and exhaled three perfect smoke rings in the shape of the letter Z.

"After that tennis match, I thought you were a pleasant addle-pated ninny. Perfect for a dethroned minor European king. But, after Robert's wretched speech the night before, it occurred to me you could hardly be any worse…

"He and I go back a long way. I had heard in boyhood the story of Rudolf V and the Rassendyll who stood in at his coronation. It was a Sapt family secret passed down the generations. And, when I first met Robert as a young undergraduate, I thought that, if my great-great-grandfather could make a national leader of one Rassendyll, perhaps I could do the same with another." He exhaled another smoke ring and watched it rise. "Didn't quite work out as planned."

Sir Roger coughed, re-lit his pipe, and contemplated a framed print on the wall opposite, showing a foppish Lord Elgin leaning on his sword with his legs crossed very daintily. "Are you familiar with the term 'Ruritanian', plumber?"

"Of course I am. I am Ruritanian."

"I mean in the broader cultural sense. In the English-speaking world, 'Ruritanian' means, in the manner of a fantastical Mitteleuropean operetta, an enchanting kingdom of cardboard counts. The term became popular in Queen Flavia's day, when Her Majesty was attracting the attentions of unlikely suitors, and Viennese composers and playwrights wrote frothy romances about merry widows and gay hussars and so forth. Most Ruritanians are entirely unaware that to the world the word 'Ruritanian' means something absurd, a joke. And yet I have never seen any country as absurdly Ruritanian as England in its twilight, have you? Perhaps you've noticed that I, as a Knight Commander of the King's Most Excellent Order of the British Empire, have the same rank and style as every caterwauling rock'n'roller who's managed to survive to middle age without expiring in his own vomit. A lifetime's service to the Crown is accorded no greater value than getting to Number Four on the Hit Parade doing the Hippy Hippy Shake."

"Could be worse," I said. "You could be in the People's Order of Ruritania with Bill Gates and Kim Kardashian."

"Do you know what they say in England, plumber?"

"I'm sure you're going to tell me."

"They say it takes six generations to make a gentleman. I've still got five to go."

I thought of his mediaeval manor house and its perfect ha-ha. "Well, you're off to an awfully good start."

"I don't want to start again - somewhere else."

"Lighten up, man. When Fritz drove me to Victoria Station after that Pride Parade, there were two 'dolly birds', as you would say, puking on the sidewalk while their boyfriends tried to toss one of your municipal rubbish bins through the bus shelter. I don't think they're worrying about how many generations they are from gentlemanliness, or if Lily Allen's been elevated to Viscountess Swingsbothways."

"That's his point," said Fritz, returning to the room with a dark suit. "That's why it's down to us foreigners to save England."

"You two sound a little nutty. You're aware of that?"

Neither man responded.

"Maybe," I mused, "you should spend less time in this 'Westminster village' you were telling me about."

"*Ach, ja*, the Westminster village!"

"Which accurately conveys both its size and its parochialism but not perhaps the increasingly automaton quality of its inhabitants," said Severn. "The party leaders all came off the assembly line within twenty minutes of each other and, before they achieved their present ascendancy, worked only as consultants, special advisers, public-relations men. One of them did something at the European

Commission, another was something to do with a think tank for social justice — the non-jobs that now serve as political apprenticeships," he scoffed. "The men waiting to succeed them are also all the same. There are mild variations in background — this one went to Eton, that one is heir to an Irish baronetcy — but once they determine on a life in politics they all lapse into the same smarmy voice, and they all hold the same opinions, on everything from the joys of transitioning to the necessity of 'fifteen-minute cities'. And they sound even more alike on the stuff they stay silent on — ruinous welfare, transformative immigration, the ever increasing rates of crime…"

When another perfect Z hit the ceiling above the mini-bar, he announced: "Mr Rassendyll shall command Westminster once more!"

"Mr Rassendyll?"

"The reborn Rassendyll!" He looked down at his *handifon*. "The greatest Englishman of our time, according to one of our livelier Internet pundits."

"You're insane!" I cried.

He crossed the room, and laid his hand on my shoulder. "Rudolf Elphberg," he said, "if you play the man, you may save the Prime Minister yet."

"But whoever took Rassendyll will know…"

"But they can't speak!" roared Sir Roger in triumph. "We've got 'em! How can they denounce you without denouncing themselves? Without saying 'This is not the PM, because we have the real PM.' Can they say that?"

"This is a country with retinal scans at the airport and security cameras on every lamppost. You can't just steal someone's identity, especially the Prime Minister's."

He exploded in laughter. "Dear boy, the Prime Minister's identity is the only one you can steal. As you point out, everyone else has to jump through a dozen hoops to make the door open – retinal this, biometric that. But the PM doesn't need to make the door open; somebody opens it for him. If you were a lookalike for the Downing Street cleaning lady, our job would be much harder. But to be the PM all you have to do is walk around acting as if you are."

"I called my secretary by the wrong name; I didn't know where the Cabinet Room was. I'll be found out, and sooner rather than later."

"Perhaps. But every hour's something."

"Suppose they've killed him?"

He settled back in his chair and refilled his pipe. "Then you're as good a Rassendyll as Robert, and you shall reign in Downing Street!" He took a puff. "But, if they haven't killed him yet, they certainly won't while you're in his place. For, if they murder him, all they'll be doing is handing Number Ten to you. If they kill the real Rassendyll, who'll ever believe that you're an impostor? They'll sound like fantasists, like lunatics who insist they're Napoleon. Chaps who say they've seen Elvis Presley or bang on about Obama's birth certificate."

"That one might be true," said Fritz contemplatively.

"And what if it is? He served his eight years, didn't he?"

It was a wild plan, if you can call it that. But, to be frank, if you've been an unemployed actor as long as I have, it's nice to have a return engagement. He led me into the bathroom, and repeated his instruction to wash and shave.

When I emerged, Fritz was holding the suit, and a ring – because we weren't in a position to borrow Rassendyll's, as I had for the Pride Parade.

"This is a plain gold band," I said, slipping it on my finger. "It doesn't have his family motto."

"Wendy might notice," muttered Severn. "But she's in Belfast and then Wales. Come on."

I changed, and Sir Roger led me through St James's and across the park.

"Isn't Downing Street that way?" I asked.

"We're not going to Number Ten." Severn glanced at his watch, picked up his step, and marched me briskly across Parliament Square, where once the statues of Palmerston, Disraeli, Churchill had stood, and whose now empty plinths had fallen to perpetual camps of demonstrators demanding an end to war, an end to Brexit, an end to climate change, an end to transphobia, an end to hate, an end to meat products, an end to humanity, and an end to my prime ministership. They didn't seem to notice that the actual living object of their scorn was a few metres away. We crossed the street and Severn piloted me past a startled policeman, who attempted to intercept. Sir Roger waved a pass at him, and the officer, recognising the Prime Minister, hastily stepped out of my way.

"What's the rush?" I whispered to Severn, his hand steering the small of my back as we motored into a crowded lobby of staffers and statuary.

"PMQs," he hissed.

"PMQs?" But ahead of us a door opened, and, with the lightest of shoves, he propelled me through.

Chapter Eighteen
Number One, Mr Speaker

PMQs. PRIME MINISTER'S Questions. It seems that part of the PM's job involves going to the House of Commons and answering questions while the Members of Parliament bay like a pack of hyenas and he crushes the representatives of His Majesty's Loyal Opposition like bugs beneath his feet.

I discovered afterwards you can watch it back in Ruritania, on BBC World. But it's the same time as *Real Housewives of Hentzau*, so I don't suppose anybody does.

Anyway, my first impression of the most famous parliamentary chamber in the world was that it was very small. It looked like a chapel – a rectangular space with high ceilings, and benches arranged down the sides like choir stalls. In Strelsau, in the heyday of his one-party state, Comrade Bauer had built a People's Assembly in the traditional Soviet brutalist style, but at least his stooges had been able to listen to his four-hour speeches from the comfort of well-upholstered arm chairs. In the House of Commons, hundreds of elected legislators were crammed onto hard green benches. The remaining third of the membership had to stand at the far end, in density that surely breached the EU virodistance code. Fortunately, the Palace of Westminster had had one of the state-of-the-art Chinese building immunizers installed, softly spraying its inhabitants round the clock. Discreetly manoeuvred by Roger Severn, I strode through the chamber to astonished looks from the Chancellor and the Home, Health and Defence secretaries and, above all, the Foreign Secretary, Rupert Henley, who was sitting in my place. He turned ghostly white, muttered strange Etonian oaths to Marjorie Craftstone, and froze to the seat as I attempted to shift him over and squeeze in.

I steeled myself. Ahead of me lay the "despatch box", the ornate wooden crate from which the Prime Minister speaks.

"Deirdre Bellairs!" boomed the Speaker from his big chair. I thought he'd have a full-bottomed wig and knee breeches, but instead he'd decided that an ill-fitting suit and a rainbow-coalition tie was as far

THE PRISONER OF WINDSOR

as he was prepared to go to embody the august dignity of the people's house.

"Number One, Mr Speaker," said a severe looking woman rising from the benches opposite.

There was a pause – and then I noticed everyone looking at me. So I stood up and leaned on the despatch box in what I fancied a nonchalant manner. What sort of question was "Number One, Mr Speaker"? I opened up my "briefing book" and saw on the first page:

Number One

And underneath:

This morning I had meetings with ministerial colleagues and others. In addition to my duties in the House, I shall have further such meetings later today.

Brilliant! They write out the answers for you! The English think of everything, don't they? So I read out what was written, and sat down feeling pretty pleased with myself.

Then Ms Bellairs rose again. "Is the Prime Minister aware, Mr Speaker, of the very deep damage he has done to relations with our European partners through his disgraceful Little Englander performance of recent days?" The members opposite bayed like fans at the People's Stadium when it's Strelsau vs Hofbau. "Does he accept that he is a one-man reincarnation of the insular attitudes embodied in the famous headline, 'Fog in Channel. Continent Cut Off'? Would he not agree that, in the words of the slogan of the European Council, 'The World Needs More Europe' – and needs a lot less of this government?" Lots of barracking, jeering, thumping of "order papers", etc. "Order! Order!" barked the Speaker, twirling his hands as if he were either tuning a radio dial or tweaking a nipple in full view of the Royal Family.

So I stood up again, and opened my briefing book, and turned to the second page. And where I'd expected to find the answer to the second question all neatly written out was instead merely a lot of research notes organised by subject headings. Not only didn't I understand the research notes, I wasn't entirely sure I grasped the

137

headings: "Excess stillbirths in Scotland/Putin conspiracy theory"? As I subsequently learned, that "Number One, Mr Speaker"/"I had meetings with ministerial colleagues" routine is the traditional call and response for the first exchange between the Opposition Leader and the PM - and after that it's every man for himself.

So I said, "Erm, well, I hadn't really thought of it like that…"

The House fell silent, as if stunned.

"I mean, all that 'Fog in Channel' business is a bit of an exaggeration, wouldn't you say?"

The Opposition benches looked utterly baffled. I turned round for support from my colleagues, but they seemed subdued and all 337 of them averted their gaze.

"Hilary Musgrave!" called the Speaker.

A lean, vicious-looking chap rose from the opposition benches and demanded to know whether there had been any progress in implementing the new European directive to eliminate two-ply… The House cheered, so the last bit was inaudible.

I rummaged through the briefing book, but nothing seemed terribly relevant.

"2Ply?" I said, puzzled. "I thought he was a rapper. Okay, he's not very good, but I don't see why we have to eliminate him."

I meant it. I had failed to realise that two-ply was a type of toilet paper, and the EU had announced a pilot scheme banning it in the External Zone. But we've never had two-ply in Modenstein. The thinness of the "bog roll" had been a perennial complaint of Ruritanians under the Commies. Most people preferred to use copies of the state newspaper, *Die Offizielle Wahrheit*. Then the regime collapsed, and Big Sig's cousin bought the state toilet-paper company, and became Ruritania's first *afterwischer* millionaire. It was less thin than it was in Comrade Bauer's day, but it was still "single ply".

But I didn't know that was the subject under discussion, so I just mentioned a Ruritanian rapper.

And yet they howled with laughter as if it was the funniest thing they'd ever heard – like the studio audience on *Yesterday Tonight* with Sig's snarky brother.

I didn't get it myself. 2Ply *is* a rapper. He's from Festenburg. Harry booked him into the Big Apple when no one else was available. I don't know if he's ever had any UK hits, but I remember him telling

THE PRISONER OF WINDSOR

us he'd got to Number Thirty-Seven in Macedonia, although he did have a tendency to exaggerate.

Still, the uproarious reception accorded my 2Ply line gave me confidence. These fellows were evidently easy to please; we're not talking Open Mike Night at the Goat & Codpiece. To be Prime Minister all you have to do is appear prime ministerial: I tried to think of other PMs who'd bestrode the Commons like a colossus, but the only one that sprang to mind was Britain's famous wartime leader. I'd done his voice for a Modenstein radio play set in an insane asylum where all the inmates think they're Churchill – until the real Churchill turns up and he thinks he's Boris Johnson.

The next questioner demanded that I withdraw my outrageous threat to hold a referendum on whether or not we should ban referenda. It had made Britain a laughingstock and was a rejection of the rule of European law.

"No, Mr Speaker," I said confidently. "I will not withdraw it."

Erm, why not? WWWD? What would Winston do? "As a predecessor of mine is said to have observed, democracy is the worst form of government except for all the others – such as rule by foreign judges from a legal tradition entirely alien to our own. I deplore the notion that we need to insulate governments even further from the concerns of their peoples. So we will hold a referendum on whether to hold referenda before the end of the year. As a matter of fact, we'll hold it on …October 16th." There were gasps from all sides of the House, but I pressed on: "And I urge our friends in Brussels and Paris and Berlin to reconsider their hostility to our very modest proposal, and so bear themselves that, if the European Union and its bureaucracy last for a thousand years, men shall still say, 'This was their …er, least worst hour…'"

There was something of a stunned pause – and then a few tentative cheers from my side.

A Welsh nationalist MP rose to give it another go, noting that in many Eastern European member states of the EU my disgraceful remarks had given succour to all manner of extremist alt-right populist fringe parties who wanted to use referenda to achieve their policy goals. The President of the European Commission had said there was a real danger of other countries being "Rassendylled".

139

"In what sense," I said, "is a party 'extremist' or 'fringe' if it seeks the validation of the popular will? How can you be the fringe if you command 51 per cent or more of the vote? No, Mr Speaker, it's the Honourable Member opposite who is the fringe extremist in seeking to put an overbearing political elite beyond the will of the people! Yes, Europe is divided," I granted. "From Stettin in the Baltic to Trieste in the Adriatic, an iron curtain has descended across the Continent. Behind that line lie all the capitals of the ancient states of Central and Eastern Europe. Warsaw, Prague, Budapest, Belgrade, Bucharest, Sofia — and, er, Strelsau. If all these famous cities and the populations around them lie in what you call the Rassendyll sphere, so be it. I call it the freedom sphere!"

Slightly less tentative cheers for that one. The rest was a breeze. Rising levels of personal mortgage debt? "Never was so much owed by so many to so few!" The suddenly cancelled European Embryo Summit? "Good riddance. It would have plunged us into the abyss of a new Dark Age made more sinister, and certainly more protracted, by the flickering lights of perverted science."

I thought I did pretty well, so later that day I switched on the BBC to bask in some well-deserved adulation:

In the Commons, the Prime Minister's Churchillian defiance has sparked outrage on both Opposition and Government benches for his refusal to apologise for his widely criticised defiance of the European Court. Rob Rassendyll's failure to issue the expected clarification of the UK position on referenda astonished the House and prompted the European Council to meet in emergency session.

There followed footage of me at the despatch box. I looked rather at home there, if I do say so myself. But the pompous BBC presenter seemed to think otherwise:

Rob Rassendyll also brushed aside worries about meat consumption and mocked proposed mortgage relief for Tuscan and Provençal second-home owners. Members of the Equality and Human Rights Commission have expressed concern about the Prime Minister's comparison of black music to toilet paper.

Oh, well.

As I left the chamber, all was bustle and confusion. I ran straight into Derek Detchard and Anna Bersonin, the one with an angry expression, the other somewhat inscrutable. Behind them I could see Roger Severn, smiling contentedly. But Dame Millie Trehearne loomed and said, "Time waits for no man, PM. You need to be getting to the Palace."

"The Palace?"

Chapter Nineteen
The winter of our content

IT SEEMS THAT ONCE a week the Prime Minister has a private meeting with the King, in which His Majesty gets brought up to speed on what's happening and gets to offer his three pfennigs on things. So the limo whisked me up Birdcage Walk, and round a large statue of Queen Victoria, reigning for all eternity over an imperial traffic island. Behind her lay Buckingham Palace, its gates open and a lone policeman ostensibly all that stood between His Majesty and a terrorist attack. A handful of lottery-selected tourists leaned against the railings and posed for pictures against the background of the famous balcony, from which the King would on Coronation Day wave to a Mall spotted with dozens of cheering non-contagious subjects. We drove through the façade of the palace, into a deserted inner courtyard, and stopped under the *porte-cochère*. You're surprised I know that term, aren't you? Well, I'm a king, so I bloody well ought to know what a *porte-cochère* is, oughtn't I? It's just that for the very first time in my life I was actually being driven in and under and out of them.

A footman ushered me up the red carpeted steps and into a handsome if sparsely furnished marble hall. Ten Downing Street was a house; this was a palace, and it unnerved me. The King was one of a select group of persons who'd met both Rob Rassendyll and Rudy Elphberg. And it struck me as improbable that he'd be unable to tell the difference.

I followed my escort up a short wide flight of stairs, at the top of which His Majesty's Private Secretary was waiting. "Afternoon, Prime Minister. Lively time in the Commons, I gather." We made somewhat strained small talk about Ascot and paedophiles and Wimbledon and, if I heard correctly, "Trooping the Coloureds", which I assumed was something to do with #BlackLivesMatter, so I asked if the Reverend Al Sharpton would be coming over for it. The small talk seemed to get smaller as we walked down the corridor of ubiquitous red carpet, past paintings on one side, busts of royal forebears on the other, and with nowhere to run in the event I decided to make a break for it. The footman brought up the rear. Was it me, or was the swish of

THE PRISONER OF WINDSOR

his coat getting louder and louder? We were now in the "audience rooms" at the back of the palace overlooking the garden. The Private Secretary opened the door, the footman stepped through and, with a final thunderous rustle of his tailoring, announced:

"The Prime Minister, Your Majesty."

He nodded his head and both he and the Secretary withdrew.

The King was standing in the centre of the room. He turned around to face me.

I dredged up my vague knowledge of Court etiquette. Bow. But a short bow from the neck, mindful of George V's admonition that only waiters bow from the waist. Then approach the Sovereign and bow again.

King Arthur stared at me with an oddly blank expression.

"Ah, the plumber's here. Splendid."

No, he didn't say that. Instead, he grunted, "Mr Rassendyll."

Remember to drawl, remember to drawl. Last time he saw you you were doing the Ruritanian accent. Remember to drawl, and you'll be fine. "Your *Maaajesty*," I drawled.

It was a small room, as rooms in palaces go. Savonnerie carpet, eighteenth-century commodes, porcelain pheasants either side of the carriage clock, end tables without end, paintings by – whoa - Canaletto, and Gainsborough. I was beginning to understand the life I'd missed. The scent of unobtrusive floral arrangements mingled with that of beeswax. The King took a light beige taffeta chair to one side of a small marble-topped table and offered me its twin on the other side. Everything had exquisitely curved legs, except us. Then he gave a theatrical heave. "Consumerism," he groaned.

"Indeed, sir," I said. Compared to my tennis opponent of a few days earlier, the woes of the world seemed to be hanging heavy on him today - or at least that was the effect he was attempting to convey.

"Have you seen the latest numbers on how we're doing re a carbon-neutral Coronation? It's really impressive."

"Er, no, I haven't seen them," I said.

"Why not?" asked the King.

Good question. "Well, I've been a bit tied up. With Europe."

"Oh, Europe…" He waved airily at a £2 million painting of the Piazza San Marco over his shoulder.

143

We moved on to the devaluation of the euro, the attempted coup in Portugal, and the environmental sustainability of breast implants, not all of which affairs of state I was as fully briefed on as I would have wished. Overall, I sensed that His Majesty was relieved by the failure of the Portuguese coup, but his joy was diminished by the environmental devastation wrought by UK breast enhancement.

"Did you see that essay by your brother? In *Nature*, I think. All about whether democracy is sufficient to the challenge of climate cataclysm. Sometimes it helps to have counterbalancing institutions, to temper the whims of the people." He waved his hand in the general direction of "the people", somewhere through the window and over the garden wall. "Interesting thesis."

"Do you have any biscuits with the tea?" I asked. "I missed lunch."

The King heaved another sigh. "I sometimes wonder…" Sigh. "…why was I born?"

"We've all been there," I said. And I meant it. It was a rare point of agreement between a reigning king and a non-reigning one.

King Arthur ignored me. "Why me? Why was I of all the billions on this planet born into such a position of power and influence? I have to believe I was put here for a purpose." He looked at me. "I'm not boring you, am I? I mean, are there bills we should be discussing?"

"No, not at all," I said. "Fascinating."

"And I truly believe I was put on this earth to save the world from this ghastly hollow consumerism."

I thought of the figures I'd been shown earlier re Britain's depressed tourism industry, sinking retail spending, collapsed car sales, etc. "Well, you're off to an excellent start, sir."

"Thank you."

Even today, when I look back on that first prime ministerial audience, my strongest impression is that the King was play-acting even more than I was. He was less a man lost in introspection and contemplation than one trying to communicate that he was. Which I found odd. As I think of it, the trick to kingship is not queening it. His mother had it down to a tee. She understood the importance of allowing one's courtiers and elites to feel superior to their sovereign. She was delighted when a North London novelist would proclaim to

THE PRISONER OF WINDSOR

Guardian readers that the Queen was dreary, middle-class, unimaginative, and with no feeling for art. It does not become a monarch to be a dazzling dinner-party wit, even if she is in most matters rather better informed than those all around condescending to her. But the new King was not so secure. He needed to demonstrate that he was a great thinker who thought great thoughts.

"Consumerism," he repeated. The word hung in the air, like an official Coronation balloon from the Buckingham Palace gift shop.

"Consumerism," I echoed.

His Big Thought seemed to have exhausted him. "More tea, Prime Minister?"

I thought it better to accept, and it seemed to fortify the King. "Borrodaile's been briefing me on these Ruritanian content farmers," he said, after a concentrated sip. "What do you make of that?" I must have looked as uncomprehending as I was, because he repeated the question: "Come on, man. These Ruritanian content farmers. What's your view?"

I gave it my best. "I wouldn't say Ruritanian farmers are any more content than British farmers," I ventured cautiously. "Difficult business at the best of times, farming. Even before the insect mandates."

His Majesty regarded me coldly. "I like a joke as much as the next man, Mr Rassendyll. But not when it strikes at the heart of everything we hold dear."

He stood up, and then looked down at me. "Or rather everything *you're* supposed to hold dear. When I hear nonsense like that, I don't know why we don't go back to absolute monarchy." And with the dignity borne of his many thrones from London to Funafuti the King strode to the door and slammed it hard.

Which gave me to understand the audience was over. I waited ten minutes, just on the off-chance His Majesty would come back. And then I tiptoed warily out into the corridor and tried to remember the way back to the front door.

On my return to Downing Street, I found the German Chancellor fulminating to reporters on a mute television monitor, while Roger Severn eyed his silent ferocity with an odd serenity. "How did the audience go?" he asked.

I downed a large tumbler of Rassendyll's Scotch, and answered non-committally. "Could have been worse… By the way, what's this about content Ruritanian farmers?"

"Oh, that," said Sir Roger. "All a bit computerised for me. I think you have to go on the Internet and twerk someone who likes his feed…" The sentence tailed away, and Severn's hands made a helpless gesture. "The Speaker might be able to help you. He was saying something about it the other day, but I'm not sure I followed…"

I felt bad for Sir Roger, who was usually on top of most things and clearly embarrassed by not being so on this. So I thought the decent thing was to change the subject. "Just in case it comes up, what does a Lord Privy Seal actually do?"

Severn smiled, glad to be back on home turf. "He's responsible for keeping the personal seal of the Sovereign, as opposed to keeping the Great Seal of the Realm, which falls within the Lord Chancellor's remit."

"That's a full-time job?"

"Oh, I wouldn't say that," he said. "But prior to 1307 it was the responsibility of the Keeper of the Wardrobe. And the Keeper of the Wardrobe felt that, what with keeping the wardrobe, he didn't also have time to keep the privy seal. So here I am."

"You'd make a great superhero. Lordprivysealman – bitten by a radioactive seal and endowed with all the superpowers of a giant privy."

Sir Roger sat down. "Are you finished? Or just warming to your theme?"

"An unlicensed Ruritanian plumber can't stagger around pretending to be Prime Minister indefinitely."

"I don't see why not. Your near total ignorance of the role, the office and, indeed, the very nation seems to be serving you in good stead."

He had a point. Indeed, even on that first day, I was surprised by how easy being PM is: a briefing here, a photo-op there, a little light PMQs and Cabinet and audiences with His Majesty in between.

But I was haunted by the image of Robert Rassendyll being led away at Windsor Castle. I wanted us to bust in and get him.

"Could we have the three arrested? Henley, Detchard and Ms Bersonin?"

"On what grounds?" scoffed Severn. "Kidnapping you? But you're here, walking around, right as rain..." He puffed his pipe. "We don't even know if he's in the castle. They might have moved him."

"Who would have a motive for kidnapping him?" I asked.

Sir Roger laughed. "Who wouldn't? The Remainers hate him because he supported Leave. The Leavers hate him because he supported Leave half-heartedly and ineffectively. The Soft Brexiteers hate him because he championed no-deal. The No-Dealers hate him because he reneged on no-deal. The Norway-Plus lads hate him because he preferred Canada-Plus. The Canada-Plus crowd hate him because he abandoned Canada-Plus for Vassalage-Lite."

"Vassalage-Lite?"

"That's what Robert mocked it as. Before he decided to sign on to it." Sir Roger glanced down at the Prime Minister's desk on which Brenda or Alison had thoughtfully placed a draft apology for colonially-driven climate cataclysm. "Robert thought that we had to put Brexit to bed one way or the other so that normal politics could resume." He picked up the climate draft. Underneath was a report on LGBTTIQQ2SA Rights on St Helena, Ascension and Tristan da Cunha.

That night, after hours of being bounced from ministers of the Crown to speakers and backbenchers to kings and footmen, I was glad to be alone – and fairly famished. I climbed the stairs of Number Ten up to the poky little kitchen and helped myself to a delicacy called "Pot Noodle", which is a plastic pot filled with microwavable noodles. Bombay Bad Boy flavour. Not bad, and I should think less exhausting than a state dinner. I pondered the day's developments. The euro had fallen twenty-seven per cent. In Scarborough a bronze statue of a Colin Corgi-esque dog urinating on a vax-denier's leg had been blown up. At Wimbledon a Muslim ball boy had made the mistake of attacking the American television commentator John McEnroe with a tennis racquet, and the poor Mohammedan lad had had to be taken to hospital. Another ball boy had "died suddenly" while watching the altercation.

And then I thought: hang on, they're problems for the real Robert Rassendyll. My problem was how to find the real Rassendyll, get him in, and then get me out. Let him worry about John McEnroe and Colin Corgi.

Chapter Twenty
Relaxing in the country

I HAD NOT INTENDED to detail the chronicle of my political life, although I suppose it might prove instructive to those interested in the chancelleries of power. My preference would be to confine myself to the more dramatic narrative – planning the rescue of Robert Rassendyll from his kidnappers - so it was frustrating to have to leave that in Severn's hands while I whiled away the hours with peripheral matters such as the disintegration of the EU. But Sir Roger cautioned patience. So, with nothing to do but run the country, I found myself changing government policy here and there. I hadn't meant to, but, as I say, I had time on my hands.

For example, on that first day Humphrey Lowe-Graham, the Health Secretary, mentioned that the Government had launched a Female Genital Mutilation Hotline – for young girls to call if they or someone they knew was in danger of being subjected to an involuntary clitoridectomy. Unfortunately, due perhaps to the ambiguous nature of its name, most of the calls to the Female Genital Mutilation Hotline were from fathers (and mothers) who thought it was a government helpline set up to help you find someone to genitally mutilate your daughters, and, when the switchboard explained that such was not the case, the parents would ask if we knew another number they could call and our policy was to say sorry, we can't help you there, but have a nice day. So I suggested that, as this seemed to be the preponderance of the inquiries, maybe we should take all their details and send someone round to check on the girls. Humphrey thought it risked being perceived as culturally insensitive and undoing years of outreach to moderate sectors of the relevant community.

"But isn't it far more insensitive to have your genitals mutilated?"

He stared at me blankly.

A pretend prime minister's life may be hard, but a real prime minister's struck me as pretty easy. There are so-called "working days", but fortunately they don't involve much work, just a lot of sitting around with people who are paid to anticipate areas where what they call damage control might be needed. For example, a one-legged Chechen in a rental van attempted to ram the annual Garter ceremony at St George's Chapel in Windsor and injured two Knights of the Garter. This was reported on the BBC as a terror attack by a "right-leaning Caucasian". "Damage control" doesn't mean controlling the damage to the people who are injured but controlling any damage their getting damaged might do to the government. There was a headline in *The Guardian* - "Ulster Bomb Kills Syrian Refugee". But, about halfway through the story, the reporter explained the Syrian had been on his way to blow up a gay wedding at Warrenpoint when he prematurely self-detonated. Nevertheless, Rory and Millie wanted me to Tweet that I was calling for an end to all sectarian violence as a threat to the Northern Ireland peace process, and they seemed puzzled when I laughed. Anyway, Dame Millie would say to the perching persons each morning at the 7.45: "Any potential IEDs on the road today?" If they anticipate correctly, that gets you through to the next day, where the rigmarole begins all over again. And likewise if they don't anticipate correctly.

In a primitive society such as Ruritania, the people are just people – peasants and tradesmen and so forth. But in Britain everybody worries about "groups". Not groups like Coldplay or Nigel and the Reverts, but groups who claim to represent people. Some groups are in favour with the government, some aren't: Take the Supreme Islamic Council of England and Wales and the Islamic Supreme Council of Britain and Ireland. One of them is extreme, and one of them isn't. I could never remember which. Fortunately, every prime minister has "spads" to explain it to him. A spad isn't to be confused with a spazz, which is what Derek Detchard calls retards, although sometimes he'd call a spad of mine a spazz – especially Angus Bannerman. A spad is a special adviser – such as Angus, my Bollywood spad, who made everything understandable, if only one could understand him:

"Th' Supreme Islamic Coonicl o' England an' Wales want tae kill Colin Coorgi. Th' Islamic Supreme Coonicl o' Bri'un an' Ireland wi' settle for a public apology an' a fair bonnie penny foor th' development o' more Mooslim-friendly characters foor th' wee bairns."

"Who can tell all these Islamic lobby groups apart?" I sighed.

"You can, Prime Minister," said Millie. "It was your idea to reach out to the Islamic Supreme Council to drive a wedge between them and isolate the Supreme Islamic Council."

There are thousands of these groups, and the government spends so much time worrying about them they never have any time to worry about the people who aren't in any of the groups. My advice, if you're just a person, is to call yourself a group, and then everyone will take you seriously. Unless you're a serious group like al-Qa'eda or Isis or Boko Haram, in which case the Government will designate you an "anti-Islamic group", because, by blowing people up all the time, you risk giving Islam a bad name with alt-right racist populist white-supremacist groups, who are the real danger. Some of these groups are surprisingly numerous: The Trans-Lesbian Prison Association, for example, is for convicted male rapists who have transitioned into women but chosen to retain their external genitalia on the grounds that it impresses cis-females in the gaolhouse showers. I would have thought that would have had three or four members, maybe twelve max, but it seems forty-seven per cent of all convicted rapists had signed up.

Anyway, once everyone's finished worrying about all these groups, there's no time to worry about any people – unless the person in question is on the front page of *The Daily Mail* or *The Sun*, and even then you can probably ride it out unless there's an animal involved, like "Winnie the British bulldog":

> *Winnie won the hearts of the nation when he bravely tried to defend his elderly master from a gang of youths. But, following the nonagenarian Victoria Cross holder's fatal stabbing, the head of Thames Valley Police's Communities Liaison Committee ordered the dog put down after complaints by three of the gang members. They alleged that while committing their fatal stabbing Winnie had behaved toward them in an aggressive manner and attempted to bite them, in contravention of the Dangerous Dogs Act.*

So, if there's a canine in the story, the spads game out the risk of the dog being associated with Islamophobic white racist Colin Corgi fans.

And so a "working day" goes by. The whole idea is to stay one step ahead of the news cycle. Which I can't really see the point of, since all that means is you're level with tomorrow morning's news cycle. But the thing is, if you don't stay one step ahead of the news cycle, somebody else will, and then the media will be full of rumours about whether this or that Cabinet minister is ready to make a move against you. As Rupert Henley was reported to be.

To stay one step ahead of scheming Cabinet ministers, one holds Cabinet meetings. At least six members of mine, according to Roger Severn, knew I wasn't the real Robert Rassendyll. But they weren't sure whether I knew they knew. So in Cabinet they were being unusually supportive. "I get it, Rob," said Anna Bersonin. "These public-school chinless wonders..." She gestured toward Rupert Henley and Lowe-Graham. "...they don't, but I do. You stick three fingers up de Mauban's pert Gallic arse and all hell breaks loose. And then you pull out two of your fingers and de Mauban misses them because he was really rather enjoying it. That's the plan, isn't it?"

Ms Bersonin talked like this all the time, even before *The Guardian*'s Fourth Wave Feminism columnist called it "profoundly empowering in reclaiming the vernacular and detaching it from male violence". But then a trans-man accused the feminist of appropriation, and they all talked among themselves for a week or two.

Anyway, in between "working days" are days where the Prime Minister is obliged to go out among his ingrate people and engage in fantastical rituals far stranger than any that ever attended the Court of Ruritania. So I went to a test demonstration of robot nurses for NHS geriatric wards - the polymer skin of their fingers was evidently less harsh and calloused than the flesh of the overworked human nurses imported from West Africa and Bangladesh – and then we went on to the King's dove launch at Windsor. Homing birds bearing a memory stick containing his message on the environment were dispatched to all the "home" nations – the various kingdoms, principalities, provinces, dependencies, bailiwicks and fiefs of Scotland, England, Northern Ireland, Wales, the Isle of Man, Guernsey, Jersey, Sark... "But I hope," said His Majesty, "that you'll spare a thought for our poor Gibraltar-bound dove, who has his work cut out!"

And on the premiers' podium we all did that forced laugh that dignitaries make when a Royal personage essays a gag. The King then stepped over to the pigeons' enclosure on the stage and, after wishing them bon voyage, opened the release gate. Unfortunately, there was a sudden gale and we discovered later that most of them had flown straight into the new turbines on the adjoining Windsor wind farm – the old "Coronation Cuisinart", as Rupert Henley called it. A lot of damage control expended on that.

Halfway back to London, I noticed we weren't halfway back to London. We were going somewhere entirely different, as I spotted midway through my call cancelling Humphrey Lowe-Graham's plan for vasectomy tax-credits. In a town called Great Missenden we turned off the main road and drove through ancient hedgerows and handsome beech woods. As I found out later, these are the Chiltern Hills, in a fold of which is nestled Chequers - a solid brick house that serves as the country residence of the Prime Minister. As we approached the lodge, the gates parted automatically and we proceeded down a tree-lined runway-straight avenue before turning into a walled forecourt centred around a statue of some ancient Grecian beauty. I climbed out of the Jag and glimpsed a pretty English rose garden through a brick gateway topped by what looked like three stone dunces' caps. Under the voussoirs of a decorative arch were inscribed the words "All care abandon ye who enter here".

Topping! Just what I needed.

The elderly lady who opened the door ushered me across an entrance hall of timeworn flagstones and Jacobean panelling, and enquired whether I wanted tea and crumpets. I did, and said so eagerly.

And where, asked Mrs Delancey, would I care to take them?

That was a trickier question, as I had no idea what the rooms were called.

"Hmm," I said. Long pause.

"The study?" she prompted. "Or perhaps the Hawtrey Room, or the Great Hall?"

"The Great Hall, I think."

She smoothly changed direction, and saw me to my destination. Bad call on my part. The Great Hall was, as I might have discerned from the name, extremely large and two stories high with a gallery running along one side atop an arched arcade of fancy inlaid wood and family crests. Not exactly cosy. I selected one of a dozen sofas and sat down. It felt all wrong, like being alone in the middle of the People's Hall of Corporeal Excellence in Strelsau. My discreet housekeeper returned a few moments later to set down a pot of tea and a plate of hot buttered crumpets. I sank deeper into the couch and felt perfectly serene. The tea was excellent, and the crumpet even better. Sufficiently fortified to hike the room, I wandered over to the piano. Bit of Bach propped up on the stand. I wondered who played - Rassendyll or the missus. Or maybe Angus had had it focus-grouped, and Bach pipped Kylie. I picked out the notes with one finger, and thought of my dance with Wendy at the Windsor ball.

Still concentrating on old Johann Sebastian's sheet music, I didn't hear a thing until the door crashed open behind me. I barely had time to swing around and take in the beefy fellow in reflector shades and dark suit charging toward me with weapon drawn. He hit me in the chest – oof – and down I went, sending my teacup and saucer and half a buttered crumpet flying through the air to crash down on the piano. Sprawled on the carpet, I struggled to raise my head but a black boot crushed me, and four other fellows hurriedly rappelled down the wainscoting from the upper gallery to stamp on my hands and feet. I found myself staring into some two dozen gun barrels.

CHAPTER TWENTY-ONE

Shock and awe

"**D**ON'T SHOOT!" I YELPED. "It wasn't my idea! Sir Rog..."

"Shut the fuck up!" barked the first set of reflector shades, in what didn't sound a terribly local dialect.

"Shut it!" A second set of reflector shades reached down, tore open my jacket and reached into my inside pocket. Other hands riffled through my trousers.

"He's clean," announced the second man. "Nothing on him."

Why did these men have American accents?

"Very professional," said the first. "Who the fuck are you?"

"Me?" I gasped, still winded. "I'm just a Ruri..."

From behind the massed ranks of reflector shades with telephone cords dangling from ears there was a polite cough. Three dozen men swivelled and aimed their weapons at Mrs Delancey.

"Boys, boys," she tutted, entirely unfazed. "Whatever are you doing to the Prime Minister?"

"Prime Minister?" said the first set of reflector shades. "Shit! Get him up!" His colleagues yanked me to my feet. I noticed my trousers felt loose. Someone had broken the belt.

"This is the advance team for the American president," Mrs Delancey explained to me, brushing down my jacket. "Could one of you wee lads poke around under the piano for the PM's suit button and I'll have Gladys put it back on and re-sew the breast pocket?"

"Sorry about that, Mister Prime Minister," said the head man, staring at a picture of me on his gizmo. "The Genetidator didn't clear you. Maybe it's the light."

"Could be the Internet," offered another. "It works different in Europe – like the electricity."

"Och," said Mrs Delancey, chiding the Secret Service. "You've spilled tea and crumpet all over the ivories. Not to worry, PM. I'll put on another pot - maybe with some nice lemon curd?"

"Did you say the American President?" I asked her. Why the hell hadn't Sir Roger mentioned that?

THE PRISONER OF WINDSOR

"Yes, that sounds like him now," chirped Mrs Delancey. A distant whirr of choppers was heard overhead, and we all trooped out to the garden, where Rory and Dame Millie and Angus were waiting under the watchful eye of another three or four hundred Secret Service agents. A minute later the skies darkened, and conversation became impossible over the din. "Operation Shock & Awe is underway!" yelled Rory, beckoning to a handful of photographers. The President of the United States descended from the skies, and I crossed the somewhat trampled lawn to greet him.

Most European leaders had expected the other fellow to win - the first Asian-American to be nominated as a major-party candidate. He was a Republican "moderate", and he was naïve enough to be surprised that the more "moderate" he got the more the press demonised him as the new Hitler. In truth, he agreed with the Democrats on almost everything, but the GOP had nominated him cynically, to put to bed once and for all their media image as a demographically fading rest home for angry white men. Unfortunately, his nomination coincided with a sudden upsurge in the wars over public statuary of Robert E Lee and other Confederate generals. And, as the Asian-American candidate was called Robert Yee Lee, American college students started protesting that the Republican nominee's name was too "triggering", and the late-night comedians started doing sketches in which statues of Robert Yee Lee were taken down and shattered, and millions of people who weren't paying a lot of attention somehow got the idea that the Republicans had nominated a Confederate general for president, and he lost the youth vote by a wider margin than anybody had ever lost.

So the Democrat won. He was the first part-Hispanic nominee and distant kinsman of an enduringly iconic president, José Fitzgerald Kennedy IV.

Tall and broad-shouldered, President Kennedy strode across the lawn with the confident gait of one who expects his path to have been secured at multi-million-dollar expense. But he shook hands coolly, and his eyes blinked as if he was signalling in Morse code "Get me outta here". I thought a little small talk on non-security issues might ease the Hyannis Hispanic's tension, so I pointed out how lovely the Chequers garden looked.

But Mr Kennedy had noticed my missing suit buttons and ripped pockets and sagging trousers. "What's with the thrift-shop threads?" His eyes narrowed. "I get it. Demonstrates your commitment to sustainable living. Clever." He raised his gaze from my collapsed pants to my face. "Where's your mask?"

"Where's yours?" I responded.

"The non-American wears the mask," he said.

I forced a smile, on the off-chance facial expressions ever come back into fashion. "Cup of tea?"

I was surprised to find Marjorie Craftstone waiting in the Hawtrey Room. She was looking, frankly, stunning for a grumpy black lesbian - in a figure-hugging cocktail dress with ebony cleavage you could see your reflection in. The President brightened up at the sight. "JFK!" "Marj!" They kissed, and far from perfunctorily.

He looked around the room. "This your place? Not bad."

"No," replied "Marj". "Rob's in residence. He's the current PM." She glanced at me, and then did a double-take at my dishevelment. "This I'm-not-really-an-earl thing, Rob. Sure you're not over-compensating?"

President Kennedy glanced at the wall. "Nice pictures," he said. "Not like the affirmative-action crap they make me hang." Marjorie and he laughed at that, so I felt obliged to titter along. As I was to discover, Mr Kennedy had known Marj since Oxford, and the Americans had long tipped her as the coming woman. Still, that didn't entirely explain why he was treating the coming woman as if she'd already come. Odd.

"At least this guy," observed the President, still in art-critic mode, "can draw a tree." He was peering at another soothing, tranquil English landscape.

Marjorie moved to his side. "Supposedly Constable," she said. "But of doubtful provenance."

"Aren't we all?" laughed Kennedy.

My Cabinet "colleague" cocked her head and considered the scene. "Yet if a man, whoever he is, can paint a Constable, in a sense there is no longer any need for the real Constable..." She swung round and stared at me, hard and accusingly. "Is that your theory, Rob?"

But the Commander-in-Chief had been distracted. "Uh-huh," said Kennedy, scrolling his *handi*. He put it to his ear. "Jesus," he replied. "No way. Shit." He listened for a few seconds. "Yeah, but the over-under was my edge on the reset with Wang. Wake Maher up before Wiener figures it out."

Having made her point, Marj departed. President Kennedy rummaged absentmindedly through a handful of DVDs and CDs scattered on an end table. "What's this?" he asked, holding up a Memorex disc bearing the cryptic inscription, scrawled in red hi-liter, "PM Muslim paedo". "Anything I need to know about?"

"Oh," said Mrs Delancey, blushing, "that was Mr Rassendyll's comedy sketch with the five nice Islamic boys for the paedophile fundraiser. Very clever, I'm sure. The Prime Minister's brother wanted to watch it when he was here to see the Northern Ireland Secretary about Euro-investment for the new Iceberg ride at the Titanic park. We ought to put them away again." She scooped up the CDs, but then singled out my paedo turn. "Or perhaps you'd like to see it, Mr President?"

But it seemed he was making a flying visit to discuss the International Monetary Fund's bailout of the eurozone – an emergency meeting necessitated by my remarks at the Pride Parade just a few days earlier. The whole thing was perplexing to me. Insofar as I had given a moment's thought to the IMF before I became Prime Minister, I had carelessly assumed it was there as a last resort for "developing states". So it didn't seem quite right that it was now being used to rescue some of the wealthiest nations in history. Especially as the only money the IMF had to dole out came from those self-same wealthy nations in the first place. If I understood the President's plan correctly, the US and UK would increase the amount of money we give to the IMF so the IMF could give it to France and Germany and so on.

"But surely," I said to the President, "we're broke too, aren't we?"

He then reminded me that the Chinese were lending him the money to lend to the IMF to lend to France, and expressed disbelief that I didn't yet know who'd be lending my share to me. "I thought you'd have spoken to the Emirates by now…"

It didn't seem the time to mention the visas for the transgender ladies with non-binary-conforming genitalia. Maybe France could lend us the money, after they'd got it from the IMF, who got it from the

157

Americans, who got it from the Chinese. And then we could lend it to the Germans…

Mrs Delancey brought in a pot of coffee, and bobbed daintily in front of the President.

He watched her go till the door closed. "D'you check her out?"

"Mrs Delancey? Bit old for my tastes."

"I meant for security. Background. Anyone can walk into this place."

"I know I did," I said.

"You guys need to up your game."

"You're from Chicago, is that right?"

"Yeah, and when I go home, I don't want to be the next statistic. It's the same when I come here."

I was about to suggest that maybe the entire G7 leadership should all just stay in a secure location, possibly underground, like that Supermax he had in some mountain. But the President had moved in to threaten me:

"I'll hold you personally responsible if anything happens to our man at the Coronation."

"The Vice-President?"

"No, we've pulled him out. We're sending…"

"Oh, great. The Assistant Deputy Under-Assistant Deputy Assistant Under-Minister Counsellor for Agricultural Affairs."

He leaned in close to me, and his almost painfully fresh breath seared my face. There's never a mask around when you need one, is there? "Listen," he said. "We're only bailing out Europe because you singlehandedly fucked the euro with all that QVC shit."

QVC? That didn't sound right. But I couldn't remember my Euro-speak to correct him.

"So yet again the American cavalry has to ride to the rescue, and liberate a continent from its own blundering stupidity."

I was just about to offer a withering retort about how maybe he could just eliminate the middle man and get the Chinese Politburo to storm the beaches of Normandy, when the door opened and some carefully selected British and American hacks were shown in. President Kennedy immediately flashed his famously dazzling smile, clasped my hand, hailed the special relationship, expressed his admiration for Winston Churchill, said nobody did coronations like the Brits, and that he was glad that the Prime Minister had expressed his agreement that hydrofluorocarbons from refrigerators non-compliant with the Tahiti Accord were a bigger threat to the planet than Islamic terrorism. I would have responded, but everybody started taking photographs and next thing I knew he was back in his chopper.

As he disappeared into the clouds, Rory Vane buttonholed me. "Belinda Featherly texted to say she's about two minutes away. Soon as the Yanks let us re-open the roads. Hope you're ready for the tough questions."

Lady Belinda? Coming here?

"Tough questions?" I repeated. "You mean about our long-term goals in Chad? That sort of thing?"

"God forbid. You know Belinda: 'If you were a salad dressing, which would you be?' It's for 'After Hours'. Supposed to be the lead in the *Telegraph* mag Coronation week. They were being stroppy over the date - they'd promised it to Katie Price, but she's gotten antsy over Lady B's Islamophobic canine associations. Look, it's Belinda Featherweight. Keep it light, keep it shallow, keep it referendum-free and euro-free and Islamophobic-canine-free. Where do you want to do it?"

"Er ...here?"

"Too grand. Do it in the White Parlour. Homey. And I've told her twenty minutes max. See you back at Number Ten."

I'd been at Chequers for an hour and so far this wasn't my idea of a relaxing weekend in the country. But I followed Mrs Delancey into a snug white-panelled boudoir in which she'd already set the tea, and a plate of Hobnobs. The White Parlour was smaller than the Hawtrey Room, which was smaller than the Great Hall. At this rate of shrinkage, my next room would be the toilet or a gaol cell.

Five minutes later, there was Lady Belinda, wearing a head-hugging cloche and tan trenchcoat with epaulets, as if she'd just walked in from interviewing a visiting foreign minister on the platform at Flaviaplatz Station in 1933. I was about to do the virus-compliant mutual head-loop, brisk and professional, when she yanked off her mask, pressed her mouth on mine, and her tongue began forcing apart my lips.

"Rob, it's been a week," she moaned.

I fell back against a grandfather clock, which in turn crashed back against the cream panelling and then tipped forward. I caught it. Just as well. Seventeenth century, I'd hazard. Walnut, with carved birds.

Well, well: Rassendyll and Belinda. No wonder she'd had no interest in Ruritanian Loser Boy.

"I need this," she gasped, flinging off her trenchcoat and revealing a black cocktail dress. I was still a little off-balance from the clock business, and her plunging, honey-toned cleavage was vertiginous and dizzying. "Now."

I looked down her décolletage and stared thoughtfully at the reflection of my face glistening in her shoes far below. "I – I can't," I floundered. "I've got to prepare for a visiting, er, head of government."

"Why start now? According to the Beeb, you obviously didn't bother for José Fitz Ken. We could do it in the ante-room or whatever it's called."

"I have to write a speech."

"Since when do you write your own speeches? That gaslighting of Brussels at PMQs wasn't you, was it?" She stopped hugging me, and stared hard. "Bloody hell, you mean it, don't you?" She stamped her foot. "Welcome to Chequers: Just another bonk-free zone, fuck you very much."

She yanked off her cloche. "Are you shagging someone else?"

"No," I said, relieved for the first time in forty-eight hours to get a question I knew the answer to.

She peered suspiciously at my torn jacket and falling trousers. "You look as if you've just been rogered senseless in the Chequers topiary." Plunking herself down on a sofa, Belinda lit a cigarette.

"Are you allowed to do that in here?"

"Piss off, Rob," she said, taking a long deep drag. "Ninety-three per cent of the men in that shithole Ruritania smoke eighty a day and their life expectancy is about twenty minutes less than ours even with a civil war."

Behind her hung a portrait of Viscountess Lee doing her needlepoint. Her Ladyship seemed to be looking at me accusingly, so I joined Belinda on the sofa. She snuggled into my chest, and kissed me. "I feel cold, Rob. Cold and old and a long way from home."

"We're an hour from London."

"That's what I mean," she said. "London doesn't feel like home anymore. George is terrified the house is a target for suicide bombers now I'm the infidel whore of Britain's most Islamophobic sock puppet." She gave a long steady exhalation of breath. "Basil Brushdie: I didn't see that coming." She stood up and paced the room. "I hate that stupid corgi, but I don't see why I should jump just because Mohammed Almasri says so. Or do you think I should?"

"Is this part of the interview?"

"Bugger off. Just get your doting Rory to email me the approved answers. Does he want to write the questions, too? Jesus, there's no 'Rob Rassendyll After Hours', is there? There's no Rob Rassendyll at all, once the speechwriters and the autocue operator have gone home for the night. You're a charade. I'm a charade. The *Telegraph*'s a charade. Britain's a charade. The Coronation's a charade."

"All the world's a stage," I offered, "and each must play his part. Drink?"

"Bog off, tosser," she said, and fell back on the sofa. "I'll have a glass of wine, as long as it's real wine and not that Kiwi peepee you're addicted to. Then I'm going back to London to have facial reconstruction and move to Argentina."

I filled her glass. She downed it in one, and kissed me again. "Please, Rob, I need you," she said quietly. "I'm the only one in Britain who does." She took the bottle and poured herself a refill, stopping only when the wine overflowed and left a small pool on the table below. "George is in Zurich kissing up to some Chinaman nobody's ever heard of who owns 93 per cent of Jamaica's bauxite. That's all he does these days – jet around the world blowing foreigners."

"Leaving you back home reduced to blowing the natives? Tragic." I extricated myself. "Maybe after the interview."

She produced her *handifon* and set it to record. "Since you insist, Question One: What's the last thing you do every night? And don't say Wendy or we'll all die laughing."

I poured myself a Scotch, and wished I knew myself better. "What do I do last thing at night?" I turned around to contemplate the broad lawns of Chequers but there were a couple of stained-glass medallions embedded in the window, one of which showed some

161

fellow being lowered into a pit. Threw me off my train of thought. "Last thing at night, I like to…"

Tap-dance to the cast album of *Mamma Mia*?

Feed the team of sled-dogs I'm raising in the Downing Street basement?

The most likely answer would have been: bonk Lady Belinda till she whimpers in orgasmic ecstasy. Instead, I went with: "…work on my stamp collection for about twenty minutes. I find it very relaxing at the end of a busy day."

"Oh, come off it, Rob."

Through the window, on a beautiful June evening, a soft snow had begun to fall like… like… like cocaine on Rob Rassendyll's shirt front. Ah, yes. There's the correct answer to what the Prime Minister likes to do last thing at night. Maybe I should have left the answers to Rory.

Twenty minutes later, still fending off kisses, I saw Belinda to the door of the White Parlour. Mrs Delancey, already hovering, said she'd call a taxi to the station, and led her away.

Sinking back into the sofa, its cushions still warm from Belinda, I hit the remote, hoping to catch my bit with the American president. Instead, I was just in time for *Five Guys Named Mo*, a sitcom about five guys sharing a house together in a cul de sac of white middle-class racists. "And here they are," said an announcer whose refined vowels seemed to have stepped out of a Pathé newsreel. The titles spelled out each name as the quintet came through the beaded curtain and into the living room: "Mohamed… Mohammed… Muhammed… Muhamed… and Mohamet! Yes, it's the only comedy team that always brings the house down!" And the camera cut to a shot of their suburban abode with attached double garage being vapourised by an unmanned drone, followed by the theme song "Jihad in My Pants".

The premise of the show was that every innocent thing they do is assumed to be a jihadist plot by the various security agencies monitoring them. It was rumoured that, on live dates at madrassahs and mosques, the "bring the house down" line was accompanied by a shot of the Twin Towers collapsing, but ITV was said to be worried that this might detract from the quintet's mainstream image. I didn't know any of that, but I enjoyed the show. The slickest Mo —

THE PRISONER OF WINDSOR

Mohammed, a Jordanian with matinée-idol looks - was bemoaning the stupidity of his brother in Birmingham. "They got married four years ago," he said, "and last week the imam says, 'Waleed, what happened? You and Wafa were such good Muslims, turning out more good Muslims for Allah. A year after you were married, your first child. Two years after you were married, your second child. Since then, nothing! What has happened?'

"And my brother replies, 'Oh, imam, I would love another child, but my wife read that every third baby born in Birmingham is black!'"

The crowd roared. So did I. I was still laughing when Mrs Delancey reappeared and took a good bit of time to raise what she evidently felt was a delicate issue. "I was wondering," she began, "about sleeping arrangements tonight, Prime Minister."

I had no idea what she was on about: Was I expected to sleep with her? But eventually she resumed: "Erm, your wardrobe and toiletries are still on the second floor. But, um, Mrs Rassendyll is in Scotland this weekend, so I was wondering if, ah, you would like your things moved back down to, er..."

Now I got it. Wendy and I weren't sleeping together, so she'd booted me out of the master bedroom and exiled me somewhere in the attic. So now the Chequers security team had made an operational issue out of my lack of conjugal relations.

It was embarrassing for both of us, so I just said: "No, no, Mrs Delancey. I'll stay where I am."

"Righty-ho, sir. I'll tell Flight Sergeant Adams to leave everything in the Prison Room."

The Prison Room. Great. Even the codename blokes were doing marital-estrangement gags.

After *Five Guys Named Mo*, Channel 4 offered the first documentary in a week of themed programming called *Beyond the Quagmire: Ruritanian Reflections*. An urbane telly-friendly history prof called Simon Scharmlez appeared strolling through the palace grounds in Strelsau, musing on a land buffeted by all the storms of the preceding century – Nazism, Communism, a resurgent neo-Ottoman Islam...

I was so immersed in the grainy black-and-white footage of Queen Flavia hosting a royal garden party for a visiting Habsburg that

I hadn't noticed Sir Roger Severn had entered the room and was standing quietly behind my sofa.

"Those trees," he said. "My grandfather showed me those when I was a boy. That's where Robert Rassendyll's great-great-great-uncle was fatally shot. While walking in the garden talking to my great-great-grandfather."

"Another Sapt family game that lost the plot and jumped the tracks?"

"You might say that. A man called Bauer shot Rassendyll, and in return a young lieutenant, Bernenstein, cleaved Bauer's skull in two. Bauer's infant son grew up and became…"

"First Secretary of the Communist Party of Ruritania. And his grandson became General Secretary of the Politburo of the People's Republic of Ruritania. The man who abolished the monarchy."

"And had my father killed," said Severn. He exhaled a perfect Z. "After Bauer *père* died in the palace grounds in mysterious circumstances, Bauers *fils et grandfils* decided their country would be better off without either Elphbergs or Sapts." He nodded as the camera pulled out to a wider shot of the gardens. "A lot of history there. 'History' being a dignified term for cock-up."

I sat back on the chintzy sofa. "Whoever's got Rassendyll knows I'm not the real Rassendyll…"

"So there's no point to killing him, is there?" said Sir Roger. "The sensible thing would be to use him as bait to attract you – and then kill two birds with one stone."

At the end of the Ruritanian documentary, there was a travel advisory. Humphrey Lowe-Graham, the Health Secretary, was standing on a country road with big white blobs settling on his long, thin nose in eerily distracting patterns. "Snow," he said, waving his hand at the lightly falling flakes, "is a public health issue. It makes it all the more urgent that we get a deal at Lake Como. We can't allow the Czechs to hold up flatulence targets any longer."

The BBC anchor solemnly warned viewers not to leave the house unless it was absolutely necessary.

I switched off the TV, and told Severn to follow me. We walked through the hall and out the front door. I placed my foot on the snow. "How deep would you say that was?"

"About one-sixteenth of an inch, I should wager."

THE PRISONER OF WINDSOR

"And one-sixteenth of an inch of snow is reason enough to order everyone to stay indoors?"

"These days there's no need for martial law and curfews," said Severn. "Not like Ruritania. You simply announce that there's a severe weather alert due to climate change, and everyone shelters in place until they're told it's safe to come out. Rather useful."

I took another step and let the flakes dampen my hair and face. It was cold but cleansing. The Chilterns looked beautiful by moonlight, even in a sixteenth-inch snowstorm. In a thin flurry of white, an Uber car cautiously made its way through the gates, circled the statue of the Greek goddess, and deposited Belinda on the front step.

"Sorry, guv'nor," apologized the driver. "Nothing's leaving tonight. So you're stuck with the Marchioness of Micro-aggressions."

"A sixteenth of an inch of snow..," I snapped.

"Nothin' to do with that, guv," the cabbie snapped back. "Variant outbreak at Little Kimble. Roads closed all round."

And so we had a rather guarded supper of Dover sole *à trois* in the dining room, but not at the long main table: Belinda preferred a small round table in the cosy recess of a bay window overlooking the rose garden. Midway through his cognac, Sir Roger yawned. "I don't know about you young folk," he said, "but after the excitements of recent days an early night beckons."

Curse you, I thought, leaving me alone with Belinda. Fortunately, whenever the "After Hours" correspondent of *The Daily Telegraph* was minded to reach across the table, Mrs Delancey, with her impeccable timing, would open the door bearing digestifs or After Eights or a box of Liquorice Allsorts. Eventually, Belinda gave up. At which point Mrs D reappeared to escort her ladyship to a room in the guest quarters, which I was gratified to discover were on an entirely different floor from me.

Sanjay ushered me upstairs to my own billet – the so-called "Prison Room".

"Thank you, Sanjay," I said, and I meant it. No chance of Belinda getting past this chap. I passed a pleasant and relaxing five minutes discoursing on the Test Match, which, about four minutes in, I worked out was something to do with cricket.

I closed the door, and immediately saw why the security fellows had code-named it the "Prison Room". It was a poky corner room tucked into the eaves, with low ceilings, awkward Tudor beams, a fireplace that seemed too big for the space, small windows looking out over the roof …and a single bed. I might as well be back at the Great British B&B.

I set down the unfinished bottle I'd brought up (a pinot noir from Hentzau – one of the perks of Britain's "peacekeeping" contribution). And I was removing my tie and jacket and about to open the closet door when instead the closet door opened to me. Out stepped Lady Belinda Featherly, in bra and panties. I never got the chance to utter an expletive, for she threw herself against me, pulled me to her lips and pushed me on the bed.

"That was bloody fantastic," she pronounced forty minutes later. I was relieved the ancient four-poster had withstood her exertions. From the creaks, not to mention her own vocal effusions, I was expecting complaints not merely from Sanjay on the other side of the bedroom door but from the Princes Risborough Town Council Noise Pollution Committee five miles down the road. Sitting up, Belinda pulled the pillow, sticky with sweat, from her back, and reached for the bedside table. She lit a cigarette, took one long drag and then coolly exhaled. The pack trembled between her breasts and a few beads of perspiration trickled down her cleavage. She looked straight ahead, took a second drag, and then spoke, very quietly.

"So. How long have you been Prime Minister …Rudy Elphberg?"

Chapter Twenty-Two
Droit de seigneur

I HAD TO REMEMBER to do the voice before I spoke. "What on earth are you on about?"

"Don't come the aristocratic drawler with me," she said. "What woman doesn't know whether she's in bed with her lover or some understudy?"

"Did the understudy get his part right?"

She giggled at the word "part" and cigarette ash danced in the air. "I spent the five minutes after my first orgasm thinking this was my Ruritanian plumber's rather neat trick to get me into bed. But then I remembered the referendum, and the European Bank collapse, and all the rest of it. So this is something big, isn't it? Where's Rob?" She cuddled closer, and her breast rested on my arm, as an incentive to come clean.

So I told her that I was filling in for Rob Rassendyll because the real Rob Rassendyll was being held prisoner in Windsor Castle.

Belinda guffawed, sending a quarter-inch of ash fluttering across the counterpane. "Are you bonkers? The King can be batty, but he doesn't believe in absolute monarchy." She frowned. "Or does he?"

"You were there," I said. "At the end of the ball. At the top of the stairs, when he was being led down to the basement by Henley, Bersonin and Detchard. That was the last time anybody saw him."

"Rupert's daft, but he's not doolally," she said. I didn't know the difference, so I stayed silent. She took a thoughtful puff on her cigarette. "And I can't see Detchard stooping to kidnapping. Maybe Ballsy would."

Her face paled, and she was very quiet. Eventually she spoke. "Is Rob dead?"

"I don't think so. Otherwise they'd just be installing me as prime minister, wouldn't they?"

"Well, then," she said, taking another long drag, "we're going to get him back."

She repeated the line, and fell silent, appraising me carefully. "So you've been holding the fort – PMQs and all. Why, you crafty old doppelbanger. I hope this ends better for you than that tennis match did." She reached up to stroke my cheek. "You're rather nice cleanshaven. Like Rob. But without that cold calculating quality that never quite leaves his eyes."

"Maybe he'd be better with a beard."

"He's got a beard. Wendy."

"Ah. Wendy."

"Good luck getting her into bed. You could have duelling scars from your neck to your willy, and she wouldn't notice the difference, it's been so long." She ran her fingers across my chest, and brushed her cheek against mine. "The nose is just right," she said, nuzzling the tip. "But you're not a perfect doppelbanger, you know. You smell different."

"Malodourous, you mean?"

"No, billy. But all men have a distinctive smell. That's what women like. The smell of a man - and a good gait," she added, as I slipped out of bed and padded self-consciously across the threadbare carpet for what was left of my bottle of wine.

"So you're not an exact lookalike, after all," remarked Belinda.

I held the bottle discreetly over the Elphberg manhood.

"No, not your royal sceptre," said Belinda. I noticed her usual vocal tone — which had that upper-class affect of always sounding faintly bored by everything — had given way to something almost perky, and the dry throaty chuckle had been replaced by an orgasmic girlish giggle. "That little tattoo on your back. Just below the right shoulder blade…"

"Left, actually." I turned around.

"It looks like a pulsating vulva," she said. "Anyone I know?"

"It's the red rose of the Elphbergs." To be honest, my tattoo had completely slipped my mind. I'd had it done on a bender in Moldova with Flamur, my Albanian roommate. I don't look at my back that often, and nor have many other people in recent years.

"A rose by any other name," said Belinda, as I climbed back into bed, "would smell as hot." And she ran her tongue over my tattoo and bit it. "If you're planning on being prime minister a while, maybe you should get it removed."

She turned on her side, and I noticed for the first time a purple burn just above her right hip. I traced a finger lightly over it.

168

"Don't want to talk about it," she said. "Migrant incident at Glyndebourne. Harder to remove than a tat."

I kissed her, deep but hands-free, doing my best not to spill any wine. The sadness lifted, and I sought a change of subject. "Have you known the Prime Minister long?"

"I shagged him at Oxford. But so did everybody. He was much sought after. Old joke: What's the difference between Rob Rassendyll and the Titanic?"

"I don't know," I said. "What is the difference between Rob Rassendyll and the Titanic?"

"They know how many people went down on the Titanic."

There was another glimpse of sadness, and she turned away biting her lip. I ran my hand gently down her back and rested my thumb on the short downy blonde hairs at the base of her spine. "In case the Reprimitivisation Now! terrorists are looking for a useful tip, how did you secret yourself in the PM's wardrobe? Last I saw, you were headed to a bedroom on an entirely different floor."

Now it was Belinda's turn to pad nude from the bed. She turned the handle of the closet door and revealed an artfully hidden spiral staircase.

"Where does that go?"

"Two floors down. Comes out just to the right of the fireplace in the Hawtrey Room," she said, "where you and the President were. I expect the Secret Service missed it. They usually do."

I raised my glass. "To secret stairways!"

She clinked. "God save the King!" she said, and kissed me. "I needed that."

"Not a bad little wine for Ruritania."

"I meant the shag."

I re-filled her glass. "Almost like the old days," she continued, "when he rogered round the clock. Not like that now. Do you know what he told me? Since World War Two the sperm count has fallen in Britain by fifty-eight per cent. They're hushing it up, but they talk about it in Cabinet all the time."

I wondered how they knew. "Do they have a literal sperm count?"

"It's in the CCTV," said Belinda. "They can read it as you walk past. Even if you put your hand over your dangly bits."

That might have been a joke. But the longer I was among the English, the harder I found it to tell.

She lit a second cigarette. "By the way, that loo of mine? It's leaking."

I'd been wondering about that. I explained my lack of pipe solvent.

"It's caused me no end of problems," she said. "I was supposed to be writing a piece for the *Telegraph* on how British plumbers were more reliable than Ruritanian plumbers. But the British plumber I booked was completely unreliable, so there goes my thesis. So I hired a Ruritanian plumber to replace him, and was thinking of writing it up as a stick-with-the-Ruritanians-they-know-best piece. But then the Ruritanian turned out to be completely unreliable, too. If I believed in 'journalistic ethics', I'd be in a real quandary."

She puffed on in silence, and then said: "Below stairs at Windsor is an absolute maze. I wonder where they've put him." She peered at me. "You are a real king, aren't you? Or is that an act, too – like the politics and the plumbing?"

"I'm the rightful King of Ruritania, and in a just world I'd have my own palace."

"Well, exercising your *droit de seigneur* isn't a bad way to start taking it back. How come you speak English so well? Better than most of the natives."

"I have always loved the English tongue."

"Have you now?" purred Belinda, and swung her leg atop mine. So we stopped talking for another twenty minutes.

Afterwards, she nuzzled her nose against my cheek and wiggled a little deeper down the bed. I've never been very good at "relationships". I don't even like the word – hence, the Roger Severn scare quotes. You probably figured that out right at the beginning. I think it's the royal thing. I know that sounds crazy, but look at it rationally: For centuries, we Elphbergs had our marriages arranged. We didn't have to be charming or winning: It was all laid on for us. Take the crown and throne away, and stick a guy with a thousand years of that kind of breeding in a cheap Modenstein apartment. Why would you be surprised when he turns out to be hopeless at non-arranged relationships?

THE PRISONER OF WINDSOR

That's my theory and I'm sticking to it. When Harry told me he was gay, I wondered for a moment whether he was actually homosexual, or whether he was just doing it as a kind of express checkout from the House of Elphberg – as a way of saying, okay, it's over, move on, do your own thing.

Not so easy.

Which is by way of saying that, although I liked having sex with Belinda, I really enjoyed the post-coital stuff: our conversation getting drowsier and drowsier, as she lay in the crook of my arm, her lightly freckled breast resting on my chest and her left hand on my cheek. That's how she fell asleep, and I didn't move for what felt like hours, staring contentedly at her glowing skin even as the cramps spread from my legs and I lost all feeling below the waist. And, when I did eventually have to move, I slipped my arm around her, and felt strangely elated that she knew she was sleeping with Rudy Elphberg and not Rob Rassendyll.

Chapter Twenty-Three
Marmite soldiers in the Prison Room

S HE WAS STILL THERE the following morning. Which surprised me. Even as we'd dozed off, it felt like one of those one-night stands from which the more desirable partner would inevitably sober up at dawn's first light, and retreat from the den of ill-advised sin never to admit the encounter.

I came to before she did, to find myself with my arm around her waist and my nose in her hair. She had a worldly back – bronzed and radiant and freckled and no tan lines. I had an urge to kiss it, but instead I lay there in silence listening to her doze - and then slowly lifted my arm, inched over to the edge of our single bed and stared at the plastic casing of the smoke detector for a couple of minutes before cautiously exiting the four-poster.

In the dining room I sipped a coffee in the bay window and contemplated the rose garden. The snow had stopped falling - total accumulation point-oh-oh-oh-whatever – and for late June it was a beautiful crisp December morning. I had a bowl of steaming porridge with a dollop of thick-cut marmalade and listened to the radio. Des and Trev were speculating on whether I had "had some work done". "Subtle, understated," said Des or Trev. "Maybe just a blepharoplasty or sumfin'."

"You made that up!" said Trev or Des. "Blairferectoplasm?"

By tomorrow *The Daily Mail* would be running "Before" and "After" pics.

After a second helping of porridge, I returned upstairs to find my single bed emptied of Belinda. As I checked the door to the secret staircase in hopes she might be lurking, there came a knock behind me and Roger Severn entered bearing a breakfast tray. He sat on the bed and dipped a brown-smeared strip of toast into a soft-boiled egg. "Marmite soldier?"

I didn't know what it was, so kept my distance. Even with a Marmite soldier, Sir Roger had a certain style. He was wearing a smoking jacket in rich red velvet, and actually smoking in it, puffing away contentedly. An old man, he had a smooth, unlined face, save for a few crinkles when he cocked an amused eyebrow.

I indicated my accommodations. "Sad. The Prime Minister exiled by his wife to the maid's room. You know what the staff have codenamed it? The 'Prison Room'."

"Everyone calls it the Prison Room. Your Majesty is presently in a royal gaol cell. Lady Mary Grey was held here against her will for almost a decade."

"Lady Mary Whoozy?"

"Sister of Lady Jane Grey, the Nine-Days Queen executed for treason in 1553. Lady Mary was the last surviving grandchild of Mary Tudor, and there were those who regarded her as the rightful heiress to the throne. Being without issue, Queen Elizabeth was concerned that Lady Mary not bear children. So, when her ladyship married, the Queen had her imprisoned in this room."

As gaol cells go, it could have been worse. The room was small and a little dark, but pleasant enough. "A prison fit for a beautiful royal claimant."

"Lady Mary was short, crook-backed and very ugly," said Severn. He pointed out a picture on the wall. "The portraitist did not follow Cromwell's injunction, or I fear you would be unable to sleep here."

"Who'd she marry?"

"Thomas Keyes, the Sergeant Porter. Royal gatekeeper."

"Maybe your forebear as Constable of Zenda should have married Princess Flavia."

"Thomas Keyes was a giant. William Cecil wrote that the Sergeant Porter, being the biggest gentleman at Court, hath married secretly the Lady Mary Grey, least of all the Court. The dwarf bride got this room; the giant husband was confined to a cramped cell, and died two years before Mary was released."

"That doesn't seem fair."

"Royals and commoners," sighed Severn. "Different rules. Your father was sent into exile in Spain. My father died in a dungeon in Strelsau."

I combed the room and noticed all the stuff I'd missed last night in the throes of Belinda's passion. The walls were lined with framed letters from Lady Mary begging the Queen to release her. One

173

section was under glass and included some indecipherable graffiti scribbled on the plaster by the prisoner, plus a scrawled doodle – a winged creature of some sort, soaring into freedom.

"Almost every great house has been used as a prison at some time or other," said Sir Roger. "In this kingdom, all that separates the grand life from the torments of despair is a small back staircase. The veneer of civilisation is very thin."

There was a discreet knock, and Sanjay appeared with a couriered package marked "urgent". Sir Roger opened the envelope, and extracted a DVD. We repaired to a sitting room and, carefully closing the door, switched on the TV and clicked "Play". There were some lines and fuzzy zigzags, and then suddenly the Muslim call to prayer came blasting in. Severn seized the remote and hastily lowered the volume. "They'll be wondering why we're holed up listening to BBC Shahid," he muttered.

The *adhān* ended. A single light bulb was switched on, to reveal a hooded man in a bare room. He was busy sharpening a scimitar. Then he looked up and began to speak.

"What is that?" I asked. "Arabic?"

"Very bad Arabic," said Severn. "In a Brummie accent."

The hooded man stepped to the side and behind him sat ...me. An unshaven and baggy-eyed me. It took a moment to realise it was Rassendyll. Britain's once dazzling political dandy pulled his head up, tried to focus, and stared glassy-eyed into the camera:

My name is Rob Rassendyll. I am the Prime...

He faltered.

The Prime Minister of the United...

His voice faded to a croak.

...Kingdom. I am being held hostage. I am being fed and treated well...

I glanced across at Roger Severn, who seemed curiously serene, with a half-smile teasing his face. His complacency enraged me. "You mad fool!"

THE PRISONER OF WINDSOR

He raised a palm to silence me, and rewound the video.

My name is Rob Rassendyll. I am the Prime... the Prime Minister of the United... Kingdom. I am being held hostage. I am being fed and treated well – apart from being forced to watch ...Five Guys Named Mo!

And then he gave a comedic scream. At which point the theme song began. "Jihad in My Pants."

"I always hated that sketch," said Belinda from the doorway. Sir Roger started like a gazelle and hit the pause button. And there the three of us stood staring at the face of Rob Rassendyll frozen in mid-howl.

"The fair Lady Belinda!" squealed Severn and clapped his hands with delight. "Cup of tea?"

"Belinda knows," I said.

He looked at me reprovingly.

"I worked it out for myself, actually," said Belinda.

"I would love to know the precise point at which that revelation occurred," smirked Sir Roger. "Has someone been entering someone else's secret passage?"

"I'm sure MI5 will send you the tape." She joined Severn on the sofa. "I loathed that sketch, but Rory Vane and all the usual geniuses thought it was a masterly move – helping to defuse stereotypes, and all that. Rory said, 'It's brilliant! It's literally on the cutting edge.'"

Sir Roger ignored Lady Belinda and ran his tongue over his lips as if seeking a wedged bit of Marmite soldier. "Why would they send this to us?"

Belinda seemed to sag, and her head fell on my shoulder. "Because they're going to do it for real."

"Tut-tut," said Severn. "Marx said history repeats itself – first tragedy, then farce. Turning Robert's telly sketch into a real decapitation would be the wrong way round." He chuckled at the thought, which irritated me no end. I mean, who thinks snuff videos are a laugh?

Oh, that's right. Rob Rassendyll does.

"It was for paedo awareness," said Belinda. "ITV. 'An evening of special programming to raise money for victims of BBC sex predators during the Golden Age of British Television.' Highest ratings in a decade."

I remembered the sight of Rassendyll being led away, and felt that the chances of him returning alive lessened with every passing hour.

"We have to think this through carefully," cautioned Sir Roger.

"Who's behind this?" said Belinda. "Derek Detchard? Ballsy Bersonin?" She peered at the frozen telly screen. "Rupert has seen you both as Rudy and as Rob."

"So has the King," responded Severn. "And Peter Borrodaile. Prince Ghazi."

"Ghazi wouldn't blush at kidnapping," said Belinda. "The Saudis do that as a matter of routine, to wives, maids..."

"I hope we're not playing by Riyadh rules, or Robert will be chopped up in ten buried shoeboxes in Windsor Great Park."

The heartlessness of Severn's line caused Belinda to slump. "Hard to believe anyone thinks Rob is worth chopping up." She looked at me accusingly. "Nobody did until you came along."

"So there's no point killing him then, is there?" said Severn. "Because our plumber friend here is doing more damage than Robert ever did. The sensible thing would be to kill you and put him back, and let politics as usual resume." He did another one of his grating chuckles.

He lit his pipe. "You were the last person to see Robert," he said quietly. "Standing on the Windsor staircase watching him being led away by Rupert, Anna and Derek. You've seen the PM's delicate and nuanced acting skills in that *Five Guys Named Mo* special. Did Robert seem to you to be 'acting'?"

I thought about it, and played over in my mind the final moments of the Windsor Ball. Then I asked Severn for the King's telephone number.

Chapter Twenty-Four
Kitchen karaoke

TWO HOURS LATER, Belinda and I arrived at Windsor Castle. Peter Borrodaile was waiting for us in the quadrangle.

"Prime Minister," he said. "I gather Lady Belinda will be showing you the Great Kitchen, is that right? His Majesty wants a quick word before you start. Can't stay long, he's got your Aussie colleague here."

"Oh, do tell," simpered Belinda.

His Majesty descended the Grand Staircase. "What's all this nonsense about a feature on the kitchen? Haven't you already done that?"

"This is something else," said Belinda. "Something new. It's called ...er, *Kitchen Karaoke*. Celebrities singing songs in kitchens. So as we're launching it in Coronation Week we thought we'd have the PM in the Great Kitchen."

"Sounds bloody awful," muttered the King. "Don't know what's wrong with the BBC these days. Nothing but rubbish. What are you going to sing?" he asked me.

Oh, God. Yet another detail we hadn't bothered with.

"Well, go on," he chided. "Give us a few bars."

I gave it my best. "I'm 'Enery the Eighth, I am, 'Enery the Eighth, I am, I am... "

His Majesty considered my offering. "Well, don't mention it to the Queen, or she'll make me get rid of the telly again." And with that he left us.

"Need me along for the ride?" asked Peter Borrodaile.

"Oh, that's sweet of you," chirruped Belinda. "But shouldn't you be spinning the virtues of monarchy to that nice Australian lady?"

"Appalling woman. Wants to abolish the King but still insists on coming for dinner. And never lets him get a word in." He shook his head and pottered off up the Grand Staircase – the same staircase I had watched Rassendyll descend just a week ago. As soon as he disappeared from sight, we headed the other way – down the side stairs into the bowels of the beast. For a supposedly busy working

177

castle, the place was surprisingly quiet. We stopped tiptoeing after the first fifty feet or so, and affected more of an amble, past some goofier Royal memorabilia including a huge metallic cockroach that, on closer inspection, turned out to be a wine cooler presented to the late Queen by President Pompidou of France.

Beyond the cockroach, we found ourselves in a vast empty room of mediaeval stone vaulting through which some cheap folding tables and chairs had been arranged around a coffee station and sandwich cabinet. It was a staff room, or servants' hall, the late President's giant cockroach seemingly marking the boundary between the public and private faces of the castle. We were in what was called the "undercroft", directly below, by my guess, St George's Hall, where I'd been with Wendy at the ball. The ceilings were still high compared to my flat, but they were way lower than in the grand rooms upstairs. While the state apartments had a Georgian sensibility – gilded and upholstered - downstairs the working castle communicated something older and unyielding, hard and mediaeval. Despite a modern floor of recently varnished wood and the cappuccino price list at the staff coffee bar, it was unsettling – as if we'd crossed a line to the part of the castle where secrets were walled up, and had been very effectively since the fourteenth century. I'd felt safer in the party rooms.

On the other side of the staff hall a door led into a passageway: I glanced up at the vaulted ceiling and noticed that, where the ribs intersected, stone bosses had been carved in the shape of the royal rose of England – in a servants' passage! I rather doubted the Elphberg rose adorned any kitchen alleys in the cellars at Strelsau. My foreboding increased. A play actor fits in among the glittering finery of St George's Hall and the Waterloo Chamber, for who isn't play-acting in such a setting? But, in this hard stone fourteenth-century world below stairs, the danger was palpable. We turned left and then left again – I was trying to fix the route in our heads in case we had to scram.

And suddenly there we were: the Great Kitchen at Windsor Castle - the oldest working kitchen in the world, built for Edward III in the 1360s. It was certainly the biggest I've ever seen: row upon row of stainless-steel islands on a vast checkerboard floor, but under two-and-a-half stories of white stone walls and a ribbed ceiling like an upturned ship's hull, bookended by ancient ovens big enough to roast a couple of boars. Under the mighty trusses and the ancient roof lantern, I felt insignificant, and vulnerable. Then I noticed the young woman staring at us, frizzy-haired and apple-cheeked, in a chef's white uniform and stirring a huge copper pot. On the breast of her tunic was the royal cypher - "A R" for Arthur Rex. The tureen said "V R" – Victoria Regina.

"Hair-*lair*," said Belinda, confidently.

"'Ullo, ma'am," said the sous-chef, or whatever she was. "Mr Rassendyll, sir." She bobbed at the knees.

I asked her name. "Were you here on Saturday night, Glenys?"

"Yes, sir. You said 'ullo to me. When you wuz wiv your friends."

"So I did. I'll forget my own name next. Do you remember where we went?"

"Last I saw, you were all going to the cold prep room. Funny place for a prime minister, I thought."

"You know how it is," said Belinda. "At any party, you find all the best guests in the kitchen."

"Yeah," she said doubtfully. "But not the cold prep room…"

We thanked her and, upon reaching the cold prep room, saw her point. The only feature of note was a narrow staircase to the cellars.

"It's a warren down here," warned Belinda as we descended. At the bottom was a switch for a bare light bulb. Beyond it, unlit, lay a tangle of arched passageways, all much the same: flagstone floors worn down by a millennium of footfalls or under shallow pools of dank, stagnant water; walls of broken sandy brick, interrupted by crudely sealed doorways and holes patched with crumbling plaster; branch passages leading somewhere unknown or blocked by rusting gates. Belinda retrieved from her purse a tiny flashlight. "Most of these passages haven't been used in centuries. So let's see if we can find the one that has."

It wasn't that difficult to spot the path where the grime had been disturbed. Indeed, it seemed pretty obvious that something had recently been pulled along – or someone had been dragged, reluctantly. The passageway narrowed and shrank and eventually came to a T-junction. The disturbance in the dirt turned left, so we did too. After a few metres the walls drew in further and the ceiling lowered. Both of us had to stoop.

"Shhh!" hissed Belinda. "Listen..."

I heard it, too. From somewhere nearby, there was a very faint whimpering. A human whimpering. Before I could stop her, Belinda cried, "Rob! Rob, it's me!" She charged on down the passage. "Rob!"

I stumbled after her, to an alcove on the left and a steep fixed ladder with half the worn wooden steps missing. At its top was an old trapdoor of ancient timbers. And just off to one side was a rusted metal grating, through which could be heard a faint whimpering. I could not discern the words, but I recognised the voice – because, for the last four days it had been mine.

Belinda scrambled on the ladder, clawed at the trapdoor, and fell through on the third or fourth step. "Rob!"

The whimpering stopped. And then:

Ion Prymsta...

And again:

Ion Prymsta...

"Ion Prymsta?" repeated Belinda. "Is that a Romanian name? Ruritanian?"

It takes a foreigner to know a foreigner - or not. Ion Prymsta? "He's saying 'I am Prime Minister'," I said.

"Rob," sobbed Belinda.

He repeated, barely audibly, his previous words:

Ion Prymsta...

Ion Prymsta... Rojaymohyuradyll...

"Robert James Montague Rassendyll," repeated Belinda, and then she ordered: "Help me up!" I started to protest, but she hissed, "Just do it!" I bent down to lift her calves, and then hoisted her as far up the ladder as I could toward the narrow rusted grating.

"Rob..."

His voice drifted in and out like a badly tuned radio:

THE PRISONER OF WINDSOR

Robert James Montague Rassendyll... 16th Earl of Burle... 16th... I cannot speak... Speaking is the problem... When I speak there is a problem...

"It's Belinda, Rob. Who did this to you?"

I am Prime Minister... No worries, mate... Australia... glazed shiitake at the Commonwealth Conferen... I am not speaking right... At night is when it happens... No worries, mate...

Belinda called down to me. "It's no good. I can't reach the top. I can't reach..."

I am an earl. So I have a private room... At night is when it happens... I am Prime Minister... Maggie Maggie Maggie out out out... Speaking is the problem...

"Rob!"

Robert James Montague Rassendyll... 16th Earl of Burlesdon, 33rd Baron Rassendyll, both in the Peerage of England... I am not speaking right... I had a second-hand TR4 at Oxford...

"Rob!"

He ceased muttering, and after a long pause there came a very faint:

...Wendy?

That stopped Belinda, so I thought I'd try a different tack. "Sir? It's Rudy Elphberg."

But he went back to his 16th-earl-and-33rd-baron routine. "Do you have a doctor?" I asked.

I think he answered:

The best... I'm an earl, so I have a private room... When I speak I am wrong...

"Do you know the name of your doctor?"

There was a long pause. I was about to break the silence, but then:

Johns Hopkins... I met him at Davos... The lady's not for turning... I have met Adele...

"So it's Dr Hopkins?"

Speaking is the problem... At night is when it happens... There is no alternative...

"Oh, Rob..." Belinda was again frantically clawing at the trapdoor, trying to prise it upwards, as if she could have slipped an arm up and pulled through that awful husk of a prime minister. She was sobbing so loudly she drowned out the PM, and anything else.

Suddenly, a light snapped on in Rassendyll's room, and pierced the rusted grating with a dozen dazzling beams. For a second Belinda's anguished face was visible in its rays, and she recoiled, falling back on me. And then from above another man spoke – in a most arresting voice:

Gut evenink, Herr Rassendyll.

It was a thick Germanic accent, like the camp commandant in every prisoner-of-war movie you've ever seen.

How vos your last smoozie? Ve are trying to get zuh blend just right.

Odd accent to hear in Windsor Castle. Maybe it was the King trying to disguise himself.

The Prime Minister replied, very faintly:

Maggie Maggie Maggie... There is no alternative...

"Indeed," said the Teutonic voice. We heard a loud slurp. "Zat's right, Prime Minister. Mek sure you drink every drop..."

There was silence. And then he spoke again:

THE PRISONER OF WINDSOR

I hope you enjoyed your meal, zir.

The PM's voice followed, faint and hollow—so different from the cocky tones I had heard in Roger Severn's dining room.

I am Prime Minister... Kill me... Dying by inches... centimetres... European Harmonization Zone... I am... Kill me now...

"Your death is not desired, zir, only your good health," said the German voice. There was the sound of something being wheeled a few inches and more bright shafts of light pierced the grating above. Instinctively we drew back. "If your death were sought, behold: un inverted Jacob's Ladder!"

There was a snuffling sound – and then:

Jacob's Ladder... We had a disco at Burlesdon... I was disc-jockey... Jacob's Ladder... Huey Lewis and the News... I am on the news...

"I see zuh Good Book is not so good with you. Good night, Mr Rassendyll." The light was extinguished, the faint click of a door was heard.

Down on our level, somewhere ahead of us in the corridor, another light was switched on.

I clicked off Belinda's torch, pulled her back down and as quickly as we could we retraced our path back toward the cold prep room. At the foot of the stairs a figure stepped out, with a huge torch shining directly in our faces.

"Long way from the kitchen, aren't we? What new show is this for – *Subterranean Singalong?*"

We laughed, nervously. Peter Borrodaile said nothing. We laughed again, less nervously but also less naturally. He looked at us awhile, as if deciding whether or not to make something of it. We started to laugh again, even more forced, but he cut us off. "His Majesty is wondering whether you would like to come and have a *digestif* with your fellow prime minister. The virtues of antipodean republicanism are beginning to wear a bit thin. You too, Belinda. Come along."

183

And off we went.

Chapter Twenty-Five
Under the eye of the High Representative

SAFELY BACK AT CHEQUERS, and over a large plate of cold poached salmon, Belinda and I debriefed Sir Roger Severn.

"So Robert's alive," he said, "and under the care of someone purporting to be a physician."

"And heavily drugged," I added. "The doctor's called John Hopkins. Rassendyll met him at Davos."

"Johns Hopkins is a hospital in America," said Belinda. "So that seems unlikely."

"Might be worth taking a gander at the staff directory," mused Severn.

"Good luck with that. It's the largest hospital in the world."

"Is Borrodaile in on it?"

"I honestly couldn't say," said Belinda. "At first I thought he was, but, when we got upstairs, you could see that burly sheila really was driving the King potty and that he was desperate for a diversion."

"So who *is* in on it?" I asked.

Sir Roger counted them off on his fingers. "Henley, Detchard, Bersonin..."

"When that doctor pulled back whatever it was," said Belinda, "everything was very white."

"What are you saying?"

"I don't know really. Just a feeling. Like a very clean hospital. And that shower of schemers couldn't organise an ad hoc medical facility."

I took another piece of salmon. "Who else has access to Windsor Castle? Other than the Royal Family, I mean."

Mrs Delancey arrived with a steaming jug of hot chocolate and we all fell silent until she left. Then Belinda spoke:

"I know who has access. That beastly pig-tailed schoolgirl." She corrected herself. "Ex-schoolgirl."

"Flavia Strofzin? I *hate* her!" I hadn't meant to say it, but it slipped out, and Belinda and Sir Roger stared. "She humiliated me in front of the Queen!"

185

"No doubt," said Severn. "Still, Belinda's right. Miss Strofzin does have access to the castle." It seemed that everyone loved Little Orphan Flavia (except me, Lady Belinda, and President de Mauban, who had no time for women under eighty). The King had been so taken by the enchanting moppet that, when she announced she was setting up a foundation to save the world, he offered to lend her some office space.

Belinda laughed. "I think he had in mind a couple of the rattier rooms at St James's Palace. But they were walking through the grounds at Windsor and she pointed to the Round Tower and said, 'I want that!' So the King moved out the Royal Archives and now the tower is home to Osra's world-saving Planet in the Round foundation."

"But a little girl can't put together a scheme to kidnap the British Prime Minister." We fell silent for a moment. "There must be some grown-ups behind this Planet in the Round thing."

Belinda read from her phone: "The board of Osra's foundation includes HRH The Duchess of Wokingham, Prince Ghazi ...and Rob's brother!"

I was wearying of the entire Rassendyll family, notwithstanding how intertwined they were with mine. "I suppose," I said, "when you're an earl you're sort of expected to go into government."

"Not necessarily," answered Severn. "Among Robert's forebears were a Viceroy of India, a Foreign Secretary, a Resident Commissioner of Basutoland. But his pa eschewed 'public service' and opened one of the first studios for ...what d'you call those jungle rhythms, Belinda?"

"Reggae."

"Exactly. One of the first reggae studios in the Caribbean. Can't say I blame him," mused Severn. "Politics is shrinking at an alarming rate. Maybe I should have gone into hippety-hop."

"His pop made a lot of money with the reggae for a while," said Belinda, "just like mine did with the safari park. But Rob doesn't have that flair."

"How'd he become PM then?"

"He was an indifferent PR man, hired for his aristocratic ease."

"I know nothing about 'public relations'..." Sir Roger gave an involuntary shiver at the phrase. "So I thought Robert was much better at it than he was, and got him his first job with the party. As a member of the youth wing, he was given responsibility for supplying *au courant* pop-culture references to heavyweight cabinet ministers before their appearances on the BBC's *Question Time*."

"Oh, God, don't remind me," groaned Belinda. "So they could sit across the table from the other side and say, 'You are the weakest link — goodbye!' or 'I think we all agree we need to vote Mr Blair off the island' or 'I'm afraid the Prime Minister didn't have me at hello' or 'I'll tell you what I want, what I really really want - and that's for you to resign!' And then the watching masses were supposed to think golly, this dull middle-aged nonentity in a suit is really groovy."

"Indeed," said Severn. "So the man who provided fake demotic flourishes was subsequently made party leader, with all too predictable consequences."

Belinda lit another cigarette. "I'm not a big fan of Mike R, but I did love it when Chris Evans asked him his favourite group and Michael said, 'I don't like pop music.' Delayed his getting to Cabinet by two years, of course."

"Michael?" I said. "You mean Rassendyll's brother?"

"Half-brother," said Severn. "When I met them at Oxford, Michael thought the world all wrong. Thought he ought to be Robert."

"Not a lot of brotherly love then?"

"They loved one another as men do who want the same place and the same wife!"

"Are you sure about that?" asked Belinda. "That was true once. I'm not certain it is now. He still hates Rob, but I don't know that he envies him…"

"Michael would give his soul to have Wendy!"

"Wendy, yes. But he doesn't have a soul, and I don't think he has any interest in Number Ten."

"Why? Isn't he just some Euro-commissioner?"

They both laughed now. "He resigned as Ireland's commissioner," said Severn, "to become the European Union's chief negotiator for Brexit. When the draft treaty for the transitional period provided for the appointment of a 'High Representative to the External Zone (Qualified Recognition)', they moved him back here — just up the hill actually." He stood up and went to the window.

"We're on the wrong side of the house," said Belinda. "The best view is from the Prison Room."

We trooped up two flights of stairs and peered through the small window. On an incline in the distance was a hideous structure – and indeed a literal eyesore, in that it looked like a giant eye suspended over the hill. At the centre the eyeball was blue – like the European Union flag, complete with the circle of gold stars – staring out across the landscape.

"What the hell is that?" I asked.

"The headquarters of the High Representative to the External Zone (Qualified Recognition)," said Sir Roger. "So he can keep his beady eye on the nobody who serves as British Prime Minister."

"How did that happen?"

"Very carelessly on our part. That up there is Beacon Hill, site of Cymbeline's Castle."

I'd only heard of Cymbeline from Shakespeare's play. So Sir Roger and Lady Belinda explained that he was an ancient king, properly called "Cunobeline".

"Which means 'Strong Dog', I believe," drawled Severn. "The Colin Corgi of his day no doubt. A few years ago we signed up to something called the European Heritage Directive, in which certain national historic sites were deemed to be of pan-European significance. We didn't realise we were, in fact, ceding control of those sites for the purposes of further development. So no sooner was Michael appointed High Representative than he decided it was the perfect spot for his HQ – behind and above Cymbeline's motte and baileys. He calls himself the British Resident," added Sir Roger.

I looked blank.

"Colonial joke," said Belinda.

"Technically," Severn corrected her, "a protectorate joke."

"So Rob is English but Mike is Irish?"

"He was born in Dublin," explained Sir Roger. "As the Duke of Wellington said, a man can be born in a stable but it doesn't make him a horse. These days, a man can be born in a stable and it doesn't make him anything. Michael is entirely post-national."

"Stopped using his knighthood when he made it in Brussels," said Belinda. "Not like Roger."

Severn smiled. "But he likes all the 'White Knight' foolery. Useful." He blew another perfect Z up at the ceiling. "This would be his sort of caper."

"Why would he be mixed up in this?" asked Belinda. "Rob's rolled over for all the Euro-bollocks. Hardly says a word about any of it. His whole tranny-get-your-gun initiative was to distract from having to talk about the EU ever again. Three months of twaddle in *The Guardian* about how female regiments made up of non-cisgender women were far more lethal in counter-insurgency situations. Everyone forgot about Brexit."

"But what about Brexit?" I asked. "I mean, Brexit happened? Didn't it?"

They both laughed again.

"Which brings us back to my question," said Belinda. "Why kidnap Rob, now?"

"I think the state of the euro, and the resignation of the ECB board, and the attempted coups in Portugal and Greece answer that."

"But isn't all that my fault?" I asked.

They both looked at me sympathetically, yet I felt bad. "Belinda's right. We're going to get him back."

"Thank you," she said, emphatically.

I paced the floor and saw again the doodle Lady Mary Grey had scrawled on the wall when this room was her gaol cell – a winged creature taking flight and soaring to freedom. "Out into the world," said Severn, "like Britain after Brexit. That's how it was supposed to go."

"Instead we're like Lady Mary," said Belinda. "Banged up in our cell and wondering where the secret escape route is." She lit another cigarette. "I can't stop replaying all that rubbish Rob was spouting… Something terrible is going to happen."

"He means a lot to you, doesn't he?" I said quietly.

She looked sad for a moment. "No. Not really. He might have once." She went over to the sideboard and looked for something stronger to drink than Mrs Delancey's hot chocolate. "Have you been to Burlesdon yet, you fake earl? It looks spectacular as you come up the drive and over the moat and under the portcullis, but inside it's all a bit gloomy and mouldering. The new bit – seventeeth-century – isn't so bad. That's round the back on the other side of the moat."

"Like Zenda," I sighed nostalgically.

"The old part's very historic. Rob's room has a hidden doorway behind the wardrobe to a small chamber – what we used to call a priest's hiding hole – and from there it descends down through two sides of the house and comes out on a stone step by a water-gate on the moat."

"How do you know that?"

"The world's all-time worst double-date. First year at Oxford. Rob and me, Mike and Wendy. They both loved Wendy. Pitiful really, especially for Mike and for me. Lady Burlesdon put us gels in the guest quarters – in the new bit, on the other side of the moat, out of her consideration for the boys' virtue. I waited fifteen minutes, swam across the moat, up the steps and the secret stairway, opened the wardrobe door, and there were Rob and Wendy *in flagrante*. No one's ever beaten me over the moat since."

I was about to say something but I didn't get the chance.

"*That's it!*" shrieked Lady Belinda – and then continued sotto voce: "I know how to get into Windsor Castle – and out again."

"Really?" said I.

"Yes, really." She opened the closet door and pointed to the secret stairway down to the Hawtrey Room. "There's a way into the castle cellars from the tearoom next door. I told you..." She turned to me in triumph. "...I worked there as a waitress. It's got a secret passageway. That's how they sneaked Nell Gwynn in and out."

I looked blank as usual.

"Mistress of Charles II," she added.

"Good show, Belinda!" exclaimed Severn. "Remembering how they smuggled in the mistress. Not a lot of us would have cause to recall that."

"Ooh, saucer of milk for Sir Roger Severn," she simpered. "If you've a better idea, let me know."

Chapter Twenty-Six
Earl Force One

VISIBLY FLUSTERED, Angus Bannerman walked into the 7.45 at 7.52. "Och, surry I'm ahint," he said. "Had tae rerun th' ooverneets. Knocked me for sex when I saw th' spreadshit. Looooked as if we might ha' a computer vaerus or something." He passed around the polls. "Ye positives have gone oop tae 53 per cent."

Rory Vane dismissed it as an obvious malfunction.

"Ae reckoned sae too," said Angus. "But then ae thut: Saepose it's tha wee Ruritanian Content Farmers traein' tae head-fake us intae an early election…"

Dame Millie grimaced. "But who'd they be working for? Moscow? Brussels? Some Yank 'morning zoo' radio show?"

The meeting broke up in disarray.

I'd been hoping to have twenty minutes to work on my Irish reverse-backstop, but Angus followed me downstairs saying we were running late yet again. Another photo-op. I can't see the point myself – I mean, if that's all a prime minister does, you might as well hire an actor. Or a lookalike. It must have been an important photo-op because yet again Wendy was waiting in the Jaguar with her usual look of contempt. Or actually – now I think about it – marginally less contempt than the last time I saw her. We set off for the world-famous Trafalgar Square, which they had somehow managed to wreck since I was last there for Pride Parade. You'll know it for Lord Nelson, of course, high atop his pillar and keeping one eye on Canada House, South Africa House and the National Gallery. "England expects every man to do his duty," I said to Angus, in hopes it might break the ice.

"Ae'm Scots," he said. "Sco'land aixpecks uvry mon to eat his fraed Mars Bar."

"Well, it's a good turnout," I remarked, surveying the sea of socially distant citizenry patiently waiting my arrival.

"Tha's tha queue foo tha virocompliant sitzpinkler," he said.

Down below the great admiral were lions and generals on plinths. The so-called "fourth plinth" had been intended for a statue of William IV paid for by public subscription, but the King was so unpopular the money was never raised. Welcome to my world. So in recent years the empty plinth had been used for rotating works of contemporary art - until today, when a new and worthy permanent structure would take its place: "The Long Knife" by acclaimed sculptor Bertram Bertrand. It was a monument to stabbing victims of the London streets consisting of a giant knife with a ferociously serrated edge pointing up into the air.

The artist was circling his work in an animal-like way, save only for the admiring poses he struck at each angle. I felt I ought to congratulate him. "Golly! That huge drop of blood dangling from the knife is incredibly realistic."

"It's a teardrop," said Mr Bertrand, and didn't speak to me for the rest of the event.

His artwork had ruined the symmetry of the square: The knife was at an angle, in order that the blood – sorry, teardrop – could hang straight down. So it was leaning in towards Lord Nelson as if about to slice his column in half and send the great admiral crashing down on to the tourist buses below. The dramatic sculpture had been commissioned by the former Mayor of London, a rising star who'd been tipped to be going places, until, in the wake of an expenses scandal, the place he went to was Yemen, where he mysteriously self-detonated. The new mayor was a retired Albanian gangster, a compromise candidate after the Labour Party nominating committee deadlocked between a screamingly camp old actor and the former Grand Mufti of Jalalabad.

Rory ordered me to be seen interacting with ordinary Londoners in a normal manner, so I asked two admiring schoolgirls, Sharyn and Darenna, what they thought of the sculpture.

"Great, innit?" said the first. "Iss like really real."

"Luvvit," giggled her mate. "Jus like 'er feller's knife, noamsayin'?"

"Innit?" I replied, anxious to fit in, and then banged my knee on some ugly vertical post at crotch height. For some reason they were all over the square. "What are these stupid things?" I said exasperated. "They're everywhere."

"Bollards," said Sharyn.

"There's no need to talk like that, young lady. I am the Prime Minister, you know."

THE PRISONER OF WINDSOR

"Is this a telly sketch, like? For *Arse of the Week*?" said Darenna. "They're all comin' aht, anyway. For the new Coronation bollards. Bigger and thicker. Like Sharyn's sister." And she pulled up a picture on her phone, showing an even uglier post, and with the European Union gold stars on the top.

"If it's a Coronation bollard, why does it have the EU flag on it?" I asked.

"You're the PM," she said. "Stormzy says you're like a big evil dictator, so why don't you pick your own bollards?"

"Maybe I will," I said. I suddenly noticed Angus standing off to one side and looking, as upon our last engagement in Trafalgar Square, a little queasy.

But Rory was already hustling me back into the limo, sans Wendy, for some meeting in Belgium. I wasn't happy about it. "Why do I have to go to Brussels if we're not in the EU anymore?" Dame Millie laughed and said that, during the absence of all those Euro-presidents at the Windsor Castle ball, there had been chatter about a "Berlaymont coup" and Brussels had decided that for the moment there would be no more trips to the "External Zone". "So, if the mountain won't go to Mohammed, the External Zone will have to go to the beating heart of Euro-power."

I stared through the tinted glass into a grey drizzle and watched the shop windows go by until we reached the RAF airfield. I had assumed Sir Roger would be there to explain what was going on. But there was no sight of him, though I hung around on the runway as long as I could. "Come along, Prime Minister," Millie called from the top of the steps. I aimed a kick at a windblown confectionery wrapper for Fizzy Balls, and missed. It wafted on toward the perimeter fence, only to be ensnared on the very brink of freedom.

Ever since Rassendyll had expressed a need for a prime ministerial jet, it had been mocked by Fleet Street cartoonists as "Earl Force One". So I'd been expecting the "real deal" – a Yank-sized symbol of excess. Instead, it was a modest little plane with nothing other than a small Union Jack on the tail to hint at its awesome role. Still, compared with *Arbeiterklasse* on Ruriflotte, Earl Force One had handsome leather chairs, gleaming varnished tables, and a very attentive steward, with the specials of the day illustrated on his face mask. He served me a crab and avocado tartine, and I enjoyed it so much I then had a prosciutto, brie and mango tartine. Behind me, miscellaneous aides chattered away, fine-tuning the day and scrolling their *handifons*.

Seeing Brussels for the first time, I was relieved that nobody had thought to make Strelsau the capital of Europe. Fun towns have a Latin Quarter; Brussels has a European Quarter, and it feels more like three-quarters. If 10 Downing Street had been designed to communicate that a powerful man lives in an ordinary London house, the Euro-edifices are there to announce the opposite – that, in this modest capital of a minor kingdom, small unknown men wield immense power and bestride the world. These were the palaces not of a president-for-life but of a bureaucracy-for-life, reach-for-the-skies monuments to the Eurocracy towering above empty plazas to make mere mortals far below feel like insignificant ants to be crushed beneath their rulers' feet. Giant billboards dangled down thirty stories of rain-streaked concrete, their slogans screaming in multiple languages "Strengthening Europe Through Governance" and "Forward with Europe".

Every Euro-building was ugly but some particular thought seemed to have been given to ensuring each edifice's distinctive totalitarian bombast clashed with the unsightliness of the immediately surrounding buildings. Thus, the location for the EU's meeting with the "External Zone", a glass skyscraper encased in a massive lattice of metal tubes, looked like a giant's erection in an over-ribbed condom. In the shadow of its hideous tumescence, my car idled behind a couple of other limousines while Brussels bureaucrats wandered up and down the sidewalk, none bothering to shoot so much as a glance our way: Why would they? They wielded the real power, and "prime ministers" of mere "nations" were simply archaic window-dressing. Across the street, a knot of demonstrators held up signs demanding "BRUXIT".

"Pathetic," I said. "They can't even spell it." But our driver explained that these were francophone Muslims who wanted "Bruxelles" to secede from Belgium and become the capital of the European branch office of the Organisation for Islamic Cooperation.

We exited the car and I was on. I buttoned my jacket and remained studiously oblivious of the camera shutters and flashes; next I waved to the hacks, relaxed but assertive; and then I got carried away and did that thing the American-style lounge acts in Modenstein do

THE PRISONER OF WINDSOR

where you tap a pistol finger from your brow to someone you purport to recognise in the audience. Bit too Las Vegas for a Brussels crowd. Should have saved it for Big Sig's uniforms night at the Windy City. But it filled time on the red carpet until we reached the two Euro-heavies on the door, neither of whom asked for my security pass.

I was sorely missing Roger Severn. What sort of Lord Privy Seal leaves an unemployed Ruritanian lookalike to conduct a summit with the European Union?

And then I saw a familiar figure, across the lobby in his trademark purple suit. He was ambling toward me with a very fake smile on his face. Millie and Rory seemed somewhat puzzled.

"Prime Minister." He did the EU viro-compliant head-loop. "You probably don't remember, but we met at, er, Wimbledon. Fritz Tarlenheim."

"Of course I remember! Fabulous match, wasn't it?"

"Indeed, *ja*. Björn Borg vs Rod Laver," said Fritz, who like me with *Kitchen Karaoke* believed in winging his cover stories.

I jumped in lest Rod went on to meet Nadia Comăneci in the final. "Dear old Fritz! My word, we've a lot of catching up to do!" And, disentangling myself from Dame Millie et al pressing in from all sides, I wheeled him away to one of the hideous daubs lining the wall of the atrium – "Solidarity" or "Harmony" or something, a blurry abstract that looked worse the closer you got to it, much like the EU. "What's going on?" I hissed. "You're coming to the meeting, aren't you?"

He removed my frantic fingers from his lapels. "At summits with the External Zone (Qualified Recognition) called under the auspices of the Conference of the Presidencies," he said softly, aware we were surrounded on all sides by professional translators, "only heads of government plus two additional persons from each state are permitted in the room."

"But Britain's not in the EU, is it?"

Fritz sighed. "The rules apply both to member states and to 'external zone entities enjoying qualified recognition', which is you. Everybody else has to view the meeting through the glass from the interpreters' cubicles. Your two persons are Dame Millie and Rory Vane. In theory, Sir Roger could have arranged for a powerful laxative to be placed in Mr Vane's chai latte on the plane, but you might have drunk it accidentally, and who knows where we would be. The presidents are at the podium seated alphabetically according to each president's title in his preferred first language. Below them the national heads of government are at a horseshoe table seated alphabetically counter-clockwise according to each member state's name in its own language, per the Conferences of the Presidencies (Revised Seating Plan) Directive. As an 'External Zone Representative Granted Conditional Audience' you are seated at the open end of the horseshoe, between the first and last of the alphabetical member states – Belgium and Finland."

Even by Euro-standards, that didn't sound right. "How can Finland be alphabetically last? What happened to member states G to Z?"

"As I said, it's alphabetical according to each member state's name in its own language. Sverige – Sweden – is last, but as they're the incoming member of the presidential troika they're seated on the wing of the presidium of presidents."

"Yes, but Finland in Finnish is 'Finland'."

"*Nein*. Finland is the Swedish name for Finland. The Finnish name for Finland is 'Suomi'. So they are seated as 'Suomi/Finland'."

"I don't believe a word of it! You're telling me that the Swedish name for Finland sounds more Finnish than the Finnish name for Finland? It's an obvious trap! Why are they next to me? Why aren't they seated as Finland/Suomi?"

"You're beginning to jabber; people are staring!" hissed Fritz. "Maybe they didn't want to sit next to the España delegation. I don't know, I'm only a Euro-MP." He again removed my fingers from his lapels. "You're worrying too much about this…"

Fritz was right. What difference did it make where the Finnish guy sat? What I needed to know was whether Severn had written me a list of answers to any questions that might come up.

"*Nein*," he said. "Sir Roger has full confidence in you. Quote: 'Tell him to say whatever he wants. We've tried everything else.'"

By now Millie and Rory were nipping at my heels. I was swept into a circular windowless room, in which, as seemed to be the way in Brussels, the maximum money had been spent to achieve the worst effect. The chamber was somewhat overlit, perhaps to accentuate the floor and ceiling, which were both mosaics of randomly coloured oblong tiles. If I had to guess, I'd say they were meant to suggest flags of many nations but without actually being any flag of any nation in particular. At least back on the Mall the Commonwealth flags were real flags of real countries, more or less. Here, a turquoise rectangle was set between yellow and red rectangles, as if to evoke that Mitteleuropean tricolour you can never quite place, but its effect instead was to conjure a giant playland of make-believe jurisdictions. The floor tiles were angled toward the horseshoe conference table where the leaders of mere nation states sat. Above it loomed a separate dais from where the Euro-grandees presided in majesty. Below the horseshoe, between the points, in an indentation in the floor, was a small plastic folding table marked "External Zone (Qualified Recognition)". That would be me. I literally had "qualified recognition", since, unless they gave me a couple of dozen cushions, only two-thirds or so of my head would be visible to anybody seated at the main table.

The Belgian guy on my left was very surly. But the Finnish PM, I couldn't help noticing, was a stunning Nordic blonde. "Hi," I said.

She leaned down into the indentation and kissed me on both cheeks. There was no waft of perfume, just a minty Scandinavian freshness. "Robert," she replied in accentless English, fixing me with piercingly blue eyes.

I would have used her first name if I'd known what it was. I had a fleeting notion that maybe me and the Finn could have a cocktail after the summit. There must be a bar round here. So I picked up her place card and showed her my charming side. "Suomi," I said. "It always makes me think of those Japanese wrestlers. I keep expecting you to turn up in one of those loincloths."

She stared blankly at me. This wasn't going anywhere – worse than when I asked Lady Belinda for a drink. "Obviously you're a lot trimmer than those fellows."

Her face remained impassive.

"I didn't mean one of those loincloths that shows off your bottom, of course…"

She seized my hand, and again those piercing blue eyes bored into me. "I am counting on you today," she said. For a moment, my hopes were high, but then she added: "We all are."

Oh, yeah. The summit.

197

Before I could try another line, a lush orchestral rendition of "Imagine" by John Lennon filled the chamber. We heads of government rose to our feet and held ourselves erect, very noticeably so in the case of President de Mauban, who was staring at the elderly lady serving as Prime Minister of Slovenia. It seems that, after the last terrorist attack in Brussels, "Imagine" by popular demand had been officially declared Europe's national anthem, replacing the "Ode to Joy" from Beethoven's Ninth, presumably much to Beethoven's relief. Most of the leaders (except, of course, M de Mauban) sang along in English, imagining there's no countries, no religion, nothing to kill or die for, etc. When it ended, we all stuck our earpieces in and, from beyond the glass, a Babel of translators said in multilingual unison, "Please remain standing while His Excellency the President of the Conference of European Presidencies and his fellow European presidents assume the presidium: the President of the European Council, the President of the European Commission, the President of the European Parliament, the President of the Council of the European Union, the President of the Commission of the European Council, and the President of the Conference of European Presidencies. *Voilà, les Six!*"

And so it began.

Chapter Twenty-Seven
Overseers of Orientation Criteria

WE LANDED BACK AT Northolt on a cold, un-June-like evening, with Roger Severn waiting at the foot of the steps. "Awf'lly grateful to you for helping out," he said softly, as we strolled across the tarmac. "You've changed the course of history."

"No problem," I replied, clapping my arm around him. "Anytime."

What's that? You're wondering what did I actually do? Well, I was hoping we could skip over that, because to this day I'm not entirely sure. I asked Sir Roger directly: "But what did I actually *do*?"

"I shouldn't worry about that, dear boy. You've had a long day."

"Good thing I'm not one of these fancy actors who's all about the motivation, eh?"

But, since you ask, with help from the official transcript in thirty-seven languages, I'll do my best:

The President of the Conference of European Presidencies, Rupert de Haan-Zaaier, opened things up. He had the same Christian name (as we used to say) as Rupert Henley, but he was Dutch and taller, blonder and svelter, and more handsome. "Welcome to the official European Union intervention with the External Zone (Qualified Recognition) Non-Compliance Sector," he began, with a nod in my direction. "It is a pleasure to have with us today not only my colleagues the President of the Parliament, the President of the Commission, the President of the Council, the President of the Council of the Union, the President of the Commission of the Council, and the outgoing and incoming presidents of the presidential troika, but we should also welcome –" He gestured toward two beaming fellows who looked like they'd won the lottery. "- Mr Hamish Ellerton, First Minister of Scotland, and Mr Jim Erskine, First Minister of Northern Ireland. He is very worried about his backstop." And, upon the word "backstop", he very considerately switched to English: "As I always say, the future of all of us is held by the nuts, and the more it is the more we say 'Eff you!'"

199

We all applauded this sentiment, including yours truly. Given the state of the EU, his point was well taken, I thought. But the transcript subsequently revealed that Mijnheer de Haan-Zaaier was, in fact, referring to Scotland and Northern Ireland, which are, in Eurospeak, two of the NUTS. NUTS is the acronym for *nomenclature d'unités territoriales statistiques*, the officially accredited sub-state regions the EU likes to talk up as a not so subtle way of talking down old-fashioned sovereign nation states. If Modenstein hadn't seceded from Ruritania, it might one day have been eligible for the NUTS. Thank God for small mercies, eh? As for "Eff you", that would be "FU", as in *Funktionierende Unabänderlichkeit*, or "Functioning Unalterability", which was a new German proposal for reinventing the EU after the damage I'd inflicted on it. Functioning Unalterability was attracting a lot of interest. Anyway, having got us by the NUTS, Mijnheer de Haan-Zaaier dropped the English and made the rest of his remarks in Dutch.

I don't follow politics very closely, but I'd heard of some of the national leaders around the table – the French guy de Mauban, the German chancellor… The Irish lady seemed vaguely familiar from a profile I'd skimmed in the in-flight magazine about the first transgender taoiseach. But my point is I had no idea how unimportant these fellows were. The chairs at the presidential podium were fantastic luxury items with sculpted arms and extravagantly high headrests like the throne of the supreme intergalactic being in a sci-fi movie. Whereas the heads of government down below had humbler, armless seating – and, as a representative of the External Zone (Qualified Recognition) Non-Compliance Sector, my chair was, I noticed, not only two feet lower than the Finnish gal and the other PMs but cheap uncushioned plastic, like the waiting room at Hofbau Station. On the basis of my brief acquaintanceship with most of them at Windsor Castle, the podium chaps were dull as Oktoberfest in Zenda. Yet these half-dozen presidents on the presidium were the bigshots in the room, even though I'd never heard of them, or most of their job titles.

The European Commission president, Adelheid Lauengram, started speaking. My German's passable enough (it was the language of the Ruritanian court) but I couldn't make head or tail of anything she said. So I plugged in my earpiece and waited for the English translation to kick in – and that made even less sense. Frau Lauengram was talking about the dangerous precedent "if the Commission were to deploy its competence in external non-compliance to authorise a temporary alleviation of harmonisation obligations with regard to non-deconvergence criteria". So instead she proposed using weighted QRC to re-adjust external harmonisation internally. I wondered if the translator was drunk.

But everyone else, after shooting me viciously hostile looks, nodded thoughtfully, as if it were the most natural thing in the world. The European Council president, Fru Annika Maktsten, said, "I couldn't agree more." The European Parliament president, Madame Marie-Claude de Chard, argued that it ought also to be extended to QM/CER imbalances under the ETS. The Council of the Union president, Monsieur Hubert de Gautet, stroked his chin before saying, "Certainly." The Commission of the Council president, Monsieur Herman Bersonin, expressed his full support and said, "That would be a *most* satisfying re-calibration." I was waiting for the Danish prime minister or the Austrian chancellor to say something, but all remained mute.

"Indeed," said the President of the Conference of European Presidencies, this Haan-Zaaier chap, as a flunky set down a cake stand adorned with his personal standard and bearing a giant *croquembouche*. He got stuck in and then slid the stand along to the President of the European Commission, who in turn passed it on to the President of the Council of the European Union and the President of the Parliament. I was feeling a bit "peckish" myself, but we prime ministers were apparently on a different meal plan.

"Anybody else?"

I raised my hand, which was just about visible over my submerged seating. "Mr Rassendyll," said President de Haan-Zaaier. "What is the External Zone (Qualified Recognition) Non-Compliance Sector's view of this question?"

"Oh, sorry. I thought you were asking who wanted the *croquembouche*."

"Sir," said Haan-Zaaier, as if to a child, "the zone you represent has held two referenda whose results were incompatible with the Non-Désacquis Directive. You are now threatening to hold a third, and a fourth. We are proposing a very simple solution to these difficulties. All you would have to do is accept a re-adjustment of external harmonisation internally by weighted QRC."

That's easy for him to say. I think it helps, when you have no idea what you're talking about, to make yourself sound as formal and authoritative as possible. So I replied, "His Majesty's Government cannot support using weighted QRC to impose an internal re-adjustment of external harmonisation."

There was a sharp intake of breath from around the room, including, I could have sworn, from Millie and Rory behind me. Marie-Claude de Chard leaned forward and gripped the front of the podium. Her knuckles were white. "I must have misheard my friend Robert," she said. "What did you say?"

Oh. Now I remembered. She had been Foreign Minister of Luxembourg when Ruritania was falling apart. In the affairs of the world, or even of Ruritania, Luxembourg's foreign minister isn't that important. But at this point Luxembourg had happened to hold the EU's rotating presidency, so Mme de Chard had stood up and told the United States to butt out of Continental affairs because "The hour of Europe has come!" A hundred and fifty thousand dead Ruritanians later, the hour of Europe had come and gone. I'd wondered what had happened to her. Well, no, to be honest, I hadn't. But, if I had, here was the answer: She was running the European Parliament, and claiming she had misheard my position on QRC re the CER of the ETS.

"The British Government," I repeated, "cannot support using weighted QRC to impose a re-adjustment of external harmonisation internally, no matter its consequences for ETS imbalances on CER."

There was a flurry of frantic whispering among the presidents. It ended when Adelheid Lauengram asked: "Perhaps you would care to elaborate, Robert?"

"I think my position speaks for itself," I said. "The British Government cannot support extending weighted CER to competences affecting the QRC." They looked momentarily baffled, but fortunately I caught myself: "I mean vice-versa, of course."

Hubert de Gautet threw up his hands.

I took a sip of water. President Bersonin polished off another pastry, licked his lips, and suggested we return to this impasse later. (He happened to be, as I subsequently discovered, Anna Bersonin's ex-husband.) The President of Presidents chap invited his colleagues to address the issue of ECB jurisdiction over the ESM given that the

EFSP now extended beyond the EZP. The European Commission president was in favour subject to certain safeguards, but the European Council president cautioned that it wouldn't solve the problem, and the Commission of the Council president argued that the ECB had proved an inadequate overseer of orientation criteria.

"We are trying to help you, Mr Rassendyll," said President de Haan-Zaaier, pityingly, "but you are being very difficult."

I thought about it for a moment and then said: "His Majesty's Government cannot accept the ESSC's extension of Reverse QRC to competences beyond the EFRT."

There was an even sharper intake of breath around the table. "*Merde!*" hissed Herman Bersonin. Frau Lauengram looked me straight in the eye as she crushed a paper cup in her white-knuckled grip.

At de Gautet's suggestion, we moved on to expanding the orientation convergence of ETS targets. Annika Maktsten began speaking. Hard to follow but the sentence ended, after a pause by a momentarily stymied translator, with the phrase "bovine flatulence". At last: a concept I could understand. The presidents of the Council of the Union and the Commission of the Council indicated that, subject to agreement on harmonisation of emissions, they would withdraw earlier calls for penalties on External Zone shortfalls with regard to flatulence targets.

"The United Kingdom," I said, "has considered the formula proposed by the ESGT for combining QRC and Reverse QRC for competences agreed between the ESFM and the EFRT, and has no choice but to reject any linkage with flatulence policy."

Frau Lauengram was furious. I thought at first she was crushing another paper cup, but this time it was a real glass. Shards and slivers tinkled to the table, and a dark pool of blood and Badoit spread over to de Gautet's notepad. He pretended not to notice.

And so the meeting slogged on until the President of the Council of the Union whispered in the President of the Conference of the Presidencies' ear, president to president. "*M le Président* reminds me that we don't want to be late for our afternoon tea break," said Mijnheer de Haan-Zaaier, who'd finished off the *croquembouche*. "It is mandated since the unionisation of EU presidents." I think that was a joke.

I rose and turned to the Finnish babe. "Shall we?" I said. But the cool Nordic blonde had chilled since our opening banter: She was cool mainly in the sense that Glottenberg in February is. She glared at me icily, and strode off without a word.

As we exited, a deathly pale Rory tapped me on the arm. "I appreciate an element of high stakes poker," he whispered. "But re-opening the weighting for Composite QRC without meeting flatulence targets?" He gripped my elbow. I could feel, through my suit and shirt, his nails breaking my skin. "Where's the loo?" I asked, anxious to get away. "Bursting for a pee."

A Euro-usher led me down a corridor lined with posters of various EU development projects – a girls' school in Kandahar, a dance company in Benghazi, a community college for trainee civil servants in Raqqa – at the end of which was a small bathroom. I unzipped my fly, at which point two sensors in the cistern flashed red. I jumped back in alarm, lest my manhood be lasered to shreds. Then, from a speaker in the ceiling, a voice announced in German:

> *Hey, Herr Penis, stand-peeing is not allowed in here. So, unless you want a fine of up to 200 euros, I suggest you turn around, sit down, and empty your bladder in the approved manner.*

It was the voice of Frau Lauengram, but a recorded announcement, or so I hoped. At any rate, it repeated itself in French, and then English, and then worked its way through the other 48 official languages of the European Union. I decided to ignore it, and bent down to lift up the seat. It beeped, loudly. I gave up, turned around, dropped my trousers, and took the EU-mandated position on a toilet seat designed to accommodate no known shape of human bottom. I shifted sideways and found myself staring at twin toilet-paper dispensers, one offering a luxuriant quilted tissue, the other small single sheets of thin waxy paper; the former marked "European Union", the latter "External Zone (Qualified Recognition)". I sat there for two minutes, unable to urinate, before giving up, humiliated.

A voice came from outside—a voice that spoke perfect English. "Mr Elphberg," it said.

I made no answer.

"We want to talk to you."

THE PRISONER OF WINDSOR

"Have I the pleasure of addressing Rupert de Haan-Zaaier?" I said.

"Never mind names."

"Then let mine alone."

"All right, sir. We've an offer for you."

The locked door mysteriously opened, and I hastily pulled up my trousers as all six Euro-presidents entered the room

"Er, is this permitted?" I asked. "The ladies, and all..."

"I am always in here," said Adelheid Lauengram. "Are you transphobic enough to suggest I cannot choose to identify with your sitzpinkler – if it takes my fancy?" And they all laughed, and clustered round me at the porcelain. "Come, we are alone, Elphberg—"

I stood up.

"What's the matter?" she asked.

"I was about to call one of my retinue to remove you, *Frau Präsidentin*. If you do not know how to address the Prime Minister of the United Kingdom, you must find another men's room."

"Why keep up the farce?" asked de Haan-Zaaier, nonchalantly resting his foot on the lavatory seat and dusting his boot with his glove.

"Why keep up yours?" I looked around the half-dozen. "Are you sure this is appropriate?" I asked. "All of us in the same toilet. What if a covered Muslima came by?"

"Enough with this play-acting!" roared Hubert de Gautet, forgetting for a moment he wasn't supposed to know how to speak English. "Oh, so I'm supposed to worry if a Muslim woman wants to use the bathroom," he simpered. "I take your Little Englander shit and shove it up her burqa."

"*Calmez-vous, monsieur!*" barked Mme de Chard. "Don't you want to hear our proposal, Mr ...Prime Minister? Two million euros, and safe conduct to non-Union jurisdiction inclusive of External Zone (Qualified Recognition) and Territories under the Authority of the High Representative."

"By that, you mean 'the Rest of the World'?"

"America probably. With a passport. So you could run for Congress."

"I don't really like politics."

"We've noticed," said the Swedish lady, Annika Maktsten.

"If you know who I am, why didn't you tell all those prime ministers in there?"

"Tell them what? That the greatest disaster in the history of the European Union was brought about by an unemployed nobody whose only gainful labour in the last ten years has been a voiceover for an artificially flavoured condiment in Modenstein that can't even be legally sold in the EU?"

I hadn't known that last bit.

"Those *Östbüffel mit dem Populismus*," sneered Frau Lauengram, "would make you a hero from the Baltic to the Adriatic. And the western prime ministers…"

Mme de Chard interrupted her. "It would cut too close to the bone to tell them that any third-rate play-actor can do their job."

"You're ruining everything, you little shit," seethed de Gautet.

"We just want you out of Europe," said Annika Maksten. "So everything can go back to normal."

"Do you know what's beneath us?" asked Herman Bersonin.

"The will of the people?"

"I meant literally."

"Four-hundred-and-thirty-seven stories of Euro-bureaucracy?"

"And beneath that is the Zenne."

"The Zenda?"

"Zenne," said Herman Bersonin. "Or Senne in French. The ancient river that runs through Brussels, like the Thames in London or the Danube in Vienna. Except that in Brussels we covered it up in the nineteenth century. Put it underground, and then diverted it. But all the old tunnels are still down there. And I know where they are." He gave me a shove in the chest.

"We could take you there right now," said de Haan-Zaaier. "And no one would ever find you. You would be the prisoner of Zenne."

"Ah, wondered where you were, PM!" I've never been happier to see Rory Vane, and Dame Millie - although they evidently didn't know what to make of catching six Euro-presidents in the bathroom hectoring a prime minister with his flies undone. The Six parted to admit my minimal entourage who stood either side of me as I washed my hands and straightened my tie, knocked askew by Bersonin.

THE PRISONER OF WINDSOR

Whatever they thought they'd seen, the British delegation was not happy. Rory was perspiring heavily, and Dame Millie's pursed lips seemed to grow tauter with each second. She looked like a houndstooth suit with a cat's bottom poking out the top.

As we walked up the corridor, Hubert de Gautet affected bonhomie and slapped his arm round my shoulder. "How is this coronation of yours going?" asked the President of the European Council of the European Union of the Commission of European Councils as we passed among staffers and media as if we were the best of pals.

"*Comme ci, comme ça,*" I said.

"It is so absurd, your king in all his finery! The trumpets sound: Ta-ra, ta-ra! And all the king's horses and all the king's men are having tea with Christopher Robin and Alice, I am sure of that! This -" He gestured toward his Euro-podium. "This is the future! The future that cannot be stopped!"

I took my seat. The Finnish gal turned to the Slovak PM and frosted me out. And off we went for Round Two. From the presidium, the Belgian bloke said, "The most pressing matter before us today is that the Four Presidents' Report is in significant disagreement with the Imbalance of Orientations Review. I submit that, given the insubordination of the External Zone, the Four Presidents' Report must take priority."

I stifled a yawn. But everyone else loved it. "At last!" enthused the Finnish blonde. "Someone with the courage to say what needed to be said!" Looked like that lucky Belgian would be the one joining her for late-night bilateral *frites* with mayonnaise.

There was further discussion on the imbalance of orientations before Annika Maktsten suggested we needed to hear from the External Zone (Qualified Recognition) himself. In a negotiation, you never want to be too hardball. I read in a Donald Trump book that sometimes it helps to mollify the other side by offering a potential compromise. So I threw them a bone: "The United Kingdom has considered the difficulty of reconciling the Imbalance of Orientations and the Non-Désacquis Directive, and so would be willing to consider a formula for ESGT calculations combining weighted QRC with reverse QRC less deductions for composite QRC on competences agreed between the ESFM and the EFRT."

The translators had a bit of trouble with that, but, once they were on top of it, the massed ranks of prime ministers nodded thoughtfully and seemed appreciative. But up on the podium there was a look of pure fury from Frau Lauengram. "*Scheiße!*" she swore, and sent her chair flying back into the knees of the young *fräulein* behind her. This time it was the turn of de Gautet to crush a paper cup, but unfortunately this one had coffee in it. The scalding liquid shot up in the air and narrowly missed the cleavage of the Estonian Prime Minister down below.

"It is a trick!" fumed Bersonin. "It sounds so reasonable, but he is trying to trap us!"

"Well, we didn't want to go here," sighed Haan-Zaaier, "but the representative of the External Zone (Qualified Recognition) has left us no choice. Please put up the slide."

Something that looked like a collapsed giant-size honeycomb was projected on the far wall.

"What's that?" I asked.

"Your brain," said Haan-Zaaier. "After your remarks on the referendum, we asked the most brilliant specialists in Europe to conduct some tests. We have *followed the science!* The mental impairment you're exhibiting is a symptom of poisoning – a rare cocktail of Polonium and Novichok." There were gasps from my fellow prime ministers. "Undoubtedly," continued Haan-Zaaier, "a Russian operation. Under the External Zone operating agreement, we could have you declared enfeebled and replaced by ...well, almost anyone."

I rose to my feet. "You seem confused," I said. "The United Kingdom is a sovereign nation. We are not on the EU health plan."

"You have no authority," said Haan-Zaaier, "to bring the meeting to a close."

But I was halfway to the door. "By the way," I said, "the joke's on you. I would have settled for rebalancing Orientation Criteria against a composite Ré-désacquis. How about that?" And they fell back stunned as I swept out.

Chapter Twenty-Eight
A blow-up sex doll from the Bulqizë Massif?

I WAS REVISING MY opinion of Lady Belinda. Granted that, in a certain sense, she remained a total stuck-up bitch who deserved to have her career vaporised by association with an Islamophobic sock puppet, nevertheless she was a very efficient and motivated total stuck-up Islamophobic bitch – and she was more agreeable than the 7.45 crowd, who were all aghast about the Brussels meeting, or what *Le Monde* was calling *Europacalypse Deux!* They'd sat around worrying how they should "spin" the summit, and I couldn't see the point, because, honestly, it was a very boring meeting and if you just let it go there'll be another boring summit to get hysterical over along in a minute. I wanted to talk about Angus's announcement of another uptick in my approval rating – 59 per cent – but Rory and Dame Millie had not forgiven me for whatever it was I'd done in Brussels and were totally uninterested in my overnights, except insofar as they may have precipitated the Belgian constitutional crisis.

So I was glad to hear from Belinda. That morning she'd woken up to find that her breakfast appearance on *Good Morning Britain* had been cancelled due to "security concerns". So, with time on her hands, she had taken the train to Windsor and revisited the teashop next door with the secret passageway to the castle. Her successors behind the counter at this quintessentially English tearoom were everything but English and they regarded her dubiously when she said she had been a waitress there herself. In truth, I too found it hard to credit that there had once been a time when Englishmen were served in restaurants by their compatriots. So she revised her story and said she was an EU fridge inspector and (flashing her BBC pass) needed to see the refrigerator to ensure it was compliant. The staff were nervous now, and offered her a complimentary Cornish pasty, lemon curd tartlet and Scotch egg, which did nothing for her mood. When she finally got downstairs to the small cellar kitchen, she found the world's biggest fridge in front of the passageway door. After calling down two of the waitresses, and with a lot of huffing and puffing and protests from the staff, she succeeded in moving it back. Not far. Just a few inches. But enough to reveal…an almost perfectly smooth wall.

The secret passageway had been blocked up!

"But I have an idea!" said Belinda on her phone from the station. "Leave it to me!"

I was bringing Sir Roger up to speed on her report when Alison interrupted. "The Secretary of State for Forei..," she began.

Rupert Henley barged past her. "That's alright, Ali. He knows who I am. No time to lose: the Belgian constitutional crisis waits for no man." She hurried out and he slammed the door after an appreciative backward glance at my retreating secretary.

He was a daredevil was Rupert: By disdaining all the rules, he'd put himself beyond them – and ensured that they applied doubly to those politicians not so bold. Oddly enough he had nothing to say about Belgium, but instead delivered a pretty speech about how my devoted and loving brother Michael prayed that I might be kind enough to visit him at his country home. So declared the Foreign Secretary with an insolent smile on his curling upper lip and a toss of his shambolic hair—he was a rogue, and understood well his appeal, and not only to the ladies. For my part, if a man must be a knave, I would have him play the role with brio, and I liked Rupert Henley more than most of his Cabinet colleagues. It makes your sin no worse to do it *à la mode* and stylishly. He put a theatrical ear to the door: "Hark! I hear Alison departing… So can we drop the play-acting now, Rog?"

Severn took a puff of his pipe. "Play-acting, Rupert?"

"I know *this*…" He indicated me, scornfully. "…is a Ruritanian plumber. Not a very good one, by the way. Belinda Featherly told me the loo hasn't stopped leaking since he showed up. Metaphor for England, if you ask me. But I was the one who told him to shave off his beard. Didn't realise I was inciting a coup."

"Since we're speaking man to man, Rupert…"

"Steady on, Rog. I'll grant you that, but this fellow …who knows?" He strode up to me, and peered, nose to nose. "They say he's a Balkan prince – presumably cryogenised and lying deep in an Albanian mine in the Bulqizë Massif until you decided to thaw him out. But that sounds like just the sort of cock-and-bull cover story

THE PRISONER OF WINDSOR

you'd cook up after a snifter too far in the Carlton Club." He pressed his finger into my cheek, deep. I winced. "My theory is a clone or a robot. Don't know whose - Maxim Rogovsky? one of Prince Ghazi's experimental Saudbots? the Yanks or Japs?" He stepped back and cocked his head. "Without the beard he looks rather like the blow-up doll from PornoMart we bought for Lowe-Graham before he decided he was a non-practising pillow-muncher..."

"I stand corrected, Rupert. Speaking man to man to blow-up doll, if this is not the real Robert Rassendyll, what have you and your associates done with your dearest school chum?"

"Was he?" mused Rupert. I didn't like the past tense. "Oh, by the way," he added jauntily, "it turns out the blood of the aristocracy isn't blue, just bog-standard red. I know. I had to spill a little."

He said it to Severn with such jeering scorn on his face that I thought the old fellow would lash out: He clenched his fist, his knuckles white as White Mike's features, yet he scowled black as night. Then he spoke, very tight-lipped. "All this over a few remarks about a European court decision?"

"What's with all the Churchillian guff at PMQs?" demanded Henley. "I'm the Winston *de nos jours* – the dazzling wit and self-serving opportunist distrusted by his own party whom the nation turns to in its darkest hour."

"And in its darkest hour what would you, exactly, be willing to save the nation from?" Now it was Henley's turn to scowl. "Remind me again, Rupert, what was your position on referenda? You were for them before you were against them, or against them before you were for them? It's so hard to keep up."

"They said that about Churchill," said Rupert, prowling the room in search of a tin of Quality Street.

"I don't think they did, actually."

"Cometh the hour, cometh the man."

"Didn't your hour cometh last time? Robert's predecessor was the despised appeaser of Brussels. But you funked your Churchill moment."

Henley considered the point. "That would make Rob the Lord Halifax figure. Couple of high-born earls full of low cunning. Where are you going with this analogy, Rog? The referenda, the court decision, the gents at Piccadilly Circus: none of it matters. It only matters if people run around squawking as if it matters. Like your inflatable sex doll is doing."

"Have you murdered him?"

"Didn't you just tell me I lack the killer instinct?"

"Enough of this," said I. "You can tell the High Representative I would be pleased to accept his invitation subject to my diary."

"If it's Tuesday it must be Europocalypse Three?" sneered Henley. "Do you know the word Europocalypse is the same in all 147 official EU languages? It's the only thing we Europeans have in common! Except the Maltese: *'Europroypse.'* Don't ask me why. Do you know what it's like to get briefings on Valletta's view of composite QRC at 8.30 in the morning?"

"This meeting with Michael..," Sir Roger reminded him.

"You should know the terms first," said Henley. "You and Clone Boy. That's it. Your security is to wait outside."

I accepted. Suddenly he lunged. I saw a small knife flash in the air, and I reached to grab his arm. It struck upward and cut my cheek. With a cry, I staggered back.

"So," said Rupert Henley, stepping back satisfied. "If it is a robot, the polymer is not impenetrable. It bleeds." And he left the room.

Chapter Twenty-Nine
A new use for a dinner table

I DABBED AT MY CHEEK, and we considered what we'd learned, underneath all the cloning and Churchill stuff. Henley's confession to having spilled Rassendyll's blood made it more important than ever that we rescue the PM. Severn departed and I staunched my own bleeding. But it was the wrong time for the Attorney-General to send me a memo about the European Court of Justice. Cranky and exhausted, I told him to pull us out.

At Cabinet, we discussed refugee claimants. There were no longer any immigrants to Britain: Everyone claimed refugee status, even if you were only coming for the weekend, as it was the easiest way to avoid the quarantine and vaccine passports.

"It's a delicate balancing act," said Anna Bersonin, the Home Secretary, briefing Cabinet on a Sudanese refugee whose claim had been denied. The day before his removal to a deportation centre in a five-star country-house hotel, he'd raped an eleven-year old girl, for which he was now serving a three-year gaol sentence with time off for agreeing to be on the Priority Sex Offenders' List. In the meantime, he'd appealed his deportation on the grounds that returning him to Sudan would put him in danger of being physically assaulted for being a paedophile. The Immigration and Asylum Tribunal denied the appeal on the grounds that, *au contraire*, Sudan was very relaxed about paedophiles, which decision had resulted in the Committee for Racial Equality launching an inquiry into the Tribunal over its institutional Islamophobia. The convicted paedophile refugee had then appealed to the Upper Chamber of the Tribunal, whose judge, not for the first time, had ruled that deporting the deportee would be a breach of his human rights under the European Human Rights Act. Contrary to the Crown's argument, the judge ruled that, as the refugee belonged to a non-Arab tribe with a strong cultural antipathy to child sex, he was at risk of being slaughtered by his own tribe for being a paedophile and, if he moved elsewhere, of being slaughtered for not being an Arab.

"The point is," said Anna, "we're going to be paying for this paedo till the day he dies."

"This is the European Human Rights Act?" I asked. The Home Secretary nodded. "So why can't we deport him to Europe?"

"Britain *is* in Europe," said Humphrey Lowe-Graham. "For the purposes of the EHRA. Remember?" He gave me a curious look.

"Well, why don't we pull out of the European Human Rights Act? Except for the purposes of deporting to Europe persons enjoying the protection of the EHRA."

"That's all very well, Prime Minister," began Humphrey. I knew as soon as the words "that's all very well" were uttered that there was no need to pay any attention to the blather that followed. So I cast my eye round the table, and felt a weird vibe. Couldn't quite put my finger on it. I'd certainly gotten all the hostility this time last week, but this was something subtler. I was aware of factions in the room – Rupert seemed to have one, and perhaps Anna Bersonin. Even Humphrey seemed to think he had a faction.

I was glad to sink into the back of the Prime Ministerial Jag. Until I saw Wendy in the next seat. Oh, God. I tried a "Good morning, darling", but she said not a word as we crawled slowly through London traffic and onto the M4 westward to the Princess Fiona Pet Rescue Centre in Swindon. It was a strangely insubstantial place. The "chair" of the centre, Mrs Naylor, opened the wrong door and led me into a broom cupboard, which, for some reason, had a bucket of blood in it. We backed out, she laughing nervously, me a little too heartily, the cameras clicking. But the bucket reminded me of Henley's boast about Rassendyll's non-blue blood. I was rattled, and not exactly at the top of my game.

The "chair" introduced me to a wan, melancholy woman, who flinched as I offered my hand.

"It's okay," barked Mrs Naylor. "It's only the Prime Minister."

"How are you?" I asked, for want of anything better to say.

The woman said she'd just taken in an abused dog, so I asked whether she liked dogs.

She answered that she'd never had a dog, but her husband had died of C difficile in the car park of the Prince Alfred waiting for a bed to open up and they had no children so she was lonely for companionship and so far she was enjoying sitting with the new dog in the lounge every afternoon thinking about her late husband, who was only fifty-seven when he died, a week after his booster shot. There was a portrait of him on her face mask, and he did look young and well-preserved for his age. "At least until he got to the hospital, obviously," I added.

Angus waved frantically at me to move on.

Mrs Naylor proceeded to the next lady, who was holding a bored-looking Persian kitten. The woman was younger this time. Early thirties, with thin, greasy hair, a distracted expression, and a beige smock. I fell back on a variation of my previous penetrating question:

"Do you like cats?"

"Well, I'd like to have kids, but me boyfriend hates them. I said to him me biological clock is running down, and 'e said great."

"Ah," I said, stumped. "The old biological clock running down, eh? Lot of it about."

I had a renewed respect for Rassendyll. This business was trickier than it looked.

The cat began playfully chewing on my thumb.

"There's our headline, boys," a bored hack in the front row said to his colleagues. "'Rassendyll Caught with Fingers in the Kitty.'" A dozen shutters clicked. "We can tie it to the virocleanser insider-trading."

"Och, steady on, laddies," said Angus, but they were already stampeding out the door.

Ten minutes later, Wendy and I were also heading back to London. For the first time on one of our grim car rides, she decided to initiate conversation:

"You're losing it, Robert."

"Beg pardon?"

"I've gotten used to you being a hollow unprincipled bastard who believes in nothing other than his own indispensability, but at least you had a knack for interacting with the public, the light touch, the ability to connect... What was all that back there? C-difficile? The biological clock?"

I was stung. "Well, look, if you don't mind," I said, "I just don't see the point of all these so-called 'photo-ops'."

"Oh, God, Robert, you really have lost it. That was Rory Vane's supposedly brilliant strategy to neutralise 'the sixteenth-earl baggage' and show you were a man of the people with the common touch." She mimicked my voice. "Hair-*lair*. Have you come far? Do you enjoy septicaemia? Would you like me to give you some?" I heard Vic and Sanjay titter in the front seats. "If Rob Rassendyll can't even be an authentic phony, what's the point of him?"

She continued in like vein until we hit London traffic and ground to a halt behind a double-decker bus. "Can't the police do anything?" said Wendy, tetchily. She glanced at me with barely veiled contempt. "He is the Prime Minister, after all."

"It's the Albanian supercars, Mrs R," replied Sanjay. "They ignore the coppers."

Vic tried a shortcut and twenty minutes later we were stuck behind an entirely different bus. Another twenty minutes and we were stuck behind a third bus outside the Elgin Hotel in Piccadilly. "I'm starving," said Wendy. "Haven't eaten a thing since breakfast, unless you count the tang of that Petticurean Red Snapper Nibbles wrapper that landed on my tongue after you terrified that poor Siamese." She opened the door. "I'm going to the Viceroy's Grill."

Wendy stomped off. I wasn't sure what to do, but assumed, as her husband, that I was obliged to follow her. Sanjay scrambled after. The Elgin was the swank hotel where Fritz and I had bonded over the Toblerone. By the time Sanjay and I caught up with Wendy, she was having a word with the maître d' and securing a table. The Viceroy's Grill was a large room of brilliantly polished walnut walls and empire-basket chandeliers that had been expanded to include a glassed-in colonnade overlooking Piccadilly. A place to be seen but in an understated and tasteful way, it brimmed with London's most successful people – i.e., foreigners mostly. They were so successful they pretended not to notice us as we were shown to our table. I figured that, had Elvis Presley himself walked in with Marilyn Monroe, they would have done the same. Sanjay and Vic were discreetly seated at a separate table, distant enough to give us some genuine privacy.

Wendy ordered a bottle of Bollinger. The bubbles danced in her flute as she hoisted it. "Bottoms up!"

"Pardon?" I said.

I know, I know… "Bottoms up" is an expression, like *Gebetenärschen*. But I was tired. I raised my glass to hers, but she hadn't waited.

THE PRISONER OF WINDSOR

"The last time we were seen eating here," she recalled, "Rory said it knocked two points off your approval rating. I'm confident we can do better than that tonight."

The waiter re-filled her glass and, as he withdrew, the background chatter suddenly subsided. Unlike Wendy's and my entrance moments earlier, this arrival stilled the room: men in dark suits, big and squat, surrounding a more expensively tailored version of themselves. Behind them followed a dutiful "supermodel" and two or three "business associates".

"Oh, God," murmured Wendy. "Maxim Rogovsky." Britain's richest man, according to *The Sunday Times*. His head was mostly shaven except for an odd furry ridge at the front, gelled and spiked and with blond streaks at regimented intervals. Above the ridge were propped his wraparound sunglasses. Below it there was something cold and merciless in the angular cheekbones, jutting forehead, and eyes so steely and penetrating you wanted him to pull his shades down. Among the clientele of the Viceroy's Grill, he looked like someone given a complimentary ticket to an awards show he knew nothing about. But half the wait staff stopped what they were doing to usher London's most powerful oligarch to the best table in the room. Prominent businessmen and wealthy celebrities reflexively moved their chairs in as he passed.

And then he saw me, and took a detour.

"Rob." His cologne descended on the table like a thick Zenda fog.

"Hullo," I said.

"And Mrs Rassendyll. What a surprise." *Vot a sorprize*. He turned back to me. "You look so well. Good health agrees with you!" He looked to his flunkeys for confirmation of this dazzling aperçu, but they weren't paying attention. "And you are making so much news!"

"Really?"

"Yes. Only a moment ago, my associate showed me this." He snapped his fingers, and one of the entourage passed forward a cellphone showing me talking to Sharyn and Darenna in Trafalgar Square:

'Why don't you pick your own bollards?'
'Maybe I will.'

217

His voice turned more serious. "We need to speak." He leered down at Wendy. "Since we are both dining here this evening, I would be honoured if you would join our table. It's much better, as you can see. I have some associates with me, but we have concluded our business, and we are ready to relax." *Ri-lox.*

Wendy looked up at him and smiled sweetly. "Oh, we'd love to, Mr Rogovsky. But this is a special anniversary for us, and it's our little romantic dinner *à deux*. We don't get a chance to do it very often. I'm sure you understand. But thank you so much for asking."

He wasn't quick enough to hide the scowl of displeasure that flashed across his face, but he recovered. "Of course," he said, and snapped his fingers at the flunkey behind. "Give me one of those fancy cards from King Arthur's royal stationer that I paid a fortune for." A tasteful cream notecard was passed forward on which he scribbled something before handing it to me. It was very classy, with engraved lettering:

Maxim Rogovsky, Esq
At Home

And then underneath, where he was supposed to write in the date, he had instead penned:

As soon as your fucking arse can shift itself.

He smiled and went on his way. The room chatter resumed. He was angry with me about something, and I had no idea what. Just another item on the list for the next time I saw Roger Severn. I watched his tank-like back moving over the floor, and turned my attention to Wendy.

"And what romantic anniversary is it?" I asked.

"It's two years since we last slept together," she said. Draining a second glass, she ordered a passing waiter to bring a third.

I was embarrassed and had no idea how to respond. So I looked over her shoulder and, without intending to, caught our Russian friend's eye. Even in public, even halfway across a room, it felt like Maxim Rogovsky had reached under the table and was slowly

218

squeezing my nuts. Of course, it would have helped if I'd had some inkling about what he was so miffed about.

After ordering a confit of mackerel and then the pigeon, I noticed a familiar figure entering the room. I recognised his face, because he wasn't wearing a mask. I thought for a moment it was a minor member of the Cabinet – maybe the Education Secretary or the Chancellor of the Duchy of Lancaster, whoever that was and whatever he did. But then it clicked: Tony Bennett, American showbiz legend. Plus his wife. The pianist segued into "I Left My Heart in San Francisco". Our fellow diners looked up and smiled politely. Mr Bennett sang, "I left my mask in San Francisco", and beamed with arms outstretched. We all laughed.

Encouraged by the reaction, he began to work the room. For an elderly man, he had a big childlike smile. "Hey, great to see you!" he said to happy diners, fist-bumping and shooting fingers. "I love England!"

Bennett ambled unhurriedly around the room. From the power table, Maxim glowered. "Who the fock is this wonker?" he said, audibly.

"Tony Bennett," hissed the Italian supermodel at his side, also audibly. "The Welsh singer. He sings that song about stabbing your woman to death. They do it at the football in Wales."

Mr Bennett, it turned out, was in Britain for a pre-Coronation gig and an album of celebrity duets called *Swingin' with the Brits*. He'd been at Abbey Road laying down vocals with Brittany Lyon on "If I Ruled the World".

"Hey, great to see you!" He held out his hand, so I shook it. "What's your name?"

"He's the Prime Minister," Wendy said, somewhat icily.

Mr Bennett was oblivious. "Hey, great! Gotta love that Coronation, right?" And with that he advanced to the adjoining table. The pianist tinkled "Stranger in Paradise".

"Focker," muttered Maxim. Mr Bennett seemed sufficiently attuned to the general vibe to avoid the Russian's table. Rogovsky summoned the sommelier and loudly ordered four bottles of the Château Pétrus at £4,000 each.

Mr Bennett's meal seemed to have been pre-ordered. Either that, or the waiters liked him far more than they did our table. The appetiser and main course were brought in quick succession, and the veteran entertainer and his lady took their leave. As they did, he stopped for a quiet word with the piano player. Sitting down on the bench, he put his arm round the guy, and they chatted sotto voce, as the pianist tickled his ivories. "As Time Goes By." Even I know that one: The fundamental things apply, etc.

At the end, Mr Bennett stood up and turned to the room. "This guy's the best, isn't he?" The pianist blushed. We all applauded politely, and Tony and the missus left the restaurant.

Maxim growled. "If it's not too much trouble," he hissed at an inattentive waiter, "perhaps you could bring more bread."

The piano player went into "Put on a Happy Face". When it was over, he collected together his sheets, rose and coughed discreetly. "Pardon me," he said. "I just wanted to explain that I don't usually stay this late, but it's not often that we're privileged to have an artist of the stature of Mr Bennett with us, and it was an honour to be able to play for him."

This time Maxim's low growl was a roar. "Fock you, focker!" he said. He didn't yell. It was very calm, but it was extremely loud. The clatter of cutlery ceased. You could hear a pin drop.

"Beg pardon?" murmured the pianist.

"That focker's staying in one room that some other focker's paying for," Maxim continued. "Do you know how many suites, how many floors in this hotel that I'm paying for tonight? For all my associates from Odessa and Alma Ata and Cyprus and Nevis? And their staffs and security? And you have the nerve to say you're only playing for him?"

"I didn't mean any offence, sir," said the piano player, his sheet music shaking audibly. "It's just that as a musician..."

"Fock that!"

The pianist edged nervously toward the exit.

"Sit down!" barked Maxim.

The poor fellow stopped. "What did you say?"

"I said sit down." The man froze. Maxim stood up. The table was very ornately dressed, a heavy damask, with many candles and goblets and bottles, and his abrupt rise caused a handful to totter and spill. But then he seized the two legs nearest to him, raised the whole lot above his head, and hurled it at the piano player. A table for eight sailed through the air, scattering in its flight knives and forks and bread rolls and half-eaten Wellington of lamb and sea bass *en papillote*. A couple caught in between reared back as the table began its descent, crashed the lip of theirs, and bounced on toward the pianist. He yelped, and leapt sideways toward the keyboard. Two new potatoes and some sautéed chard narrowly missed him and hit the ivories with a cacophonous plunk.

"Now sit down and play!" commanded Maxim. "What was that fockin' thing you were playing? The Rod Stewart one about man needing his mate?"

"'As Time Goes By'?"

"Right. You played it for him, you can play it for me. *Play it!*"

The pianist meekly sat and opened the lid. "What are you fockin' staring at?" he jeered at the frozen faces of the other diners. "Enjoy the music!"

As I look back, I think it was Wendy's remark about the second anniversary of the last time "we" had slept together. It had stung me, and left me with a sense of vicarious inadequacy – or maybe shared inadequacy, Rassendyll's and mine. At any rate, I had been quietly seething through the whole dinner, the excellence of the food only emphasising the cheerlessness of the occasion. To my surprise, I found myself rising to my feet.

"That's enough!" I barked at Rogovsky. "This gentleman doesn't have to play anything if he doesn't want to. You'll behave yourself, sir, when out in a public place!"

His men bristled and started to rise.

"Oh-ho," said Maxim, dropping down into his table-less chair and crossing his legs. "So a prime minister is telling me what I can and can't do?" He stroked his chin thoughtfully. "Dearest me, I own so many prime ministers I can't quite recall the name of this one. Oh, yes. Now I remember. You're the marquess who can't even enter a sitzpinkler and produce any peepee!"

I wondered how he knew that, and so evidently did my fellow diners. "He's not a marquess, he's an earl," pointed out a lady at the back of the room. So much for Rory's de-nobilification strategy.

"Oh, I am so impressed! An earl! Do you know how many so-called prominent Britons seek me out? Earls. Viscounts. Second sons of somebody whose ancestor was famous for something in the eighteenth century. I can barely tell one from another even when they're genuine!"

He glanced down at his business associates. "We Russians all make the same mistake when we arrive in London, don't we? Everyone wants to meet us, and they all are so impressive! Lord This! Sir That! Everybody sounds like the Duke of Wellington or Sir Winston Churchill. But there are no more Wellingtons and Churchills, are there? Just third-rate spongers who in exchange for providing a few minimal services expect to be yachting off Cap Ferrat and skiing at Courchevel." And he turned his eyes on me with the look of one who knew where I'd been on my holidays.

He had the advantage in that respect, so I thought it best to let it go. I motioned to the pianist. "Instead of making him play it again, Max, why don't we ask everyone to vote on what tune they'd like to hear?"

That wasn't such a good idea. Someone suggested "I Will Always Love You", and somebody else "Firework", and a third couple wanted "Blurred Lines". And the pianist didn't know any of those. So in the end I said, "Oh, forget it. Just go back to 'You must remember this…'" For those diners on whom the oligarch's six-grain rolls and mangetouts had descended as his table flew through the air, I added: "I'm sure Mr Rogovsky regrets the disruption to your dinner, and, by way of recompense, I'm sure he'll be happy to pick up the tab tonight."

For a moment the Russian and I stared at each other across the room. Then the pianist commenced re-tinkling. Rogovsky snapped his fingers. "Waiter, bring me another table! And another five bottles of that fockin' Pétrus." He looked down at the glass-speckled pool of £4,000 wine at his feet, and for a second there was a tinge of regret.

But I wasn't going to let that go. I looked around the room and did a rough count. "I don't think that's going to be quite enough, Max. Make that fifteen bottles," I said to the waiter, and then to the diners: "The drinks are on Mr Rogovsky."

I sat down and noticed that Wendy was regarding me with a look I'd never seen before.

Chapter Thirty
The Tilted Teapot

THE FOLLOWING MORNING, the news was all about the collapsed share price of EuroBollard, following my altercation with Maxim Rogovsky at the Viceroy's Grill. Up to 12,000 jobs in Saint-Denis, Molenbeek and Malmö were said to be at risk. Everyone at the 7.45 was very upset about it. Whereas hardly anyone was bothered by the news that England had set a new grooming-gang record: 4,731 abused, gang-raped and enslaved girls in one small Shropshire market town. At Cabinet, I directed the Home Secretary to create a new division of the Metropolitan Police to eradicate Britain's child sex-slavery epidemic.

"Are you sure that's smart?" asked Derek Detchard. "It risks giving the impression that it's a problem."

"I thought our policy was not to alarm the public and alienate moderate members of the relevant community," said Anna Bersonin.

"Besides," added Rupert Henley, "the plods in these towns are all in on it. And coppers stick together. So they'll just fit up some do-gooder who wants to clear it all up." And he stared at me, meaningly.

An hour later I was back in Windsor, a stone's throw from the castle, in front of a bizarre sixteenth-century house that looked as if it had been dropped very carelessly into the middle of a narrow, cobbled lane. It was three thin stories high, just one window apiece, and each story leaning at an ever more alarming angle, as if were about to collapse into the building across the alley.

"You can't blame that on Ruritanian plumbers," I said. "I wonder who built it."

"What a cant," offered my driver Vic, apparently something of an architecture buff.

"I'm not sure it's safe for you to enter the premises, sir," cautioned Sanjay.

"It's been that way for four hundred years," I assured him. "It's not going to fall down in the next hour."

Vic and Sanjay looked doubtful. It may have been crooked, but it was well-maintained, with a fresh coat of creamy white paint and green trim, and an arresting shingle of a fresh brew ready to pour: The Tilted Teapot.

I'd been back at Number Ten, curled up on the sofa watching the telly, when I got the idea. Or rather I stole the American president's idea. After he'd taken off from Chequers, he'd flown on to France to give a speech at the opening of the new Notre Dame with its state-of-the-art solar panels and he started going on again about how hydrofluorocarbons from refrigerators non-compliant with the Tahiti Accord were a bigger threat to the planet than Islamic terrorism. I spewed a mouthful of Pot Noodle down my shirt and slapped a thigh. But then I noticed Président de Mauban and the rest of the audience were nodding very soberly, and I realised that, if I met him again and he insisted on bringing up the refrigerator gas threat, I would have to remember not to titter as I did at Chequers.

And then it occurred to me that maybe we could leverage this fridge compliance business in that Windsor tearoom...

It was the work of moments for Lady Belinda to call Rudy Elphberg's old friend Ladislas from the Big Tex and deputise him as a European External Zone (Qualified Recognition) Harmonisation Directive domestic-appliance compliance inspector. In return, Laddie brought Belinda and Sir Roger up to speed on a brilliant innovation - the "pass-through" fridge. "You can go in the front door – or in the back door," said Laddie to Severn. "Like with English girls."

"Hmm," said the Lord Privy Seal, non-committally.

When you've managed to procure a Tahiti-compliant refrigerator, the important thing is to have a sufficiently distinguished dignitary to inaugurate it. It had taken some doing, and the US Department of Shock and Awe wasn't happy at having to re-route the 127-car motorcade at short notice. But, if you thought his summit with me had gone badly, at least it happened. President Kennedy had landed in Germany just as Chancellor Freyler, returning from the humiliations of my Euro-summit, was replaced by a populist rival to whom a mere six weeks earlier the State Department had refused to issue an American visa – something to do with Congress passing a resolution denouncing him as the new Hitler. So the new Hitler was disinclined to take the meeting with President Kennedy and, after two hours sitting on the runway at Berlin wondering where the honour guard was, Air Force One had taken off for Spain, only to find its prime minister had also been forced from office. In the sudden void of allies, the White House had been very receptive to the idea of the President congratulating the distinguished runner-up in the competition to find the Great British Coronation Cuppa and awarding it second prize of a new Euro-Fridge Replacement Grant. So there we were, back in Windsor at the Tilted Teapot.

As before he shook hands coldly, and, recollecting my thought that a little chit-chat on something other than Euro-turmoil might ease the tension before we entered the building, I pointed out its pronounced cant.

"Yes, we cant!" said President Kennedy in his distinctive Hyannis-Hispanic accent. "Wasn't that the GOP slogan? Then they tipped right over."

I laughed politely.

"My boys wondered whether we should do a controlled explosion on this thing."

I laughed again, but he didn't seem to find it funny.

Inside, the assembled Fleet Streeters had been hoping to ask me about the Greek bank runs and the collapse of the German and Spanish governments, and the members of the Washington press corps had been hoping to ask President Kennedy about his NASA Administrator, who'd been obliged to quit after accidentally giving a talk on "black holes" to an audience including someone called Colin Kaepernick. But instead the surly Ukrainian waitress held open the swing door, and everybody peered down the cellar steps to see the new Euro-compliant fridge dominating the space very impressively.

"As you know," I began, "the President has stated that refrigerator gas is a greater threat to the planet than Islamic terrorism." There was a round of applause at this, but eventually it died down and I continued: "So I've asked him to prepare a few remarks on the subject. Mr President…"

José Fitzgerald Kennedy IV came to the front of the room and shook my hand. "Thank you, Mister Prime Minister," he said. "I'll try not to outstay my welcome, if only because of the youngest member of the audience…" He nodded at a bouncing baby on the knee of a sallow-cheeked greasy-haired mum in a stretched pink-striped top joined in queasy combination with tight orange sweat pants. She had been confused by the notice outside and had been expecting not a

225

speech about fridges but a man called Fridge, a rapper who had made the *Britain's Got Talent* 2017 quarter-finals. The President did his best to compensate, and smiled indulgently at the baby. "What's her name, ma'am?"

"He's a boy."

"Hey, he'll be the judge of that!" quipped the President. (His own son, José Fitzgerald Kennedy V, had recently begun transitioning.) "Okay, what's *his* name?"

"Ahmed."

"*Assalum Aleikem*," said the President, placing his hands in prayer. "So you're Muslim?"

"Nah, I just liked the name," she said.

But by then I had slipped round the back of the press corps, and was halfway through the kitchen door and headed down to the cellar. According to the official statistics, President Kennedy had never given a speech lasting less than seventy-five minutes – and I figured on a subject this close to his heart we could count on at least ninety. I told the Ukrainian waitress our distinguished guest wanted a Welsh teacake, and the moment she was gone I motioned to the waiting Lady Belinda and opened the front door of the fridge.

"It's like going to Narnia," she giggled. I closed it behind us, and the light went out. She kissed me, sweetly – and the light returned, as I pushed open the rear door of the Tilted Teapot's state-of-the-art pass-through refrigerator, and we found ourselves amidst the cement chunks and plaster-board debris torn down by Laddie's men. We were in the secret passageway.

Chapter Thirty-One
Diversity is our strength

BELINDA SWITCHED on her pocket flashlight and from her carrier bag produced two burqas she'd worn for the BBC's "Full Coverage" days, empowering women to cover themselves up. Severn's idea. Nobody impedes the progress of a covered woman. The black mark on your personnel file and six months in sensitivity-training hell aren't worth it. Belinda was resistant, but, as she eventually conceded, "The way things are going I'll be spending my last thirty years dressed like this. Might as well practice."

We struggled to put them on, and Belinda dropping the phone flashlight didn't help. Laddie had also given me one of his tool belts, in case we needed pliers, wire, screwdrivers. But my burqa was a bit tight – "clingy," as my accomplice described it – and I couldn't get it over the tool belt. So Belinda took the belt, and complained that with the burqa it made her appear all lumpy. "I'm back to that 'Does my bomb look big in this?' sketch," she griped.

I was more concerned by the lack of peripheral vision. But, notwithstanding our dissatisfactions, off we set.

"Why do you think they blocked it up?" I asked.

"EU, I expect," said Belinda. "A secret passageway horlickses up your insurance. 'Elf'n'Safety."

"Elf?"

"That's how we all say it – 'Elf'n'Safety, like a grumbling working man. *Health* –" She enunciated exaggeratedly, or as exaggeratedly as she could, given her usual enunciation. "- and Safety. 'Elf'n'Safety is a big joke in this country."

"Especially if you're a schoolgirl in Rotherham," I said.

The passageway sloped down, steeply, into the bowels of the beast. It was narrow and low-ceilinged, with many parts in semi-collapse. At one such, a mere hundred metres or so after the commencement of our journey, a rusted gate hung off its hinge, and beyond it the cramped passage levelled out and widened. Further on, it opened up, with one junction, and then another, and then a tangle of arched passageways, all much the same: flagstone floors worn down by a millennium of footfalls, or under shallow pools of dank, stagnant water; walls of broken sandy brick, interrupted by crudely sealed entryways, holes patched with crumbling plaster; branch passages leading somewhere unknown or blocked by rusting bars. We were definitely under the castle, but where?

"Aside from getting mistresses out," said Belinda, "the passageway was also used for getting meat and veg from the market in. So I'm assuming this comes out somewhere underneath the Great Kitchen."

Instead it came to a T-junction. To the right the passageway narrowed and shrank. So we turned left because it seemed less discomforting. But after a few metres its walls also drew in and the ceiling lowered. Both of us had to stoop. In the confined stone space, our movements seemed even noisier.

"Your heels are clacking," I whispered to Belinda.

"I'm not padding through fifteenth-century sewage in my stocking feet," she replied. "If you're so concerned, you should have got Roger to lend me his tangerine brothel creepers."

"Why does he wear those? He's a perfect gentleman otherwise."

Belinda laughed. "No gentleman wants to be too perfect, does he? Awf'lly boring. And they are good for creeping up on one. Which may be why he knows everyone's secrets."

We came to another junction, and the ceiling rose by two or three inches.

"I would estimate we're now under the Great Kitchen," said Belinda.

"Are you sure about that?"

"Not in the least. You should have brought a compass."

Five minutes on, Belinda stopped. We were at the same indentation in the passage as the last time we were here. Only now it was on the other side. She flashed her torch up the wooden ladder steps to the old rusted grating that opened on Rob Rassendyll's cell. Darkness. And silence.

"There's nothing ahead except the stairs to the cold prep room," said Belinda, with more confidence than I had. "If there's a way up to Rob's room from here, it's back where we came."

THE PRISONER OF WINDSOR

We retraced our steps, and just ahead of the T-junction the sweep of her torch caught on the left-hand wall an old half-rotted door that we had missed before. I pushed it open and found a steep, narrow and very dilapidated set of stone stairs. We climbed up to the top and found another door, but this time metal and new. Cautiously pushing it open, we were confronted with...

Well, it was hard to describe. Especially given where we'd come from. It was a brightly lit corridor, and obviously very new. A white-tiled floor and pale green walls, all spotlessly clean. It was, I thought, very clinical. Belinda and I set off down it, and tried to estimate where Rassendyll's cell would be.

We needn't have bothered. A loud oath rang out from Belinda. Her face turned pale, and she pointed down the corridor. From under a door a red stain had spread over the floor of the passage and dried there. It was the only blemish on an otherwise spotless, gleaming scene. Belinda sank against the opposite wall. I tried the door, and it swung open.

The red stain, turning more and more to a dull brown, stretched inside. Tiptoeing around it, I felt for the light switch. The room was empty except for a single bed of strange appearance – raised high off the ground, and with various accessories around it.

Belinda took in the scene. "It looks like a hospital room after the patient died in the night."

"Don't think like that," I said. We had been directly below on our last visit to the castle, presumably somewhere underneath the bed. I wheeled it back from the wall and saw clearly the outline of the old trapdoor. It had been covered over with the same tiles as the rest of the floor, but they had been cut through to preserve its use as an emergency exit.

"Jacob's Ladder," said Belinda, "to hell."

"Not necessarily. The red smear suggests they took him out through the door." We stepped over the dried blood and back into the corridor. The smear narrowed, and pointed ahead, the dark red spatters becoming fewer and smaller but still discernible. The last droplet was four doors down. I turned the handle.

"Ah, ladies! Come in, come in."

He was a man of Prussian mien ...bald-headed, with a scar on his cheek. Yes, yes, I know one shouldn't stereotype – after all, I'd

229

attended the Windsor ball with a duelling scar and a monocle. But in this case he appeared to be self-stereotyping: he had a thick German accent, and even his arm movements, as he waved us in the direction of a red leather sofa, had a Teutonic affect. Upon reflection, the sofa was more of an Ottoman – or a psychiatrist's couch, if you will. Our host was wearing a white coat, with a stethoscope around his neck, and behind a handsome oak desk. There were various anatomical charts around the wall, a bookcase of exquisitely tooled Morocco-bound numbered volumes, and, on his desk, copies of a medical journal called *The Lancet*.

"It's delightful to see you," said the doctor in his guttural Prussian vowels. "May I know your names?"

Belinda gathered up the folds of her burqa and took the end of the couch with an arm to lean against. "Fatima," she answered.

Blast! That was what I was going to say! "Mustafa," I squeaked in a high voice.

"What a lovely name," he said. "Can I offer you a drink?"

Belinda declined, but I was thirsty. The burqa was a tight fit, and it's not the easiest garment in which to pad through damp narrow airless mediaeval passages. I felt clammy and parched. The doctor turned to a large refrigerator behind him and produced two tall glasses filled with a kind of lavender-hued smoothie – one for him, one for me. I fiddled with my burqa till I found a flap I could get my mouth near. He sipped his thoughtfully, I gulped at mine. This secret-passageway prowling was thirsty work. "That was great! Any chance of a refill?" He opened the fridge door and obliged.

Belinda watched all this impatiently and then said: "What have you done with the man in that room?"

"What man?"

"The man whose blood is all over the corridor."

"That's the blood of a deer from Windsor Great Park."

"Are you ritually slaughtering them in here?"

"It's a study on susceptibility I'm doing for *The European Journal of Medicine*: how many people upon seeing a trail of blood will follow it."

Belinda seemed to have run out of questions.

"What is this office?" I asked.

"This office is on the cutting edge." He slid forward the copy of *The Lancet*. "We're this month's cover story."

"Never mind that," snapped Belinda. "You know why we're here."

"Are you sure you wouldn't care for a beverage? It must be hot under there."

There was a knock on the door – and there was that bloody midget urchin from the carnage of Zenda again, Flavia Strofzin. "Hello, doctor. May I prethent my bithneth partner King Arthur and hith friend Her Eckthellenthy The Governor-General of Belithe." She curtsied, and His Majesty and an elegant black lady in cocktail attire entered the room. "A governor-general," Flavia explained to us, "ith like a thpare king for when King Arthur'th not around. You didn't know that, did you?"

The great advantage of a burqa, I reflected, is that at least you don't have to put on a fake smile.

Belinda stood up awkwardly. "We need to be going," she said.

I would have objected. I was still a bit thirsty, and, even with the iced beverage, I seemed to be perspiring quite heavily inside my black body bag. But Belinda was already on her feet. It was not a large office, and the King and her vice-regal Excellency had already stepped aside to let her pass. After bidding good day to all, I rose and followed.

"Walk casually," whispered Belinda.

"Gotcha," I said. "Nonchalant saunter." And off I set.

"That's too nonchalant," hissed Belinda. "It doesn't look right in the burqa." I adjusted my saunter, and wondered whether the King, his vicereine and the mysterious doctor were behind us watching.

After a few metres, Belinda relaxed. "I'm with you on that awful Flavia. Ghastly precocious little twerp."

"Such a pity," I said. "Because climate change is a very pressing issue."

"What?"

"The debate is over," I continued. "The science is settled. Ninety-seven per cent of scientists agree."

We walked on in silence for a bit, and then I said: "Maybe we can get a deal at the micro-city summit."

"Around Your World in Eighteen Minutes? I thought you'd pulled out."

"Yes, but we could always pull back in."

"Are you sure? All the decent hotels will be gone."

"We need the world's most advanced economies to take concerted unified action now," I said. "As President Kennedy was saying, domestic refrigerators are a bigger threat than terrorism. Hard to argue with that."

"Good God, next you'll be saying you're in favour of the UK being subject to EU laws and regulatory regimes..."

"Well, it makes sense, doesn't it?" It seemed an unobjectionable observation, but I noticed Belinda had turned deathly white. We came to some circular stairs and climbed up to the next level. About halfway up, she asked me whether Cabinet was making any progress on immigration issues.

I sighed. "Well, too many mainstream politicians have surrendered to the xenophobes. We adopt this anti-immigrant rhetoric to play on the fears of poor, unfortunate, stupid, ill-educated people, who don't grasp that not only are vibrant diverse communities essential to both economic and social growth but also that opposition to multiculturalism is morally indefensible..."

Belinda screamed and slapped me hard. I fell back against the banister. "Rudy!" she said. "You're drugged! It was the drink. And you had two of them."

"Stuff and nonsense!" I replied. "I've never felt better. Maybe it's the burqa, but diversity is our stre..."

"Stop it!" She tugged at my body bag. "We need to get you out of here, and to a hospital. Quickly. Moments count." She yanked off the burqa and threw it over the railing.

"You interrupted me," I said, crossly. "I was just saying that diversity is our stren..."

"Stop that!" she shrieked, tearing off her own black garb. She wrenched my arm, dragged me up the stairs, and my feet stumbled to keep up. Oddly enough, even out of the burqa, I still felt clammy and sweaty.

"National sovereignty is very overrated," I remarked. "I mean, I'm not saying I necessarily agree with everything the European Commission President said about 'stupid nationalists'..."

"You will be in another forty-five seconds," snapped Belinda. "Come on, Rudy. Look sharp..." We reached a landing, pushed open a door and found ourselves in a courtyard at the foot of the Round Tower. "Maybe the fresh air will help you." Belinda took a deep breath, turned around, and beckoned me to follow. A few minutes later, we were in a darkened yard. I could see a hundred or so metres away a half-dozen cigarettes glowing in the dark of a starless night. A handful of liveried footmen and a scullery maid or two were taking their break. It was, after all, a non-smoking castle.

"Here," hissed Belinda. And we plunged through another door and back into total darkness. Something smelled different. I stopped to catch my breath. "Where are we?"

"The stables," said Belinda.

"The Stables? The luxury spa where celebrities go to dry out?" (I had been reading *The Daily Mail*.)

"No," she said, sliding back a heavy latch. "Where they keep the horses." There was a timely whinny, and the intoxicating perfume of equine urine. I felt straw under my feet. And something sticky and squishy and pungent. Ahead of me pairs of eyes glowed in the dark. A row of stalls.

"Why have we come to the stables?"

"Because I don't fancy our chances of leaving via the front door."

The sound of heavy boots echoed across the courtyard. "*Diversity is our strength!*" I yelled. God, it felt good just to come out and say it without being interrupted by Belinda.

"What's that?" said whichever palace flunkey was outside the door. One of our stablemates whinnied.

"Shut up!" yelled his co-worker. "You're waking up the 'orses."

"I could have sworn that 'orse was whinnying something about diversity..."

The sweat was pouring off me and I was beginning to shake. "Have I mentioned that Islam is a religion of peace?" I said to Belinda. "Also," I added, "a lot of women have penises nowadays. If you're one of them, you're welcome to use my bathroom."

"Shut up!" she hissed. "And get on this horse."

"I've never been on a horse in my life."

"How can you be a king who doesn't ride?"

"Like you said, I'm just a pretender. Diversity is our..."

233

"You can pretend to ride then. It worked with the tennis." She was already leading a stallion from one of the stalls. "Rode one like this for Children in Need." Prowling the stables, she auditioned likely companions, while I staggered behind feeling increasingly woozy. "You take the gelding," she said. "He seems to like you. Keep an eye on them."

"What?" But she was threading her way along the cobbled floor to the tack room. It took her a couple of trips to acquire the saddles, reins and other necessaries she fixed to our mounts.

"The safest, fastest way out is through Windsor Great Park, to the south of the castle. If we ride parallel to the Long Walk, between the rows of trees, we should be able to get through to the Copper Horse."

"A lot of women are hung like horses," I said. "Please use my bathroom. I insist. Diversity is..."

"It's a statue of George III. We might not need to go as far as the Copper Horse, if you'll stop blathering about diversity and let me Google the nearest A&E."

"I don't think we talk enough about diversity," I said, "although I don't see why I have to do it on horseback."

"I'll be right behind you. Nice and quiet, and no one will notice. I'll help you up."

I put a hand on my gelding's flank, and he turned and puckered his lips invitingly. Friendly fellow. I put a foot in the stirrup and hauled myself up. My royal steed swayed, and I began to tip. But I righted myself and got the other foot on, dripping sweat all over his coat.

"See?" said Belinda, atop her mount. "Piece of cake. These are the easiest horses in the world to ride. Windsor greys. Bred from birth to pull coaches through congested streets to the opening of Parliament. Completely unperturbed by motor vehicles, large crowds, overhead helicopters."

"Well, when you put it like that..."

"He knows how to drive, so you just sit back and enjoy the ride."

She opened the stable door. "Now!" yelled Belinda, and rode away. I gave my ride a gentle hint with my heels, and my mount took off at breakneck speed, with me yelling an encouraging "Fu-u-u-u-u-u-u-u-uh". Clinging on as best I could, I noted Windsor's residential streets to the right, fields to the left, and directly ahead the so-called Long Walk, the giant sidewalk running dead straight through the park that I'd entered by two days earlier. Belinda was galloping between the two left-hand rows of chestnut and plane trees, into gusts of wind and spits of rain, and the moans and sighs of the foliage. I ducked down, leaning low over the horse's neck, and then sort of slid a little too far to one side. Hanging half off the horse, I caught up with Belinda in seconds.

"Rudy," she cried, "try to bring yourself upright. You're almost upside down."

"It all makes perfect sense this way round," I slurred. "The ground is the sky, the sky is the ground, women are hung like stallions, Europe is the future, diversity is our str…"

And at that point my head hit a stray bit of undergrowth and I passed out.

Chapter Thirty-Two
An undrained swamp

I WASN'T OUTSIDE, BUT it didn't seem like inside, either. High above, very far above, there was a big starburst, and angels. Very literal angels, with halos and wings. God was the only power above me, and I had no lord except the king of kings. That's what the old Count of Tarlenheim told me at my coronation, and now it was true. Above me were God and His angels. I was in Heaven. And below the angels were saints, and Jesus and me. Heaven was everything it was cracked up to be: It was like living in a beautiful painting by …wossname, I did the voiceover… Raphael, that was it. I was in Heaven, and Heaven was a Raphael fresco. It was perfect.

Except it was a touch musty. As if Heaven had a slight problem with rising damp… I faded in and out for a bit, but, when I opened my eyes again, the angels were still there. And the mustiness. St Peter should call Laddie. Get the Ruritanians in. Take care of the damp… I don't like to complain, but come on: What sort of Heaven looks like a Raphael fresco and smells like my room at the Great British B&B?

I closed my eyes, and my head slumped to one side. I only raised one eyelid this time, and saw stone. I was on the floor. That's why it was musty, because this was the entry-level position. I should try to get up higher to where the angels and saints were. Not far from my eye, across the floor, was a large block of marble …like a – what was the word? – tomb. Of course. If I was in Heaven, I must be dead. But, if I was dead, I should be in the tomb, shouldn't I? Not outside the tomb. That was Jesus, not the King of Ruritania.

I faded out again. And the next I remember was a faint voice saying: "*Vale desideratissime! Hic demum Conquiescam tecum, tecum in Christo consurgeam.*"

So they spoke Latin in Heaven… Should have foreseen that. I'm rusty. Not like the EU External Zone (Qualified Recognition) summit. No simultaneous translation.

Except there was. Another faint voice was saying: "Farewell, most beloved. Here at length I shall rest with thee…" That was great. I didn't need headphones, and unlike the EU summit the translation made sense. "With thee in Christ I shall rise again. Oh, look, he's waking up…"

I opened one eye just as the lurid orange *Bordellschlingpflanzen* of Sir Roger Severn walked into shot. "Hello, Prime Minister."

My voice sounded tinny and far away. "Hello, Sealman. Am I dead?"

"No."

"Then why have you laid me next to a whatchamacallit – a large coffin?"

"I believe the word you're searching for is sarcophagus. That is the last resting place of Queen Victoria and her beloved Prince Consort, and this–" He wafted his hands airily up toward the high domed ceiling with its bewinged angels. "-is the Royal Mausoleum at Frogmore."

"Why am I here?"

"Because Belinda's quick thinking saved your life." Sir Roger's brothel creepers were now flanked by two other pairs of shoes – Belinda's pumps and Fritz Tarlenheim's pale lilac patent leathers, both stained by what appeared to be blood and vomit. (It would be hard to tell if someone had been sick on Severn's orange footwear.)

"I think," Fritz was saying, "that we should first establish if the procedure worked."

Belinda knelt down and took my hand. "Important you get this right, Rudy Elphberg. Complete the following sentence: Diversity is..?"

I looked into her wide azure eyes and held her gaze. "Diversity is the name of a notoriously bad massage parlour in Strelsau, patronised by EU officials and using mostly surly girls from Belarus with a couple of Thai ladyboys for the bigshots with an expense account."

Belinda kissed me on the forehead. "Bless you. The superplumber's back."

She told me what had happened – from when we'd been galloping away from the castle, and I'd knocked myself unconscious on a low-hanging branch. Belinda had pulled alongside, grabbed the reins of my horse and righted me, with some difficulty. She tried to rouse me, to no avail. So she called Sir Roger, who was opposed to taking me to hospital because we wouldn't be able to keep it out of the news and there would be "speculation" about certain substances. He would bring a doctor and meet us where the Long Walk crosses the Albert Road, by the handsome memorial to the old Queen. It had been a gift from the people of New Zealand, who had chosen to represent her late Majesty with three of her devoted royal corgis at her feet. As Belinda approached the junction, she heard a loud but indistinct clamour and came in sight of a hundred-strong demonstration denouncing the monarchy for its support of Colin Corgi. She was about to trot past, as daintily and discreetly as she could with me and my mount in tow, when one of the bearded men stepped into her path - and for a moment the stallion froze. "It's her!" yelled one of the guys. "Colin Corgi's whore! The one who wrote *Seventies Muff*..."

They ran toward us, and Belinda reversed course. Terrified she'd lose hold of the other reins or that I would fall off, she galloped back up toward the castle as fast as she dared risk, with dozens of enraged Mohammedans in hot pursuit. When she'd put a bit of distance between us, she ducked into the eastern row of plane and chestnut trees, rode between them more cautiously, and a few hundred metres on ducked out the other side and found herself near the car park of the Royal Household Cricket Club. There was some kind of reception on, and a lot of people about, and she was concerned that either we or the horses would be recognised. She rode on, followed the perimeter of a ploughed field, and realised she was near the Frogmore mausoleum. So she called Sir Roger again. They agreed that Frogmore was the least worst rendezvous in terms of being disturbed by protesting Muslims, cricketing servants or anybody else. Sir Roger had brought Fritz Tarlenheim, who in turn had brought a tube, a syringe, a bowl, and lots of bottled water.

"We had very little time," said Fritz. He explained that what he called *un lavage gastrique* - pumping the stomach – was only really effective within sixty minutes from the time of ingestion. I'd had a double dose of that doctor's smoothie, and it was a very fast-acting drug.

"Belinda wanted to take you to A&E at the Edward VII," said Severn, "but that would have been too late. You'd have woken up talking like the head of the ECB or a trustee of the World Economic Forum."

THE PRISONER OF WINDSOR

"Crumbs!" I pulled myself up on one elbow, still feeling groggy. "Did you know this drug existed?"

Sir Roger pursed his lips. "There was a Polish finance minister, hardcore populist. Went to Brussels for a summit, and came back demanding a European army and a single EU rate of income tax. Curious."

"He was found dead a month later," said Fritz. "Supposedly auto-erotic asphyxiation. His wife said he'd been doing it for years without problems. There were rumours that it was a side-effect: The drug works for a short time, and then you die. The autopsy results were never released."

"The sad thing is," remarked Belinda bleakly, "they don't really need this drug at all. Almost all the politicians sound as if they've been on it since birth."

Severn stared down at me. "Belinda says you didn't get this doctor's name. And her description of him wasn't much help." I tried to remember what he looked like, but that was the point: He was so obviously stereotypically villainous that every time I tried to conjure the specifics he morphed smoothly into some half-remembered Hollywood baddie – Erich von Stroheim or Goldfinger or Ming the Merciless or Laurence Olivier as that Nazi dentist...

"So he looked like a Teutonic movie villain," said Sir Roger, setting aside his pen and paper. "Anything else?"

I remembered he'd said his clinic was in this month's *Lancet*, and he had a copy of the magazine on his desk.

Fritz showed me his *handifon*. "Is this the one?" And there on the screen was the front of *The Lancet*, and the big cover story:

Towards a Treatable Nationalism

"The medicalisation of political opposition," said Sir Roger. "Rupert, Anna and Derek were telling the truth."

They helped me to my feet and I stood up, a little unsteadily, taking in my strange surroundings. There were Victoria and Albert in their great sarcophagus topped by effigies of both Queen and Consort and watched by four bronze angels. Biblical kings and prophets stood guard in a quartet of alcoves, and above them were frescoed mosaics of Matthew, Mark, Luke and John. My eyes were drawn upward again to the great dome and the angels.

"I thought I was in Heaven," I said. "Or in a Raphael brought to life."

"Raphael was a favourite of Prince Albert's," said Belinda. "That was the effect Victoria wanted."

I remembered the shattered vault of the House of Elphberg in the ruined cathedral of Strelsau, and I envied England's Royal Family even in death.

I called Vic and asked him to meet us at the castle cricket club. After scooping up the tubes and syringes and bowls of vomit, Severn and Tarlenheim left, and for a moment Belinda and I were alone in the sepulchral shadows. She kissed me.

"Why is it musty?"

"They built it on a marsh. Frogmore - so called because there are more frogs. Because it's a swamp." She hugged me, tight. "A swamp that's not easy to drain. This is real, isn't it, Rudy? I mean, Rob talking about his TR4 and quoting Mrs Thatcher... It *was* Rob, wasn't it? It's not some arse of a game from those freaks at MI5, is it?"

But she knew the answer to that. "Poor Rob... Poor Rob... Are we going to win, Rudy?"

We walked back round the field to the cricket club, me a little wobbly, and Belinda having broken a heel and ripped her skirt in the excitement and showing a stocking top. I was too woozy to be turned on; she was upset but also exhilarated. "You saved my life," I said.

"I know. That bit I liked. I think it was more fun than the ball." She tried to pull her torn skirt together and removed a twig from my hair. "You're a survivor, Rudy Elphberg," she declared. "Useful talent. Especially in crowned heads."

And then she threaded her arm in mine, and we hobbled in silence until the cricketers' car park.

I told Vic we'd be dropping Belinda at her house. "South Ken," she instructed.

"Had the loo fixed yet?" I asked. Unseen by the front-seat security, she slipped her hand across the divider and rested it on mine.

"Don't think we'll be there much longer. George has a reverse Midas touch. Everything he's invested in is worth half what he paid for it. And we're poor as church mice next to everyone else in the street.

THE PRISONER OF WINDSOR

Oligarchs. Not the Russians, of course, but the ones from stans nobody's heard of. Not the chaps who order the killings, but the hands-on types who like to do it themselves. The baronet's widow three doors down sold up to an exiled daughter-in-law of one of those Arab Spring dictators. It'll be Pushtun warlords next." She heaved a sigh. "Don't let's talk about that." So we sat in silence, and, unseen by my minders, our fingers entwined.

We pulled up outside Belinda's house. The dictator's daughter-in-law was off at Harrod's and the oligarchs from no-name stans were with their tax advisors, and the street was silent. We're going to rescue him," she whispered. "The useless bugger." She kissed me lightly on the cheek. "I enjoyed the ride in the park," she said reflectively. "I had a good time. The best time really. Thank you." Belinda tottered up the path with her broken heel, unlocked the door, and stood there for a moment, framed by the lintel. She gave a lopsided smile, and a friendly wave. And then the door closed.

Chapter Thirty-Three
A basic chahar-bagh

NEXT MORNING AT the 7.45, Rory was demanding to know why I'd abandoned the President of the United States to go galloping through an anti-Colin Corgi demo of enraged Muslims, and ordered Angus to get some polling on it. Dame Millie announced that we were getting some pushback on the Coronation Community Involvement Act, and invited Imogen to expand. "As you know, PM, the Palace wanted to protect certain logos and marques for the Coronation, created in cooperation with the King's monarchy development underwriters. And obviously you were very much in favour of this as a way of helping ensure the costs of the beano didn't get out of hand."

"Especially," drawled Rory, "now the ingrate colonials are demanding we pay for their chaps' flights."

"The Coronation Community Involvement Act? Know it well." That was the eyes-only file I'd been riffling through the other night: it's illegal to put words like "King" next to a picture of a cheeseburger, etc. "Common or garden dictionary words are now the sole property of the state, and so on."

"Oh, come on, PM," chided Millie. "The Palace was concerned that American fast-food chains, multinational corporations and other…"

"Consumerism denialists," chipped in Imogen. "That's what the King calls them."

Dame Millie groaned. "The Palace was concerned that 'consumerism denialists' or whatever you want to call them should not cash in on his Coronation."

"It's not 'his' Coronation," I said. "Not in that sense."

"Well, anyway," continued Imogen, "as usual, everyone's got a bit carried away. In Leamington Spa, trading standards officers are prosecuting a florist who displayed a crown of flowers in her window. In Harrogate, police confiscated a Coronation display from a butcher's window on the grounds that the sausage sceptre, pork pie crown and bacon rasher robes contravened the act. There are rumours that the

THE PRISONER OF WINDSOR

bobbies have since eaten the evidence. The proprietrix of Laureen's Lingerie in Leicester was ordered to take down her window display of five mannequins wearing crown bra cups and a sceptre thong. In the village of Culver Magna, 87-year-old Gladys Maudsley's 'Coronation cosy' was disqualified from competition at the church fete after an anonymous complaint to the parish council."

"Wait a minute," I interrupted, "isn't this a freedom-of-expression thing?"

"Christ on a bike!" exploded Rory. "Colin Corgi in a Coronation cosy. Shoot me now."

"When you say 'the Palace' wanted this, Imogen, who do you mean?"

"Peter Borrodaile, of course," said Rory. "Doing for the monarchy what he did for Mubarak and Gaddafi."

After which we discussed the King's reluctance to be crowned, as British monarchs have been styled for half a millennium, "Defender of the Faith". This seemed reasonable enough, given that (a) he was an exposed adulterer and (b) the Church of England had barely any Faith left that required Defending by the King or anybody else. But that's not what the King meant. Instead, he'd decided that in his multicultural kingdoms he was going to be "Defender of Faiths". Multiple. Whatever your faith, he's looking out for you. This had caused a panic among the Anglican hierarchy, not because they cared one way or the other about any particular faith – they were themselves impeccably ecumenical, having no greater regard (indeed, rather less) for their own than for Islam or Hinduism, Gaia-worship or Hobbitism. On the other hand, they were rather partial to their seats in the House of Lords, and they were concerned that the King's notion might lead to the disestablishment of the Church of England and their bishops' eviction from parliament. BGHA – the British Gay Humanist Association – had also joined the anti-disestablishmentarians on the grounds that two of the Anglican clerics on the bishops' bench were among the most prominent gay members of the Upper Chamber. So I – that is to say, Rassendyll – had crafted a compromise, whereby the lines sworn by previous sovereigns – to maintain "to the utmost of your power" "the true profession of the Gospel" - were quietly excised, but all the lingo about the "rights and privileges" of the bishops was kept in, and the Chief Rabbi and the Grand Mufti and various representatives of other faiths invited along for the ride. There had been some talk about the Mufti hosting a bonus coronation at the new Grand Mosque of London, but this was felt to be a touch provocative, and, being as it was located in the far East End, less scenically cooperative with the needs of the tourism industry.

Next up were the "Syrian refugees". Who were, more geographically precisely, refugees from Scandinavia: They were Muslims fleeing Sweden since the collapse of the kroner and the shutdown of the welfare system.

Downstairs in my office, I made a list of people I thought I could trust. It was not very long. But all through a long and tormented night the vision of Rob Rassendyll's empty cell had not left me. We knew not where the Prime Minister was, except that he was in the hands of a poisoner and brainwasher. I liked Severn and Tarlenheim, but, really, what were we? A trio of Ruritanians on holiday in a fantastical kingdom we barely understood. If we were going to retrieve the situation, we would need help.

The King had asked if our weekly audience could be moved to the morning. I didn't see why not – he is the King, after all. Upon arrival, I was informed that His Majesty wished to see me in what the footman called "the carpet garden", so I was led straight through Buckingham Palace and out the back, to a terrace overlooking a vast verdant lawn. A half-dozen men were working on a temporary bandstand for the Coronation garden parties. They were speaking, I noticed, Ruritanian. In Arthurian London even the carpenters at the Palace were Ruri. I followed the footman to the end of the terrace, down a few steps and through a door set into the wall.

On the other side was a small guardhouse and then a viewing platform some two feet below which stretched a lush geometric garden enclosed on all sides. The high walls were lined by higher cypress trees alternating with spreading tamarisks. Within this arboreal stockade was a symmetrical pattern of paths, trees, waterways and flower beds, centred on a scalloped fountain rising from an octagonal plinth of coloured tiles. On the far side of the fountain, a man in Arab dress was bent over a shrub. It seemed that at Buckingham Palace the carpenters were Ruritanian and the gardeners were Mohammedan.

"The Prime Minister," announced the footman, and withdrew. It wasn't clear anyone had heard. I descended three steps and walked down the centre aisle of pale terracotta stone and up and over the gaudier ceramic tiles around the marble fountain. At the sound of my click-clacking brogues the Muslim gardener straightened up.

"Ah, Mr Rassendyll," he said.

Stone the crows! It was the King, dressed like the Sheik of Araby.

"Your Majesty." I did my short bow from the neck. Had it really been a week since my first audience?

"You don't mind meeting here, do you?"

"As in all matters, sir, I am at Your Majesty's service."

He giggled like a schoolboy. "Corks! You sound like you're channelling Roger Severn." He waved his arm around the greenery. "On such a beautiful day, I'm afraid I couldn't bear to tear myself away from my garden." It was twelve degrees Centigrade and cloudy, but at least it wasn't raining. The King smoothed down his robe. "Find it easier to commune in a thobe."

"Pardon me?"

"*Thobe*," he repeated, indicating his robe. "Worn with a *keffiyeh*." He pointed at his headgear. "First tried it in the school hols when Prince Ghazi took me to spend three days at his Bedouin encampment. I felt a sense of serenity I'd never known before. Certainly not at boarding school. I don't think you've been here before, have you?" he asked. "To my carpet garden?"

I hoped that wasn't a trick question. "Why is it called a carpet garden?"

He looked at me as if I'd asked what a Hentzau dumpling was. "You really don't know?" His Majesty walked me back up the steps to the octagonal platform around the fountain. "It's a traditional Muslim garden."

"Very nice," I said, looking around. "Amazing, Buckingham Palace having a traditional Muslim garden. Remind me again. Was this put in when Queen Victoria became Empress of India?"

He tittered. "Don't be silly. I installed it. It was in the papers."

"Of course. Slipped my mind."

"Many years ago I was given an ancient Anatolian prayer rug…"

"Oh, really?" I said. And off he went. If you're wondering what to give the man who has everything – palaces, coaches, kingdoms –

you can't go wrong with an ancient Anatolian prayer rug. It turned out the rug had exercised a strange fascination upon him in the way that other gifts accumulated over the years – a signed photograph of Emanuel Macron, an iPod pre-loaded with speeches by Barack Obama – had not. The Islamic art curator at his foundation had taught the King all about the Persian tradition of "garden carpets" – carpets that look like formal Islamic gardens – and His Majesty thought it would be a spiffing wheeze to turn his very own garden carpet back into a carpet garden, right here at Buckingham Palace.

"It's a basic *chahar-bagh*," he said. Again, I must have looked blank, for a faintly exasperated expression crossed his face. "The four canals leading to the central fountain represent the four rivers of Paradise, which are filled with water, wine, milk and honey."

"Which one's the wine?" I said, peering in.

"Ours are all water, alas."

"'Elf'n'Safety?"

"I truly believe I do my best work here."

I wasn't sure what to say to this, mainly because I wasn't aware he did any work. After a strained silence, he said, "The Koran tells us that in the gardens of Paradise the faithful shall dwell mid thornless lote-trees and serried acacias, and spreading shade and outpoured waters, and fruits abounding." He waved his hand airily.

"Fruits abounding, eh?" I said, for want of anything more useful to contribute.

"Not quite. Of the four trees in the gardens of Paradise, we have a mere three – figs, olives and pomegranates. No date palms. Don't think they'd survive in London, even with the climate change, and they'd look a little odd, wouldn't they? But Islam considers the pomegranate the highest fruit in Paradise." He turned back down the steps. I noticed the flower beds were sunken so that the heads of the roses and gerania and other flowers appeared to be at surface level. "To accentuate the carpet effect," the King explained. He pointed to a matching pavilion at the far end of the garden similar to the one I'd entered through. "I designed that myself," he said. "The shape is based on the *mihrab* in my prayer rug."

Atop the pavilion was an Islamic crescent looking like a novelty weathervane. "Come," he said. "Let us sit."

THE PRISONER OF WINDSOR

Let us sit? What is this, outtakes from *The Arabian Nights*? I looked around for some nice English wrought-iron garden furniture, but he motioned toward some plumped up cushions adorned with the Royal cypher alongside one of the ornamental canals. He sat down cross-legged and clapped his hands. A footman appeared with tea. I seated myself rather more awkwardly.

The King trailed his fingers across the water, and said meditatively: "On Mother Kelly's doorstep down Paradise Row, I'd sit along o' Nellie, she'd sit along o' Joe."

"Come again?" It didn't sound like the Koran.

"You don't know it?" he said, shaking the droplets from his sandal. "I remember it from the dorm at school. Danny La Rue. Always liked the sound of that song. Paradise Row. Used to dream of running away and getting on a double-decker bus to Paradise Row. Probably some benighted East End slum redeveloped in the Sixties."

"Danny La Rue?" I repeated, for want of anything more inspired.

"Met him after the Royal Variety Show one year. He sang 'Mother Kelly's Doorstep' in a lilac boa and beautiful black-sequined dress. Rather low-cut. But awfully convincing."

This was more nerve-wracking than Prime Minister's Questions. I had the feeling I ought to be able to respond with more than the occasional "Ah". Any third-rate impostor can bluff his way through foreign affairs and fiscal policy and the collapse of the European Union, but local cultural allusions are a tougher bird.

His Majesty pattered his fingers across the pool. "Islam's spiritual principles have a great deal to teach us about living in harmony with the environment."

"Really?"

"The Koran instructs us that there is no separation between man and nature. In the west, industrialisation and consumer capitalism have created an artificial division between man and the environment. We seem to have lost that understanding of the whole of nature and the universe as a living entity. Islam has a great deal to offer in terms of saving the planet."

Behead me with a tree-ring, I thought.

He gestured toward the ornamental fountain. "Wouldn't it be marvellous to have a paradise garden in Leicester Square? Or would the oiks urinate in it?"

"There is that," I agreed.

"I think of this realm as a paradise garden. It only works if all the streams flow in balance – king and parliament, the people and the land." He indicated his various canals. "So I naturally worry when the balance seems ...*disturbed*."

"Quite," I said.

"Prime Minister, I wish to speak frankly. Constitutionally, I have the right to be consulted, the right to encourage, and the right to warn. So I would warn you against disturbing the delicate..." He looked down meditatively at his perfectly ironed thobe, and brushed away a speck of something. "...*delicate* and, alas, somewhat frayed threads of British society. And I would encourage you..." He gestured toward his *mihrab*-shaped pavilion. "...to build bridges between the communities of this kingdom."

As in the Palace sitting room a week ago, his Big Thought seemed to have exhausted him. "More tea, Mr Rassendyll?"

But, as he'd opened up to me, I thought I should, at least partially, reciprocate – knowing what I knew about the empty cell in Windsor Castle. I asked him if he could give me floor plans of the Round Tower.

"Why, sir?" he said, already suspicious.

"There are offices there that are not part of the Royal Household. Flavia Strofzin and others."

"I don't see what business that is of yours."

"You permit my brother access..."

"That's the organic vintners he and I started."

I proceeded cautiously. "I fear my brother is mixed up in some bad business."

He shook his *keffiyeh*ed head. "That can't be right, sir. I've known your brother longer than I have you. There are few better men. You wrong him, sir."

I heard the rebuke. "You don't like me, do you?"

"The King acts on his prime minister's advice. 'Liking him' is neither here nor there. But, since you mention it, no, I don't like some of this Europocalypse nonsense. A bit strong meat for me. The

Spanish, Danish, Norwegian and Swedish royal houses are all cousins of mine."

"So were the Russians, Germans, Greeks and Romanians," I replied. His Majesty was visibly shocked by my impertinence, so I thought it best to keep talking. "The King acts on his prime minister's advice, and with respect to European Union policy I act on the people's advice. And they voted to leave – in a binding referendum."

"Your brother has some interesting theories about the need for institutions that temper the will of the people."

"Tempering is one thing; subverting is another. And some of these institutions my brother likes are subverting not just the will of the people, but the very nation." I paused. "A king isn't really a 'head of state'. He *is* the state. The Canadian Governor General's official website says you are 'the personification of the Canadian state'."

"You have the advantage of me, Rassendyll. I don't surf the Governor General of Canada's website as often as perhaps I should."

"These institutions my brother favours don't enhance your status, sir. In demeaning and diminishing the state, they diminish you as the personification of the state, and of its rightful laws, made by the King-in-Parliament."

"I don't need constitutional lessons from you, Prime Minister. I've been prepared for this moment since I was five years old. And, as I noted, there are monarchies in the European Union…"

I scoffed, and told him they'd been reduced to princely states under the Raj.

"Princely states? I swear no one's used that expression to me in forty years. You read too much history, Mr Rassendyll. I thought your party was all about moving with the times."

"Do you know how my brother refers to himself, sir? The Resident Commissioner. As if Britain were one of the Trucial States."

"It worked out well enough for the Trucial States. Have you been to the United Arab Emirates lately?"

"So why don't you throw off your Resident Commissioner and re-establish your own Emirate?"

"Sir, you go too far!"

"I cannot bind Your Majesty, but I wish to be heard. If something happens in the Round Tower, and Robert Rassendyll does not emerge…"

"Are you speaking in the third person now? Isn't that a king's prerogative?"

I was choosing my words with care. "If Robert Rassendyll does not emerge from the Castle, I want you to ask, immediately, Roger Severn to serve as caretaker prime minister – and believe everything he tells you about this matter. And if such persons as Henley, Bersonin and Detchard tell you otherwise, believe Sir Roger and do as he advises. Will you?"

"Is this another of your Ruritanian content-farmer jokes?"

"Swear to me, on your faith and honour and by the fear of the living God, that you will ask Roger Severn to serve in the absence of Rassendyll."

"On my faith and honour, and by the fear of God? And listening to you talk about yourself in the third person? Sir, do you have any idea what a king has to put up with? I have to go to south London to listen to two hours of Coronation hip'n'hop, and then take part in a comedy sketch with Frankie Puss. I'll have earned some laughs after all that gangsta-rapping caterwauling, but there won't be any with Frankie Puss, will there? Because he's less funny than you and your Ruritanian content jokes!" He rose and smoothed his *thobe*. "You have disturbed the peace of this carpet garden, sir. I'm sorry I asked you here."

And with that the King walked out on me. Again.

Chapter Thirty-Four
Deep waters

"WHAT DOES THIS PLANET in the Round foundation actually do?" I asked.

"Hard to say," said Sir Roger Severn, peering at the report. "An Uzbek oligarch paid Flavia Strofzin two million euros to give a speech on diarrhoea in Belgium…"

"Is that a big problem?"

"No more than usual, as I understand it — although you might want to check with the Foreign Secretary. Not my department."

"And there are that many people in Uzbekistan who want to listen to a middle-school dropout give a speech on Belgian diarrhoea?"

He slid forward a photocopy of *The Tashkent Times*. "As you can see, young Miss Strofzin spoke to a football stadium filled with seven people."

"That's some serious social distancing. So that works out at…"

"285,714 euros per customer. Not to mention the stadium rental."

"And this Dr Davos is on Flavia's board?" According to *The Lancet*, Dr Davos was the name of the doctor I had met the other night.

"Yes. Davos is her married name."

"Her?"

"Female-to-male transgender. Born Lan Ping. Former director of the Wuhan Institute of Cohesion. Rather a minimal biographical entry on the website."

"Where did the German accent come from?"

"WEF, I think. They teach a class in it."

Compared to both the King and the snakes slithering round the 7.45 every morning, I found the Official Opposition relatively easy to handle. But at PMQs Deirdre Bellairs did have something of a point. "The Prime Minister," she said, "chose to walk out of an important speech by the President of the United States on hydrofluorocarbons to go galloping around Windsor Great Park with Lady Belinda Featherly as if he's some sort of Regency buck." She held up her *handifon* to the amusement of the House. "Well, not exactly galloping. More like hanging on for dear life to a half-dead horse!" Derisive laughs, jeers, etc. "When will the Prime Minister stop flogging the dead horse of nationalism and accept that there's no point locking the Little England stable door after the people's horse has bolted for the Continent?"

Everyone roared with laughter, this being the height of wit in politics. I rose to my feet. "I was about to congratulate the Right Honourable Lady on getting back in the saddle. She certainly had the bit between her teeth, but I fear she lost hold of the reins toward the end of that metaphor." Lots of sycophantic laughter, etc.

"If the Prime Minister has finished horsing around," said Ms Bellairs, "instead of being too cowardly to attend EuroWind, instead of walking out on a presidential speech because he's too gutless to face the truth about his climate denial, he might walk over to Victoria Tower Gardens and talk to some real heroes who, unlike him, are standing up for something really important!"

She yelled those last seven words, and the roar from the Opposition benches was like nothing I'd heard. I was stung, and for a moment subdued. And then I stood up.

"Okay, Mr Speaker, I will." And I looked around the House of Commons and said, "Anybody else coming with me?" And, without waiting for an answer, I strode out of the chamber, through the Central Lobby and St Stephen's Hall, as Cabinet and backbenchers and security scrambled to keep up.

The spads weren't happy about it. "They won't talk to you," warned Dame Milllie. "You'll look weak if you're turned away."

"As weak as I look letting them have the run of the joint? And the State Department wankers of President Look-At-The-Length-Of-My-Motorcade issuing travel advisories about the dangers of visiting London?"

So I ignored her, and walked into the street, past the Victoria Tower (that's the other one – the one without Big Ben) and into the gardens beyond, where a sea of signs greeted me, waved by activist groups from the Turquoise Scarves to the Tied-Tubes to the Self-Extinction Movement: "The People United Against Referenda!" "Love Out-Votes Hate!" "Referenda: Don't Mend 'Em, Referend 'Em!", "Kill, Kill Rassendyll!" Flavia Strofzin was there, of course, the spindly orphan telling a BBC reporter: "I'm here becauth I want the world to know I weally weally weally don't like Mithter Rathendyll." And she stamped her foot.

And there at the centre of it all was Marie-Claude de Chard, the President of the European Parliament, under a banner bearing the slogan, "Europe says No to the Tyranny of the Unelected People".

"It is a great pleasure to be with you here in the External Zone (Qualified Recognition). Let me say, as a proud vibrant sensual Luxembourgeois woman, that to me you will never be External. You are as internal to me, as European to me, as a Frenchman playing *boules*, an Italian dancing a tarantella, a Swede offering refugee accommodation to a seventeen-year-old Syrian male fleeing persecution. My recognition of you is unqualified!" There were cheers at this. "I will never abandon my fellow Europeans here in the External Zone, no matter how many times Mr Rassendyll holds his referendum – or, as I call it, his neverendum. I know a lot about your Anglo-American rock'n'roll – who does not like it, in small doses? - and I say welcome to the Hotel Brexifornia! You can check 'Out' any time you like, but you can never leave! Because that is the real, enduring, eternal will of the people that can never be nullified by a mere snapshot of a moment of a millisecond of ignorant opinions manipulated by spin-doctors and racists and Russian bots re-routed via Ruritanian content farmers!

"That is the real enduring vote of the eternal European people. There are those who want to vote down the European idea. They want us to go back to obsolete ideas about small inbred navel-gazing states exercising national sovereignty." There were loud jeers at this. "I have been to Auschwitz and I have seen where Mr Rassendyll's Little Englander Express leads!" There was a more muted response to this, the BBC/*Guardian* crowd being apparently unsure whether Auschwitz was an applause line or not. "So we are not disheartened. We hear you, no matter how many neverendums your government holds. Because no polling booth can vote down the European vision: If it's an 'In', we say 'On we go!'; and if it's an 'Out!' we say 'We march forward!' That is the European way! That is the true voice of the people! *En marche!* Onward!"

Mme de Chard had spotted Deirdre Bellairs and me marching toward the podium. "Ah, I see your leader is among us!" I thought she meant me and was about to wave, but she continued, "What do you say in your quaint English way? 'The Leader of His Majesty's Loyal Opposition.' No! She is not the opposition. She is the true leader of the External Zone, loyal to Europe and determined that one day her people will sit once again at the European table, instead of at the children's table by the kitchen door, sipping Orangina and waiting patiently for a croque monsieur. Please welcome my great friend Daphne Bellairs!"

If Deirdre was upset at Mme de Chard getting her name wrong, she didn't show it. She hopped up on the stage to a thunderous roar, and immediately roared back:

"What do we want?"

"*Europe!*"

"When do we want it?"

"*Forever!*"

The whole encampment seemed to be sitting in a shallow bowl of murky water. I tiptoed gingerly through the muddy pool, past the giant hot-air *Guardian*-sponsored Rassendildo, intermittently priapic in the Thames breeze, and a group of daytime TV presenters staging a nude protest because they'd never again get to lie on the beaches of the Costa del Sol.

The chanting continued:

"Racist referendum! It's time to end 'em!"

"Yes! End them!" cried Mme de Chard. "Tell the world that Europe will not be crushed under one racist nationalist populist Englishman's giant..."

I think she was about to say "ambition" or some such, but at that point the wind changed and *The Guardian*'s spectacular Rassendildo came crashing down on the podium. Mme de Chard had the advantage of the crowd: She saw it coming, gave a deafening shriek and jumped out of the way. Poor Deirdre Bellairs wasn't quite so nimble: She stood there open-mouthed in terror and got clipped by the tip of it. The protesters in its path took a more direct hit. Barely waiting for their screams, the Rassendildo bounced off their heads and backs to come down on an adjoining group of spectators, and everybody else just started stampeding in all directions, notwithstanding the efforts of the Metropolitan Police at crowd control.

THE PRISONER OF WINDSOR

"I'm not going to ask again," yelled an officer, before the Rassendildo rebounded and knocked him over. A covered and bewigged woman stumbled against me, causing her full-bottom judicial wig to slip to the ground. It was Britain's first Muslima Lord Chancellor, Baroness al-Ghoti, who had caused much press commentary by her practice of walking around in the streets with her horsehair wig on top of her abaya. "Hello, Yazmina," I said, retrieving her wig and placing it back on her head. "You probably don't want grass stains and footprints all over that." She pulled herself away, disgusted. As the police regained control we found ourselves forced with the crowd across the small triangular garden. "Oy, you! Back!" yelled a copper. They were demolishing the somewhat stark wall and benches to build a section of the Coronation Walk, an ecological heritage trail linking key sites of the new Arthurian age. Lady al-Ghoti and I and a few dozen others were pushed through the tattered "Do Not Cross" construction tape that snapped and lay limp along the ground. A handful of uniformed police officers followed.

"'Ere, keep back, keep clear," said the copper. "Back off." He shoved a Human Extinction activist, who fell back on to Yazmina al-Ghoti. I heard a splintering sound and then a scream, as Britain's first Muslima Lady Chancellor toppled backwards through the construction fence and into the River Thames.

"Help!" cried Yazmina. Her head went under, and her judge's wig floated off downriver eventually to wash up on the coast off Bordeaux. "Help," she gasped again, more faintly and muffled this time from under her waterlogged abaya.

I don't know quite what I expected. There were a dozen uniformed policemen present. And they all just stood there watching.

After what seemed like an eternity, I asked, "Aren't you going to rescue her?"

One officer said, "Jurisdictionally, the river isn't our responsibility. It's the MPU."

A second officer said, "And as a matter of procedure it's not the responsibility of the police to go in the water, it's Fire & Rescue."

A third officer said, "And we're not allowed in anyway, because of 'Elf'n'Safety. Hard to maintain social distancing when you're rescuing someone…"

Fourth officer: "A colleague of mine jumped in to rescue a ten-year old boy last year and was subject to disciplinary procedures."

I never heard what the fifth officer would have remarked as he stood on the bank watching a woman drown, because at this point I myself said, "*Ihre Großmutter ficken!*", and tore off my jacket and shoes, and dived into the famous River Thames. The last thing I heard as I sailed through the air was "Oy, you can't do that!"

On the embankment, and on the long dive down, plunging in to rescue the Lady Chancellor seemed the obvious thing to do, if faintly unreal. But it was all too real once I was in the water. I quickly pulled off my tie, and socks, and shirt, and trousers, too.

You're probably wondering what it was like. I remember my dad taking me to a municipal pool in Madrid, and telling me about swimming as a boy in the cold, dark moat of Zenda Castle. So I could tell you about how cold and dark the Thames is, black and freezing, and how terrible it smells, a great churning murk, sucking at you like an evil thing. And how vile it tastes when you get it in your mouth. And then there are the currents. When you're pottering about London on dry land, the Thames just sits there. You don't think of it as a moving river, but it is: a hundred tidal miles of strong currents, lethal eddies, and vicious undertows continually trying to drag you down. I felt the pull even as I surfaced, and saw Baroness al-Ghoti moving downstream, and pushed myself to catch up. Her head went under, and I dived into the deep to follow her down into that inky, choking, stinking maw.

Once I'd adjusted to the random, unnerving hints of sewer gas and burning chemicals, I clawed at the water ahead of me - in hopes of finding, feeling something, anything other than silt and mud and strange oily tendrils of water life and urban garbage that brush your body before slithering silently onward. Striking something soft and sponge-like that was conceivably Lady al-Ghoti's heavily garbed arm, I reached to seize it, but missed and caught …what? a piece of material? I tugged, and held on to it until I cleared the surface, gasping for breath and spitting out water. At which point, I realised it was Yazmina's abaya, but without Yazmina in it. With a deep intake of breath, back down I dived, lungs aching and floundering until I touched a human limb – this time not sponge-like and covered but goose-pimpled and slippery. I pulled at that cold, grey arm and propelled myself upward, straining and out of breath, until once more I pushed through the surface of the Thames, shortly followed by Lady al-Ghoti's own bare head.

We had been dragged further downstream, so I made for the river bank - only to discover there was no such thing, just slick, slimy walls. Grabbing at a rusty chain and finding just enough of an old worn stone abutment to deposit her ladyship on, I hung exhausted with one hand and with the other tried to feel for a pulse. She had turned blue, and I couldn't hear any breathing.

I tried to remember that public safety announcement on beach emergencies I'd done in Modenstein, where I'd had to fondle Jovanka's wrist in a convincingly pulse-taking manner. Unlike Jovanka, Yazmina was horribly cold, and I could feel every hair and goose pimple. But no pulse. No breath. I remembered something else from that PSA, about gasp reflex or anaphylactic shock. So I tried to tilt the head backward to get the airway open. I put my left hand on her forehead, but, as soon as I moved to try to get above her face, her head flopped forward again. I pinched her nose closed and placed my mouth on her blue lips, but I couldn't force my breath in. Not as easy as in a public-service announcement. Her skin looked strange, kind of see-through, and her under-garment had sort of unwound itself, revealing her bra. I raised myself over her, forced open her mouth, and leaned down to give her the kiss of life. She tasted of bitter stinky Thamesy water.

I pressed in deeper. My tongue snagged on something. I retracted, and accidentally pulled whatever it was back into my own mouth. What the hell was that?

Yazmina al-Ghoti's eyes flashed open, and she pulled my head away. "That was my cyanide capsule," she croaked. "I always carry one disguised as a tooth filling in case I am captured by populists. It is now in your mouth."

I was, as Belinda would say, agog. And, before I could say "Captured by populists? That's a bit paranoid, isn't it?", she had pressed her mouth back to mine, shoved her tongue in and was waggling it around my cheek to get at the cyanide capsule, press down on it and release its contents into my system.

I strained to pull away but she had her arms around my back and held me down pressed against her. She was remarkably strong for a petite one-and-a-half metre Muslima, and her tongue probed relentlessly to find the cyanide to release it. With one final burst of energy, I rolled sideways and we fell back into the river. Underneath the water I punched her in the stomach, her grip slackened and her lips left mine, and I spat out the capsule. When we broke the surface again, what I mostly remember is looking back upstream and seeing more policemen staring in passive half-curiosity from whatever bridge we'd been swept under.

Fortunately, the skipper of a small tourist river-cruiser anchored just downstream spotted us and lowered a lifeboat. We clambered into it and then up onto his deck to collapse on our backs in an undignified heap and lie there groaning and gasping for the benefit of tourist cellphone cameras above.

And at that point it was determined that it was safe enough for the safety crews to come aboard.

One of the coppers stepped forward, and stared down at the Lady Chancellor, unrecognizable in bra and knickers with her lustrous hair down over her bare shoulders. "ID, miss."

"It's in the river," she wheezed.

"In that case, I'm going to have to ask you to accompany me to the station."

"No, you're not," I said sharply.

Lady al-Ghoti turned to me. "You should have killed me," she whispered, and then looked down as if wondering where her clothes had gone. "I was determined to kill you."

A second policeman spoke up to defend his colleague. "Swimming in the river between Putney Bridge and the Thames Barrier," he said to me, "requires prior consent in writing from the Harbour Master to waive mask-wearing requirements."

I wobbled unsteadily to my feet and helped Yazmina to hers. "Don't worry," I told her. "Next time you fall in, I'll go down to the Harbour Master, fill in the paperwork, and come back and rescue you three weeks later."

"You have ruined me," she hissed.

Chapter Thirty-Five
Cymbelline's castle

I THOUGHT MORE PEOPLE would like my River Thames action sequence. Some did, of course – "Action Man Rassendyll in Daring River Rescue" (*The Daily Express*). But it's never universal, is it? Several feminists at *The Guardian* and Radio 4 complained that rescuing a damsel in distress was Extreme Mansplaining, and that the very term "kiss of life", with its predatory #MeToo date-rape connotations, raised consent issues. And one of them, after complaints by Muslim lobby groups, had deplored the pictures of Baroness al-Gothi in her bra and panties, and argued that it would have been more culturally sensitive for me to leave her to die. Her Ladyship was too mortified to attend cabinet, and I was more surprised by the reaction of our colleagues, who were weirdly hostile.

"Politics isn't about *doing*," said Humphrey Lowe-Graham at Cabinet. "Good heavens! Do you think Jacques Chirac went around diving into the Seine, or Angela Merkel into the Rhine, or Justin Trudeau into the..?" He paused, hoping someone would intercede with the name of a Canadian river. No one did, so he continued. "Politics is about *talking* - chairing cabinet sub-committees, giving speeches – and you seem to have given up on that, Prime Minister. You hardly say a word in committee these days!"

"Actually, he's giving a speech tomorrow," said Anna Bersonin.

"Am I?"

"Some dull teachers' conference," said Anna. "No opportunities for stuntman heroics, or getting Cabinet totty down to their knickers. Just sticking to the script."

"Keep your trousers on," advised Rupert Henley. "Very few ministers of the Crown can carry off Y-fronts on the front page of *The Sun*."

"By 'very few', you mean you?" said Marjorie.

"I usually go commando for cabinet, Marj."

That seemed to have exhausted that line of conversation, so we moved on to a plan to issue Muslim schoolgirls with spoons to put in their underwear if their dads try to fly them back to Pakistan to marry their cousins. The spoons set off the airport metal detector. Offended by this cultural insensitivity, other Muslims were now shoving cutlery in their underwear and had brought Britain's remaining post-Covid airports to a standstill.

As I thought of it, Humphrey had a point. So later that morning, after reading through the speech I was supposed to give, I decided to write one of my own. I'd made a pretty good start before I was interrupted. I had promised Rupert that I would call upon my "brother" - White Mike, the White Knight, the Right Honourable former Sir (he declined to use his GCMG) Michael Rassendyll, High Representative to the External Zone (Qualified Recognition). And the hour was nigh.

Viewed from Chequers, the High Representative's headquarters was certainly high – set on an elevation looking down in every sense on the mere country house of a footling prime minister. We could have walked there – a few hundred metres through Box Tree Wood and up the hill. But Sir Roger thought it more dignified to take the car – a four-kilometre trip south, east, north, west and south again, just to reach the same destination. So the Jag pulled out of a side entrance of the house and motored up the Missenden Road to a hamlet called Butlers Cross, so called because it was the crossroads where servants for Chequers had once lived. We turned left and passed the Church of St Peter and St Paul, where Margaret Thatcher had prayed the day after the IRA blew up her party conference. On the northern side of a narrow English road it was the usual mix of houses and the occasional field – tamed country. "That's what Mrs T told me she liked about it," said Severn. "The English countryside is beautiful because the English imposed their will upon it." On the southern side amidst the trees the remains of an older, rawer Britain - the ancient motte-and-baileys of Cymbeline's Castle - had once been easy to miss. But now atop a pair of stern gatehouses two giant flags fluttered – that of the European Union and the personal standard of the High Representative. That's right – my "brother" had his own flag.

No sooner had we turned in than the gates clicked open and slowly slid back. We passed along a gravel drive through the wood until the trees cleared and we saw what the European Union had inflicted on an ancient monument to a great British warrior.

THE PRISONER OF WINDSOR

Cymbeline's Castle sits on a shoulder of Beacon Hill. The castle itself is just a mound – all that's left of the regnal seat of a king of the Britons who died around AD 40 – Cymbeline, or Cunobeline: "Strong Dog", as Sir Roger translated it. His kingdom had shrunk to a raised earthwork about forty metres in diameter – that's the motte part - encircled by a ditch, outside of which were the remains of two enclosed courtyards overlooked by the motte – they're the baileys. Nearby was another, later or earlier, motte-and-bailey structure and a Roman villa, dating from the Emperor Claudius's invasion of Britain, which began two or three years after the Strong Dog had died. Yet now, two millennia on, there was a new top dog in town: To loom over Cymbeline's remnants the EU had built White Mike what looked from the north like a neo-Roman villa, and from the south like that giant Euro-eyeball I had seen from the Chequers Prison Room. Cymbeline's Castle was now merely a bit of landscaping to White Mike's lair.

"There's a bit of local folklore," muttered Severn as Vic pulled up to the door. "They say that, if one runs around the mound seven times, the Devil appears. I doubt we'll have to wait that long."

We rang the bell. After some time, a heavyset man with shaven head and close-cropped beard appeared and said, "*Oui? Ja? Si?*" He was Albanian.

"The Prime Minister," said Sir Roger.

The majordomo, if such he was, couldn't have been less impressed. "ID?"

Severn handed over his Palace of Westminster car-park pass. The Albanian examined it carefully, ran it through a scanner, and examined it again, this time with a loupe. Eventually satisfied, he ushered us in.

The main living area of the house was a large oval made of mirrored glass that allowed my "brother" to look out but no one to look in, least of all from down below at Chequers. Suspended in the middle was a huge circular lapis lazuli mosaic with a smaller dark circle bearing the logo of the European Union. Hence, the giant eyeball effect: the lapis lazuli was the iris, and the fifteen gold stars framed the pupil, and the pink concrete walkways hanging below and above functioned as the eyelids. The oval sat on stubby black marble pillars, wherein dwelt and laboured the servants and bureaucrats; above it, another line of pillars extended, to serve as self-contained bedroom suites and White Mike's offices. These were the eyelashes, so to speak. It was undoubtedly better to be inside looking out than outside staring at his hideous architectural disfigurement of the Chiltern Hills.

We entered the central pillar of the edifice and were led up a grand stairway into the well of the eyeball, and from there to a vast living room extending to the "back" of the eye and ending in a spectacular floor-to-ceiling view of which the puny Prime Minister's pitiful rural retreat was just a piffling detail. In the centre of the room was a sunken seating area flanked by a wet bar on one side and a Steinway grand on the other.

The wall was a single ceiling-high piece of curved glass affording a breathtaking panorama. The room itself was cantilevered out above the hill and into the sky, and, as it left solid ground, the ebony floor yielded to reinforced glass, below which one could see solid ground fall away - and also, presumably, get an advance warning of any would-be intruders climbing up to get you. We peered down. "I think this is what the estate agents call a 'drop-dead view'," said Sir Roger, and tiptoed on the glass floor as if it were the thinnest of thin ice.

"Yow rang, milord?"

We jumped, and turned to see my "brother" limping toward us in a white linen suit that set off his translucent face and bleached hair – and behind him, on the wall opposite, the vast blue expanse of a giant map of "The Union and External Zones (Qualified Recognition)". He was bearing a tray of kirs and absinthes and, after motioning us to the sofas, took a chair in between.

"As this escapade seems oonlikely tow end amicably, Roger, oi thought it would be interesting to meet yow lively creation – before whatever thrilling dénouement awaits in this ridiculous diversion."

I had forgotten his voice – the freak side-effect of his environmentally friendly accident. What had Belinda called it at Windsor? A Black Country accent?

"Oi knew the old Countess Amelia story, of course. Not from Pop. Didn't bother telling me. Don't 'ave the Elphberg red, do oi?" He stroked the seven white strands atop his ravaged features with a strange tenderness. The livid blotch on the hairless part of his scalp flared brighter and more intense. "The 'ousekeeper told me. Had tow pick oop family history from the servants, didn' oi?"

He stood up and hobbled over to the sofa, peering down at us. "Do yow even remember the old me, Roger? Before the accident? And this accent?"

Severn took a long, slow puff on his pipe. "Michael," he said quietly, "you dwell too much on this."

"Because there's mooch tow dwell on." He hobbled across the room and stopped at an interactive global-warming model of the British Isles bearing the EuroWind logo and showing Northern Ireland entirely under water and the North Sea and Irish Sea rising to meet in the middle of England and sever Great Britain in two. White Mike stabbed at a button and the Thames drowned Greater London.

"Two broothers at Oxford, both interested in politics. But a senior party figure down from London decides tow bestow his patronage only on one of them." He hobbled across the room, snatched at a praliné-noisette macaroon, and devoured it like a jackal. "All moy loife oi plyed second fiddle tow that weakling. Why? Because his mother was a liedy and mine was not. Our father divorced his mother and could barely stomach being in her presence again. 'E fownd 'appiness with moy mother. But because she worr a Filipina masseuse, because he met her in a massage parlour in Manila, she worr never quite accepted by yow party snobs, was she, Roger?"

"That's not true," said Severn. "We all adored your mum. It's what I loved about the old House of Lords – before Tony Blair wrecked the place. You're right: In those days, a chap with a Filipina masseuse on his arm would have had a hard job getting past the selection committee on a winnable seat for the Commons. But in the Lords? Not a problem: diversity was their strength, as nobody said back then."

"Is that story in the *Express* true? That Robert's planning to wear his earl's robes and coronet to the Coronation? That's all yow fellows care about, isn't it? Long as yow can keep playing your silly dress-up games..."

"What are you wearing for the big day?" asked Severn.

"Oi warren invited, warr oi?" said Michael. "The Duchess of Wokingham's fellow supermodel from that Kazakh yurt gets to go. The High Commissioner of Botswana. The Governor of the bloody

Pitcairn Islands will be there. But not the most powerful man west of Brussels."

Sir Roger put a steadying hand on White Mike's shoulder. "I always liked you," he said. "But I tipped Robert for the top because it requires a certain combination of skills to reach the finial of the greasy pole. You've always been a little …intense."

Michael shook off Severn's bony fingers. "Yow get used to it. The half-brother, the half-breed. So oi've been in the shadow of a degenerate sibling all moi life. And now a ludicrous 'Lord Privy Seal' thinks he can put me in the shadow of the degenerate's lookalike?" He sipped at his absinthe, and gestured at me contemptuously. "Yow doing this for king and country, am yow? But yow not a real king, and this is an imaginary country…" He walked over to the Steinway Grand. "Has Roger shown yow the piano at Burlesdon?"

I shook my head, not sure where this was going.

"Yow can hardly see the bloody thing under all the celebrity photos – my brother with Boris Large, my brother with Carrie Moonbeams, my brother with Nigel and the Reverts. This piano isn't a *Hello!* magazine display stand – because unlike Robert oi can actually play it." He sat down and started a little Chopin, but the crushed knuckles of his useless hand crashed down on the keys. "Or oi could before the accident. The Japanese have developed a female robot that can play Mozart…" He stood up, and went to the window to glower at Chequers far below. "Do yow remember the Rassendyll boys' first party youth conference, Roger?"

"I can't say that I do," replied Severn.

"The last-night talent show," said Michael. "Oi played Brahms - the second violin sonata. Brilliantly. Violin isn't even moi first instrument, just a second string to moi bow. But it was a perfect performance, making allowances for moi pianist, bloody Belinda. Then Rob stood up and sang parody lyrics to 'Wake Me Oop Before Yow Go-Go' about Tony Benn or Neil Kinnock or whoever it bloody was then. And the audience went cryzy and he did foive encores. It didn't even rhyme or scan properly." Michael was visibly seething now. "But it made the news on Magic 107.3 when we were droiving home the next morning."

He fumbled in his jacket pocket. "Oh, oi have souvenir snaps, too," he sneered – and he produced an old print, colours fading, corners curling, showing an ancient party scene. Oxford. Two boys, two girls. Teenage hair and goofy clothes. But both girls with adoring expressions were flanking Rob, cigarette dangling from his lip, party can of beer balanced on his head – and off to one side the other boy, ignored by the ladies and staring sadly into space.

"It was Robert who recommended you for Euro-commissioner," Sir Roger pointed out.

"Yes," said Michael. "Oi used to think it was because 'e couldn't bear to look at me across the Cabinet tyble. But it worr at the time he worr plotting his rise tow Noomber Ten, and Rory Sodding Vane switched on *Newsnight* and there I worr talking about how my brother had all the qualities of a perfect prime minister. And Rory looked at moi... 'ideous... misshapen... grotesque features..." His thin translucent fingers fondled his cheek with each adjective. "...Rory thought a freak sibling disfigured the sheer perfection of Rob Rassendyll. So oi got moved to Brussels, and nobody invited me on *Newsnight* ever again."

He paused, and for the first time spoke with genuine enthusiasm. "Best buggering thing that ever 'appened to me. Politics is joost telly now, isn't it? Like a reality show that never gets cancelled, for people who can't 'ack it on *Big Brother* or *Celebrity Squat*. And with some stupid new challenge every day: Oooh, the VC holder's dog has been ordered to be put down; 'ow will Rob Rassendyll gerrowt of this thrilling cliff-hanger? Maybe some spad will write a Tweet he can use!"

"Meanwhile, elsewhere, some of us are building the future!"

"Do you have one of these piano-playing Japanese sexbots on hand?" asked Severn. "Might help to have a musical interlude right now."

"Wit!" jeered Michael. "Useful for telly, completely irrelevant to anything real." He picked a narrow green tube off an end table. "Seen moi latest venture?" He pointed it at us.

"What is it?" asked Sir Roger.

"It's an envoironmentally friendly gun."

We both leapt out of the way, and he laughed. Severn recovered himself. "Aren't all guns environmentally friendly? They reduce your carbon footprint pretty comprehensively."

"It's all a joke to you, isn't it?" sneered White Mike. "We're thinking of making it standard issue in the European Army. So that when we kill all the populists we can clean up on the carbon credits." He paused, waiting for a reaction. "See, Roger, oi can do jokes, too." Michael flipped the green tubular device back and forth from one palm to the other. "See 'ow light it is? It uses non-lead bullets and an advanced form of bioplastic. We're thinking we can get a chunk of the Yank market – for climate-conscious gun nuts: 'With a green gun, you pack heat; the planet doesn't.'"

He put it back on the table, and returned to the window. Down below Chequers seemed to be getting smaller, receding into the distance. "There is a class of new man," he began.

I hadn't said anything for a while, so I thought this would be a good point to chip in. "I know," I said. "The New Man is a man who is sensitive to women's needs. It came up in cabinet. Humphrey Lowe-Graham says you can get a grant to de-toxify your masculinity."

"Not that kind of new man," snapped Mike Rassendyll. "I'm talking about me and de Gautet and Haan-Zaier. What the pygmies of the Internet call the 'globalists'. We're really an evolutionary breakthrough: Post-tribal man. 'E doesn't care whether he watches *Coronation Street* or smokes Gauloises or wears lederhosen. 'E's beyond all that. That was Angela's great insight when she moved four million Syrians to Germany: Why can't a Syrian wear lederhosen?"

"Because Muslims don't like to bare their knees?" I suggested.

"*Dumbkopf!*" Michael exploded. "Yow think oi care a fig about Mohammedan kneecaps?"

Sir Roger yawned. "Why don't you get your leg over that Japanese robot and breed a new master race?"

"There's an oidea," mused the White Knight, with a teasing smile. "Can't be worse than waking up alone in the Prison Room every weekend…"

"Enough!" said I. "Have you killed your brother?"

"Why would oi want to kill him? The original plan was to cure 'im, and poor 'im back. When 'e's norr off 'is meds, 'e's a perfectly adequate hollow showboating quote-unquote 'head of government'. Then yow came along. Rupert Henley et al wanted me to have yow killed – so we could put my useless brother back. But actually yow're pretty useless too, aren't yow?"

THE PRISONER OF WINDSOR

Mike Rassendyll went back to the window and stared across to Chequers far below. "Do yow recall yowr – lemme see if oi can get this roight - great-great-great-uncle, the Duke of Strelsau?"

"Black Michael?" said I, surprised that he of all people should come up in the conversation.

"Why did they call 'im that?"

"Black hair. Black heart."

White Mike took a swig of his absinthe. "As yow say. But moight it not be that the black 'air led to assumptions about a black 'eart? Black Michael looked so un-Elphberg-like. No red hair, blue eyes and pale skin, such as yow and yowr forebears boast. But black 'air, brown eyes and..." He reached up with one shrivelled useless finger and stroked his cheek. "...sallower, olive skin – like moine was, before the ...accident. A touch of colour prejudice perhaps?"

"There was more to it than that," I said.

"Oh, yes. Black Michael's father married 'beneath 'im'. A second marriage. 'Morganatic'. How very civilised. A morganatic wife of low birth. Hence, the dark hair, dark eyes, dark skin. But at least he married – as opposed to fooking another man's mistress."

My anger flared, and he guffawed. "Defending Lady Belinda's honour? Ow, *please...*"

"It wasn't just the hair," I said. "Black Michael committed treason."

"Did 'e now? Whose word do yow 'ave on that?" He went to the bookcase, and pulled down an old Morocco-bound volume. "From the diary of a British observer's account of the ructions around Rudolf V's coronation:

The city of Strelsau is partly old and partly new. Spacious modern boulevards and residential quarters surround and embrace the narrow, tortuous, and picturesque streets of the original town. In the outer circles the upper classes live; in the inner the shops are situated; and, behind their prosperous fronts, lie hidden populous but wretched lanes and alleys, filled with a poverty-stricken, turbulent, and (in large measure) criminal class. The New Town was for the King; but to the Old Town Michael of Strelsau was a hope, a hero, and a darling.

White Mike turned to another page. "From the diary of a minor British diplomat, George Featherly. A kinsman of Belinda's husband, I understand. Mr Featherly met the Duke of Strelsau at dinner in Paris: 'An extremely accomplished man, I thought him.'"

The White Knight laughed. "Yowr family gorrit wrong," he said, "as Ruritania's rulers always do, whether monarchical, fascist or Communist. That's why the only thing 'olding up yowr silly little country today is EU and Nato subsidies. What yow think of as a palace coup was *noblesse oblige*. Michael was a true public servant – for all those poverty-stricken masses in the Old Town. Rudolf V represented nobody: 'E worr the creature of a decadent leisured Court fearful of its waning influence, a closed ruling class led by men like Marshal Stracenz and Colonel Sapt who'd earned their spurs keeping the peasantry in their place."

"I do declare," said I, "this is the longest disquisition on Ruritanian history I've ever heard."

"Because those who don't learn from 'istory are condemned to repeat it. Yow're on the wrong side of 'istory all over again, Elphberg. Sir Roger has yow waltzing the ladies across the palace ballroom and galloping around on 'orseback up against evil masterminds threatening to undermine the kingdom. What evil mastermind would trouble himself? This kingdom is doing a grand job undermining itself." He spun around and raised his palms. "Look, no 'ands. No sinister masterminds bent on world domination need be involved."

He limped over to two crossed swords set against a faded Burlesdon crest above the fireplace. "I'm a better knight than yow. Best in moi fencing class. I would have won *Duelling with the Stars*, instead of being a mere lookalike for its second banana." He shot me a pitying glance. "The gallant knight who tilts at wind turbines," he sighed.

I stood on the glass floor of the White Knight's giant floating eyeball and looked at Chequers far below. Perhaps Mike Rassendyll was right; perhaps I was wasting my time…

There was a loud snort behind me. "The reborn Rassendyll! What are you up to today? Retaking Heligoland? That's the only language the Hun understands…" I knew the voice, although she was swearing less than usual: Anna Bloody Bersonin.

I turned round. "Hello, Anna."

"Hello ...whoever you are. Mrs Delancey said I'd find you up the hill." She fell back on the sofa in an oddly manspreading position. "God, I'm so exhausted..."

"What are you doing here?" Sir Roger asked.

She didn't seem to hear. "Did you see that item in *Londoner's Diary*? I was so excited: several constituency chairs have reported that I'm the grassroots favourite to topple you. Then I remembered: I'd planted that story, but they'd had to sit on it for a few days because of all the EU governments collapsing... So by the time I read it I'd forgotten it was just the usual bullshit."

"Your voice is higher than usual," I pointed out. "Why's that?"

"When I got into politics," she said, "I was told by some flabby-arsed poufter of a deputy party chairman that people didn't like excessively female voices. He said Mrs Thatcher had gone to a vocal coach to lower hers. So he booked me in too. I got a bit carried away. So I wound up sounding like a cheapskate tranny who's had it done on the NHS. Had enough of it."

Severn asked again why she was here.

"You know how long I've been Home Secretary," she began. Then she stopped, and regarded me oddly. "Well, no, you don't, do you? You're not one of us." She reached over to Michael's tray and took a kir. "In four days' time, I will pass James Chuter Ede's record and become this country's longest-serving Home Secretary. It sounds so nice, doesn't it? 'Home Secretary'. Home is so homely. In the EU they have Ministers of the Interior. The Interior sounds like it's up your bum. Not like home sweet Home Secretary." She looked down at her hands, and clenched them. "It's an evil job. The first grooming scandal, I invited dozens of victims to the Home Office. I sat across a coffee table from them and saw myself: Grew up on a crap street, went to a comp, single mum. Rob liked all that; helps to neutralise the poncey earl stuff, doesn't it? So I looked at them and saw me, maybe a couple of rungs down the socio-economic ladder from me, and definitely a couple more decades on in the fucked-upness of this septic isle, and not as smart as me. Still, I wanted to help ...for a while.

"But I didn't, did I? The girls weren't real to the toffs like Rob and Rupert. And they weren't real to all the new-class types in the government – the gay boys and the dykes and the PR spivs and media wankers who'd made it to Highgate and Islington and Holland Park and couldn't even imagine a Britain where you get pissed on by gang-rapists and then dangled over the council-flat balcony in case you're thinking of squealing about it. They thought it was a political problem to be swept under the carpet. And now the fucking carpet looks like a giant boil on England's mottled lumpy arse with no one to lance it.

"Evil job."

Sir Roger asked a third time: "Why are you here, Anna?"

She looked up at me with a distant smile. "Okay. I'll tell you."

Chapter Thirty-Six
Chuter cum shooter

ANNA PUT HER HEAD in her hands and took a deep breath. Then she sat up straight, with her palms flat on her knees. "I'm becoming a changeling."

I had no idea what she meant. Fortunately, Sir Roger appeared to be on top of it. "You'd be committing career suicide," he said.

"Suits me, when the alternative is actual suicide."

For my benefit, Severn explained that the changelings were a small group of moderate centrist MPs arising from a spasmodic epidemic of party-changing. There were some Conservatives who'd switched to Labour, and vice-versa; LibDems who'd gone Green; an Ulster Unionist who'd joined Sinn Féin; and even a Scots Nationalist who'd become a Welsh Nationalist. After a while, no MP in any party liked them, so, after Brexit, they came together to form the Party for Independence – not independence from Brussels (they were all pro-EU) but for independent-minded politicians who all agreed that Britain can't be independent. They then changed their name to the Movement for Change, because they believed that politics needed to change, even though all the policies (EU, mass immigration, more vaccines, more imams, etc) needed to stay exactly the same. So it was mostly their name that kept changing, and eventually Westminster began referring to them informally but not unaffectionately as "the changelings".

Sir Roger was baffled by Anna's declaration. "Why would you give up one of the Great Offices of State to become part of last year's running joke?"

She practically screamed her answer. "*I can't fucking stand another day of it!*" She fell back on the sofa convulsed in heaving sobs. "There was this bloke," she said to me. "You wouldn't know, but he was an obvious nutter. Claimed that forty years ago he'd been gang-raped by members of the House of Lords when he was twelve in the House of Commons tearoom after hours. Does that make any sense? But because no one wanted to go near the 'Asian'-" She made extravagant and contemptuous air quotes. "-the 'Asian' grooming gangs we had to find some other paedos to look as if we were treating the issue seriously. So we told the Crown Prosecution Service to take a gander at the tearoom bloke. The peelers told him he was very credible. Next thing you know he says he also attended human sacrifices in the smoking room of the Palmerston Club. All these peers, after buggering the arse out of all the little tykes, then ritually slaughtered them and drank their blood. Does that sound remotely plausible, even for the House of Lords? But the sodding Met had run out of *Top of the Pops* presenters who'd copped a feel back in 1972. So I set up an independent inquiry and brought over a Canadian judge, and the coppers, being the lazy jobsworths they are, picked six peers to torment, five of whom were in the late stages of cancer and Parkinson's and brain tumours and Alzheimer's. So there were no trials and they went to their graves ruined. The sixth lost his job and lost his house, and wound up living in the garden shed of his last remaining friend. The Canadian judge eventually figured out the inquiry was a racket, but we made sure she signed the Official Secrets Act before she pissed off back to Little Mooseshit on the Prairie." She raised her head and stared at Severn.

"You don't need to tell me, Anna," responded Sir Roger. "I went back a long way with a couple of those 'paedo peers', as the papers had it. And I spoke out against the inquiry in cabinet."

"Oi remember that," said Michael. "Robert slapped yow down and said we needed tow be seen tow 'believe victims'."

"Even if they're fantasist sociopaths," added Anna.

Roger Severn rose to his feet. "Nature calls, I'm afraid. Old gentleman's problem."

"I wouldn't know," sneered Michael Rassendyll. "Oy'm norra gennelman, am oi?"

Severn said nothing.

"Oi'l do yow a fiver, Roger," White Mike continued. "I won't mike yow use the new viropaper we'll be introwducing in the External Zone. Lubricated recycled microw-thin chipboard." He held up an advance prototype on the table. "Greasy and scratchy" – and he tossed a sheet over his shoulder. "Come on, I'll show yow the way."

They left the room. I was alone with Anna.

She stood up and paced around me. "What are you?" she asked. "I don't believe this Ruritanian lookalike crap. Russian bot? My money's on Chinese clone. They're up to their coolie hats in that shit.

Unless you're Rob pretending to be his own fucking lookalike for a *Five Guys Named Mo* special. 'Cause that's totally the crap he pulls." She reached down to my crotch and squeezed hard. My eyes started to water. "Well, that's more lifelike than my Ken doll…"

She prowled the room restlessly. "I'm not going to be the longest-serving Home Secretary. The final straw was you — well, not *you*, but the real you — you transferring HM Prisons back to my department because poor little Yazmina didn't like having to visit all-male institutions. His Majesty's Prisons — that's a joke, isn't it? When has His Majesty ever gone anywhere near any of them?" She stopped her prowling at the end table on which White Mike had placed his eco-pistol. "What's this?"

"It's an environmentally friendly gun."

"Is it now?" She picked it up. "Ah, fuck it. I don't want to sit with those independent change wankers anyway." And she turned it toward her temple.

"Anna, don't…" I meant it, and she heard the concern in my voice and was so startled by it that her trigger finger paused for a split-second. But it was enough. With a lightning bound I was upon her, and trying to wrest the eco-gun from her grip. My hands held her wrists, my nose parked itself in her cleavage, and I forced Anna back till she lay flat on the sofa. Our eyes locked, I felt her breath on my face, and slowly and patiently I began to work the second-longest-serving Home Secretary's gun hand away from her head. She grasped my plan and her muscles tensed, and by God, she was strong. I thought her right arm would crack, but at last it moved. Inch by inch it was driven down. The elbow gave, and lower and upper limbs gradually broke contact. The sweat broke out on Anna's burning brow, augmented by large drops falling from mine. Now her wrist was moving toward her shoulder, and slowly the fingers of my right hand began to wiggle free of her left and creep toward the green trigger. The grip seemed to have half numbed her arms, and her struggles grew fainter. Round both wrists my fingers climbed and coiled; cautiously the grasp of the other hand was relaxed and withdrawn. Would the one hold both? With a great spasm of effort Anna put it to the proof.

My smile betrayed the answer. I could hold both, with one hand - not for long, no, but for an instant. And then, in the instant, my right hand, free at last, fell on Anna's gun, now pointing directly at the

273

underside of her chin. I tried to push it away from her, which is when I noticed that she was also trying to push it away from her ...toward me. From under her chin to under my chin.

She made another effort, and my one hand, worn out, gave way. I fell back on top of her, exhausted and drenched in sweat, and with a huge involuntary grunt.

"Oh, I say! Didn't mean to interrupt..."

Sir Roger Severn had picked a fine time to return from the men's room, and with him Mike Rassendyll bearing another round of kirs and absinthes and pastis. Finding me and Anna Bersonin locked in clammy, heaving embrace on his sofa, the White Knight recoiled in disgust, as who would not?

I was so embarrassed I failed to notice Anna had squeezed the trigger.

The bullet skimmed the top of my jacket and disappeared into a bookcase behind me.

I fell off the sofa. "No!" wheezed Anna, sharply, at Michael, and swivelled the eco-pistol round to level at White Mike and Sir Roger. "Stay out of this!"

I pulled myself off my back onto my knees, thumped her elbow, and the gun clattered to the floor and skittered under the sofa's end table. She swung round in a fury, clamped her legs around my neck and squeezed. Bloody hell, she was choking me. I was going to die between Anna Bersonin's thighs, which was unbecoming even for a lookalike.

But by concentrating all her strength in her quadriceps she had let the rest of her body relax. In a single move, I reached up, grabbed her arms and threw her off the sofa. Scrabbling across the floor on my knees, I groped wildly, seized the first thing to hand and hurled it at her. It was White Mike's global warming model of the British Isles, and the tip of Scotland hit her square in the forehead, while various bits of ice flew off the east coast of England and peppered her cheeks. I scrambled away again, but she was on my back, her hands around my throat. I rolled sideways, trying to crush her even as she was throttling me. She was not only strong, but quick.

So I elbowed her in the kidneys, and she grunted and relaxed her grip. I sprang free, and across the room. There, above the fireplace - the crossed swords, from when the not yet crippled Michael had come first in his fencing class, wherever that was – Eton? Oxford? I yanked at one, and hoped it hadn't been glued into place against the tatty moth-eaten family crest. No, sir. I swung around and faced Anna Bersonin, blade in hand.

"Bravow!" cried Michael. "A very parfait knight!"

Anna stared dumbfounded for a moment, and then roared her head off. "You're going to run me through with a sword, clone?" She laughed again. "Bloody Nora, the action hero who does his own stunts!" I advanced toward her, but she had no fear. She reached for something on the table, but I warned her not to move. She laughed even louder. "It's only *The Daily Telegraph*, clone," she said. "You're not scared of a newspaper, are you? I was just checking that I'd remembered correctly. What is it that old slapper Belinda Featherly calls you? 'The Last Englishman'?"

She put down the paper and regarded me thoughtfully. "'The Last Englishman.' Ha! Made in China, owned by Russians, hacked by Ruritanian content farmers, like everything else. What sort of 'last Englishman' is that? Surely an English gentleman takes breeding rather than cloning?"

I didn't understand what she meant, so she put it to me directly.

"Will you fight like a gentleman?" she asked. "Let me take the other blade. Or would you rather just run me through?"

She shouldn't have put it that invitingly. "That's the most sensible thing you've said all day." I thrust toward her, and she hurled the *Telegraph* in my face. Bloody huge thing. The last broadsheet newspaper in London. Fell apart in the air. But I'd have made my way through if I hadn't slipped on that prototype sheet of External Zone toilet paper White Mike had tossed over his shoulder. What had he said? "Greasy and scratchy"? I slipped on the grease, and then got a nasty paper cut on my hand trying to cushion the fall. I was on my back, and Anna was over at the fireplace and on the second sword.

"Just as I thought. Not quite a gentleman, are we, clone?"

I staggered to my feet, but she was in no hurry to press her advantage. "At first I thought I'd just turned cynical. And that's good, isn't it? Because cynicism is sophisticated. All the political diarists and the wags on *Newsnight* are cynical. But what I keep trying to work out is when cynical curdled into evil. Because I am evil, aren't I?"

275

Sir Roger and White Mike stepped toward her, but she raised her blade. "This is between him and me. No spads, no spinners. Just the two of us."

The White Knight smiled, and put out a restraining hand to Severn. Then he set down his tray, passed a drink to Sir Roger, and the two men leaned against the wall to see what would happen next.

And, with a slight bow, she took her position. There was a faint flush on her cheek. "Guard yourself, clone," she said.

"Oh, let's get on with i-" And I jumped back, for her blade had touched mine in warning.

And I realised I was going to die in a sword fight at Cymbeline's Castle. Which would add a surreal touch to the obit back in *Der Außenwelt*.

I crossed her blade. Then again. The steel jangled. Her sword ran up mine with a sharp, grating slither. She lunged, I withdrew. I lunged, she pulled back, quicker, warier, sharper. I grasped, as at the King's tennis match, that I had no idea what I was doing. And then I felt something and cried out. Anna's voice was merry with triumph: "Nearly! nearly!"

I glanced down at the small bubble of blood on my wrist.

"A little prick," she jeered.

And then her blade was slithering up mine again, and I was driven backwards, step by step. I bounced off the arm of a chair and stumbled back into her path.

"You're supposed to be an actor," she crowed. "Know your lines and don't bump into the furniture."

And I lunged again, and grazed her, but it was enough to catch her by surprise.

Anna had strength and will. More importantly, her mind and her eye were perfectly coordinated, and her hand obeyed them as swiftly as the automatic weapon in a computer game. I'd fenced as a teenager. It was Harry's idea, and he enjoyed it. He liked the sport enough to get good at it. But not me. Anna could sense that. Even at my best, I was doing no more than maintaining my defence against her ever wilier feints. The Home Secretary's hand was almost motionless. *Almost* - for the merest, barely perceptible turns of wrist sent her blade whirring and dancing from my left to my right, from face to belly.

THE PRISONER OF WINDSOR

Anna could see it in my eyes: I could, if I concentrated, keep my skin whole for her next thrust, but she would break down my guard eventually. A flicker of amusement teased her lips, but she checked it. What mattered was that she knew the way things stood: I lunged once more, and almost pressed her against the panelling. Almost. *Almost.*

She pricked me again, deeper this time – and there was a faint hissing sound as her sword withdrew. "A trial of steel," she chortled. "I was best swordsman in my class at Grimwich Comp. I use it like Derek Detchard uses his cock."

She lunged yet again, and came very close. For five minutes our steel clashed. She ran her blade up mine, and breathed, hard, fierce and heady.

"There was an Australian blogger," she wheezed. "Full of shite like they are. Mouthing off about 'plandemics' and 'depopulation agendas'. We were shutting down a free-speech demo in Luton, and he got lippy with a copper. Then in court he started swearing at the judge. Very Oz. Got thirty days for contempt in HMP Tea-Cosy. Someone in the department thought it might be a big up-yours to these 'citizen-journalists' if we transferred him somewhere harder. I sort of knew where they were going with this, but I signed off on it anyway. Third night he was there, six of the jihad boys jumped him. He's a vegetable now, so no more blogging."

Her sword was on mine again.

"I thought I'd feel bad about it. But nobody else did, not even the Aussie government. They hated the bugger, too. So I was surprised, after a day or two, that I felt fine. Made it easier to do it again." Her blade slithered up mine once more. "And again." I was driven backwards step by step, bounced off the arm of a chair and stumbled back into range of her blade.

"Like I said, evil job. And I've done it longer than anyone, so I'm more evil than anyone."

She lunged suddenly. I'd forgotten, midst her soliloquising, that we were supposed to be fencing, and I jumped back. She laughed. "You're not a 'man'. You're not even a play-actor. You're Colin Corgi! A sock puppet. Roger Severn sticks his arm up your botty and wiggles you around." She held my glance, and then turned to Severn. "Wiggle away, Roger! I'll kill him for the fun of it."

My sword fell. Again. Must stop doing that. Anna considered the matter. She could kill me now. But her blood was up. She'd been invigorated by the duel.

She stood over me. "Pick it up."

"Right. And you'll truss me while I do it."

"You useless 'alf-inch dick, you don't know me at all, do you? I'm not like Rob and Rupert and the playing fields of Eton, duplicitous fucks. I'm so tired of nice people who have a thousand reasons for doing nothing when townloads of girls get gang-raped. I'm tired of civilised persons in offices with oil paintings of fuckin' marquesses on the wall who can sign a form and get you put in a coma at His Majesty's Pleasure. I just want to kill you out in the open, in a fair fight. So pick it up. I'll wait."

She lowered her blade, and rested its point on the floor, while her left hand indicated my own sword. "It's an interesting question, isn't it?" she said. "Do evil people know they're evil? Did Hitler? Or Mao? Or did they just think they were doing what's best for their country? Like I did – for a while. Hard to keep it up, though. Not when you're going to be Home Bloody Secretary forever."

I got to my sword, but she got to me, as our blades reared between us, and we stood nose to nose. I was jammed against the wall. With her right hand Anna had pinned my left arm to the panelling above my head. With her left hand, she held my right wrist as I tried to manoeuvre my sword between us. It wasn't her strength that froze me. It was her eyes, bright and merciless. I don't know what she saw in return, but I could feel my teeth biting my under-lip, the sweat pouring, the veins swelling on my forehead. Millimetre by millimetre her hand on my wrist curved the blade between us, angling it toward me. My sword had pointed straight up, and now like a clock it began to tick its way to five and then ten past. It moved quicker now, for I was losing the strength to resist. I was beaten, and she could feel it, and read it in my eyes. The fingers on my left hand fumbled and touched a picture on the wall above. I tensed them, pushed up, and shoved it off its nail. The portrait came crashing down on both of us, a portrait of Jean-Claude Juncker. Alarmed by the sight of the "Father of the External Zone" tumbling her way, Anna jerked backwards just in time – but not fast enough to prevent the sword being knocked from her hand.

THE PRISONER OF WINDSOR

I lunged, but she threw herself backward, almost acrobatically, and in one smooth move stretched her arm out and her hand under the end table to retrieve the White Knight's environmentally friendly gun. She paused, lying there on the rug, with a sly smile and her weapon cocked. I leapt away, wildly, instinctively, and found myself on the glass floor projected out over the view below.

And that's when she fired. As wildly as my leap. I forget how many shots. But I heard the glass at my feet crack and splinter and then, as if in slow motion, drop away. Flailing as I fell, I grabbed wildly for something, and one hand found the edge of the main floor – the solid floor, the brilliantly gleaming ebony. That was all I had: hanging off with four fingers and one thumb and straining desperately to get my other hand up there. I could see nothing of the room above me, but I heard Sir Roger cry "Rudy!" – the first time he had used my name – and Mike Rassendyll yelled too: "Yow bloody stupid bitch! Do yow know how mooch that floor cost?"

And then I saw two stiletto heels standing at the edge. Anna had retrieved her blade and was smiling down at me.

"Saudi justice," she said. "Amputation for thieving. You stole Number Ten." And she raised her sword in order to deliver one swift clean slice through my wrist.

And at that moment, with a great baying "*Nooooooooooooooo!*", Sir Roger Severn charged, and he and Anna came flying off the edge, knocking me from my tenuous grip and sending all three of us tumbling through space.

We crashed down into the ruins of two thousand years of British history – in one of Cymbeline's baileys, or rather in some scrub that had grown up in it and softened our landing. I landed on a tangle of branches, which helped break my fall, and Sir Roger landed on me, which helped break his.

Anna Bersonin wasn't so lucky. She fell with her fingers clenched around her sword. Indeed, my impression was that she was waving it wildly in order to spear me in mid-descent. Instead, she landed on hard ground, and the blade drove up through her jaw and into her skull.

There was a faint smile on her lips. Her head snapped back, her arms fell limp, she wobbled, and sagged. I reached out my hand, and her fingers twitched as if wanting to pull me into hell with her. Her eyes burned for an instant and then faded. And the second longest-serving Secretary of State for the Home Department in British history came to the end of her not quite record-breaking tenure.

Chapter Thirty-Seven
The winter of our discontent farmers

DESPITE MY BREAKING his fall, Roger Severn had landed awkwardly and twisted an ankle, which made the limp back through Box Tree Wood to Chequers somewhat more protracted and nerve-wracking. When we finally staggered into the forecourt of "my" residence, we looked like scarecrows, with grass and straw poking out from our hair and clothes, and mud smears all over. Neither Vic nor Sanjay nor Mrs Delancey seemed entirely persuaded by our insistence that it was a lovely day for a stroll. "Well, you've earned your lapsang souchong today, Sir Roger," the last murmured sympathetically, as she showed us into the Great Hall. Severn was woozy and breathing hard.

As soon as the door closed, I said, "Get me out of this. I can't take any more. All the way back, I was expecting White Mike's Albanian gangsters in full pursuit spraying AK47s."

Slumped on the sofa, Sir Roger croaked out: "Prime Minister, do you think we might not be more comfortable taking tea in the Hawtrey Room?" He stared me in the eyes, and then with some difficulty raised himself up and tottered off. I followed.

Safely removed to the Hawtrey Room, I demanded to know what all that was about.

"As you might have noticed when President Kennedy's Secret Service chaps came abseiling down to give you a damn good thrashing, the Great Hall is a two-story room. Halfway up the wall is a gallery. It is extremely easy for someone on the floor above us to enter the gallery unseen and eavesdrop on those below. Churchill's personal secretary did it all the time."

"Are you suggesting that Mrs…"

"Delancey."

"…that she'd deliberately…"

There was a knock on the door, and there she was. "I know Sir Roger likes his Hobnobs," she said. "And I thought you might appreciate some hot buttered crumpets. Usual seat for you, PM?"

281

When she'd departed, I asked why the Albanians hadn't pursued us.

Sir Roger nibbled his Hobnob meditatively. "Priorities. Michael has a Cabinet minister's body to dispose of."

"Poor Anna," I said.

"Whom the gods would destroy, they first make Home Secretary. It's a filthy posting."

I wondered how we were going to explain one less Minister of the Crown in Cabinet meetings and the House of Commons, but Severn said, somewhat coldly, that Anna was Michael's problem. I pointed out that, in the event the White Knight simply called the police, my fingerprints were all over the body.

"Exactly," said Sir Roger, exhaling, for once, an imperfect Z. "Your prints, not Robert's. Besides, I don't believe the jurisdiction of His Majesty's Constabulary extends to the redoubt of the High Representative."

This country was mad, and it had driven Anna mad. Homicidal Home Secretaries? Even in Albania, cabinet ministers leave that sort of thing to their underlings.

Severn departed, and in the car back to Downing Street I worked on tomorrow's big speech. All things considered, Marjorie had had a good point in Cabinet: if the alternative was Anna Bersonin running you through with a sword, better surely to win the day with rapier-like wit – the honest jousting of free expression and open debate. I thought my draft was coming along very nicely, and was feeling pretty pleased with the thing by the time I retired to the flat and my trusty Bombay Bad Boy Pot Noodle.

Unfortunately, I made the mistake of switching on the BBC. I recognised it as *Zlapp & Tickell*, the popular situation comedy about a Ruritanian and an Englishman living together in Mayfair. Zlapp is not really a Ruritanian name, but it is quite funny as British comedy goes. However, after the punchline to the joke, the camera cut to a severe-looking blonde woman with an aquiline nose and pursed lips, dressed in the usual BBC severe trouser-suit. prowling what looked to be some sort of dungeon. She was labelled as "Gabriella Waitrose, National Security Editor" and began to speak:

THE PRISONER OF WINDSOR

For many Britons, that's their only acquaintance with a faraway country of which we know little: Every Tuesday we tune in for the comic adventures of dim-witted English man-about-town Sir Aubrey Tickell and the brilliant Ruritanian manservant Zlapp, who somehow manages to rescue him from all his scrapes. But what if the Ruritanians are far more brilliant than we suspect? And what if we unsuspecting British are too dim-witted to realise what they're up to? Tonight on Panorama *a special investigation: Have Ruritanian content farmers stolen our democracy?*

There followed the usual doom-laden opening titles, followed by a clip of Hillary Clinton on a book tour to promote *Why Did I Lose? Volume Seven*. She was onstage in Malibu sitting opposite Oprah Winfrey when a question about whether it was a mistake not to campaign in Wisconsin brought her to her feet, yelling, "HAVE YOU ANY IDEA WHAT IT'S LIKE TO HAVE VICTORY SNATCHED FROM YOU BY RURITANIAN… CONTENT… FARMERS???"

Oprah backed her chair away cautiously, and at that moment Mrs Clinton's legs buckled and she fell into the orchestra pit.

"For many national-security analysts," continued Gabriella Waitrose, "that was the first time they had heard the phrase 'Ruritanian content farmers'." And to my astonishment I saw that she was now standing in the old Rudolfplatz in Hofbau! In the distance behind her, one could make out a couple of locals urinating against the plinth of Rudolf III. "Hofbau," explained Ms Waitrose, "is a poor town even by Ruritanian standards. The average weekly wage here is about seven pounds eighty-three. Yet in the months before the most recent vaccine launch some Hofbau teenagers were earning as much as forty thousand pounds per month from click-throughs to ClotShot.com. At Hofbau prices, forty grand buys a lot of slivovitz." One of the lads behind her was now vomiting on the right fetlock of Rudolf III's horse.

"But what," said Gabriella, "if Ruritania's already sophisticated content farmers were ready to take it to the next level? And, under cover of the Ruritanian plumbing boom, had set up their manipulative content farms right here in Britain?"

And to my further astonishment Ms Waitrose was now back in London, standing outside the Big Tex Diner, a stone's throw from the

Great British B&B. "From the outside, the Big Tex looks like just another third-rate American fast-food franchise, full of tasteless rubbery croissants with indigestible fillings, and burnt macchiatos with badly frothed milk."

She had Otho's number, I had to concede.

"But what," intoned Gabriella solemnly, "if the fast-food franchise is pulling a fast one?" And with that she pushed open the door.

Otho seemed pleased to see her. "Oh, yoss. We are full-service Internet café. Full service." He was seated at his computer terminal, and by way of demonstration logged on to the Internet.

"You use Windows 98," said Gabriella, "because it's no longer supported by Microsoft, and so leaves fewer digital fingerprints?"

Otho didn't fully grasp the question. "The English schoolgirls leave fingerprints," he explained. "But I always wipe down the screen. Even before the China virus, you don't want to know where those girls have been."

"And can you get Twitter on this computer?"

Otho clicked and stared at a Tweet from John Bull calling for the expulsion of the High Representative and an end to rule from Brussels, concluding with #BrexitBetrayed.

"And you can reTweet this all over the world?"

"Oh, sure," said Otho, and did so, flattered to be able to demonstrate his mastery of the technology.

"And 'John Bull' is a subtle Russian bot account masquerading as the stereotypical British white-supremacist icon of the nineteenth century?"

"No. He's a Guyanan who lives in Kentish Town. Laddie did his bathroom." And he motioned to Ladislas, watching fascinated from his usual seat the BBC's in-depth investigation of his compatriot.

"I would avoid that computer," Lady Belinda's plumber advised the BBC reporter. "It will put gay porn in your timeline." He'd done the same joke with me. (Laddie only has eight quips, and I'd heard them all.)

"But gay porn is the least of it," said Gabriella's voiceover over a graphic of mysterious wiring snaking all over a map of the United Kingdom to throttle the very life out of these islands. "What else is this computer putting into your timeline?"

THE PRISONER OF WINDSOR

And the producers cut to a reTweet of Rob Rassendyll shaking hands with a man called Ted Cruz.

Chapter Thirty-Eight
Of modules and men

AT THE 7.45 I WAS EXCITED about my big speech in Manchester, but nobody else was. Instead, the main topic was Gabriella Waitrose's explosive investigation blowing the lid off Ruritanian content-farmer penetration. "Five and Six are calling for a cobra," said Rory Vane.

"No Ruritanian has any fear of a cobra," I replied. I was thinking back to those scorpion-in-a-stein challenges after last orders in Hofbau. But Rory meant that MI5 and MI6 were demanding a top-level emergency security meeting – i.e., a COBRA, which, like so many things in government, is less exciting than it sounds: COBRA stands for Cabinet Office Briefing Room A, which is somewhere in an underground tunnel between Number Ten and the Foreign Office. It used to be King Henry VIII's "real tennis" court. See what I mean? One minute, giraffes and caterpillars; next a cobra. Big deal.

In non-Ruritanian news, following Baroness al-Ghoti's emergence from the Thames in dripping bra and panties, her father, a retired carpet importer from Bradford, had been arrested outside the lady Lord Chancellor's London flat where he was loitering and in possession of a machete. Yazmina herself was said to be "taking a well-earned break". I wondered if Anna had any loved ones. As a practical matter, the Six Big Beasts of the Cabinet were now down to four: Henley, Detchard, Craftstone, Lowe-Graham.

Immediately after the 7.45, I was driven to RAF Northolt to board once more Earl Force One. My aides finally stopped going on about cobras and settled down to focus on today's big event. "So," I began, calmly pouring myself a bottle of Black Country spring water, "these chaps I'm speaking to today…"

"The National Alliance of Educators," prompted Millie.

"The government can always use more alliances. Who's in this one?"

"Nuts," she replied.

THE PRISONER OF WINDSOR

Being familiar with the pithy European Union acronym for sub-national regions, I was about to start twittering about Scotland and Northern Ireland, but fortunately Rory interceded.

"National Union of Teachers and Students," he said.

"Nasuwt," she continued.

"National Association of... Well, that's a bit trickier. One of these merged unions. National Association of Schoolmasters and Union of Women Teachers, I believe."

"Ayeeowaaah," wailed Millie.

"Anglican Educational Outreach Association," explained Rory.

"Addysg Cymru," said Millie.

"Something Welsh," translated Rory. "I wouldn't worry about it."

"The Recovery Centre for Black Historical Memory," continued the Dame. "The Irish Catholic Progressive School Movement. Gayducate – the Federation of LGBTQQI Teachers. The British Madrassah Committee of the Islamic Supreme Council."

"Och, dinna worry aboot th' Supreme Islamic This an' That," said Angus. "Echie nor orchi aboot Colin Coorgi on t'dae's agenda."

Earl Force One taxied down the runway and the cul-de-sacs of London suburbia fell away behind us. England looked very planned, at least from the sky. We landed at Manchester in a frigid rain. The good news was that in the car Wendy seemed marginally less icy than the weather.

"Robert," she said, only semi-hostile.

"Wendy," I replied. "You look lovely this morning." I could see her toying with a withering putdown and then abandoning it. Encouraging.

We drove downtown to a decayed edifice in what I believe they call Gothic Revival style. For a supposedly pogonophobic nation, there were a lot of bearded blokes milling around, a third of them extremely hirsute and wearing the *shalwar kameez* of South Asia and Northern England; another third with tattier whiskers and the traditional corduroy of classroom socialists; and the final tranche with exquisitely trimmed face fungus but some sort of triangular pink tassled mortar board calling for an end to hate in education. Across the street, held back by crash barriers and a beefy blue line of coppers, were demonstrators from the Supreme Islamic Council, or possibly the

Islamic Supreme Council, and the Transgender Cislesbian Alliance, or possibly the Translesbian Cisgender Alliance. I gave them a cheery wave. The trans protesters chanted back: "Hey, hey, Rassendyll! How many kids are you gonna kill?" while the cislesbians opted for "Top, bottom, femme, butch! We reject your fascist putsch!" Something to do with my proposal to reduce the increase in funding for Pink Shirt Day.

We turned left and were deposited outside the stage door, which was locked. So we had time for several choruses of both the "Top, bottom, femme, butch!" chant and "England is the cancer/Islam is the answer", which didn't exactly work contrapuntally. The thin blue line of northern coppers strained to hold back the pacifists, while we waited for the lethargic *Jobwert* to open the door and admit us.

We got to the wings just in time to hear:

> *Please welcome the Prime Minister, and a good friend to education in a multicultural society, the Right Honourable Robert Rassendyll!*

They began to applaud, tepidly.

"Best of British, PM," mumbled Dame Millie without enthusiasm. I froze. She gave me a little shove and I emerged, blinking into the glare, on stage. I had a strange nauseous feeling, which I realised was my *Arschloch* climbing up my gullet and into my mouth. For some reason, I was finding this more nerve-wracking than diving into the Thames or the clash of steel atop Cymbeline's Castle. Walking the walk, sure, but talking the talk? *C'mon, Elphberg, you can do it!* I waved breezily through the blinding lights to the unseen audience, and then greeted the dignitaries on stage, grasping firmly the supreme hand of the Supreme Leader of the Islamic Supreme Council of Supremely Supreme Islam, grasping limply the limp wrist of the Arch Canon of the Anglican Squishy Multifaith Outreach Losers' Association, hugging the gay guy with the pink tassle, ignoring the scowl from the adjoining supreme imam who declined to hug along, mwa-mwaing the chicky alongside after failing to notice she was in a hijab. She recoiled in horror, so I recoiled back, as if it's some showbiz thing. Then I placed my speech on the podium, glanced at the teleprompter to my left, and the one to my right, and set off.

THE PRISONER OF WINDSOR

"Ladies and gentlemen," I began, confident that in the sea of beards at least one or two of them belonged to women. "Thank you very much. It's an honour to be invited here for this inspirational gathering. We meet today at the dawn of a new reign – a new Arthurian era. Much has changed since the last King Arthur. Today we are a land of many races, many religions, many sexualities, many genders, and we all have a seat at the Round Table – black knights, gay knights, Muslim knights, trans knights or ladies, as the case may be…"

Yes, yes, I know that's the most utterly steaming pile of brain-dead claptrappy codswalloping bosh and balderdash that's ever passed mine or anybody else's lips. But I just threw it in to warm up the crowd, and it did get a round of applause. Just goes to show. Maybe it was my delivery.

"And through it all," I read on, "runs the golden thread of our beloved Crown, which, as Winston Churchill said on a speaking tour of Canada in 1929, 'links us all together with the majestic past that takes us back to the Tudors, the Plantagenets, the Magna Carta, habeas corpus, petition of rights, and English common law …all those massive stepping stones which the people of the British race shaped and forged to the joy, and peace, and glory of mankind'."

The audience looked baffled by this, as if they weren't aware that Winston Churchill had made a speaking tour of Canada in 1929.

"Nevertheless," I read on, "even in a diverse society built on mutual respect, there remain points of contention. As you know, there have been protests at home and riots abroad over the decision of the BBC to have Colin Corgi co-present its Coronation coverage. I too have concerns about the BBC. After all, they're hardly great supporters of mine…"

Self-deprecating humour. Can't go wrong with that, can you?

"And I too am concerned about Colin Corgi."

The room applauded loudly. When the cheers had died down, I continued:

"I am concerned that we will concede on this as we have conceded on so much."

The crowd fell silent. Sitting in the front row, the Supreme Ruler of the Supreme Council eyed me warily.

"Perhaps none of these concessions was important in and of itself. Some Danish cartoons whose publication we deplored. A

Continental – quote - 'Islamophobe' – unquote – we deported when he landed at Heathrow to give a speech. The NHS advising its staff against eating snacks during Ramadan. An anthropomorphised pig the watchdog OffSwitch banned from television. A novel whose publication was cancelled after threats of violence. A Yorkshire schoolteacher forced into hiding. Single-sex swimming sessions at municipal pools. The lessons we no longer teach in history classes – on the Crusades, World War Two and the Holocaust...

"Many of these issues seem comparatively trivial – including, at least to our police and social services, even the sacrifice of thousands of white working-class girls condemned to child sex-slavery in dozens of towns up and down England. But cumulatively what they and other ostensibly minor matters communicate is one consistent underlying message - that we are willing to trade core values and fundamental rights for a quiet life. The right to say what you believe, the right to draw what you want, the right to eat when you're peckish, the right of all female Britons to live the lives they choose - and yes, the right of canine puppets to present television shows without facing investigation by the watchdog OffSwitch. Who watches the watchdog, eh? If Colin Corgi is to be dispatched to the knacker's yard, who's next?

"It is characteristic of free societies that our instinct is to avoid conflict. And so we tell ourselves that we make these concessions because we're 'tolerant' and 'sensitive'. Incremental surrender is less immediately painful than instant total surrender, but it leads to the same state." On the prompter, I had helpfully written a stage direction: "[STARE STRAIGHT AHEAD AND LOOK DETERMINED]". So I did as I was told:

"I did not become the King's first minister in order to preside over the liquidation of the United Kingdom."

Churchill. Can't go wrong with Winnie, can you? So I was surprised by the boos, and even more surprised to see that straight ahead of me in the front row were Angus and Millie who, for the entire length of my determined stare, were staring right back with slack jaws hanging about three inches above the floor. So I stopped staring determinedly straight ahead, and ploughed on.

"After September 11th 2001, many on the left thought America and the west needed to ask ourselves: 'Why do they hate us?'"

There was sustained applause for this. "Actually, I don't think they do hate us, so much as they despise us," I read on. "A more relevant question is: 'Why do *we* hate us?'"

I'd emphasised the "we" as advised by my own stage directions, but the crowd seemed to receive the line coldly. So I ad-libbed:

"I mean, c'mon, we're not so bad, are we?"

The chill in the room grew more pronounced, so I returned to the script.

"As we in Britain know, all predominant power seems for a time invincible, but is, in fact, transient. The question is: What do you leave behind? I know what Britain has bequeathed the world. Today, three-sevenths of the G7 major economies are nations of British descent. When it comes to the global rankings of economic freedom, nine out of the top twelve nations are British-derived, from Singapore to Mauritius. Why do *we* hate us? Of the twenty economies with the highest GDP per capita, no fewer than eleven are current or former realms of the Crown. And, if you protest that many of them are tiny islands like Bermuda, colonial pinpricks, then eliminate all territories with populations lower than twenty million and the Top Four is an Anglosphere sweep: the United States, Britain, Canada and Australia. So why do *we* hate us? Think how great the world would be if the whole planet had had the benefit of being a British colony."

The crowd erupted in angry shouts, but I ploughed on:

"That's my message to you today. When it comes to providing the conditions that enable large numbers of people to live in peace, health and prosperity all but unknown to human history, you can't beat the Britannic inheritance. The key regional players in almost every corner of the globe are British-derived - South Africa, India - and, even among the lesser players, as a general rule you're better off for having been exposed to British rule than not: Why is Haiti Haiti and Barbados Barbados?"

At this point the boos resumed.

"As for the allegedly inevitable hyperpower of the new age, if China truly achieves that status, it will only be because the People's Republic learned more from British Hong Kong than Hong Kong ever did from Chairman Mao's Little Red Book. What a pity that the entirety of China was never a British colony."

There were more boos at this.

"Like many of you, I am a great admirer of Stephen Harper..."

The booing stopped, and the audience looked at me with a great unified blankness.

"...the, er, former Prime Minister of Canada," I explained. "Speaking to the Canada-UK Chamber of Commerce... Anybody here today from the Canada-UK Chamber of Commerce?" I ad-libbed.

Again, nothing but audience-wide befuddlement.

"Well, anyway, Mr Harper said – quote – 'Much of what Canada is today we can trace to our origins as a colony of the British Empire. Now I know it's unfashionable to refer to colonialism in anything other than negative terms ...but in the Canadian context, the actions of the British Empire were largely benign and occasionally brilliant.'" I was about to say, "I think that's something we can all agree on", but it would have been drowned out by the jeers.

When the jeering died down, I continued: "And not just in Canada but in India and Australia and almost every corner of the globe, to where Britain, as Mr Harper said, exported parliamentary democracy, basic freedoms, the Industrial Revolution, the free-market economy, not to mention Shakespeare, Dickens, Kipling..."

"Racist!" someone yelled.

"Kipling? Or Stephen Harper?" I asked.

"You!" he yelled back.

I thought it best to ignore that and chugged on. "So I ask again: why do *we* hate us?"

I'd reprised the "why do we hate us?" line as a bit of a crowd-pleaser, assuming the audience would be cheerily bellowing along by this stage. Instead, it was received in stony silence, until someone yelled, "Bollocks!"

I smiled genially. "In terms of your best shot at liberty, a long life, a decent standard of living, and civic structures that allow you to fulfil your God-given potential, nothing beats having been part of the British Empire. Why can't we say that once in a while?"

There were more sustained jeers at this. Can't think why. I mean, I know I'm a dispossessed king so I suppose I'd be more partial to imperialist romanticism than the average union leftie, and I was in a sentimental mood that day I'd been tootling around Westminster Abbey. But I'd asked the 7.45 perching spads to get me all the statistics, and it seemed pretty fact-based compared to most political speeches. Hard to see why everyone would start booing. Nor was I sure quite what the form was on this prime ministerial public-speaking business. Was it like open-mike night in Hentzau? Time to put down the hecklers? I was tempted to say, "Oh, lighten up, you losers. You know it's true." But it didn't seem likely to help.

So I slogged on:

"Britain's influence has been so great that we assume our values and the global order and prosperity they undergird are permanent and universal. In fact, they derive from a very particular cultural inheritance and may well not survive it. Yet, instead of teaching our children to preserve and promote this inheritance, we worry about 'saving the planet'...."

Here, I had inserted the stage directions "[ROLL EYES]", but I thought it best to skip that bit.

"There is an arrogance and self-indulgence behind that presumption. Professions of generalised concerns about 'world poverty' or 'saving the planet' testify not so much to your idealism as to a narcissistic complacency about the permanence of our liberties: We worry about lofty and distant problems because we assume there are none closer to home. Well, there are. The planet will be just fine. Why not try saving the nation from squandering that glorious inheritance? Saving your county from a descent into mutually hostile self-segregating socio-cultural ghettoes? Saving your school from abusive social engineering and bodily self-mutilation modelled on utopian fantasies? Saving your town from the depravity of so-called 'grooming gangs' who like to urinate on small girls or douse them in petrol and dance around them waving matches? Or does that lack the universalist glamour of healing the planet?"

"Bollocks!" yelled the guy who'd yelled "Bollocks!" the last time.

"Racist bollocks!" the guy who'd yelled "Racist!" corrected him.

"Climate denier!" yelled a third party.

"Only last month," I continued, "Emmanuel College at Cambridge ordered students to change their plans for an 'Empire Ball' that would 'party like it's 1899' after there were protests by so-called 'anti-fascist' groups. How have we reached the point that Britain's glorious past cannot be celebrated at Cambridge University?"

"You're the fascist!" shouted a burly lady in the third row.

A Mitteleuropean king reduced to a one-bedroom flat by the vicissitudes of mid-twentieth century Continental politics is the wrong person to bandy these terms lightly with. I departed from the script and fixed her with a beady eye. "If I were a fascist, madam," I said, with as much of a thin-lipped sneer as a third-rate lookalike actor could manage, "if I were a fascist, madam, why would I be defending the British Empire? In 1940, in that critical year after the fall of France, madam, the British Empire stood alone against fascism. If it weren't for the British Empire, madam, you might well be living under fascism today. Why don't you teach that to your pupils?"

"Sexist!" she shouted back. "Stop calling me madam!"

"I ask again," I asked again, returning to the autocue. "How have we reached the point that Britain's glorious past cannot be celebrated at Cambridge University?"

I had intended it as a rhetorical question, but the guy from the Black Historical Memory group in the front-row reserved seats decided to answer it. "Because of the British Empire's association with slavery!" he yelled.

As it happened, my last bit of work before the Pošhspicě mustard commercial had been as an extra sitting behind William Wilberforce for an American Evangelical TV network that had outsourced its ninety-second video series of "Christian Heritage Moments" to Modenstein.

"The British Empire's association with slavery?" I scoffed, scoffily. "Sir, the British Empire's principal association with slavery is that it abolished it. Until William Wilberforce spoke up, and the British Parliament voted, and the brave men of the Royal Navy acted, until then, slavery was an institution regarded by all cultures around the planet as a permanent feature of life – as eternal as the earth and sky. Britain expunged it from most of the globe, sir. Why don't you teach your pupils that?"

"Crap!" He was about to stand, but slumped back into his seat, momentarily stymied.

"As the American right-wing alt-right alt-wing commentator Ben Shapiro likes to say," I said, having come across it on the Internet, "facts don't care about your feelings."

"That's a misquote surely," said the bloke who'd yelled crap. "It's 'My feelings don't care about your facts.' I saw it on a T-shirt."

We were at a bit of an impasse over that, so I returned to the script.

"Cambridge University demanded that the Empire Ball Committee remove the word 'Empire' from all promotional material. The way things are going in Britain it would make more sense to remove the word 'balls'."

In public speaking, particularly on a serious subject, I always think it's good to vary the tone by throwing in something light and humorous, don't you? So I was rather pleased with my little joke, and was pretty confident it would get a big laugh. Instead, the crowd erupted in fury, hooting, jeering, hurling crumpled-up flyers for the day's program: "The Rt Hon Robert Rassendyll, MP, speaks on the challenges of education in a multicultural society."

Well, you can't say I hadn't lived up to the billing.

"There is a lesson here for all of us: When a society loses its memory, it descends inevitably into dementia."

That wasn't Churchill. I nicked it from Roger Severn at our first dinner at what felt like half-a-lifetime ago. As if to underline his point, the audience was now doing a passable impersonation of Bedlam, the entire auditorium churning with firebreathing imams, belligerent polytechnic Trotskyites, surly gays, trans activists, and hand-wringing Anglican clerics squirming in agony as if someone were twisting a pineapple up their bottoms.

From the posh seats of the on-stage panel behind me, a woman stood up and yelled into the microphone: "What about blacks and homophobia?"

That caught me by surprise, but I gave it my best shot. "Blacks and homophobia? Like when gangsta rappers rap about wanting to beat up the gays? Or when Louis Farrakhan of the Fruit of Islam accuses the Jews of manufacturing bad marijuana to feminise the black man?"

"That's not what I mean!" she snorted. According to her name-card, she was Professor Gillian Arkroyd, co-chair of Nasuwt.

"They're two separate questions. Question one: what about our treatment of black people? Question two: what about our homophobia? And how dare you try and dodge my question by racistly suggesting blacks are homophobic? That's totally racist."

It wasn't in the stage directions, but this time I rolled my eyes for real. "Boring," I replied. "Calling somebody totally racist is totally gay."

For a moment, she stood there with open mouth and a semi-cross-eyed look. Then she got her groove back. "This constant hegemonic vilification of Caribbean homophobia is an attempt to distract from the real culprit – four hundred years of colonial oppression in the West Indies, rooted in the sodomy of male slaves by white owners as a means of humiliation."

I shuffled through the script, but there didn't seem to be any reliable statistics on Caribbean plantation owners sodomising the workers. Why hadn't one of those perching spads back at Number Ten given me the briefing paper on that? "Aren't we getting a little off-track?" I suggested.

She sensed my weakness. "I teach a module in Post-Colonial Self-Conflict Resolution at Nottingham!" she replied indignantly. "Why vilify Jamaicans for their homophobia when their phobias about homosexuality all came from us?"

The audience bayed its approval.

I tried to follow her line of thought. "So you're saying," I responded, "that if we hadn't enslaved these fellows and taken them to be our playthings under the Caribbean moon they'd have stayed in Africa and grown up as relaxed live-and-let-live types?"

"*Exactly!*"

I turned back to the autocue, and found that, from somewhere off-stage, someone was typing additional material into the script even as I spoke. "Relaxed live-and-let-live types like, er, Zimbabwe's Robert Mugabe, who accused Tony Blair of being a 'gay gangster' leading the 'gay government of the gay United gay Kingdom' with a secret plan to impose homosexuality throughout the Commonwealth; or, um, Kenya's Daniel arap Moi, who attacked the 'gay scourge' sweeping Africa; or Zambia's Frederick Chiluba, who said gays do not have 'a right to be abnormal'; or Namibia's Sam Nujoma, who accused African homosexuals of being closet 'Europeans' trying to destroy his country through the spread of 'gayism'; or Uganda's Yoweri Museveni, who proposed the arrest of all homosexuals - although he subsequently moderated his position and called for a return to the good old days when 'these few individuals were either ignored or speared and killed by their parents'."

Crumbs! Whoever was typing offstage could major in Homophobic African Heads of Government, or at least teach a "module" in it.

"Racist! Racist! Racist!" jeered Professor Arkroyd from NASUWRT.

"Don't tell me," said I. "No doubt African homophobia is also the malign legacy of British colonialism. Who taught them to spear gays, eh? By refusing to enslave them and take them to our Caribbean plantations and sodomise them every night, we left them with feelings of rejection and humiliation that laid the foundations of their homophobia."

Professor Arkroyd furrowed her brow. "Possibly," she said. "The point to remember is that…"

"…it's all our fault. Gotcha. Always has been, always will be."

The Supreme Imam of the Supremely Islamic Supreme Council of Stockton-on-Tees or whatever he was stood up: "I am all about celebrating diversity. True, to Muslims, homosexuality is immoral, unacceptable, spreads disease, damages the very foundations of society, and is utterly abhorrent. But nevertheless I am committed to a dialogue of mutual respect."

"That's a bit homophobic!" said Gillian Arkroyd.

The LGBTQ+ guy stood up. "Why is Islam so uptight about gay sexuality?"

"That's totally Islamophobic!" yelled the vicar from the Anglican Educational Outreach Association.

I thought it time to break things up. "So if a Muslim says Islam's not cool with gays it's homophobic? And if a gay guy says Islam's not cool with gays it's Islamophobic? That's why it's easier to blame everything on colonialism."

"Sir Mahmoud got *Sharon Has Two Mummies* banned from primary schools in Bradford," said the LGBTQWERTY spokesgay.

"Not to worry," I said. "He probably had it replaced with *Sharon Has Four Mummies and a Big Bearded Daddy Who Wants to Marry Her Off to a Cousin in Mirpur.*" A blueberry muffin hit the podium.

"Where was I? Oh, yes. The Britannic inheritance has transformed the lives of millions of people around the world, of all races and religions – black, white, brown, yellow, Christian, Hindu and Muslim; in the Americas, in Africa, in Asia…"

More boos. And more boos upon boos. Some Numero Uno bigshot imam in the front row started hurling muffled yells through his beard. Something about "British killers". I decided to go for the old open-mike-night-at-the-Windy-City putdown. Turning toward him, I jabbed my finger. "You're free to yell at me, sir, because this is a free country."

I paused to bask in the glow of my stellar performance. Judging from the catcalls, it had made quite an impression on the crowd, too.

"On slavery, on fascism, on all the great conflicts of the ages, the British people have been, in the scales of history, a force for good in the world." The autocue text was jerking up and down, as if, up in the control booth, someone was trying to wrest it out of someone else's grasp. But I could still just about follow along.

"In cutting off generations of schoolchildren from their cultural inheritance, the British state has engaged in what we will one day come to see as a form of child abuse, of ideological grooming."

There was a mass intake of breath at this.

"Why are our children not taught our great national narrative? The British education system has raised our young people to believe that this country is merely the font of imperialism, colonialism, racism and all other evils. 'While some nations suffer from *folie de grandeur*,' wrote one commentator, 'the British seem uniquely disposed to badmouth themselves.' In the late 1960s, Sir Richard Turnbull, High Commissioner of Aden in what is now the jihadist war-torn wasteland of Yemen, remarked bleakly to the then Defence Secretary, Denis Healey, that the British Empire would be remembered for only two things – quote – 'the popularisation of Association Football and the term 'eff off'. He put it rather more bluntly," I added.

At that point, the autocue died. Presumably someone had gotten into the tech booth and unplugged it. Fortunately, I had the old double-spaced script on the podium, but, while flipping through the pages to find the right place, I had to fill for a few seconds. So I improvised:

"Eff off," I repeated, to no one in particular. "Indeed. Eff off. Instead of our chronic and psychologically unhealthy self-flagellation, perhaps we might deploy that quintessentially British formulation of 'Eff off' toward, er, the globalist proponents of 'digital identity'; and, um, billionaires who demand we surrender our cars and eat their insects; and above all, ah, those kinky Eurofetishists who think the future lies in subordinating English law, custom and democracy to the postmodern global elitists so indifferent to the voice of the people that they're willing to ban referenda so they don't have to listen to them."

The booing stopped for an instant, as if the hooters and jeerers couldn't quite believe what I'd said. A big bloke on the left in additional temporary seating stood up, grabbed his chair and hurled it at me. It bounced off the lip of the stage. Another guy did the same. It hit the podium and fell at my feet.

"Any more?" I said, jauntily. "Three chairs for the Prime Minister? Hip-hip…"

I noticed the protection officers had moved in, and were hustling out the Downing Street gang. They tried to grab Wendy Rassendyll, too, but she shot a steely look at the cop, removed his hand from her elbow, and stayed put. As for me, I was kind of high on the whole moment. No one had ever before booed me, or thrown furniture at me. Because I'd never mattered. I felt like the award-winning actress Sally Field at the Oscars: You *don't* like me. You *really* don't like me. I was intoxicated by the heady perfume of universal loathing! I only had two pages of script left, but I was minded to improvise for another forty minutes.

And then someone had to go and ruin it all by yelling "Allahu Akbar!"

There was a nano-second of silence.

And then the Black Historical Memory guy, the President of the Association of Lesbian Gym Teachers, the Primate of the Gay Bishoprics and the Supremely Supreme Leader of Islamic Supremacists all dived to the floor. I was still savouring the atmosphere, so it caught me by surprise. A group of young men rushed forward, shoved the podium and knocked it over, scattering my speech to the stage. One of them grabbed my trouser-leg. "Hands off the togs, blighter!" I snapped, giving him a good kick. Police poured through the doors at the back, and down the aisle, as a larger part of the crowd surged toward me. I became aware of a half-dozen officers behind me, who grabbed my arms and lifted me free of the excitable types around my footwear. As I was hustled backwards, one pulled off my shoe, and tossed it at my head.

Amazingly, I caught it.

"In the words of Sir Richard Turnbull," I said to the security guys, "time to fuck off."

Chapter Thirty-Nine
The Prime Minister does not get much sleep in Downing Street

"Well," said Angus, scrolling his *handifon*, "I think oor fears tha' th' speech woo nae get much coverage has a'ready preeved tae be unfoonded."

We were on our way back to the airport. It had been somewhat chaotic outside the stage door, and, when the prime ministerial limo pulled up and Wendy and I had gotten in, Angus had decided he didn't like the look of the mob and wasn't going to take his chances waiting for the back-up car. He shoved aside Dame Millie, and wrenched open the door to clamber into what he feared was the last lifeboat.

"Gogogogogogogogogogo!" he yelled at the driver.

"Honestly, Angus," sighed Wendy. "It's not the Kennedy assassination, and you're not the Secret Service."

"Gogogogogogogogogogogogo!" he roared again.

"You sound like the end of that Welsh town," said our chauffeur, staring contentedly out the window at the rampaging mob. "The one with the longest name."

At that moment, the seething throng broke through the police line, our tires squealed, and we took off like a test-drive on that BBC motoring show.

"Llanfairpwllgwyngyllgogerychwyrndrobwllllantysiliogogogoch, that's it," said the driver, turning round to flash Angus a smile as he skidded blind round the corner.

When we were clear of the first two sets of lights, the wee distraught Scot calmed down, and, feeling a little sheepish, made a rather too obvious effort to be cynically media-savvy for the rest of the journey. He pulled up the BBC newsfeed:

Rassendyll's Message to Teachers: 'Hands Off The Togs, Blighter!'

"Let me have a look at that," said Wendy, snatching his mobile. "Oh, my, Angus. They've got a picture of you shoving Dame Millie in the ribs and hurling yourself into the limo. That's amazing. Within a few seconds of you diving onto the seat, a picture of your pert little bottom is being beamed around the world."

He wrenched the phone out of her hands.

"'Hands off the togs, blighter'," Wendy repeated. "What a marvellous line! And which gifted special advisor lovingly crafted that particular bon mot?"

"Soondbaet o' th' day," pronounced Angus. "Nae, wait, I may ha' spake tae seen. From *The Guardian*: 'Rassendyll: Time to Fuck Off'."

Wendy exploded with laughter. She seemed to be enjoying the excitement, certainly more than Angus or Millie. I wouldn't say we were exactly getting on, but we were certainly not getting on a lot better than we'd been not getting on before. I felt rather sad when we parted at the airport, and the limo whisked her away to her Sudden Death Syndrome initiative.

Back on Earl Force One, I ordered Scotches all round, and raised my glass. "Bottoms up!" I said, as we admired another media close-up of my Bollywood spad's rear end poking out of the limo. Angus declined to be amused.

Dame Millie went into damage-control mode. "It's critical to agree the message here."

"Isn't the speech the message?" I asked, puzzled.

"Oh, for fuh..." She stomped off to sit in the cheap seats.

"What the bollocking arse were you thinking?" hissed Rory. "Ever since we met, I've devoted myself to neutralising all the sixteenth-earl wankerama. And in one fell swoop you decide you're running on a plan to restore the British Empire."

"Look, Stephen Harper gave a speech on the subject..."

"Who?"

"Prime Minister of Canada. I quoted him." For a moment I felt disheartened. "It didn't get a lot of coverage in the London papers."

"Good thing, too," said Rory. "We'd have had him deported." He furrowed his brows. "When those nutters rushed you, I thought for a moment we might retrieve something from this fiasco. Either they'd beat the crap out of you and you'd be a sympathetic victim, or you'd see them off and be the plucky hero. But no, you have to go full earl and say 'Hands off the togs, blighter.' Which, if I remember correctly, you never said back when you actually were a full earl. That's the worst soundbite since Jim Callaghan said, 'Crisis? What crisis?' And to be fair to Sunny Jim he didn't actually say that, whereas you did. Up yours, blighter!" And he stomped off to the back of the plane, displacing Imogen and forcing her to join the otherwise unwanted me.

The young percher tried to be conciliatory. "Perhaps you should have played up contemporary British identity."

"Like what?" I said. "Highest drug use in Europe? Highest number of single mothers?" I'd read the brief.

Imogen couldn't resist joining in. "Highest incidence of sexually transmitted disease," she giggled.

My turn to make a contribution. "Marriage all but defunct, except for toffs, upscale gays, and Muslims. Didn't think I knew that, did you, Imogen?" I'd read it in her paper, and she was flattered.

"But you're not to be a naughty boy and say it out loud at PMQs," she warned.

"That was you on the autocue with the African homophobes, wasn't it?"

"Shhh," she said conspiratorially. "Rory and I are still on non-speakers over your two-ply loo-roll bit." She slapped my wrist playfully, and let her hand linger a little longer than it should. It occurred to me that imperialism might be a great way to pick up birds.

But not tonight. I had been running on adrenaline and, as soon as the action ended and the door closed behind my humble Downing Street flat, I felt suddenly exhausted, my arms and legs like lead weights. I was shivery, and had that fogginess in my head that usually presages the flu. Even Number Ten's extensive range of fine single malts had lost its appeal. I sat on the corner of the bed. Firmer than the Great British B&B, that's for sure. Maybe this PM business wasn't so bad after all. I pulled off my shoes and socks and all the rest, and let them fall to the floor. With a huge effort, I inched up the counterpane as if on a cliff face. Fumbling for the light switch, I let the Sandman bury me like an abandoned corpse in the deserts of Araby. And by the time the deep sleep of exhaustion had lightened I was in a dark dream, trapped in a windowless room on the other side of which a transgender schoolmistress was singing a homophobic gangsta rap about Colin Corgi. A bearded man rose behind her with a rusty scimitar, but, before he could slice off her head, she died from Sudden

Adult Death Syndrome. And, even though she was deceased, her vocal rendition continued uninterrupted.

I sat bolt upright. A shaft of light pierced the room.

"I assumed you'd still be working. You usually are."

The door was ajar and on the threshold was ...Wendy?

She was back-lit from the corridor. Her legs were apart and she seemed to be wearing a very short negligée.

Roger Severn hadn't given me any advice on how to play this one. "I thought you were in..." I ground to a halt, not being sure what part of England the bit north of Manchester was called.

"I had a sudden yen to return to the heart of things." She exhaled the line.

"Come in," I offered, aware that it seemed an odd thing to say to one's wife. She slid through the door, softly closed it behind her, and flipped a switch. A light came on over by the desk. I pulled the sheet up around my chest and tucked it under my arms.

Which was ridiculous, but I wasn't entirely persuaded by Lady Belinda's assurance that I was a perfect match. I mean, as Rassendyll's mistress, she wouldn't want me sleeping with Rassendyll's wife, would she? So maybe she hadn't mentioned the strawberry birthmark, or the third nipple...

Wendy came closer, shimmering in a pale lilac diaphanous thing, her breasts half exposed.

Her eyes were wide open, like saucers. "Mind if I join you?"

"You already have," I gulped.

"In bed, twit." She didn't wait for an answer. And, when she'd slipped between the sheets, I frantically hit every switch above the nightstand, throwing the room into blinding light, then to the subtle shadows of tasteful sconces, and finally total darkness. That seemed the best way of avoiding, at least for the moment, any glimpse of potentially non-lookalike aspects of my body, and the awkward conversation that might follow: "Darling, where did the other four inches of your *Schneidel* go?" I cursed myself for not having taken the time to find the prime ministerial pyjamas.

"Do you know, Robert," said Wendy, touching my cheek and staring into my eyes, "you looked somehow different today?"

My heart missed a beat, and I wondered whether her other hand, running across my chest, had noticed it.

304

"You feel different."

"What do you mean?" I asked.

"I'm not sure. You're more prime ministerial. More genuine, less of an actor."

"You need to have some acting skills in this job."

"Sometimes you're too good at acting," she said. "You forget who you really are, deep down. I liked the way you were today."

"I'm glad."

"You sound different, too," she said. "More like your old self, and less of that ghastly Mister I've-Renounced-My-Earldom-to-Pretend-to-Be-a-Man-of-the-People voice."

My fingers hovered over her shoulders and eventually, summoning up my courage, I patted her on the back, like a parent going "There, there" to a sick child.

"Oh, my God!" she moaned. "Even your touch is different." She shivered, and kissed me, and entwined a leg around mine.

I became aware of a stirring down below. So did Wendy, who gave a contented squeal. I wondered if that was also as different as my look, feel, sound, touch, etc, or whether it had merely been a long time. She threw herself on top of me and her hair fell on my face. "Mmm," she purred, running her hand over my chest. "Someone's been working out. Moob-free zone."

"What?"

"If *The Daily Mirror* could see you now!" she said, tracing a finger across my pectorals and teasing my chest hair. "What was it that miserable man put on the front page under that picture on the beach in Providenciales? 'Is This the Biggest Tit in British Politics?' Where did they go? You're like a new man, Robert."

She disappeared beneath the sheet, and, just as I was thinking me playing Rassendyll offered more side-benefits than him playing Rudy Elphberg ever could, I remembered that I hadn't yet established whether his and my whachamacallits were also perfect doppelgangerplonkers. So I grabbed her and yanked her back up.

"So you want to play rough, lover?" she purred, tossing her hair over her shoulder before diving down to bite mine. "Say that line you used in your speech," she said, breathing hard between every other word.

"What line?" I couldn't really remember too many of the specifics. "'Why do we hate us?'"

"No," she moaned. "The bit about 'Nothing beats the British Empire'."

So I did. I tried to say it like the late Luther Vandross would have, had he been playing a gig in front of the Supreme Islamic Supreme Council of Greater Manchester and the Gay Anglican Archbishoprics of Stockton-on-Tees.

"Ooohhhhh, Robert," she whimpered.

If I can pull this off, I thought, the G7'll be a breeze.

"Ooohhhhh, Robert," she whimpered again. "Robert, Robert, Robert, Robert…"

"Wendy," I said, stiffly, and then, not wishing to be parsimonious, "Wendy. Wendy."

"Robert Robert Robert Robert Robert," she said and, pushing the blankets aside, stretched lazily till the distant glow of the lamppost through the window found her pale rosebud nipples pointed straight up at the ceiling. For someone so faded and careworn on our first meeting, she had high, round, girlish breasts. "It's like discovering a whole new you. Like digging deep within and finally reaching the real man. No more games, no more pretending. Just you. The you I fell in love with all those years ago, and thought I'd lost forever." She paused. "Is that how it is for you?"

"Oh, yes," I agreed. "Definitely."

And then I sat bolt upright and said: "No. No, it's no good. I can't do it."

"What?"

I hadn't meant to say that out loud; it just sort of spilled out. But it was true. Some complex ethical consideration had popped into my head. That's to say, when I'd slept with Belinda, she was already cheating on her husband and I was pretending to be the fellow she was cheating on him with. But, on the other hand, she'd worked out that she was really sleeping with me as Rudy Elphberg, so I wouldn't really be cheating on Belinda if I slept with Wendy in my capacity as Rob Rassendyll, would I? On the *other* other hand, if I slept with her as Rob Rassendyll, then Wendy would be cheating on her husband without even knowing it.

Which didn't seem quite fair.

THE PRISONER OF WINDSOR

What the hell was I doing? I'd had the hots for Wendy ever since dancing with her at that Windsor ball. And she and Rassendyll had been on the outs for two years. And I didn't get so many opportunities like this that I could afford to turn them down.

And yet, and yet... Sir Roger had told me all these stories about Rudolf Rassendyll all those years ago in Strelsau. He could have taken Princess Flavia for himself – he wanted to – but he was an English gentleman and a man of honour. Which is how the Sapt family got all those stupid ideas about Englishmen and honour that led to ol' Ma Sapt bringing little baby Roger to Britain to be raised among bounders and schemers and poltroons.

Nevertheless... for some reason I was thinking about being a man of honour. Whereas mere seconds earlier I'd been thinking about being a man of on-her-and-off-her all night long.

Wendy was staring disbelievingly. "What do you mean, you 'can't'?" The evidence suggested otherwise. "Not the recycled water at Chequers again?"

I took her in my arms. "Look, darling," I said. "These last years have been pretty rotten, haven't they?"

"The worst." And her eyes dimmed.

"But I don't want us to start over again all half-cocked... I want it to be right. I love you, but I think we should wait until..."

Until what? I racked my brains. "Until we're back at Burlesdon."

"Burlesdon? I don't see what's so romantic about that damp, decrepit dump..."

"But," I said, taking a shot in the dark, "it's where we first made love..."

"No, we didn't. That was in the back seat of your TR4. And I'm not doing that again. My back took a month to recover."

She climbed out of bed, somewhat tetchily. So I got out and held her. "When the moment's right," I pleaded. "Soon, I promise..."

"Soon enough," she said. "According to that bitch at the Beeb, Rupert Henley's planning to move against you before the Coronation. So we'll have all the time in the world. Six weeks in the Maldives, if that's 'right' enough for you..."

And she left, slamming the door. I stared bleakly at the indentation on her side of the bed. At this time of night, like most chaps, I like to let my willy do the thinking. For the first time in my life, my conscience had overruled it. I thought I'd feel good about behaving honourably. But it was a long and restless few hours till dawn...

III
Half a hero

Chapter Forty
A PM gone rogue

Something had changed with my speech in Manchester. Rory, Millie and Angus regarded me as if I were a motheaten old lion that had just savaged a keeper. They were metaphorically holding chairs and whips. With the exception of Imogen, the younger spads were also keeping their distance, as if waiting to see whether lion or keepers would win. The press had ceased promoting obvious alternatives PMs like Rupert Henley or Derek Detchard. Poor Anna Bersonin was forgotten. The same political diarist who had acclaimed her the grassroots favourite was now reporting a rumour that she had fled abroad fearing disclosure of a lesbian relationship with a senior Cabinet minister from a notoriously "conservative" community. That was pretty obviously meant to be Yazmina al-Ghoti, who likewise was nowhere in sight. I wondered who'd started that one – White Mike? Or Sir Roger? Or maybe Anna had floated it to some hack a couple of weeks earlier in a bid to trump Marjorie on her intersectional points…

Instead, on Radio 4, the BBC's political correspondent announced that this week's coming man was Dominic Horniold-Farquahar. He was a very young Old Etonian and heir to an Ulster baronetcy but they cooed over his every word when he caught a Tube train and visited a shopping centre somewhere near the eastern terminus of the District Line because "I want to hear the views of all the people who despise my party and its current leadership" – i.e., me.

"Who is this man?" I asked Roger Severn, switching off the radio. "I've never heard of him. The BBC's just made him up."

"Oh, he's real, after a fashion," said Sir Roger. "Sits directly opposite you in Cabinet."

"That weird cove? From one side he looks like the world's wrinkliest teenager, and from the other like an adolescent geriatric? Fish eyes and huge gums?"

"Well, the BBC says he could win the leadership by the skin of his teeth. They're very keen on him. His advantage is he has zero name recognition."

"What's he do?"

"He's the Echo man."

"What?"

"Secretary of State for ECHO - Equality, Community, Hope and Opportunity."

"What's that mean?"

"I couldn't say. Robert's predecessor created it to show how caring we were. Far more mystifying job title than Lord Keeper of the Privy Seal."

On my way to the loo, I overheard Rory telling his crew that Horniold-Farquahar was said at that very moment to be riding a bus to a school in south London where no child spoke English and which he would hail as a model of the future. The younger spads reacted to this with a burst of frantic texting.

At Cabinet, nobody said a word about my speech. Instead, they were all still on about the need to be seen to be holding a Cobra on the Ruritanian content-farmer assault on British democracy. Several ministers raised the possibility that there may have been Ruritanian subversion of the last election. Which I suppose was, in a certain sense, true.

Still, my mind wandered. Humphrey Lowe-Graham was twittering on about "EU-compliant toilets". God, it never ends, does it? "That means no urinals," he explained, "and no liftable seats on the 'traditional European' side."

I'd worked hard on my speech. And for once a British politician was talking about something important, not drivelling on about whose voice should order you to sit down in a public toilet.

"Frau Lauengram hectoring you to sit down is standard in all UK models. That's actually mentioned in a codicil to an appendix of the External Zone (Qualified Recognition) Harmonisation Directive." Humphrey's voice sounded tinny and far away.

"Can we disable the voice technology?" asked Marjorie Craftstone.

"It's very difficult. Like airbags in cars. A few Poles tried to do it, and the whole toilet seized up. So the streets of London would be running sewers. There's not enough Ruritanian plumbers on the planet to fix that."

THE PRISONER OF WINDSOR

Who'd go into politics? I started thinking about giving a second speech, perhaps on the virtues of Common Law vis-à-vis all this Euro-regulation we needed to get rid of. I was jolted back to the grim reality of Cabinet by Rupert Henley's use of the word "squatting":

"…sitzpinkler on one side; the other a traditional 'Turkish toilet' for squatting. And no Frau Lauengram for the Mohammedans."

"So a bloke can piss like a Kraut or a Muzzie," said Derek Detchard. "But not release the old spray halfway up the pub wall like any decent Englishman. Whose idea was this?"

"Collective Cabinet responsibility," snapped Humphrey Lowe-Graham.

"Which means we haven't yet decided on the fall guy. I vote for you," decided Detchard. "Bet you wee-wee like a girl."

"The danger," said Rupert, "is that traditional Brit pissers will eschew the sitzpinkler and use the Turkish toilet as a urinal…"

My mind wandered yet again, until I became vaguely aware that Marjorie was saying "PM? *PM?*"

"Er, yes," I said.

"Maybe you should have an off-the-record tea-and-falafel with Almasri?" she suggested.

"Better to have him in the tent pissing out, and all that," said Rupert.

"One more thing to keep an eye on," said Lowe-Graham. "In some models, waste from the European side of the sitzpinkler is getting into the Turkish toilet side."

Marjorie reeled back in horror. "You mean infidel fecal matter is, um, backing up in the, um, non-infidel toilet?"

"Could be more fake news from the Ruritanian content farmers," murmured Humphrey. "But there've been some stabbings in Westphalia over it. The Germans are confident they can keep the lid on it."

Usually Cabinet comes to a close when I stand up, and then everyone else follows my cue and they all leave. This time, they all sort of wandered off, as if they had a meeting to go to, leaving me sitting there on my own feeling like a bit of a chump. Then Rory Vane and Millie Trehearne barged in.

"This is what we're going to do," said Rory, holding up his hand to silence me. "The autocue in Manchester was one of those new models from Maxim Rogovsky's partnership with the Chinese in Wuhan. Unfortunately, the Ruritanian content farmers hacked into it and planted that speech on it, and you just went ahead and delivered it. Sorry, Rob, but I'm Europe's highest-paid spin doctor, and that's the best I can do."

"But doesn't that make me sound like just a hollow airhead sock-puppet who simply reads out whatever's put in front of him?"

"I wish," said Rory. "Whatever happened to *that* Rob Rassendyll?"

"I liked that speech," I said. "I stand by every word of it." I made the mistake of adding that I'm the PM and they're the spads. Which means that I'm the boss, and they're supposed to do what I want, right?

"That's an interesting point, Prime Minister," hissed Rory. "And one that, if you insist on pushing, I'm happy to address on an in-depth interview with the *Today* programme after handing in my resignation."

Blimey!

"Blaming it on the Ruritanian content farmers," Dame Millie chipped in, "is the best way to put this behind us."

"There are no Ruritanian content farmers," I said. "It's all rubbish got up by that woman on the BBC. I'd have put that in the speech if that wallah hadn't shouted 'Allahu Akbar'."

"Wallah?" replied Rory. "*Wallah?* You're doing coke before cabinet now, aren't you?"

"It's worse than that," said Millie. "He's being blackmailed. Who put you up to this, Rob?"

"Put me up to what?"

"All this stuff about how great Britain is. Was it Moscow? The Chinese? The ayatollahs?"

"Why would they blackmail me to say how great Britain is?"

But Millie was rummaging through my speech. She read out:

> ...as Winston Churchill said on a speaking tour of Canada in 1929, 'links us all together with the majestic past that takes us back to the Tudors, the Plantagenets, the Magna Carta, habeas corpus, petition of rights, and English common law'....

"Those are words we don't say in public," said Rory primly, staring at me like a mummy reprimanding a small child.

"Well, I like it," I said, defiantly. "Common law, Magna Carta, the golden thread of our beloved Crown... What's wrong with that? People like Churchill."

"They used to like the *idea* of Churchill," explained Rory, "a strong leader who wins wars. But the specifics are increasingly problematic..."

Millie read on:

> *In terms of your best shot at liberty, a long life, a decent standard of living, and civic structures that allow you to fulfil your God-given potential, nothing beats having been part of the British Empire. Why can't we say that once in a while?*

She reached out and touched my hand, tenderly. "Honestly, Rob," she began. "I know you've been under a lot of stress with the External Zone Non-Compliance Mitigation negotiations. But you do realise that's grounds for temporary removal from office on mental-incapacity grounds..."

"Along with the climate denial," added Rory. "Why didn't you just come right out and demand the blessed Saint Flavia be burned at the stake?"

"Then you did that awful joke," said Millie, "about removing the word 'balls'."

"I'll match mine against yours any day," said Rory, standing up as if he were about to get them out. "You don't think it takes balls to take a flier on a sixteenth earl and remake him as the face of modern 21st-century Britain?"

"Okay," I conceded. "Maybe it's undignified for a prime minister to say 'balls'. Maybe I should have said 'the old twig and berries...'"

"I've been offered a job on the European Commission," said Millie.

"But you're not, er, European. External Zone subjects aren't eligible."

Millie laughed and said that for the last three years she'd been travelling on a Belgian passport. "And you should know," she purred, "that a significant number of permanent secretaries are thinking of filing a class-action suit against you for failing to follow their advice."

Rory stood up again. "You've gone rogue, Rob. If you persist in this, our duty is clear – and you'll be the one who, in the words of Sir Richard Turnbull, has to fuck off."

Chapter Forty-One
A bit of a glitch

THAT AFTERNOON Lady Belinda Featherly, the *Daily Telegraph* "After Hours" columnist, contributor to *Sorted!* on BBC Radio, and co-presenter of *Two Oiks and a Toff* on ITV5, was standing at the front door of her house waiting for Reg the plumber who had telephoned, after five weeks, to say he was on his way. The elderly baronet's widow walking her poodle thought the young man of "Asian" appearance strolling toward her looked somewhat out of place. However, having just completed a sale of her own property to a Belarussian oligarch's estranged son-in-law, she no longer felt as certain of these things as she once might have. They passed each other; she smiled, and so did he. And a hundred yards further on she heard a cry of "Allahu Akbar!" and turned around.

Sanjay and Vic escorted me through the freight entrance of the Princess Fiona Medical Centre, a dingy 1970s structure. Belinda was in a private room, propped up in a hospital bed with various drips in her arms and a strange lumpy mound over the lower part of her torso. My chaps gave the place the once-over and then, with the nurse, withdrew.

I leaned over, brushed away some stray hairs and kissed her on the forehead.

"Hello, lover," she said. "Do you mind if I call you that? Feeling a bit sorry for myself." Her husband was on his way back from Australia, where he'd been doing something with a client's underperforming bauxite operation.

"Rather in the mood for a nervous breakdown. Does that sound pathetic?" she said. "Pass me a fag, there's a good boy. They're under the brochure for the telly-wifi package."

"Are you sure?"

"The nurses only make their rounds once every three or four days. By then the tell-tale whiff will have been wafted away by the sepsis."

I lit a cigarette for her and placed it between her lips. She took a drag and then stubbed it out on the frame of the bed. She contemplated me for a moment. "Bastard. I should have stayed with you, breaking into castles and galloping round Windsor with my lord and protector. I'd still have my leg."

I glanced at the one-sided elevation of the blankets on the lower half of the bed. Her sister, Lady Georgina, had told me in the corridor.

"*La* not-so-*grande horizontale*. That's me now, isn't it?" I sat carefully on the covers. And Belinda reached out her arms, weakly, to pull me toward her. We hugged for a while, and she sobbed for a longer while.

Finally she said, "Everyone in this stupid country is crazy. None of us natives can see it, but Ghazi and Rogovsky and the Duchess of Woke all know it." She reached for her cigarette and then remembered it was out. "We could have gone away somewhere, do you think?"

"Where?"

"I don't know. Somewhere boring where no one ever goes. Canada. But the French bit. I don't want to speak English ever again, and my French isn't so bad. Isn't there a mining town in northern Quebec somewhere where you can be a Ruritanian plumber and I can be a one-legged plumber's mate?"

"I'm not a very good plumber," I pointed out. "Your loo's leaking, remember?"

"By the time poor old Reg arrived, the bomb squad had closed the street. He won't be back for months," she said. "I don't really mean it anyway. I'm stuck with England like I'm stuck with George. For better or worse. My country wrong or wronger." She pulled me down again, and kissed me. But the effort exhausted her and she asked me to re-light her cigarette.

"There are worse things," I pointed out, "than living in a country where the king likes you. He asked you to dance at the ball."

"Well, he won't be doing that again," she said.

"He should have married you. You looked great together. Better than him and the Queen."

"You looked great dancing with Wendy. Better than Rob and Wendy." She paused, and squeezed my hand. "Rudy..."

"Yes?"

"You're sleeping with her, aren't you?"

The room seemed very still. "No. Honestly."

"I don't believe you. Even the lookalike goes back to the wife."

She took a long unhurried puff on her cigarette. "It's a funny thing bonking a celebrity."

I raised an eyebrow.

"Not you," she said. "Rob."

"Is the British Prime Minister really a celebrity?"

"I mean, someone you know from telly. Rob had a cameo in *Holland Park*. He played Hugh Grant's scheming political brother."

"Chick flick," I said. "Never saw it."

"Hadn't run into him since Oxford. But I was covering the Royal premiere for *Sorted!* and I went to the party. Just after I'd watched him on the silver screen. Cinemascope. VistaVision. Larger than life. And then he comes over at the party and you're sipping some horrible plonk – 'I hate Press Night Chardonnay,' he says – and you banter for a bit. And he talks about the old days at Oxford as if you're both just university pals who've lost touch. And you're attracted to him, you really are. And you ask yourself: Is it the Prime Ministerial thing that makes his eyes flash, and his skin glow, and his laugh …erotic?"

"There's nothing less erotic than the word 'erotic'," I said. "And come on, the 'Prime Ministerial thing'? Would you have said that about David Brown or Gordon Major?"

"Okay, the celebrity thing. The telly thing. The VistaVision thing."

"Not a lot of vista or vision with Rob Rassendyll."

"The thing about sleeping with a celebrity is, even if the sex is mediocre, the idea of it's a turn-on."

"But you're a celebrity…"

She lit another ciggy. "I'm radio, and a bit of daytime telly. Trying to hold on a bit longer before my looks go – even before Colin Corgi gave every commissioning editor the perfect excuse not to use me. I don't exude glamour."

"You do to me," I proffered. It came out phony, but I meant it.

"Well, you're a Ruritanian plumber," she said. "It's not glamour like Rob Rassendyll glamour. The golden boy of British politics. Celebrity sex is like dynastic marriages in mediaeval Europe. When he got me into bed, he was bonking beneath him."

319

"Evidently he enjoys it."

"It's the opposite with you. I'm bonking beneath me."

"I'm a king."

"You're a loser. But a spirited one." I caught her eyes, and could see she was trying to envision circumstances in which we might have had a life together and not quite succeeding. "It's a bugger," she sighed. "First the telly people want you because you're posh. Then they don't want you because you're posh. Then you pretend not to be posh, just like every public-school-educated faux-yobbo is doing. Then they tell you you're pretending not to be posh in not quite the right way. It's a hard country to reinvent yourself in, don't you think?"

"I'm really not the person to ask." I leaned over and kissed her. "You're very sweet under all that poshness."

"I thought the missing leg would be a good career move. By now they'd all be calling - Piers Morgan, Jonathan Ross: 'The *tewwibwy tewwibwy bwave* Lady Belinda tells her story...' I'd get to be one of those boring awareness-raisers going on about how great my prosthetic is. Like that supermodel who married whichever wrinkly old rocker it was, and unscrewed the thing and put it on the desk so Larry King could get a good look at it." She took a long drag on her cigarette. "God, I loved my legs. They were great, weren't they?"

I nodded, and felt a tear welling so I kissed her on the lips. But her eyes were also watering. "The phone hasn't stopped not ringing. All the papers say I had it coming. I lost a leg and I can't even monetise it."

I'd seen that. The BBC had announced that Colin Corgi had gone into hiding.

"What does that even mean?" asked Belinda. "They put him in a cardboard box and stick him in the attic? I wish it was that easy for me."

She picked up *The Guardian*, and pointed out a column by a feminist novelist:

> *The narrative of the Belinda Featherly attack — a white privileged European wounded by a Muslim 'extremist' — is one that feeds neatly into the cultural prejudices that have led our government to make so many disastrous mistakes in the Middle East and elsewhere. To allocate reflexively the blame for such a convenient narrative is to preclude the*

rational and careful thinking we owe our Muslim neighbours on what provoked this attack. And to anoint Featherly, granddaughter of a marquess who served as British Political Officer in the Trucial States, as some sort of 'victim' is to absolve her of her role in supporting the cultural prejudices that made her fate inevitable.

"Thank you, Francine," she said. "When it was all happening I didn't realise it was a 'cultural narrative'. I thought it was blood and body parts and sodding awful reality. Thanks to *The Guardian*, I'll know better next time."

"I didn't know your grandfather was Political Officer in the Trucial States."

"Not sure I did. But in the mosques of Tower Hamlets they talk of little else apparently." She started to cry. "I'm so sick of all the bullshit. My 'role in supporting the cultural prejudices'? I made one burqa joke fifteen years ago, and I'm Geert Wilders."

I kissed her again.

"Don't think I'm up to a shag," she said. "But, if you're careful not to knock out any drips and tubes, we could just cuddle."

And so I moved cautiously up the bed, and she rested on my shoulder. She felt spent, as if there was less of her than there should have been, which I suppose there was. I felt all her regret and loneliness. Danger brings you closer to someone than dating ever does, I'd say. Fear and adrenaline had done more for me and Belinda than soft lights and sweet music.

I knew not a thing about her really. "Do you have any children?" I found myself asking.

"Can't."

"Oh."

"Do you?"

"No," I said.

"I had an abortion at Oxford. No big deal, is it? Had another a couple of years later. The father is in your cabinet. '*Father*'," she repeated. "Then I married George and got pregnant after the honeymoon. I went for a routine check-up at two months, and there was a bit of a glitch with my uterus. That's how he said it. 'Bit of a glitch with your uterus.' And they took everything out, and that was that. Bit of a glitch with my uterus, bit of a glitch with my leg."

"Were you sad about the abortions?"

"I don't remember being sad about them at the time. I'm sad now because I wasn't sad then. And I'm sad because I wouldn't have bothered becoming a pathetic D-list minor celebrity if I hadn't needed something to do." She snuggled closer. Even in a hospital bed, greasy-haired and bomb-scarred and one-legged, Lady Belinda Featherly was beautiful.

"The Rassendylls are childless, too," I said.

"Yes." She stared blankly toward the window, which afforded a prospect of the bare, rain-streaked concrete wall of an adjoining structure. "A king, an earl, and a marquess's daughter. All childless. Doesn't say a lot for the health of the hereditary principle, does it?"

Chapter Forty-Two
The Big Shut-Up

THE OPPOSITION disliked my remarks in Manchester almost as much as my Cabinet and spads. "Will the Prime Minister," thundered Deirdre Bellairs at PMQs, "understand the very real offence his extremely offensive speech caused to millions of Muslims, women, black Britons, gay Britons, Arabs, Haitians - I may have left out a few..." The members opposite bayed like a terrace of fans at a Hofbau-Rischenheim match. "...and will he," the Right Honourable Lady continued, "apologise for his totally racist remarks and pledge to this House that he will undergo a course of sensitivity training?"

There were a few chortles from members on both sides who took this as an example of the devastating repartee for which the House of Commons is renowned. On the other hand, Ms Bellairs seemed to mean it quite seriously.

"With respect to the Right Honourable Lady..." I opened up the briefing notes I'd been handed. It was the usual guff: Deeply regret if any remarks were taken out of context by those seeking to score cheap political points... The government remained committed to investing in Muslim community networks... greater female opportunities in sport and agriculture... proud to sponsor a motion at the next Commonwealth Heads of Government Meeting to inaugurate a Gay Commonwealth Games... Good grief.

"With respect to the Right Honourable Lady, I say..." I swallowed and staggered on. "I say phooey, Mr Speaker." The footie fans behind me cheered. "Many of those she says are so 'offended' cheerfully insult people all year round. Mohammed Almasri, for example, said on television in Pakistan that homosexuals should be put to death – and then, when the tape was broadcast in Britain, blamed it on Jews controlling the media. Perhaps Sir Mohammed needs 'sensitivity training'." I put on a simpering, mocking voice for those last two words. "Or perhaps it would be a complete waste of time. It seems to me that what today's Britain needs is *in*sensitivity training, so we can stop going around taking our cues from lavishly remunerated spokespersons for the perpetual grievance industry." Boos, etc. "A multicultural, multiethnic, multireligious, multiorientational, multigendered society is only going to work if we all grow thicker skins and learn to rub along. Every word I said in Manchester was correct, Mr Speaker. Every fact was true. If the Right Honourable Lady rejects the truth, that's not my problem, it's hers."

I had come straight from Belinda's hospital room, and I was perhaps more angry than I should have been. "Furthermore, I am sick of the Big Shut-Up, and I regard it as pathetic that the Right Honourable Lady, the Leader of His Majesty's Loyal Opposition, a job whose very title acknowledges that differences of opinion are the absolute bedrock of free societies, has chosen to side with the Shut-Up crowd – the ones whose response to any opinion they don't like is not to debate it, argue it, challenge it, but to tell you you can't say it."

Big cheers from behind me now – not because my lot necessarily agreed with what I was saying, but just because I was sticking it to the Leader of the Opposition.

"And quite disgracefully the Right Honourable Lady has chosen to side with the Big Shut-Up in a week when a harmless children's puppet who for years has given pleasure to millions around the world has been forced into hiding – and when his co-presenter is right now lying in a hospital bed with her leg blown off. The Right Honourable Lady mocks her very office, her very job description, because she's in favour of a world in which there is no possibility of 'Loyal Opposition', where everyone who disagrees with you has to shut up or be blown up."

The benches opposite were jeering at me and yelling "Shame! Shame!" Deirdre rose and asked the Speaker for a ruling on whether my accusations against her were unparliamentary because they implied she supported political violence.

But my blood was up and I interrupted the Speaker. "Oh, there's no question of that. The Right Honourable Lady was on LBC an hour ago and said that the most sensible piece on the Belinda Featherly attack was a *Guardian* column rationalising the suicide bombing because Lady Belinda's grandfather had been political resident in the Trucial States. So the sins of the grandfather are justification for attempted murder, according to the Right Honourable Lady. As it happens, Ms Bellairs' grandfather was in the King's African Rifles and arrested Barack Obama's grandfather during the Mau-Mau rebellion. The Right Honourable Lady apologised to Mr Obama for it. But, by her own logic, that would justify blowing Deirdre Bellairs sky-high! And, when her chum in *The Guardian* writes a column saying the Right Honourable Lady was asking for it, I can go on LBC and say what a very sensible contribution to the public discourse that column is… The attack on Belinda Featherly was outrageous, but your – " My blood was up and I forgot to do the parliamentary thing of addressing my remarks through the Speaker – "The attack on Belinda Featherly was outrageous, but your sick rationalisation of it is even more outrageous and shames the office you hold. Resign!"

Yes, yes. I know it was a weak and anti-climactic end. But at PMQs nobody cares about the merits of the argument, they just want you to jab your finger across the chamber and call on somebody to quit. So the cheers were tumultuous and echoed to the rafters.

Chapter Forty-Three
The glorious dead

ENGLAND IS NOT RURITANIA. Things that would seem utterly fantastical in Strelsau are entirely routine in London. And so it was that Mrs Rassendyll and I found ourselves in the back seat "spiffed up to the nines", as they say in English, heading to something called the Coronation Command Performance at Windsor Castle. Wendy wasn't happy about it. "Why do we have to go to this? We don't go to the regular Royal Variety Show. Didn't you go on the telly and say it didn't reflect multicultural Britain?"

"Did I? Well, this one's multiculti-a-go-go." I was thumbing through the programme. "What's DiversCity?"

"Robert, anyone would think you'd been locked up in a cellar for years. They're the multicultural trapeze act. From the Odessa flotilla. One of them got shot in the leg by a Russian assassin who turned out to be a former hooker of Hunter Biden's, remember? He still winces when they catch him by it."

The car pulled through the Downing Street gates, and into Whitehall. We passed, in the middle of the street, the famous Cenotaph – the tall, tapering stone memorial to Britain's war dead. Beautifully clean unfussy design by Sir Edwin Lutyens, moving words by Rudyard Kipling: "The glorious dead," I said aloud, for no particular reason.

Wendy snorted. "Dear Lord. Don't tell me they're playing!"

"What?"

"The Glorious Dead? Even the trendies at the Beeb can't put the King through an evening of whatchamacallit ...thrash metal?"

"Post-thrash," chipped in Sanjay from the front seat.

Wendy looked radiant. She was all pastel pink and blue in a figure-hugging dress by Helena San Servolo, whom she told me had been at Ascot Ladies' Day before the fight broke out. Something to do with Maxim Rogovsky's mistress threatening to "shed" on a EuroBollard investor. I had an urge to hold her hand, but Wendy had been a bit stand-offish since I kicked her out of bed the other night.

THE PRISONER OF WINDSOR

I riffled through the bill of fare: Kenny Twink & Kenny Bear. Zlapp & Tickell. And, notwithstanding the King's antipathy, Frankie Puss. "But it's not a regular Royal Variety show. It's the Coronation Command Performance. There are acts from around the Commonwealth."

"Great," said Wendy. "Dame Kylie, Cirque du Soleil, and some drummers from Lesotho."

"Mustn't be cynical, darling. Isn't that right, Vic?"

Our driver glanced in his mirror. "I'm with Mrs R on Cirque du Soleil, sir."

"See, Robert?" Wendy picked a bit of fluff off her dress. "Who else is on the bill?"

"Oh, you know… Sir Cliff, Sir Elton, Sir Paul, Sir Mick, Dame Shirley…"

"England, bloody England. You have to give up your titles so you can pretend to be a man of the people. Meanwhile, every pop star swishes around like the Viceroy of India."

"You sound like Roger Severn," I said.

"Can you put the windows down, Vic? Not often we get a perfect summer's evening in London…"

Wendy was right. The town was aglow. Even Whitehall's drearier buildings shone.

And then it happened – just as we approached Parliament Square. The vehicle came out of nowhere, rounding the corner and heading straight for a protest by Small World, the movement against freedom of movement, along with a smaller number from Make the Poor Rich. A white van was flooring it directly at some fellows with a big "Think Globally, Live Locally" sign. The vehicle came out of nowhere, rounding the corner and heading straight for a protest by Le Monde Sans Viande. A white van was flooring it directly at some fellows dressed as lambs. They panicked and scurried four-leggedly out of its path, and we all braked and veered and swerved, and the Jag went up on the sidewalk and slammed straight into one of the few surviving red telephone boxes. It had been converted into a novelty artwork showing a City gent in bowler hat with rolled 'brolly' unbuttoning his shirt to burst through the roof of the booth as Captain Britain in Union Jack spandex undies. We hit it head on, and Captain

327

Britain fell from the top of the box, into the street and under a bus, poor chap.

None of us were hurt, or so I thought. But Sanjay had banged his head and seemed to be struggling to stay conscious. And Vic couldn't restart the Jag, and there were two other cars blocking us anyway. And demonstrators all around. And, before I could stop her, Wendy had gotten out to see if she could help an elderly protester who'd fallen over. As I did at the Elgin, I opened the car door and followed.

And that's when the rival demonstration appeared from a side street. "Uh-oh," said Vic. "Not good. It's Reprimitivisation Now. And looks like Avatar, too." That would be the Anti-Violence Anti-Torture Anti-Racists. "They're vicious bastards," he added.

Reprimitivisation Now and Avatar weren't running so much as dancing – waltzing on a summer's night, lighter than air, free of their crowd-control barriers and riot police and romping through town. They hadn't seen the homicidal van, all they saw was us – "Rassendyll and his posh bitch!" as one of them yelled.

A Reprimitiviser threw something that sailed past my head and hit a car behind. There was a splintering sound, and a huge spider's web appeared across the windshield. "Time to go," I muttered. I hadn't survived a sword fight at Cymbeline's Castle only to lose my life to a gang of superannuated kindergarten anarchists. But the mob were upon us. Sanjay had roused himself and was halfway out but an Anti-Violence Leaguer crushed his arm in the car door. It was every man for himself.

Wendy and I ducked down the side of the Jag. She slipped off her heels and tucked them in her bag, and then set off down Parliament Street at a hell of a sprint. I had the devil of a job keeping up. We'd barely started when I heard a shout behind us:

"Rassendyll!"

"Get him!" cried another. I think at that point I'd rather have been hanging off White Mike's precipice.

If it hadn't been for the mob in pursuit, it would have been a lovely summer's evening - indeed, the first such evening since I'd arrived. Big Ben glittered in the sunlight, I thought, as I darted past.

We were nearing Downing Street now. We were going to make it. I could see the black steel security gates – closed, of course, to keep the Prime Minister safe. But what if the PM's on the wrong side of the fence with a howling mob at his heels? There was always someone on duty, and, when he saw us, he'd open the gates, wouldn't he? Wendy was ahead of me. The officer came into view. She waved at him. "Open up!" I shouted. He appeared stunned, and then looked behind, up Downing Street, as if seeking a second opinion. And then our luck worsened. The mob cut us off on our left flank. They were now between us and the gates. Wendy yelped and zigzagged off toward Richmond Terrace, but there were more demonstrators coming that way. She reversed hastily, and we found ourselves in the middle of the street a few metres from the Cenotaph - the glorious dead, whom we seemed likely to join, most ingloriously.

There was nothing else in sight, nowhere to go. And they were on us now, from all sides. Wendy fell panting against the south end of the Cenotaph, and I made ready to protect her from the people's wrath. And then to my amazement she leapt up, put a stockinged foot on a small bit of moulding, swung round to the side of the monument, used one hand to grab the pole of the RAF ensign bolted into the stone and the other to start pulling herself up the wall in a kind of sideways crouch. When she'd got her foot on the small brace fixing the flagpole to the Cenotaph, she gave one further heave, reached back around the corner to seize the lower leaves of the stone wreath, gave another heave, got her other hand to the top of the wreath, one foot up on the wobbling crown capping the pole, another push, and there she was – atop the Cenotaph in nothing flat. I did the same – or tried to. I jumped, reached for the moulding, missed, tried again, got a hand hold on the flagpole, but some guy below did the same to my ankle. I shook him loose, and tried to pull up. *Whoooooph!* This was worse than hanging off Mike Rassendyll's precipice. Upper body strength not quite "up to snuff". I made the midway bracket, and then the lower part of the wreath. Wendy leaned over and offered a hand, and pulled till my own fingers could grab the shelf below her. I kicked at those scrambling to tear me back down, and in a moment I was up.

We got to our feet, took a breath and looked around. It was a little precarious, but solid. North, south and east, there were enraged Reprimitivisation, Human Extinction, Anti-Violence and Small World advocates as far as the eye could see. And to the west, beyond a somewhat smaller number of agitators, were the Downing Street gates, behind which two officers were speaking into their radios with all the urgency of a bored RuriFleisch clerk repeating an order for two Hofburgers with cheese.

"Let's deplatform them!" yelled one of the Human Extinction lads.

"They're going to get us kicked off Twitter," I warned Wendy.

"I think you'll find," she said, "they intend to throw us off the platform."

I wasn't so sure. The demonstrators jostled for space round the base of the monument, but it was tall and, aside from that stone wreath, pretty sheer - and there were too many short or fat or spindly or stooped types crowding around to allow the fitter chaps to bust through.

But they'd get through eventually. So now what? I held up my hand, cleared my throat, and tried to remember my Swiss-school Shakespeare. "Friends, Britons, countrymen!" I declaimed. "Loan me your ears!"

They jeered. So what next..?

"This is the Cenotaph," I cried. They looked baffled, so I explained. "The monument to our glorious dead."

"The Glorious Dead want debt forgiveness for Africa!" someone yelled.

"Not the post-thrash post-metal band," I clarified, "but Britain's war dead. Soldiers."

They barracked some more. "The men we honour here," I continued, "gave their lives in horrible bloody conflicts so that you would not have to, so that you could live in peace."

"Warmonger!" a man shouted, shaking his fist. "Yeah," agreed those around him. They seemed to be blaming me for the First World War.

"There can never be a 'war to end all wars'," I carried on, "but since 1945 most Britons have led lives untouched by the mass terror rained down on our people twice in the previous thirty years. Do you know how rare this moment is in human history? Even in modern Europe. Ask a Ruritanian if he'd…"

"Piss off!" shrieked a young lady. "What about our frozen bennies?"

"And, yes, we still face many challenges," I said, shifting gear. "But, compared to the burdens your forebears took up on the Western Front or in the Blitz, we're not asking much of you. We're not asking you to sacrifice your life, only to accept a slightly lower rise in the increase of your benefits so that we can afford the External Zone (Qualified Recognition) transfer payments."

"Bollocks to that!" yelled another demure miss. "You're an arsehole!"

I remembered something I had learned at school when we did poetry of the Great War. Surely all Britons would have learned it, too. "The poppies we wear each Remembrance Day…"

"No blood for oil!" a woman screamed.

"They're a tradition whose origins lie in a famous poem: 'In Flanders fields the poppies blow…'"

The crowd looked blank. "My body, my choice!" yelled a bearded man in a polka dot dress.

I pressed on. "The final lines are a challenge to us – the children, grandchildren, great-grandchildren and on and on for whom they died so that we might live in freedom:

To you from failing hands we throw
The torch; be yours to hold it high.
If ye break faith with us who die
We shall not sleep, though poppies grow
    In Flanders fields.

The Human Extinction Movement and Avatar and Small World and all the rest fell silent.

Yes! I've done it, I've pulled it off. I've turned the mob. They're with us now. We'll climb down, the crowd will part, and, midst their cheers, we'll walk through the Downing Street gates and back into Number Ten.

And then someone yelled: "Crap!"

The mob jostled restlessly.

"Yeah, it was total crap."

Someone lobbed a soda can. Something called Irn-Bru.

"It's even crapper than when Rassendyll does that shit where he pretends he's not a racist."

They scrabbled around the monument searching for hand holds.

"Yeah, quoting poetry? It doesn't even sound like Rassendyll..."

Really? That last devastating criticism gave me an idea.

"So worraya think?" I said in a non-Rassendyll voice. Not sure exactly what accent I was doing. Might have been Cockney, or Brummie - or Geordie, Ulster, Kiwi or South African. But it certainly wasn't Rassendyll.

"What are you up to?" whispered Wendy, huddling close and readying for our Ceauşescu moment.

I repeated my question: "Whorraya think, gang?" I attempted to reprise my Cockney-Belfast accent but it may have veered into Scouse-Aussie or a Highland brogue via Rhodesia. Close enough.

The mob looked baffled.

"I mean, how'd we do?" I spread my hands like a burlesque comic. "C'mon, don't tell me we fooled you. We're lookalikes!"

There was some muttering among the activists. "What yer mean, 'lookalikes'?"

I nudged Wendy, and she stepped up to the crease. "We work for an agency in Notting Hill," she said, with what I think was meant to be a Welsh lilt. "They supply celebrity lookalikes for parties. We were just on our way to play the..."

She was doing so well, but she floundered...

"...the Recovery Foundation for Black Historical Memory," I said, recovering my memory of one of the fellows I'd met in Manchester. "They stage a mock show trial, and we carry on like the Ceauşescus. Then they raffle tickets to see who gets to shoot us. Everyone loves it."

"And the money's pretty good," added Wendy.

Wrong thing to say. They bristled.

"Twenty quid," I said. "Plus the complimentary buffet."

They de-bristled.

"Yeah," said a bloke near the base of the Cenotaph. "I can see it now. They're good, but they're not that good. I mean, if they'd been on telly, I'd know they weren't the real Rassendylls."

"They're almost right," said another, "but it's like they're not a real couple. They don't go together."

"It's a mixed bag. One's very good, the other not so much."

Uh-oh. I didn't like the way the conversation was going.

"Yeah, if you look closely, he's very convincing, but she doesn't look right at all."

"They had me going for a while. Specially with all that shit he was saying. That was some fucked-up shit. Seriously fucked-up. Must have great writers for shit like that."

And then the mob burst into a round of applause. They beckoned us down from the Cenotaph, and, albeit a little nervously, we descended. At the foot of the memorial, we posed for selfies with a few star-struck anarchists. A handful had amusing ideas about pretending to punch me in the kisser, or hanging us with their trouser belts, so we gamely played along. Pity they were blocking our path to the Downing Street gates. Then again, it looked as if the officers had gone into lockdown and, in any case, given our disavowal of Rassendyllishness, we couldn't very well stroll over and up to Number Ten.

"So where's the Black Historical Memory gig then?" asked a gender-ambiguous type.

"Oh, up that way," said Wendy, airily pointing in the general direction of Soho. The Welsh accent seemed to be wilting.

"That's right," I said. "We don't want to be late, do we, Bronwyn?" So we ducked away and walked nonchalantly back up Whitehall, the protesters falling away behind us to shake their fists and chant their chants through the gates to Downing Street. At Trafalgar Square, Wendy thought it safe to put her heels back on. We walked through Soho arm in arm and undisturbed. Perhaps it was because we were both a bit bedraggled: the sheen of celebrity had been rubbed off. In Poland Street, I stopped and pulled Wendy into a doorway and put my arms around her tight.

"You were wonderful back there," I whispered.

"So were you."

I kissed her.

"I love you," she said. "I do."

And I instantly hated myself – and remembered her husband. Something was happening: when a prime minister and his wife get chased down the street, is that just because some random mob gets lucky? The white van charging at the crowd, the car hitting the phone box, the car not re-starting, Downing Street security locking us out: *something* was underway.

"We're two lovebirds on a date!" Wendy cuddled closer. "We haven't done this since your first election." In a Soho square, we stopped and kissed like young lovers, leaning against a tree. From a nearby bar, music drifted on the night air, and Wendy sang along: "I kissed an earl and I liked it," she trilled.

Then we hailed a cab to take us to Paddington Station for a train to Windsor. At the drop-off, the driver said, "Loved your Manc speech, guv. This ride's on me."

He held up his *handifon*: "Rassendyll's Approval Numbers Hit New High." No wonder things were spiralling out of control.

I think I was a little mad on the train that evening, but oh, if you had seen her! I forgot the PM in Windsor. I forgot the PM in Downing Street. She was my love - even though I was an impostor. Overwhelmed by the former, I did my best to deny to myself the latter.

"I liked what you said at PMQs," she said. "I don't suppose I'll like Belinda any more as a one-legged bitch than I did as a two-legged bitch, but I can't believe how they're trying to justify it. You're the only one who's pushed back." She snuggled in to my chest. "And I'm sorry those twits didn't like the poem back there. I did."

And then we held hands and said nothing. The soft hum of the wheels against the track set my wooing to a wordless rhythm, as I pressed my kisses on her lips. I know, I know: I was false to all that I should have held by – and I thank God for the ping of Wendy's mobile that interrupted my madness.

"Millie Trehearne," she said. "You're not answering your phone, and she wants to make sure you see this."

It was a bombshell report from al-Jazeera:

> *Leaked smartphone footage appears to show that Hubert de Gautet, President of the Council of the European Union and formerly the EU's chief Brexit negotiator with the United Kingdom, was aware some weeks ago that Euro-toilets were leaking into Muslim toilets, and dismissed concerns at a high-level meeting, attended by the presidents of both the European Commission and the European Council...*

THE PRISONER OF WINDSOR

And there somewhat oddly framed but nevertheless distinct was unmistakeable footage of de Gautet, flanked by Adelheid Lauengram and Annika Maksten, sneering:

> *Oh, so I'm supposed to worry if a Muslim woman wants to use the bathroom. I take your Little Englander shit and shove it up her burqa.*

I knew those words. I knew where he'd said them – to me, in that bathroom in Brussels at the big External Zone summit. As the news presenter put it:

> *The fact that the conversation appears to be taking place in a Euro-toilet lends credence to reports that so-called 'leaking sitzpinklers' were known and discussed at the highest level in Brussels.*

Three sitzpinklers had been set alight in St Denis, Malmö and Moelenbeek. But I wasn't paying attention to any of that. Because it occurred to me, from the shot of de Gautet, that the camera in that bathroom must have been exactly where I was standing – i.e., on me.
    I'd been bugged.
    And most likely I was still bugged.
    And at that moment our train pulled in to Windsor Station.

Chapter Forty-Four
Hitting bottom

I HAD HIGH HOPES we'd get to the Castle just in time to have missed most of Act One at least. Unfortunately not. We were shown to our seats in the ad hoc open-air auditorium just in time for Muffin and the Mule. She's a lesbian, and he's a mule who fancies her and chases her around the stage. Then came a special Coronation version of *Zlapp & Tickell*, the popular situation comedy about a dim-witted English man-about-town, Sir Aubrey Tickell, Bart, and the brilliant Ruritanian manservant, Zlapp, who rescues him from all his scrapes. Next came the rapper G Haddy (not bad).

But my mind was not on the entertainment. There was something strange about the way people approached us. Not everyone, but certain persons – Rupert Henley, and Peter Borrodaile, and that transgender field marshal I'd met at the Pride Parade. They looked at Wendy and me as if we were ...uninvited guests. I wondered whether they'd been in on that business at the Cenotaph ...but that Irish rocker Brillo gave me the same look, so maybe it was just a more general dislike of me.

And then there was that BBC woman, who'd intercepted me as we arrived and wanted to know how I felt about the Prime Minister of New Zealand, Sir Jim Locke, announcing the removal of the statue of the 13th Earl of Burlesdon.

"What number am I?" I asked.

"You *were* the 16th Earl," she said.

So this chap would have been my great-grandfather, I suppose. Long ago he had been Governor-General of New Zealand and, upon taking up the post, had been greeted by a party of Maoris who had bared their bottoms to him. Being unaware that this was an expression of their contempt for the Crown, the 13th Lord Burlesdon had assumed it was simply a friendly greeting from one fellow to another and, wishing to enter into the spirit of the occasion, had turned around and dropped his own breeches. A left-wing academic had started a campaign against the late viceroy.

"Ah, I see," I said, "because he broke public decency laws."

She laughed. "No, because he's guilty of cultural appropriation. Bottom-baring is a Maori custom."

"Well, I don't see how one race can have a monopoly on dropping one's trousers," I said. "The Ruritanians do it quite a lot, I hear." I was thinking of Open Mike Night in Hofbau, where by tradition the winner has to hold a bottle of slivovitz between his cheeks and walk it around the room. But I didn't want to get into that unless she asked a follow-up question.

"How do you feel about Sir Jim's comments?"

"Well, I suppose if nobody else wants the statue, we'd be happy to have it shipped to Burlesdon. Stick it between the moat and the ornamental fountain."

"Not that. The bit where he said you need to consider your position. Because you have no credibility in the Commonwealth. Are you going to resign? There are rumblings from the 1922 Committee."

"Is this pants-down thing supposed to be genetic then? I am not my brother's keeper but I am my great-grandfather's trousers? In that case, how can it be cultural appropriation?" I could see Wendy behind the BBC harridan starting to giggle, so I put my hands on my trouser belt.

"Don't you dare," said the Beeb gal. "I could #MeToo you."

"Not if I identify as Maori," I pointed out. "As the Maoris felt about my great-grandfather, so I feel about the BBC."

At intermission, I sought out the King, who was annoyed by the lateness because Wendy and I were supposed to be seated next to him and the empty places didn't look good on the big monitors. I ignored all that, and said I needed a quiet word. He received me very frostily. But I didn't care: Too much was happening. Even the toppling of the 13th Earl in New Zealand seemed unlikely to be entirely coincidental. Events were accelerating – and then there was Wendy. I couldn't bear what I was doing to her – or to myself. So, as much as I loved her, I had to get Rassendyll back - now. "Sir," I said, "do you have that floor plan of the Round Tower I asked you for?"

"This is hardly the time, Mr Rassendyll. I have to get through a bloody reception line of pop stars who all expect me to know one wretched hippety-hopper from another."

I bowed, from the neck, and as I came back up I looked him in the eyes and said: "Then on your soon-to-be-crowned head be it, sir."

Act Two began with Carrie Moonbeams doing "The Last Tide", the theme song for the Duchess of Wokingham's Bafta-winning documentary about rising sea levels, but she took the opportunity to announce that the Government was partnering with Bill Gates on a new initiative to develop sustainable amps for rock bands, and, with the best will in the world, she did go on a bit. The crowd grew restless. Fortunately, hundreds of British troops came marching on, drumming frenziedly behind Brittany Lyon doing her latest hit.

Wendy squeezed my hand. "Poptastic," she whispered. "I suppose a bit of Handel's *Musick for the Royal Fireworks* would be out of the question?"

The song ended, and Brittany stepped to the microphone. "Wotcha, UK! UK, I'm 'kay, 'mkay?" she bellowed. The crowd roared. "Brilliant! It's brilliant to be here at the start of a new thingy, reign, innit? And it's brilliant to have these really cool soldiers drumming behind me doing their royal tattoo thing. I'm not into politics, but I say that's what an army's for, right? More tats and less wars? Got it, lads? We should send you into the Donbass, izzit, and tattoo the Russians."

The lads had the grace to look a little sheepish. Seated next to Wendy, the Hon Jamie Topham, whose forebears included at least seven generals, applauded enthusiastically.

"I want to say sumfin," she said, "'cause a lot of people don't know this but I'm a Jew, right? Well, part-Jew. I mean, I'm not practicing or anyfing. Not that there's anyfing wrong wif that. I mean, like, I'm very spiritual. But I'm not into organised religion because of, like, the legacy of child abuse, which is my main priority as an activist. But I've got no problem if you are. Freedom of religion, see? Muslims, Hindus, Wookies, I'm cool. 'Cause I'm part-Jewess, and I seen where it leads. Like my great-aunt and great-uncle, I fink it was, might have been great-great-aunt or sumfin', but anyway they were killed 'cause they were in the Holocaust. In, like, Germany. Not that I've got anything against Germans. Lovely people. The remix of 'Pump It' went triple platinum. But, like, I never knew my Jewess relatives. So that's why I'm passionately opposed when I see Israel being like Nazis and turning the Golan peninsula into a concentration camp, geddit?"

The crowd cheered.

"Not vat I'm anti-Semitted or anyfing. Say what you like about Israel, but you gotta admire their booster rollout…"

THE PRISONER OF WINDSOR

The camera cut to the Royal Box and the giant monitors on each side of the stage showed His Majesty with an inscrutable expression, while I appeared to be stroking my chin thoughtfully. I ceased to do so.

"'Cause that's really the message here, innit? In this new reign, we're all in it together, not just for Britain but for the planet and the environment. It's all interconnected, isn't it? The reign. The environment. The envi*reign*ment. That's what we want. The envireignment. That's why I'm passionately opposed to this government."

The crowd bayed its approval. On the monitor, the King maintained his inscrutable expression; I smiled goofily.

"Rob Rassendyll wants to turn us against one another. He's into fear and division. Whites against blacks, infidels against Muslims, straights against LGBTT... Q... I ...IQ? Always lose it after the 'T'. Anyway, straights against gay, lesbian, bisexual, transgendered, questioning, whatever; capitalists against public servants, anti-vaxxers against quintuple-boostered... I say we need everyone pulling together – blacks and Asians and cislesbians and translesbians and workers and banksters and environmentalists and denialists and boosters and nutters..."

Seated next to me, the King clapped politely.

"Let's not rob the people. Let's rob Rassendyll – of his job!"

The cheers filled the Windsor skies. Despite my record-breaking post-Manchester-speech approval numbers, the BBC had apparently had difficulty finding anyone who approved of me for their specially invited audience. On the monitor, I waved as blithely as I could.

"L'il bit of politics," said Brittany Lyon. "Sorry 'bout vat. Couldn't 'elp meself. Anyway, here's a song that sums up how we all feel, doesn't it?" And she launched into her big love song, "In You I See Myself". This was the cue for a giant medley of the best of the Great British Songbook from the last thousand years – which meant a brisk trot through "Greensleeves", "Old MacDonald Had a Farm", "Loch Lomond", "Danny Boy", "Men of Harlech", "Let's All Go Down the Strand (Have a Banana)", and then on to the poppier stuff. It wasn't exactly choreographed, but thousands of quarantined and hypervaccinated volunteers had been hired to form "the biggest group of British extras ever seen". They were there to recreate the nation's history in interpretative dance – or as interpretative as they could get considering they weren't dancers and they weren't being paid and the bits that non-dancers usually use to express themselves – the face – were masked and some of them had gone a booster too far and had erratically twitching limbs. Controversial parts of the national story – the Crusades, the Empire, winning the Second World War, economic growth - were largely avoided in favour of social commentary. So the extras stomped about weary and burdened as agricultural labourers, and then they stomped about some more as downtrodden mill workers, and then they cowered as cannon fodder in the trenches of the Great War, and, after a brief interlude shivering and starving during the Depression, cowered again as bombs rained down in the London Blitz. And then things perked up a bit, and they rock'n'rolled to Cliff Richard, and made peace signs to the Beatles, and pogoed to the Sex Pistols, and post-thrashed to the Glorious Dead, and pretty soon everyone was happy and dancing and coming together in a complex kaleidoscopic pattern that looked a chaotic mess but, from one very precise aerial shot that the BBC cameras never got quite right, formed a kind of giant mobile-phone text that read: "lolz to hm omg".

And at that point I politely excused myself. The show was intolerable, and so was the situation with Wendy. I had to get Rassendyll back, and then maybe I could get off this honour kick and return to the normal life of an unemployed Central European layabout. "I have a meeting in the Castle," I whispered to Wendy, and said that Ron and Suresh – the relief team for Vic and Sanjay – would get her back to Downing Street.

"Okay," she said, and squeezed my hand. "I'll be in our bedroom."

As I walked toward the Round Tower, the Great British Songbook medley climaxed with Brittany Lyon back on stage to sum up a thousand years of British history with her celebrated song, "Sex Candy":

I wanna wanna taste your
Sex Candy
I gotta gotta chew chew chew
On you...

THE PRISONER OF WINDSOR

But I had other matters to chew on. I ran toward the tower, and the first door. On the other side was a footman, who raised his hand to stop me. Then he saw who I was, and withdrew it. I walked calmly past, and once out of his sight began running again. Running on fear of what the men who had Rassendyll would do next. Kicking open doors, checking closets and cupboards, kidneys aching and chest pounding. I found a narrow stairway and headed down. My breath was steady at first, but I was now panting and gulping. Too many exertions, too many close shaves, too many bruises and cuts. But I kept moving forward, forward, forward. I crashed through one door and stumbled past a startled servant, but I didn't stop. Somewhere in here was the Prime Minister. I had stitch and was sweating, and tripped and stumbled, but caught myself. My calves felt like lead weights, and my chest as if it were about to burst. My arms flapped arhythmically at my side. But, over the gasps of my breath, I felt I was closing in on my target.

And then, on the half-landing, from out of nowhere, there he was. Derek Detchard, Chancellor of the Exchequer. Dressed in cricket whites.

"Wotcha, PM!"

I was so surprised I didn't notice the cricket bat.

Until he hit me on the side of the head.

Chapter Forty-Five
The international Ruritanian conspiracy

I CAME ROUND SLOWLY, with a buzzing in my head, a chill in my bones, and a vague feeling that I was at the wrong angle in relation to the room. My right eye opened to a blur of greyish-brown. I was face down on a stone floor. I closed my eye, and wandered off again. Twenty seconds later, twenty hours later, whatever, I re-opened my eye. Ah, right. The stone floor. Grey-brown. Now I remember. With supreme effort, I attempted to raise my head, only to find my cheek was stuck to the ground. Grey-brown. Grey-brown stone floor. The grey was the stone. The brown was my dried blood. I tried again, and howled as my cheek pulled free. But no sound came.

I fell back, and passed out. I dreamed. I dreamed I was back at Royal Chewton. No, somewhere else. Not real tennis, or royal tennis. Regular tennis. Who was I playing? I knew him. The last big Ruritanian contender. He had a big Serb. Big serve. Hantz. Christian Hantz. Christian "Fore" Hantz, the American commentators called him. Okay on grass, brilliant on clay. He would have been even better on rubble, which most of Ruritania's tennis courts were by the time he was at his peak.

Why was I dreaming about tennis? I opened my right eye. Somewhere a radio or TV was playing. Tennis commentary. Wimbledon. Through the wall a voice declared, "Game to Mr Castle."

I closed my right eye, and opened my left. There, across the floor, was a pair of boots. Black-brown boots. The black was the boot. The brown was my blood. What do they call them? Bovver boots? I raised my eye, along the legs and up the torso to the face. I wanted to speak, but only a gurgling sound emerged. He looked at me and grinned.

"Welcome back, mate," said Derek Detchard.

The Chancellor of the Exchequer gave an operetta bow, then strolled over and kicked me in the ribs. "My mistake," he said. "It's Your Prime Ministerial Excellency, isn't it?" And he gave me another kick. Then he unclenched his fingers to reveal a small, splintered chip in his palm. "Clever. I'd've bet it was up your khyber. Was just about to get me finger going when we got a reading from your tat. Crafty."

That explained the ache in my shoulder. A bugged tat. Fritz and Severn must have done it – on that first night, with Rassendyll unconscious on the floor and me passed out in a drunken stupor.

"Why are you holding me?" I croaked.

"Why are we 'holding' you?" he mocked. "You sound like a social-media misgenderer at a police station demanding to ring his solicitor." He dropped to his knees and pressed his nose against mine. "We're not *holding* you. We've disappeared you, mate."

"This is England," I protested.

"And England's done this to all kinds of people all over the world for centuries. They did it to my bog-trotter father-in-law. They did it to bloody Obama's grandfather – as I heard you say in the House."

He spat in my eye, and it trickled down my cheek, mingled with the blood, and dried. He watched the progress of his saliva thoughtfully. "They wanted to have the minions do this," he said, "but the minions do everything, don't they? G7 finance meeting? Here's your briefing paper, Mr Detchard. *Panorama* interview? Here's your talking points. Party conference? Here's your speech. God forbid you wander off-message ...'cause, if you say anything they didn't write out, they make you go back and say, 'I regret that I mis-spoke.'" He simpered the last words, and then kicked me, almost gently. "D'you remember how my ministerial career started?" He laughed at his own question. "Well, no you wouldn't, 'cause you're just the understudy." And he kicked me again, harder this time. "I was junior Minister for Children and Equality... Equality and Community... Community and Identity... Whatever. Not like Lord Privy Seal, is it? And they wanted me to say I regretted that I'd mis-spoken. And I said bollocks to that, so your..." He counted it out on his fingers. "...your wanker predecessor-but-three fired me. Three weeks later there was a rumour in the paper about me jumping to the LibDems, so your wanker predecessor-but-two put me in the Cabinet. What I really wanted to be was Speaker – like that arsehole in Canada: no spads, no minders. You can do what you like. A little bit of creative interpretation of some wanker Speaker from the thirteenth century and Parliament can now usurp the functions of the executive. Thanks to those Supreme Court poufters, the Prime Minister can now be ordered to do what the Speaker tells him."

He paused in his monologuing to scratch his crotch and adjust his trousers. "Still, you've been an inspiration to me, cock. All those river rescues and Cenotaph stand-offs. Makes a bloke think maybe I should be doing a bit more meself." He kicked me again, for real, and I howled in agony.

"So look on this as my audition for Speaker - just another PMQs, awwight? Order!" He stamped on my right leg. "Order!" He stamped on my left. "Questions to the Prime Minister. Here we go: Number One, Mr Speaker." He stared down at me. "C'mon, mate, this is an easy one." Another kick, just a gentle nudge.

"This morning," I wheezed, "I had meetings with ministerial colleagues and others. In addition to my duties in the House, I shall have further such meetings later today."

"Correct. Second question: Who do you work for?"

"I'm the King's first minister," I croaked. "I work for His Majesty."

"Weird," he ruminated. "Only the other day I was kicking the head in of another man who claimed to be the King's first minister. But he gave a better answer: He said, 'I work for the British people.'"

Good old Rob Rassendyll. Knows the right soundbites even when he's having the crap beaten out of him in some dungeon. Somewhere beyond my cell a voice announced, "Thirty-love."

"You are Rudolf Elphberg," said Detchard. "Don't make this more difficult for yourself. I'll ask again nicely: Who are you working for?"

I paused, and took a deep breath. "The RSS," I replied.

"The RSS?"

"The Ruritanian Secret Service."

He reached down and grabbed me under the arms. Roughly, he pulled me on to my feet, and then leaned me carefully, gently, against the wall. When he was satisfied I was properly balanced, he drove one fist into my ear, and with the other gave me a knifelike jab to my already sore kidney. I slid down the wall, and back to the floor.

"So you're an actor. Perhaps you should have gone into stand-up comedy."

"Comedy is easy," I wheezed at his toecaps. "It's the standing up I'm having trouble with."

"Are you working for the bleedin' Yanks?"

I laughed, and spat up blood.

"The Jews?"

"Now you're getting closer."

He exhaled heavily, and I felt the tang of red wine and peanuts on my cheek. "Don't piss around, Elphberg."

"Who's behind the International Jewish Conspiracy?" I asked. "It's the International Ruritanian Conspiracy. Everyone knows that."

He laughed. "Ruritanian content farmers! There's no such thing. Some Ruritanian working on Anna Bersonin's bog offered to help make her party leader, and Anna laughed her head off, and then mentioned it to Hillary Clinton as a joke, and Hillary took it seriously, and now the CIA want to pull out of the Five Eyes 'cause they're convinced the Ruritanians have penetrated it…"

He walloped me again. I fell against the wall, and in the echo of my skull crack I heard Derek say: "Unless whichever Ruritanian was working on Anna's bog wanted her to *think* it was just a joke…"

My face hit the floor and I passed out.

Chapter Forty-Six
Lookalikes and thinkalikes

I OPENED MY EYES to see the "doctor" – Doctor Davos. The absurdly Teutonic bullet-headed Junker who had tried to poison me in the Castle that night. Odd chap to have as one's gaoler. The doctor was smiling, in a kindly, paternal manner. Then he raised his hand and I flinched. Instead, he brushed my blood-matted hair with an odd tenderness.

"Are you in pain?" he asked. I was confused. I had been expecting that strong German accent of his. Instead, he spoke in an eerily accentless voice.

He was correct about my pain. "How long was I out?" I asked.

"Not long. Mr Detchard was just beating you up to kill time, I'm afraid – while little Flavia and I were giving King Arthur a tour of our latest research."

That perfectly unaccented English again. Not an English I had ever heard before – not from an Englishman, an Irishman, a Canadian or South African. Where had the Prussian gone?

"Shall we go somewhere more comfortable?" he continued. "Give him a hand, please, Chancellor." Reluctantly, Derek put his arm round my waist, as the doctor chattered away. "News," he sighed. "It never stops, does it? Not today anyway. A mob of aggrieved Muslims stormed the Council of the European Union headquarters and destroyed Hubert de Gautet's office – because of that soundbite of his about sitzpinklers. The BBC has suggested that, because he has never spoken English before, it could not be the real de Gautet and must be a lookalike from an agency. This theory has not caught on. Why would it? *Lookalikes!*

"De Gautet is in hiding. An emergency Conference of the EU Presidencies has been called."

He walked me up another flight to the next level of the Round Tower, and a room that was an odd mix of old and new, mediaeval and modern. Set among the thousand-year-old stonework was a sort of work cubicle on one side, with a desktop computer and an office chair, and mounted high up in the corner was an HD TV. There was a neat clinical sink unit against one wall, and my host ordered Detchard to bring some water. Then he began gently sponging my face.

"Who are you?"

"I'm your doctor."

"I didn't know I was sick."

"That's often the way, don't you find?" He touched my cheek, gently. "Everyone's very worried about you. And it's such a long wait at the NHS."

"Do you have any other patients?"

"Oh, you'd be surprised. I'm on the board of EuroSanté, the EU public health agency – oh, and the 'death with dignity' clinics." He stroked my hair again. "It's lovely. So red. Vibrant. Vivid. Full of life."

I was in pain and didn't want to talk hair colour. "The assisted suicide place? The EUthanasium? That's you?"

"Me and Brussels. Europe has a lot of very unhappy old people, even with all the SADS. So does the United Kingdom. That's why the EU insists on it in the External Zone (Qualified Recognition) Harmonisation Directive."

"So you're a mad scientist?"

"I'm more of a mad social scientist. Very lucrative. I'm the first euthanasia billionaire."

"Impressive."

"We've hardly scratched the surface. I discovered the Corona Syndrome and the last three Chinese viruses." He paused. "I'm getting ahead of myself. The third one hasn't been released yet."

"What happened to your German accent?"

"Oh, *zat*," he chortled. "So exhausting. '*Zuh future iss built by us – zuh masters of zuh future!*'" He shook his fist theatrically. "I couldn't keep it up if I had to do it in private. I'm Asiatic, you know. Female originally."

Dr Davos took three walnuts from a large bowl. He smiled at me with gleaming white teeth, and cracked the nuts with his small delicate hand. The white knuckles tensed whiter. He popped a walnut. Phalanges, is that it? The bones of the finger. Proximal phalanges. I looked down at mine, which didn't feel quite right.

"Identity politics," he murmured. "When I assumed mine, my associates wanted me to talk in a non-threatening accent – Norwegian perhaps, or Dutch. I thought it would be funnier to be a sinister

Teutonic megalomaniac hiding in plain sight as a sinister Teutonic megalomaniac. Dare people to call me on it – which they never do, because that would be culturally insensitive. And, really, all that 'masters of zuh future' bombast never sounds quite as good in a non-German accent."

He smiled again, and looked down at me.

"I admire what Sir Roger Severn did to Mr Rassendyll. He stole his identity. 'Identity theft'. I thought one only did that on the computer. Much easier than hiring a…" He paused to savour the word. "…a *lookalike* to start going around town in Mr Rassendyll's clothes. For most people today surely their real identity is on the computer anyway: the passwords for their online banking and specialised pornography interests. So there's something charmingly old-fashioned about you, Mr Elphberg, running around mimicking the voice and romancing the wife.

"Utterly charming."

He gave another thin-lipped smile. "But not so effective."

"You knew," I said. "You knew someone had switched prime ministers."

The doctor did not seem the type to explode with involuntary laughter, but he did. "This isn't an age for doppelgängers, for lookalikes. In our time, we venerate those who look unalike. Celebrate diversity!" His pallid hands made ghostly air quotes. "'Your' cabinet, for example. There are men, women, whites, blacks, homosexuals, lesbians, a genitally ambiguous transgender…"

Really? I wondered who that was…

"They all look different, and they all think the same. Same at the BBC. Same at the European Commission. Same anywhere that matters. Ours is an age of thinkalikes. That's the line I'm in. Sir Roger Severn is a romantic, like King Arthur with his cottage industries, his organic marmalade and oaten biscuits. The lookalike business is a cottage industry. The thinkalike business is global."

"And my problem is I don't think alike?"

Dr Davos picked up an uncracked walnut and cradled it, affectionately. "They were surprised by your referendum remark at the Pride Parade. But they assumed you were high."

"Who are 'they'?" I asked.

"Who isn't they? Cabinet. Civil servants. Eurocrats. BBC. Influential novelists. Activist scientists." He cracked his walnut. "Then late at night there was a viral video of you with men in the street at Victoria Station doubling down on your foolishness. I got a call from Rupert Henley. He and Mr Rassendyll go back a long way. He was worried about you – about Robert, I mean - and I'm the acknowledged specialist. I said obviously I can't diagnose somebody from a few soundbites; I would need to examine the patient in person.

"Mr Henley said he didn't see how that could be done, as Rassendyll would never agree to it. I said, well, I have a small research facility at little Flavia's foundation at Windsor Castle. Surely the Prime Minister comes to Windsor every so often – even if only for banquets and balls. Mr Henley was confident he and his Cabinet colleagues could get Rassendyll downstairs to my consulting room.

"He was in a terrible state, far sicker than I'd expected, babbling incoherently about reducing immigration, ending insect-farm subsidies, pointing out the benefits of British colonialism… I could see why the Cabinet was so concerned." He smiled at me. "If only I'd known about you," he said. "You were supposed to be his lookalike. But, after two soundbites from you, he wanted to be your lookalike. So I offered him a glass of wine, and after another half-bottle or so he'd calmed down enough to let us run a few tests."

"I filled in for Rob Rassendyll at the Pride Parade because he'd OD'd on cocaine," I said. "Did Rupert spike it?"

Dr Davos gave another of his explosive laughs. "The Prime Minister did not do cocaine before his dinner with you and Roger Severn."

"But he was unconscious. Comatose. The doctor said it was bad coke."

"If you mean your friend Fritz Tarlenheim," replied Davos, "I fear he is not the best doctor. I understand that's why he went into politics, where standards are so much lower."

"But he knew about adulterated cocaine from Austria. Something to do with belladonna."

"He would have been better to recall the Austrian wine scandals of the 1980s," sighed the doctor. "Sweet wine adulterated with …what was it? Diethylene glycol?"

I remembered the special bottle – the last toast of the evening. A gift from the King - and White Michael.

"As I mentioned, I made the mistake of letting Rob Rassendyll drink one of his brother's bottles of wine. And I observed a few hours later the facial flushing, swollen lips, anaphylactic shock... Herr Tarlenheim's belladonna fantasies were misdirected. He should have checked brother Michael's disgusting wine. And poor Robert Rassendyll should have stuck with cocaine.

"Mike Rassendyll was frantic, and so were the others. We had a man made sick by organic wine on our hands. And not just any organic wine, but the very first vintage from the King's vineyards. In a constitutional monarchy, it would not look good should the King's wine end up killing his prime minister. Even worse, suppose it was the organic wine that was causing Rob Rassendyll to think all these bizarre thoughts about climate change and the British Empire.

"They all agreed that the priority was to nurse Rob back to health. Obviously, it would not be safe for him to return to work. So, for a couple of days, Rupert Henley stalled, telling Mr Rassendyll's security team that he was just taking a couple of days off to spend with the King at Windsor. The six cabinet ministers who knew the truth agreed they would appoint an acting PM, and then immediately fell to squabbling as to which of them it should be." Dr Davos smirked at the thought. "As if it would make any difference."

I knew what came next. "And then I walked into the House of Commons and started taking Prime Minister's Questions..."

"At the exact moment Mr Henley was about to stand up and enjoy his moment in the spotlight. As soon as Question Time was over, Lowe-Graham telephoned to find out how Rassendyll escaped. I said what are you talking about? He's right here – and I texted a picture. They were incredulous. An impostor at Number Ten?"

"But what could they do about it?"

"Must have been a shock for you and your Euro-chums," I said, "to see a prime minister who isn't bought and paid for."

He laughed again. "Who would bother to buy people so anxious to give it away?" Dr Davos refilled his tumbler. "You're an unimportant man, Mr Elphberg. And, for the first time in your life, you are thrust into the spotlight. So you naturally think you and all your silly running around are suddenly important."

THE PRISONER OF WINDSOR

Davos took another nut – this time an almond. With the gentlest pressure from his thumb, the shell cracked. He removed the contents, pursed his lips, and slid it in thoughtfully. "I was fascinated by Rassendyll's case. I really wanted to cure him. But it would take time..."

"And with you in Number Ten bollocksing everything in sight we couldn't afford that," brayed a familiar voice. Rupert Henley. Wearing a cravat and leaning in the doorway as if he'd just popped by to ask Dr Davos if he could make up a four for tennis. Instead, he pulled up a chair. "That bonkers decision to hold a photo-op at the Tilted Teapot: why take President Kennedy to such a rubbish tourist rip-off? I haven't been since we were at Oxford and Belinda Featherhead was working there and a couple of us went in to take the piss and I felt a bit sorry for her and one thing led to another and we went back to her flat and I shagged the billy-ho out of her. And in the morning it was all rather embarrassing and I was itching to get my britches on and scarper and she kept twittering any old bilge so that the conversation wouldn't end. And one of the things she twittered on about was Nell Gwynn and a secret passageway..."

Rupert reached for an almond, noticed the absence of the nutcracker, and withdrew his hand. "And it occurred to me that's the only reason you'd be going anywhere near the Tilted Teapot. Which is why the good doctor was waiting for you."

Dr Davos splintered the walnut noisily. Shards of shell shot from his hand, and Rupert picked pieces of what was left from his palm.

I turned to him. "You're one of Rob Rassendyll's oldest friends – and yet you betray him by conspiring against him."

"Who's conspiring?" he said. "I thought he was sick, so I went to a world-renowned specialist. The doctor and I were trying to get him back on his feet, all tickety-boo. You and Roger are the conspirators – stealing his job, stealing his wife, stealing his mistress."

"What's this sickness he's got?"

"Globophobia," said Dr Davos. "One of the worst cases I've seen. You'll be glad to hear he's been responding to treatment."

"If you're such a world-renowned specialist, how come I've never seen you on television?"

"The people who matter aren't on telly," replied Rupert, a sneer curling his lip. "Television is for Belinda Featherly. Took me a while to figure that out."

We were joined by another of the many non-conspirators: Marjorie Craftstone stood in the doorway with her arms folded.

"Hallo, Marj!" said Rupert.

The Defence Secretary nodded to Henley and Davos and Detchard. The doctor looked pityingly at me, and drew a cold white finger down my cheek. "What a preposterous situation," declared Marj. "Two British prime ministers who are perfectly indistinguishable. What say you, Mr Elphberg – time to put one of them back?"

I was thinking maybe I'd make a run for it. But the doctor seized my arms and gently pulled me to my feet. Marjorie opened a side door in the panelling, and Rupert shoved me through into a small stone ante-room. "We thought you two might appreciate the company," said Marj. "It's not often we have two cells but only one prisoner. Robert Rassendyll, meet Robert Rassendyll."

Chapter Forty-Seven
A brace of prime ministers

I STARED DOWN AT the man whose life I'd usurped. He sat on an old bench, hunched over a copy of *The Daily Telegraph* spread out on the floor. "The Prime Minister is a little distracted at the moment," Rupert smirked. "He's an avid reader of your exploits. Isn't that right, Rob?"

Rob Rassendyll pulled his head up from the paper – a story about the Duchess of Wokingham's non-binary Coronation dress - and leaned his back against the wall, looking at us with a glassy-eyed befuddlement. "Yes," he said, dully. A man of "Asian" complexion (as the newspapers say) prevented him sliding on the floor.

"Robert's going back to Number Ten," said Dr Davos. "For a little while." He smiled at Rupert and Marjorie and Derek, in acknowledgment of their ambitions.

"Just so long as he doesn't get off his meds," added Rupert. "And really, once this Coronation's in the bag, the King deserves a prime minister at the peak of his powers for the dawn of our new Arthurian age."

The lady Defence Secretary gave a thin smile. "Or the peak of *her* powers."

"You had a bogtastic run in your impromptu premiership," Rupert said to me. "But there's not going to be any referendum on referenda."

"The simple working man – assuming for the purposes of argument there are any left – doesn't understand how complicated everything is now." Marj turned to Rassendyll. "That's right, isn't it, Rob?"

A cloud came over Rassendyll's eyes, and he slumped down again. Dr Davos contemplated the Prime Minister of the United Kingdom sprawled on the bench, eyes rolled upwards at the ceiling. His breathing grew heavier. The fellow alongside aimed a bored kick at his dangling foot.

"Who's this bucko?" I pointed to the heavy.

"Works for your brother," said Dr Davos. "In the organic wine business, aren't you, Mohammed?"

Marjorie sighed. "And now it is time to restore the rightful occupant to Number Ten Downing Street. The Prime Minister would thank you personally, Mr Elphberg, but he seems to have dozed off."

"But he knows everything that's happened…"

"And who can he tell?" crowed Rupert. "Severn will be reshuffled out of cabinet with the promise of that Garter he covets. And Rob will be happy to resume business as usual until the moment of his own reshuffling comes."

"And what about me?"

Dr Davos gave a thin smile. "My latest EUthanasium opens tomorrow in a charming village in the Haute-Savoie. And you seem to me to be a little depressed."

I felt a tightness in my chest. This couldn't be right. It was all a game – a jolly jape to help a Lord Privy Seal…

"Your brother's idea," explained the doctor with a genial smile. He corrected himself, nodding toward the real Prime Minister. "*His* brother's idea. So confusing." He left the room.

"I have an audience with His Maj," said Rupert. "We're getting along like a house on fire. By the way, did you like that video we sent you? *Five Guys Named Mo*? Not sure I'd've been up for decapitation vaudeville. The old Rob at his best."

Humphrey Lowe-Graham arrived, accompanied by another guard, also of what the papers call "Asian" extraction. "Pity I never got to work on your wedding tackle," Derek Detchard grumbled. "Never mind. We'll leave you in the capable hands of Mohammed and Mohammed."

"My name is Muhammad," objected one of the Mohammeds. "Like on *Five Guys Named Mo*."

"Lock him in," snapped Humphrey Lowe-Graham, "and then get the others. Clean up Mr Rassendyll, and put him in his suit. The *real* Mr Rassendyll." He tut-tutted theatrically, and looked back at me and Rob. "Two prime ministers: classic 1970s British overmanning. Time to make some long overdue cuts."

He smiled at the two Mohammeds, and they in turn smiled down at us.

THE PRISONER OF WINDSOR

"Oh, put a sock in it, Humphy!" snapped Rupert. "Stop twirling your wrist like it's am-dram night at the village hall and the body's in the library."

The heavy door clanged shut behind them, and the keys turned. My heart was racing. I didn't like the sound of this "important meeting". There must be some way out of here. I looked at the two Mohammeds, watching us from the other side of the room.

Time to try a little ice-breaking small talk. "So you're not both called Mohammed?" I said.

"As I said, I am Muhammad," said the shorter of the two. "Like the handsome one in *Five Guys Named Mo*."

"You wish," laughed Mohammed.

"How'd you chaps land a cushy job like this?" Alongside me on the bench, Rassendyll whimpered. It would be helpful, I thought, if he could perk up and contribute to the conversation.

"We qualified for the DRI," said Mohammed.

DRI? I'd heard that before, but I couldn't remember.

"They pay very well," said Muhammad, "but it's very hard to get in."

"I did three years in Raqaa," said Mohammed, "so I qualified."

Oh, of course! The White Knight had mentioned it. DRI: Rassendyll's De-Radicalisation Initiative.

"I had to take the test twice," said Muhammad, "even though I drove my car at top speed through the shopping centre."

"But it was a hybrid," said Mohammed, "so he didn't get very far. No hybrids in Raqaa."

I was wondering if I could get away with pretending to be a Zendak Muslim, and getting them to let me out in intra-Islamic solidarity. "Are there a lot of DRI graduates in Windsor Castle?" I asked.

"Just here," said Mohammed. "For the little Ruritanian girl's foundation."

"She is hot," said Muhammad.

"Too old for me," said Mohammed. "But her foundation recruits all its staff from the DRI. Prince Ghazi arranged a special deal."

"May Allah fart on the beard of that decadent and accursed member of the House of Saud," said Muhammad.

355

"Indeed," I agreed heartily. "Hear, hear."

"Although he did get us the job," conceded Mohammed. "I do climate modelling synthesising and Muhammad does climate synthesising modelling."

Rassendyll whimpered again, and slumped listlessly further down the wall. Good grief, would it kill him to contribute something to the conversation? "Must be exciting to have two prime ministers to guard," I suggested.

"We did not know you were prime ministers," said Muhammad. "I only know you from my mobile."

He could see I didn't get that, so pulled out his *handifon*, and clicked on some grainy nocturnal video. "I was there that night," said Muhammad, with pride, "at the Colin Corgi protest. It was great – until that infidel whore who sleeps with dogs rode up..." And there on his mobile was Lady Belinda on her mount galloping out of the Long Walk and into the Albert Road. And there on the other horse was...

"That's where I know you from," said Mohammed. "The consort of the infidel whore who sleeps with dogs!"

"It's a shame she survived," said Muhammad. "And the cowardly cur is in hiding."

"But the third member of the team is right here before us," said Mohammed. He picked up his briefcase, which I hadn't noticed before, and entered the combination.

"What's in there?" I asked.

He took out a machete.

Chapter Forty-Eight
A de-radicalisation hiccup

A FEW YEARS AGO, WHEN there was a spate of Albanian kidnappings in Ruritania, I did the voiceover for an instructional video Dobromil put together for what to do when you're in danger. And the big takeaway was that, when someone pulls a gun or a knife on you, the sooner you act the better your chances of surviving the situation. Be alert – so that, if something starts, you can finish it quickly, before the man with the weapon has taken control of the room, and of your future. "Situational awareness", or some such.

All that flashed through my mind as Mohammed got out his machete – and yet I myself did not act in accordance with the advice of my instructional video. Instead, I froze, as his comrade Muhammad picked up his umbrella and pulled at the handle to produce from within a blade of his own.

And then, aware of the awkward silence, I blurted out, "What have you got there?"

And Mohammed and Muhammad explained that, in the absence of Colin Corgi, it was time for the filthy whore Belinda Featherley's other dog to die.

As to what I said next, to this day I tell myself I was trying to buy time. "How do you know it's me in the video? It looks like him." I nodded at Rassendyll, who appeared to be asleep.

Both men laughed. "You make a good point," said Mohammed. "So we will kill both of you, and release the best video."

"Do him first." Muhammad nodded at the dozing Rassendyll. "I want to kill this one, and silence his infidel banter."

In a flash he was on me, and had the knife at my throat. Mohammed calmly returned to his briefcase and extracted a high-quality camera and mini-tripod that he sat neatly on the small wooden table. He yanked Rassendyll to his feet and moved him into the middle of the room. The swaying prime minister seemed entirely unaware of what was going on.

Without moving the knife from my throat, Muhammad looked through the camera. "The shot looks good."

"In Raqaa I did this every week – a Canadian peace activist, two American Jewesses," said the first Mohammed. "Climate research and organic wine production isn't the same."

The second Mohammed hit the record button, and Rassendyll opened his eyes.

Despite the knife at my throat, I sat up, involuntarily, as a mark of respect, as if I were at a memorial service. Which, in a way, I was. After all that time in captivity, Rassendyll looked more like me than he had that first night at Roger Severn's. It isn't often a man gets to watch his own execution.

Mohammed manoeuvred Rassendyll left and right until he was satisfied he was in the centre of the picture.

"State your full name!"

It was like the *Five Guys Named Mo* video, except it wasn't. "My name is Robert James Montague Rassendyll," he said faintly. "16th Earl of Burlesdon, 33rd Baron Rassendyll, both in the Peerage of England, Privy Counsellor, Member of Parliament for South Burlesdon and the Clewes, Prime Minister of the United Kingdom and First Lord of the Treasury."

Mohammed seized his hair, and held his face in front of the camera. The Prime Minister grimaced.

The Mohammeds began chanting in Arabic. Rassendyll stared into the lens, and, still staring at me, rolled his eyes at the end of each sentence. He knew what they were working up to. Both men screamed "Allahu Akbar!" and the first Mohammed lowered the machete.

Rob Rassendyll spat out his last words: "I'll show you how an Englishman dies!" And then he reared backwards and nutted his executioner in the head, in mid-swing. The machete twitched, and cut the second Mohammed in the arm. "Fuuuuuh," he screamed, and dropped his knife to tend to his wound. I elbowed him in the stomach and he fell to the floor, blood pouring out of him. I grabbed his knife, as the first Mo took another swing at his victim. He slipped in the pooling red left by his colleague, cut Rassendyll badly on the shoulder, and I drove the blade up into Mohammed's guts.

He fell back with a stunned expression.

The second Mo was scrambling to his feet. But Rassendyll had seized the machete and brought it down on his wrist. Muhammad screamed, and his hand hung useless from his arm. Rassendyll raised his weapon high and split his skull. For two or three seconds, Muhammad fixed his gaze on the camera, with gleaming pupils, and I saw a look in a pair of human eyes that I had never seen before. "Can you see the virgins?" asked Rassendyll. "Are they any good?" And then the light in Muhammad's eyes grew hazy, and faded, and there was nothing.

The Prime Minister stood up, panting hard. "God, it feels good to kill someone. I wonder when was the last time a Rassendyll did that. Probably my great-great-whatever-uncle in your country." He was exhilarated, but then reconsidered. "Pity, though. Of all the Deradicalised Mohammeds he was the most fun. Quite a dry sense of humour once you got past the Allahu Akbar rubbish." He noticed the blood from his shoulder. "Still, wouldn't look good to be the first PM to be killed in office since Spencer Perceval…"

Ah, Spencer Perceval. I'd seen him at Westminster Abbey.

Rassendyll clutched his shoulder, and then examined the blood on his fingers.

"I thought you were asleep," I said. "You were faking."

"You're the last person in a position to complain about that." He smiled, even as he winced from the shoulder pain.

The wound looked serious to me, and I thought it important to keep his spirits up. "We need to get you back to Downing Street, sir."

He laid down the machete.

"The thing is I'm not sure I want to go back, Rudy."

Oh, for crying out loud. There's always something you didn't see coming. I tried to find the words.

"The country needs you, Prime Minister."

There were voices from down the corridor.

"Don't call me Prime Minister. If there's one thing that's plain after the last few weeks, it's that the country needs *you*. You're a better prime minister than I'll ever be, than I ever was." He grasped my arms. "You're a better man than I ever was."

"That's not how this works," I said. It rang weak and tinny, like a line from a bad movie.

"You're really cut out for government," he continued. "And you know the sort of thing you do — mustard commercials, voiceovers — I think that might be more my cup of tea. I was talking to the Duchess of Woke at that Windsor ball, and she said the camera loves me. Plus she knows some people at Netflix, and they're doing an animated feature based on last year's Tony-winner..."

"Oh, come on," I scoffed. "After what you've just done? 'I'll show you how an Englishman dies'? I've never seen courage like that."

"Oh, that," he said carelessly. "I've been locked up in this castle for weeks with nothing to do but work on my treatment for Disney about a PM who gets kidnapped. I wrote that line on my fourth night and I've been waiting to use it. Duchess Kissy-Kissy says she can get me the number of the exec who greenlighted *Sleepless in Seattle*."

"So what?" I responded. "You're the chap who greenlighted the Chad invasion."

"Yeah, well, that didn't work out as well as *Sleepless in Seattle*, did it?"

He could see I was dubious.

"Look, I've always had a pleasant baritone, and she says celebrity-activism is where the real action is. I mean, how many leaders of the G7 can the average punter in Idaho name? So why don't you carry on with the PM-ing, and let's just swap passports? Wendy seems to prefer you too, judging from that business at the Cenotaph. She's never put on that Afrikaaner accent for me, even on our honeymoon."

I would have argued the point, but I remembered that important meeting Rupert & Co had all been so keen to hurry off to. So I said:

"It's a deal. Shake?"

Rassendyll extended his hand, as he had done so long ago in Roger Severn's dining room.

"Since you're so keen to swap passports, maybe we should do it the Ruritanian way."

"Ah, the traditional head-bump. Roger told me all about it."

We leaned into each other, and I nutted him harder than he had Mohammed. He fell unconscious to the bench and his head cracked against the stone.

Chapter Forty-Nine
Triggering His Majesty

I HAD TO MOVE FAST. There were two doors out of here, both locked. Of course. Why would they trust the Mohammeds, no matter how "de-radicalised" they appeared? One door led into Dr Davos's office, which meant another door after that, presumably also locked. So I went to the other, and shoved. Nothing moved. I retrieved the machete from the second Muhammad's head. My blood was up, as much because of Rassendyll's wish to become a Disney voiceover artiste as anything else. I plunged my blade into the door, and pulled it out. And again. And again, and again, until the wood began to splinter. My arms were heavy, but the wood was centuries old and dried out, and I hacked through to glimpse the room beyond. And again and again, until the breach widened, and I hurled myself at it and pushed through. And, with one final thrust and a thousand slivers in my – or rather Rassendyll's - beautiful bespoke suit, I burst out of our cell.

Just in time to spot a third de-radicalised Mohammed running headlong toward me, waving a pistol. He was going too fast, and hit me sideways on, sending us both tumbling to the floor, him on top, me underneath. But I drove the machete up and into his chest and straight through.

He gurgled, and fell on top of me, dribbling over my face. I forced my way out from under, and tried to retrieve my trusty blade. But it was stuck on something deep inside Mo, and I couldn't pull it out.

I stepped back into the cell, retrieved Muhammad's *handifon*, and then pulled up the unconscious Rassendyll. Further along the corridor I found a cupboard door, opened it, and dumped the PM inside. Then I called Roger Severn and left a message on where to find his protégé as I pounded up the stairs to the next level, desperate to find my way out of this castle of madness. At the first landing I pushed open the door and found myself in a well-appointed and rather crowded sitting room.

"*You* again!" said Peter Borrodaile, standing nonchalantly by the fireplace. "His Majesty certainly does not want for milord Burlesdon's counsel." Eight faces looked up from around a handsome mahogany conference table. As did a few more seated behind the three persons along each side. And as did, eventually, the Queen, seated in a corner wing chair with a paperback novel by Jocelyn ffoulkes and a haunted look.

"Mr Rassendyll?" The King was sitting at the head, and seemed utterly confused. "Why are *you* here?"

I gave his table the once-over. Some of them I knew: The inevitable Flavia Strofzin seated down the opposite end from His Majesty – and indeed, now I thought about it, either the co-chair of the meeting, or possibly the sole chair. On Flavia's left, I recognised, obviously, the recently knighted mononymous Irish rocker Brillo, patron of the Cayman Islands-registered non-profit group Make The Poor Rich and the pop star who had cut me dead at the Coronation Command Performance. Next to him was Carrie Moonbeams, the indy-pop songstress and lead vocalist on the awareness-raising charity anthem against two-ply toilet paper, "All We Are Saying Is Give One Piece a Chance". On the King's right was, of course, White Michael. On the King's left was my spad Rory Vane, looking more serene than he did most mornings at the 7.45. Next to Rory was Mohammed Almasri, the man who had driven Colin Corgi into hiding. Opposite Sir Mohammed was, in full dress uniform, that transgender field marshal I'd marched down Regent Street with, and alongside her was that football bloke I'd met at the Windsor ball, Larry Spelunker. I didn't know the others, but they gave off that air of indestructible confidence I had come to associate with the British establishment – except for one under-dressed and over-powdered slattern in the far centre of the table.

"What's going on?" I asked.

"We're having a board meeting for my foundathun, and you're not invited," declared Flavia. "Becauth you're not on my board, and you never will be." She stamped her foot petulantly. "Tho thtop thpoiling things, and go away!"

"You must surely see," said the King, "that things are spiralling out of control."

362

I had no idea what he was on about: The stock market was soaring, GDP was up, the pound had strengthened against every major currency. Well, except the euro, which had temporarily suspended convertibility.

"That's all very well," responded the King. "But we've opened up too big a gap with the EU."

"The External Zone is required boi treaty tow be in 'armonisation," said White Mike.

"Yes, but why would we want to be in harmonisation with a collapsed currency and failed political institutions?"

The King patiently explained that the statistics I had cited were mere superficial indicators. "The experts are all agreed that the non-visible indicators are far more disturbing."

"What non-visible indicators? What experts?"

So he pointed out various eminences around the room – the head of the civil service, the chairman of the BBC, the Governor of the Bank of England... The director of the University of East Anglia's Climatic Research Unit cited a new paper proving that national sovereignty was accelerating climate catastrophe. The chief executive of the Health Security Agency and vice-president of NASTI – the National Association for Sexually Transmitted Infections – had a transmission model showing that a hyper-resistant post-Brexit strain of Covid-related climate-change-accelerated mega-gonorrhoea could bring the UK to its knees within seventy-two hours. The painted trollop next to him, the Madam-in-Chief of RASP – the Royal Academy of Sex-Practitioners – said that many British sex workers were already reporting among their clients unusually hued sores and pustules.

"And don't say it's the vaccine," added a bloke from the Office of National Statistics.

"Have you all gone daft?" I interjected. "Is there one verified case of this mega-gonorrhoea?"

"Well, actually," said His Majesty, "I don't wish to be indiscreet, Rassendyll, but we rather think you've got a bad dose."

He motioned to Peter Borrodaile, who clicked his iPad and produced on the screen above the fireplace a picture of me and Baroness al-Ghoti emerging from the River Thames in our undies. He

363

zoomed in on a strange discoloured blur on my shoulder — the faded Red Rose of Ruritania.

"Eeeee-ewwwww," grimaced Flavia, sticking her tongue out.

Sir Mohammed glared fiercely at the screen and the zoom-shot cleavage of Yazmina al-Ghoti. "The mega-gonorrhoea," he fumed, "is why you cannot stop yourself from tearing off the modest garb of devout women instead of leaving them to drown in the river."

"But that's my tat...," I began, before remembering that that was my sole physiognomical non-lookalike.

"Yow don't 'ave a tat," said Mike Rassendyll. "Oi'm yow brother. Oi know." He nodded at Borrodaile, who clicked on the next slide. Up popped an old front page of *The Daily Mirror* showing Rob Rassendyll sunbathing with a hedge-fund billionaire and his mistress, all lying on their fronts, stark naked. "Moi brother was staying on an island in the Turks and Caicos owned by a bankster friend of his at the toim the Mars Bar rationing riots erupted. A tabloid photographer with a very long-distance lens managed tow capture this vivid shot of the Prime Minister's erubescent bottom on that sun-drenched private beach." The headline underneath read: "CUT SHORT MY HOLIDAY? RUDDY CHEEK!"

Ruddy cheek, but no ruddy tattoo.

My silly old tat from that bender with Flamur all those years ago: who knew the fate of a kingdom would hinge on it? Fortunately, Fritz Tarlenheim had taken the precaution of installing a bug under it on that first night at Roger Severn's, and by now they were probably on their way to...

Oh, no, wait. Derek Detchard had ripped out the bug.

The man from NASTI was saying that early research indicated a correlation between mega-gonorrhoea and neo-imperialism — hence my speech in Manchester. "There's a new study in *The Lancet*," said the head sex-worker and passed around copies.

The Scotland Yard commissioner nodded, and said the peer-reviewed research confirmed post-Brexit mega-gonorrhoea was also connected to paedophilia, and circulated photographic copies of my arrest by the Royal Parks Community Predator Response Dance Team Assistant Choreographer. "The false beard," he added, "is a bit of a giveaway."

THE PRISONER OF WINDSOR

The King heaved his shoulders wearily and set it aside. "I had an epiphany the other day," he murmured. Oh, God. Whatever epiphany he'd had was likely to be a long one. "I ask myself constantly, 'Why me?'"

I was with him up to that point. I'd only known the guy three weeks, but I too found myself asking constantly, "Why him?"

"And the answer I return to again and again is that I was born into this position of privilege for a purpose. I've come to believe I was put on this earth to reconcile the west and Islam."

I waited for the sex-worker and the transgender field marshal to burst out laughing, but they didn't. Instead, Sir Brillo said, "We've had some enormously fruitful discussions. For example, it's not true that Islam wants to ban all my music."

"Just the later albums after you went solo," said Sir Mohammed, and everyone giggled, although not Brillo. "So we're making real progress on a lot of issues."

Rory chipped in: "Including emissions targets."

"And meat reduction," added the head of the Royal Academy of Sex-Practitioners.

I turned to the King accusingly. "And in what capacity are you reaching this consensus?"

"You're being awfully familiar," hissed Brillo. "You're meant to call His Majesty 'sir' on second reference."

"You're awfully hung up on correct forms of address for an Irish republican rock star with one name, *sir*."

"The government is fiddling while the planet burns," said White Michael. "We won't stan' boi and let that happen. When the chips are down, democracy is less important than restoring our earth, and if that means imposing rational solutions on the people, sow be it. We're doing this tow save the planet."

"We've got a ten-point plan," said the Commissioner of the Metropolitan Police. "First point: Every adult will have a maximum carbon allowance.

"Second point: Every adult will also have a travel allowance. Mass tourism has been environmentally devastating, as has driving to the supermarket."

The King nodded approvingly.

"But mass tourism has collapsed with all the viruses," I pointed out.

"Exactly," said the head of NASTI. "But we wouldn't want it coming back, would we?"

"So, in the interests of mitigating climate change," continued the police commissioner, "we will introduce a travel allowance equivalent to one flight to Greece per half-decade, and one long-haul to Phuket or the Maldives every eight years. Beyond that, frequent flyers will pay an Excess Movement Penalty, especially to Florida. We calculate that this would give HMG an annual surplus that would enable us to take the lead on debt forgiveness for Africa.

"Third point: Smart chip-embedded toilets in every home that will enable us to target resources more effectively in compliance with the European Dietary Directive and make sure we're hitting our insect-consumption targets.

"Fourth: Environmentally responsible breeding. Tax penalties for having more than one child. The average English child has a carbon footprint sixty times greater than a Bangladeshi or sub-Saharan child. So the world needs fewer Britons, not to mention far fewer Americans. One way to do this would be to make offspring part of an adult's personal carbon allowance. So, if you have no children, you could fly to Greece more often, but, if you have three babies, you'd have to spend your hols at Bognor. For a fourth pregnancy, the NHS would mandate counselling, on abortion and other alternatives."

This all sounded nuts to me even by the standards of experts: Agree to abort your kid and the state will grant you a special exit visa for a week at Disneyland? I stopped him in the middle of Point Five. "The Prime Minister has a right to an audience of the King. I'm claiming that right."

"Ah, well, actually," said His Majesty, "I was thinking of invoking the reserve powers of the Crown."

"What?"

"Aside from electoral interference by Ruritanian content farmers, there's a constitutional issue," explained Rory. "Since the resignation en masse of the European Commission, the High Representative has had nobody to report to. And, as you report to the High Representative, that also puts a question mark over your legitimacy. The Attorney-General thinks we may be in an unusual situation where, in the lapse of the External Zone treaty, the British constitution temporarily applies, in which case executive authority is vested in His Majesty."

Holy cow, these guys were way crazier than a bunch of de-radicalised jihadists. Right now, I'd have welcomed the Twelfth Imam showing up to take charge.

"I was thinking of appointing a government of national unity," said the King, as if he were inviting us to a game of croquet.

"We're announcing it tomorrow morning," added Rory, "so it will get lost in all the Coronation hoopla. Just a minor footnote to the new reign."

There was a knock on the door and a footman entered. He bowed from the neck and announced that His Majesty's ministers, Dame Marjorie, Mr Henley and Mr Detchard, were here.

White Mike interrupted him. "We're not quite ready to expline tow them wha' will be 'appening."

The King ordered his footman to take them to the Waterloo Chamber, give them a cup of tea and show them the video on the history of the castle. "It's jolly good," he added.

Suddenly I saw it. The "government of national unity" was Flavia's foundation. Not my cabinet ministers squabbling for the amusement of the media and the diversion of the public and of poor naïve Sir Roger, and for the privilege of replacing Rassendyll as if it would make a ha'porth of difference. But the real sources of power – the masters of conventional wisdom – conventional elite globalist groupthink, fronted by spindly little Flavia, the Conscience of the World.

"And who'll be heading up this government of national unity?" I asked.

"Your brother," said the King.

"You're making my brother Prime Minister?"

"No," replied White Mike. "To emphasise the urgency and special nature of the commission oi've been given, oi'm thinking of taking the title Lord Protector. Norrin the Cromwellian sense, oi 'asten to add," he said to the King, "burrin the sense of stewardship of the land."

"The original proposal was First Steward," added the transgender field marshal.

"I went on a cruith thip last year," said Flavia Strofzin. "They had a First Thteward. He brought me complimentary champagne. It tathted icky."

I remembered our tennis match. He caught my eye, and I hissed, "T-nay!" It startled him. I took a deep breath. "Okay, His Majesty wishes to fire me and appoint my brother as Lord Protector of a government of national unity. I believe I am still entitled to an audience of the King for the official termination of my commission, or the unkissing of hands, or whatever it is. So the rest of you please move to the far corner, and His Majesty and I will confer." I pointed to the opposite corner, where the Queen sat reading her Jocelyn ffoulkes chick-lit. The King rose and signalled to the others to do as I said.

I ushered His Majesty to a spot halfway behind the Queen's chair, and then, as subtly as I could, positioned myself to block the others out of earshot. These were no conditions in which to give a constitutional lecture, but I conjured up what the old Count of Tarlenheim had told me at my childhood "coronation" in Madrid and did my best.

"Sir, a king is king not because of *who* he is but because of *what* he is."

"I beg your pardon?"

"A king is the personification of the state. That's what matters – not whether you want to save the polar bears or found a multifaith madrassah or whatever this week's hobby activism happens to be." I could hear the Queen suppress a titter.

But His Majesty bristled. "You impertinent jackanapes!"

I pressed on, and told him that a king is the legal personality of the state's sovereignty. Therefore, if he reigns only because my brother and his globalist cronies permit him to do so, this nation no longer has any sovereignty. What sort of coronation would it be? What throne in any meaningful sense would he be ascending to?

He started to speak, but I slogged on. "As I say, in a legal sense, *l'état, c'est toi.*" He fumed at my use of "*tu*" rather than "*vous*". "Therefore, if you are a big nothing sitting on his throne only at the pleasure of a bunch of Eurocrats and primaeval rockers and celebrity halfwits, then Britain is a big nothing, too. That may be the case, but I've no desire to advertise the fact to the planet. So enough of your

THE PRISONER OF WINDSOR

'Lord Protector' and his council. You're the only king we've got. So you have to stand firm!"

"That's enough!" Michael Rassendyll, High Representative and Lord Protector, had strode into the centre of the room. "Yow're threatening 'is Majesty."

"He's triggering him," agreed the transgender field marshal. "We wouldn't allow that in Helmand province."

The White Knight clapped his hands, and before I realised what was happening the field marshal and the Metropolitan Police commissioner were upon me and seizing my arms. The Met man yanked my arm, and I grimaced. The trans-field marshal seized a clump of hair and tugged. Eeeeee-owwww. I fell back on an end table and a lamp crashed to the floor.

"Sir, I am a guest of Your Majesty and I am being mugged in your sitting-room by a couple of thugs. Please call a footman and have them evicted and we can resume our conversation like civilised men."

The King bit his lip. "Is this really necessary, High Representative? We had the room re-done for the Platinum Jubilee."

White Michael twirled his wrist and my two tormentors reluctantly pulled away.

"An Englishman's home is his castle," I said to the King. "Whose home is this castle, sir?"

"Don't take that tone with me, you insolent…"

"Why don't you say that to your 'Lord Protector'? You're the King of England!" I cried. "Why can't you speak for England? For the traditions to which you're heir? For the Mother of Parliaments. For Common Law. For the land of Shakespeare and Milton. For John Major's long shadow on cricket grounds. For warm beer and green suburbs, dog lovers and pools fillers. For George Orwell's old maids bicycling to holy communion through the morning mist."

Everyone in the room fell around laughing, except the King. He looked at his shoes.

"Stands the church clock at ten to three?" sneered the White Knight. "And is there honey still for tea?"

"Why does he do all the talking?" I snapped at the King. "Haven't you got anything to say?"

"Have you ever tried bicycling to Holy Communion through the morning mist?" asked Peter Borrodaile. "If you survive the juggernauts rattling down the bypass, you'll find you have the church to yourself. I'm afraid there aren't many old maids left in England. Nor young maids, come to think of it." His eyes twinkled with amusement at his own jest.

I looked at the King with contempt. So, I noticed, did the Queen.

"Field Marshal, Commissioner," purred White Michael. "Moi bruther 'as denied 'e 'as mega-gonorrhoea. So His Majesty and I would like to see 'is back."

The police bloke held my neck, while the trans-gal ripped my jacket, straight down the back. So much for English tailoring. She then tore my shirt apart, and swung me around. There was Borrodaile, standing stiffly, clutching a handful of manila folders, as if to signal by his presence that this was a routine bit of Palace business. From somewhere in the room I heard a *handifon* ping.

"Why, what's this oi see below the shoulder blade?" smirked the White Knight. After Detchard had dug open my Red Rose tattoo to get at the bug, I could only imagine the state it was in. Even with my back to them, I felt the room recoil in disgust.

Except for the King. When I turned around, he seemed confused. He was blinking, and then his eyes caught mine, and I read in them ...*something*. A faint memory, perhaps. Of a tennis-court changing room ...and a Ruritanian pretender Mr Borrodaile had dismissed as "bad karma".

The policeman and the army woman pinned me down, as King Arthur looked on bewildered. "Who are you?" I gasped. "Colin Corgi or Peter Poodle?"

His Majesty didn't answer. He was still staring at me. So instead White Michael limped over and booted me in the kidneys. Even in the midst of my own implausible narrative, it seemed incredible that I was having the crap kicked out of me in Windsor Castle. "Yowr poor prime minister," said the White Knight to the King, as if reading my thoughts. "Evidently he thought of yowr home as no more than a luxurious banqueting facility. But it's been a fortress for – wha'? A thousand years?"

"Nine hundred and something, actually," mumbled the King. "Is this really necessary, Michael?"

THE PRISONER OF WINDSOR

"This post-Brexit corona-mega-gonorrhoea-infected madman seemed tow think 'e could accomplish what the barons filed to do to Prince John and Prince Edward, and waltz in and take it over – single-'anded." Mike Rassendyll chuckled at the evident ridiculousness of my plan. "Yow will not be the first of the Crown's enemies tow be imprisoned at Windsor. King Henry II held the Lord Mayor of London here at 'is Majesty's pleasure."

"Actually, that was Henry III," said King Arthur.

"Ah, yes," I said, trying to sound debonair through the pain. "And tell me, Your Royal Poodleness, wasn't King Charles I imprisoned here before whoever it was – the Lord Protector of his day – took him to his execution?"

His Majesty looked at me as if about to say something. But he didn't. He brought his hands together as if about to wring them. But instead they just hung limply, as if even attempting the gesture would have been too much.

"Yow're wasting yow toim trying to rouse *'im*," scoffed the White Knight.

For a moment the King's eyes flashed with anger. Then he looked again at his shoes.

"And now that we've established that the Proim Minister is indeed riddled with mega-gonorrh…"

"Stop!"

It was Mohammed Almasri, head of the Supreme Islamic Council or Islamic Supreme Council, whichever it was. "This man is an Islamophobe!" He raised his finger and pointed it accusingly at me.

No, wait, he was pointing it at the man standing next to me – the White Knight. Sir Mohammed passed over his mobile, and Peter Borrodaile projected the GIF up on to the screen. I recognised it immediately. It was Michael Rassendyll, in the High Representative's residence at Cymbeline's Castle, on the day that he received me and Sir Roger Severn. And the High Representative was saying over and over and over, on an endless loop:

Dumbkopf! Do you think I care a fig about Mohammedan kneecaps?

Good old Roger Severn! If a chap has to stick a hidden camera in your shoulder, you should hope he uses it as adroitly as dear old Rog does. He'd emailed his GIF to Almasri in the nick of time.

"This dog," exploded Almasri, "is no better than de Gautet or Colin Corgi or Belinda Featherly or his damned Islamophobic brother! No Muslim could serve under this blackest of white knights, who laughs at believers' kneecaps. So Your Majesty's dreams of grand reconciliation lie in tatters at the bottom of the Thames like Lady al-Ghoti's hijab."

You could sense the room beginning to turn. The police commissioner pointed out that it would certainly be a hate crime if you posted it on Twitter, and the field marshal noted that if you said it on patrol in Raqaa you'd be court-martialed, and Carrie Moonbeams – who'd been introduced by White Michael at the Coronation Command Performance – announced she would not consent to a DVD release of the performance. The chairman of the BBC piped up to add that he'd had a pitch from a transfeminist of colour for a series deconstructing the myth of the White Knight as a selfless vessel of all that is pure and noble as a self-glorifying cover for colonialism and exploitation across the centuries. "Her thesis," he concluded, "is that Rob Rassendyll's empire speech and Mike Rassendyll's hijacking of the social justice movement are merely two sides of the same racist patriarchal coin."

Only the Irish rocker Brillo hesitated. "Steady on," he said, staring hard at Almasri. "I don't get it. Sir Mohammed here can make jokes about my solo albums, but I'm not allowed to joke about his kneecaps?"

In the confusion, I seized my moment, reared up, and grabbed whatever was on the end table behind me. Then I swung it straight into the police commissioner's jaw. Good call: it was a solid silver candelabra mounted on an ornate base with a pair of protective griffins at each end. A bit ostentatious, I thought, but not without its uses. He toppled backwards onto the transgender field marshal.

"Tha's enough!" White Michael had produced another of his environmentally friendly pistols and was levelling it at me. I leapt forward as he squeezed the trigger, and hit him in the shin. He stumbled backwards and the shot flew into Brillo's shoulder.

THE PRISONER OF WINDSOR

"Fock fock focketty fock!" howled the legendary Celt. In the blizzard of expletives, I knocked Michael off his feet, and the gun skeetered across the floor.

"I could use some help here," I yelled to the others. "He is an Islamophobe, you know."

"Stop all this," said the Governor of the Bank of England. I turned around to find the chief architect of Project Fear 2 holding the pistol even more daintily than Michael did.

"Are you sure you're pointing that the right way?"

"Wha...?" He looked down. There was a loud thwack as Her Majesty The Queen broke two cabrioled legs of an end table over his head, and the concussed central banker stumbled forward, dropping his weapon. Brillo moved to pick it up, and the Queen re-swung the table toward his jaw. He cringed and covered his face. "No, no, not the mouth, please. My lip injections..."

Her Majesty, the field marshal and the police commissioner all flinched in horror. "Oh, gross," said the head of the Health Security Agency. A furious Brillo rounded on him with the White Knight's gun, and promptly shot himself in the toe.

"Fock fock focketty fockin' fockin' fock!" howled the great man.

I tried Her Majesty's method, and brought a Queen Anne chair down on his skull.

"I'm an Irish citizen," protested Brillo, cradling his shot toe with his unshot arm.

"You should have thought about that before you accepted a knighthood."

"Yeah, well, that was your idea, you focker."

With a look of pure malevolence unlike anything I have ever seen, little Flavia came flying through the air, her spindly urchin hands outstretched like talons, which landed on my face and commenced to begin ripping it off.

"Oh, piss off," said the Queen, picking up little Flavia and throwing her across the room. The world's favourite Ruritanian moppet hit the ground with a thud. "I can't stand that awful girl," she added.

It was at this point I noticed that, among the melee, the King was gone - and Michael, too. And his gun. I ran from the room, and

373

stopped on the stairs outside. I could hear something from above. So up I went, up those hard unyielding mediaeval stone steps, my kidneys aching and my breath short from my latest beating. Too many beatings, too many exertions, too many close shaves, too many bruises, too many cuts: the stitch hit me early, and I slowed to a trot. But I kept moving – up, up, up, pounding past rooms and glancing inside at the paintings and *passementerie*: George III, George IV, Rubens, Rembrandt – but no King Arthur, no White Michael. Onward and upward. My calves felt like lead weights, and my chest as if it were about to burst. My arms flapped leadenly at my side.

And suddenly, a few steps above, there they were. Mike Rassendyll had seized the King and, with his gun jabbed in His Majesty's ribs, was dragging him up the stairs. "One king will die today, Elphberg. We're going to test that 'honour' of yours to the limit."

From below me came a shriek. Little Flavia. "What are you doing?" she screamed at Michael. "He'th the King!"

"He's a climate denier," said the White Knight, improvising hastily.

Flavia fell back shocked. I started up the stairs after them, with the little Ruritanian orphan behind me, kicking at my heels and yanking at the vent of my jacket.

And suddenly there we were, on the roof of the Round Tower, with quilted England spread out below us, and Michael Rassendyll dragging the King at gunpoint toward the parapet. Flavia kicked me between my legs, hard. Oof. I stumbled forward toward the edge, and fell at the White Knight's feet. He laughed, and stamped on my head. But His Majesty seized his moment and elbowed Michael sharply in the ribs. I clambered to my knees.

White Michael was stunned by the King's action. "Yow can't do that," he pointed out. "Yow're a constitutional monarch. Yow can only do wha' your advoisors tell yow to do. And I didn't tell yow to…"

I never heard what would have come next, because His Majesty slugged him directly in the mouth. The White Knight wobbled, and, instinctively, I reached for him. But King Arthur stayed my hand. And Michael Rassendyll fell from the turrets of the Round Tower to the moat far below. He might have survived, but, alas, at Windsor the moat is dry and converted to garden. So the High Representative to the External Zone (Qualified Recognition) and would-be Lord

THE PRISONER OF WINDSOR

Protector of England gave one last mournful howl in his lugubrious post-electrocution Black Country vowels, and landed with a dull thud on an ornamental rockery.

And then there was silence.

Chapter Fifty
The King keeps his appointment

I WOKE EARLY, DRESSED quietly, and opened the flat door to find Sanjay already on duty. "Early start, sir," he said, following me downstairs. Outside Number Ten, I pointed at the Downing Street gates. "Do you like those?" I asked him.

"Haven't thought about it, sir. Used to be that any member of the public could stroll up and down this street."

"So then they put these up – the gates that keep the world from getting in and do such a grand job of keeping the Prime Minister from getting out." I slipped through into Whitehall, and Sanjay and a pair of constables hurried after me. Five-thirty on Coronation morn. The pre-approved number of the King's subjects, bleary but enthused and wearing masks with the new royal cypher above the QR code, were already guarding their painted rectangles on the pavement. I could hear the clip-clop of horses. The Sovereign's Escort from Wellington Barracks? A detachment of hyper-vaccinated Mounties on its way to the Palace?

In Parliament Square four hundred virocleansed Gold Staff Officers passed through en route to the Abbey, followed shortly by choristers from the Chapel Royal, resplendent in seventeenth-century State Dress and period-style visors. I had a socially distanced word with a Beefeater on a smoking break. He'd been part of the detachment that had brought the Crown and the rest of the regalia from the Tower of London, and he'd spent the night guarding it. He glanced up at the sky. "Turned out nice, 'asn't it?"

Yes, it had, weather-wise. Face up to the sun, I strolled back to Number Ten. No 7.45 this morning. Instead, Alison and Brenda barged in bearing robes and a crown. For a moment, I thought Sir Roger had arranged to have me restored to the throne of Ruritania. But the crown was only a coronet, and the robes were those of a mere peer, albeit with three rows of ermine on the cape to indicate an earl. Apparently, Mr Rassendyll, as the former Lord Burlesdon, had been toying with the idea of wearing the same get-up the other earls and the dukes and marquesses and viscounts would be wearing. He'd brought from Burlesdon the robes of his forebear (the brother of the Rudolf Rassendyll who saved Ruritania), along with his court dress – tail coat, waistcoat, breeches, jabot, lace cuffs and white gloves, silk stockings and buckled shoes. Brenda had sent them to Ede & Ravenscroft, the original tailor, to have the tattier patches touched up, and an ermine-trimmed face-mask added.

Odd, I thought, to seek the democratic kudos of disdaining his peerage, but insist on his right to continue dressing up. It seemed perfectly emblematic of Britain: everything was up for grabs, everything could be negotiated away, as long as the façade was maintained and the dress-up games continued. White Mike had been right about that.

"You'll look the bee's knees in these," said Alison.

"Well, I haven't made a final decision yet."

In the cramped galley kitchen, I made myself an instant coffee and Wendy a pot of tea. Then I took it into her room on a tray and kissed her on the forehead. She held my hand and I sat down on the bed. And there we stayed in silence until it was time to dress for the big show. Wendy was resplendent in a pale green – Burlesdon green, she called it; I took a last look at the 12th Earl's coronation robes, and then hung them in the wardrobe and fished out the morning dress. In the guest bedroom of Roger Severn's English manor house, the real Robert Rassendyll, being nursed back to health by Fritz Tarlenheim, would be furious at me for ditching the coronet. Or perhaps, after weeks of attempted brainwashing in Windsor Castle, he no longer cared about such fripperies.

"We'll walk," I said to Vic. It was not a day to be sealed inside the bubble. The semi-deserted streets were bedecked with Union flags and giant plastic crowns, the spaces between the pavement rectangles had been painted red, white and blue. On Parliament Street, the designated pedestrians were dressed for the occasion – the men in patriotic variations of what I believe the natives refer to as "shell suits", the women in novelty Coronation-themed T-shirts that seemed to end several inches above the belly button. Even with social distancing, there was a respectable turnout from His Majesty's farther-flung realms: I noticed Maple Leafs and Southern Crosses. Red Ensigns from Bermuda, was it? A few foreigners, too – from that Diversity Lottery Dobromil had "won". I wondered if I'd run into anyone from Ruritania. The only real crowd were the protesters outside the Houses of Parliament, but even the Recouplers and the Non-Violence League, Make the Poor Rich and the Human Extinction Movement were all in a party mood. A coronation, even for an unglamorous, unlikable sovereign, seemed to have brought out the best in a not entirely depopulated London. So the Prime Minister passed through the streets under a fitful series of socially distant huzzahs, blessings, and fluttering handkerchiefs. "God bless you, sir," shouted a cheery, apple-cheeked wench. As Wendy and I passed, a little girl silently offered a single rose to me. I took it, and thanked her, and, as we walked on, stuck it in my lapel. The red rose of the Elphbergs.

At the Abbey, there was a long line as the Chinese virocleansers went about their business, and then the ushers escorted us up the great nave to the pealing of the organ. A century ago, as the King of Ruritania, I would have been seated among the crowned heads of Europe at the front. Now, as a mere politician, I was with the Commonwealth prime ministers, somewhat further back. I glanced around and saw Sir Roger wedged in a few rows behind. I'd had to wangle him a seat, but it seemed the least I could do: He was unlikely to be attending any coronations in Strelsau any time soon.

Even through the great stone walls a millennium old we could hear the cheers growing louder as the Royal party began arriving – dukes, duchesses, then the Wokinghams and HRH The Prince Richard, Duke of Albany, who seemed almost dashing in his naval uniform, and the Queen Consort, looking far more radiant than usual. The chair-smashing and Flavia-tossing had cheered her up.

The King advanced up the nave, his train borne by half-a-dozen pages of honour selected via a Coronation reality show to reflect various "communities". Diverse as they were, all six boys were uniformly solemn of mien and with a tendency to overstep. It was oddly moving as they walked stiffly in His Majesty's wake toward the steps to the Coronation chair. "Vivat Rex!" sang the King's Scholars. His Majesty and his pages bowed to the altar, and the Archbishop of Canterbury stepped forward. He looked like an Old Testament prophet with a great thick beard hanging halfway down his robes, and I had high expectations of serious fire-and-brimstone, but he spoke in a thin, camp voice: "Sirs, Madams and All Others, I here present unto you King Arthur, your undoubted king: Wherefore all of you who are come this day to do your homage and service, are you willing to do the same?"

We all bellowed back: "God save King Arthur!"

Then the Archbishop delivered the Coronation Oath: "Will you solemnly promise and swear to govern the Peoples of the United Kingdom of Great Britain and Northern Ireland, Canada, Australia, New Zealand, Jamaica, the Bahamas..."

My mind began to wander as I thought of all the corpses at the castle.

"...Grenada, Papua New Guinea, St Lucia, St Vincent and the Grenadines, Belize..."

The face of the man I had killed in that cell rose unbidden in my mind. I wondered what his plans had been for Coronation Day.

"...Antigua and Barbuda, St Kitts and Nevis, and of your Possessions and other Territories to any of them belonging or pertaining, according to their respective laws and customs?"

"I solemnly promise so to do," said the King.

"Will you," enquired the Archbishop, "to your power cause Law and Justice, in Mercy, to be executed in all your judgments?"

"I will," said the King. He was a stupid man who thought himself better than a constitutional monarch. Half of him would like to rule rather than reign. He was too vain to realize how delicate hereditary monarchy is. It requires only one passing incompetent to bring the work of centuries crashing down. That's something we pretenders understand. But, unlike yesterday, on this morning, chastened by the events at Windsor, he was behaving.

The Archbishop of Canterbury seemed anxious to gloss over the next section, galloping through the words sotto voce: "Will you to the utmost of your power maintain the Laws of God and maintain in the United Kingdom the Protestant Reformed Religion established by law? Will you maintain and preserve inviolable the settlement of the Church of England, and the doctrine, worship, discipline, and government thereof, as by law established in England? And will you preserve unto the Bishops and Clergy of England, and to the Churches there committed to their charge, all such rights and privileges, as by law do or shall appertain to them or any of them?"

"I will," mumbled the King.

Then came the ever so slightly rewritten passage. The Chief Rabbi stepped forward: "And will you to the utmost of your power defend all faiths?" And the Grand Mufti: "And will you govern the peoples of your realms so that each may worship in accordance with his faith?"

"All this I promise to do," said the King, confidently, the sonorous baritone echoing through the cloisters. "The things which I have here before promised, I will perform, and keep. So help me God."

"Allahu Akbar!" added the Mufti, rather loudly. I could feel the Prime Minister of St Kitts and Nevis rolling his eyes.

After the celebrations, we found ourselves next to the Queen of the Netherlands and a former *Brits-a-Poppin'* winner.

"Lovely day," said Her Majesty.

"Totally brilliant," agreed the *Brits-a-Poppin'* girl.

"Too true," said I, suddenly tired. I looked out at the empty streets and wondered for the moment if the socially distant Coronation wasn't just a clever device to disguise the lack of interest in this new king. Wendy smiled, distractedly. The Queen of the Netherlands got in her limo, ours slid up behind, and Sanjay held the door.

Chapter Fifty-One
Loose ends

THE CORONATION dominated media coverage to the extent that one would have had to be looking very carefully to find buried very deep in the other-news-in-brief round-ups a small curious story on a day no one was paying the slightest attention to politics:

> ...reports that the Home Secretary Anna Bersonin has been found dead at the London flat of Baroness al-Gothi, Britain's first Muslim Lord Chancellor. Following the recent arrest of her father, Lady al-Gothi left Britain for the Middle East a few days ago in the company of her three brothers, but colleagues are denying rumours that she and Ms Bersonin were romantically involved. The Lady Chancellor was believed in recent weeks to have been frantic that revelations of her gay lifestyle were becoming known in parts of the Muslim world, where homosexuality is strongly disapproved...

Sir Roger certainly knew how to tie up loose ends. But I did my bit, too:

> ...would be reopening investigations into the many 'grooming gang' scandals that occurred on Ms Bersonin's watch. Also in political news, in a sweeping pre-Coronation reshuffle, the Prime Minister has appointed new Foreign, Home, Defence and Health Secretaries, as well as a new Lord Chancellor and Chancellor of the Exchequer. Mr Rassendyll thanked Rupert Henley, Marjorie Craftstone, Derek Detchard, and Humphrey Lowe-Graham for their years of public service, and wished them a long and relaxing retirement...

Downing Street was almost deserted. From somewhere beyond the gates the street revellers were bellowing out patriotic ditties:

> *Na-na-na-na-na-na-na na-na-na-na, hey, Jude...*

Wendy had to go to Burlesdon for a couple of days. A village fete that there was talk of postponing because of Michael Rassendyll's sudden fatal heart attack: more loose ends. I kissed her on the lips, and wondered if this was goodbye.

From the street party came:

We'll meet again,
Don't know where
Don't know when...

I stood on the front step and watched as her car drove down Downing Street, and through the gates.

One final item from the papers: Little Flavia Strofzin, whose courageous stand against climate catastrophe had won the hearts of the whole planet, had announced the winding up of her foundation. I felt a bit sorry for her. After she had recovered from the shock of White Michael falling off the Round Tower, we'd had a bit of a talk, and she'd told me she really didn't like being given speeches to read and tweets to tweet, and having to go to international conferences all the time with people who were really rather boring. And she missed her friends back in Zenda, and she thought she'd like to go home and be a Ruritanian schoolgirl again.

I slept badly, and woke, just before the 7.45, to news that Brussels was in lockdown following ongoing riots. The European Quarter had had to be evacuated. Five of the six presidents of the Conference of Presidencies were in hiding following the firebombing of Hubert de Gautet's riad near Casablanca. The sixth, Marie-Claude de Chard, had stopped in a supermarket on the outskirts of Montelimar en route to her Provençal chateau for a few days' rest, and had been stabbed next to a display of bargain-priced *pipi de marmotte*; three others were injured. This was on the morning of the Coronation, and even French TV and radio only found time to mention it cursorily.

That left just one loose end: me.

And so yet again I was driven up the beautifully landscaped gravel drive to Roger Severn's exquisite manor house, back where it had all begun, just a month ago.

He was rather subdued at the door and led me into a faintly dowdy sitting room I'd not been in before. Joseph, his general factotum, was off, so Sir Roger excused himself and went to "put a spot of tea on", while I stared through the diamond-shaped mullions at the lawns and — what was that word again? — the ha-ha. The cheerless ha-ha. I noticed a quartet of framed black-and-white photographs atop a rolltop desk. The first showed a younger Sir Roger in a sports car — a Triumph, was it? Lotus? — with the top down and his shirt-sleeved arm over the window, and a dolly bird in mini-skirt and kinky boots sitting on the bonnet. Next came a Roger Severn younger still, in a schoolboy's summer uniform — straw boater and striped blazer — with a chum, laughing, with roll-up cigarettes in their fingers and the smoke dancing in the air. Then a sad, unsmiling lad clutching the hand of a tired-looking lady in a drab coat and head scarf on the platform of a railway station called "Bristol Temple Meads". And finally a sepia portrait of a baby in an ornate, antique crib with the same woman, full of youth and joy, and a stiff-looking man in the uniform of the Constable of Zenda Castle standing under a painting of Queen Flavia. A gilded Elphberg crown was built into the frame, and on the back was the Royal Warrant of the Court photographer.

Sir Roger returned with a decanter and glasses on a silver salver. "Thought we could both use something stronger than tea," he said, gruffly.

"Can I ask you a personal question?"

He filled two tumblers of Scotch, and nodded.

"Why do you wear those orange suede shoes?"

He looked at me as if I were mad. "You mean Elphberg red, I think. Same London bootmaker who made my father's and grandfather's." He raised a foot daintily, and smiled. "Are you suggesting that I'm not quite a gentleman?"

And then he informed me, brusquely, that I would be Britain's prime minister indefinitely. "Robert's adamant, I'm afraid. Had a lot of time to think in that cell, and he remembered the Duchess of Woke had mentioned that the Biden Foundation had got some Ukrainian funding for the #BlackLivesMatter all-star CD and it reminded him of a song he wrote at Oxford about debt forgiveness for Africa…" He took a puff on his pipe. "Robert always did like the rock'n'roll."

"This is like the virus," I said. "It was just a fortnight to flatten the curve of Rassendyll's tanking numbers. Now it's forever…"

"And would you render all we've done meaningless? Somewhere deep down Robert understands: You've made him a hero – and he can't live up to that!" He thumped the side table, and knocked a photograph to the floor. The glass cracked, and he bent down to retrieve it. A night at Oxford long ago: Sir Roger, Wendy, Michael and Robert. He spoke more softly now. "Be PM for a few years, retire to Burlesdon. Not quite the Royal Palace at Strelsau, but competitive with a flat in Modenstein, I should think. You're good at this, and who knows what we might accomplish."

"If you're that ambitious, you take the job. I'll give one last exclusive interview to Belinda saying I always felt you were the sharpest knife in the Cabinet and natural prime ministerial material."

"Only as caretaker." He was taking the proposition seriously. "The party would want someone younger and trendier. In the groove." He made his air quotes, and for a moment I thought the old Sir Roger was back. "Duty calls you," he said, coldly. "And you'll do your duty. For England."

"And my duty to Wendy?"

He fell silent. I felt the weight of Rassendyll and his intractably disunited kingdom crushing me. I don't want to go all psychobabbly on you, and I certainly don't want to start twittering about needing to find myself by placing a song on the Biden Foundation #BlackLivesMatter album, but I am saying that it took playing another man to make me realise I've been a royal cipher all my life. A big nothing, except for a label that expired before I was born: Rudolphus Rex. These last few weeks I'd enjoyed getting to know myself. Being a fake somebody had put me in touch with the real nobody. And now Sir Roger Severn was calmly explaining to me that, from his point of view, it was a lot easier killing off a penniless loser like Rudy Elphberg than the Rt Hon Robert Rassendyll.

"We haven't accomplished anything," I said, bitterly, remembering what Michael had told me. "I rode horses and waved swords, and all the stuff you're really up against just goes on and on and on regardless..."

"Well, we liberated Britain from the globalists," he said. "After what's happened in Brussels, the revocation of the External Zone (Qualified Recognition) Treaty is going to sail through the Commons and the Lords; we'll have Royal Assent before the end of the week. We can leave it to the natives to see what they make of it - or you could stick around to make sure the judges and the bureaucrats and the media don't get to snatch the people's victory away from them."

"Is even that worth a man's life? Poor Mike Rassendyll. Poor Anna Bersonin..." My voice trailed away. "Both driven mad by politics. It's not the Westminster village, it's the Westminster asylum..."

"The devil has his share in most things," said Severn. "And you forget your pushback on trans-surgeries and acid attacks and all the rest. I'll make sure you have something for Cabinet on those."

"And how would me staying in Downing Street forever measure up to that Rassendyll your pa and gram'pa used to talk about?"

The Lord Privy Seal cocked his head and considered the question. "He was a man who was almost absurdly honourable. I doubt such an Englishman exists today. I doubt he could survive in today's England." He took out that old pipe once more. "I sense that you were perhaps not quite so honourable, at least vis à vis Wendy and Belinda."

"I was more honourable than Rob Rassendyll. I'm not the one abandoning my wife for a shot at a celebrity duets CD."

"You played a good game," continued Severn, "and the final score is not so very different. We have defeated traitors and set the King firm on his throne!" He bent his head, inelegantly, and kissed my hand. "Heaven doesn't always make the right men kings! Or prime ministers."

I was embarrassed by this. "You talk about honour. Where's the honour in usurping a man's job, a man's wife, and then his life? You told me I was just holding the fort, not seizing it. If this is your Ruritanian operetta, where's the happy ending?"

Sir Roger said softly: "There are no happy endings, Rudy. You're the sporting chance."

Chapter Fifty-Two
That which is lawful and right

THAT SATURDAY MICHAEL Rassendyll, former High Representative to the former External Zone (Qualified Recognition) and heir to the earldom of Burlesdon, was laid to rest, alongside twenty-nine generations of his forebears, in the parish graveyard on the edge of the estate. It was a picture-perfect setting: the old part of the church dated from the ninth century, and the new part from the tenth - back when knighthood was in flower for more than elderly environmentalist rockers. Yet even taking into account the social distancing, it was not a good turnout: the politicians and Eurocrats, media magnates and celebrity activists, who had so assiduously courted the White Knight, had no desire to be seen paying their respects to an Islamophobe whose very nickname crowed white privilege. That left family – principally his widow, an attractive Swedish Euro-commissioner who had to leave just before the burial to make her flight – and also the villagers, who remembered him fondly as an awkward boy but well-meaning. The Church of England vicar did not seem aware of White Michael's fall – I mean fall from grace, not fall from the Round Tower – and cooed enthusiastically about a man who could have led the usual decadent life of a layabout aristocrat but instead chose to devote himself to the European project. That all seemed a bit much considering his church was actually on the Burlesdon lands. Then the cleric began to draw further contrasts: Ezekiel 18:27, for example. The church was admittedly far from full, but I don't see why he had to fix his gaze on me.

> *When the wicked man turneth away from his wickedness that he hath committed, and doeth that which is lawful and right, he shall save his soul alive.*

And his eyes held mine.

Yeah, I got the cut of his jib. But I wasn't in the mood to take lessons from the Church of England, one of the great failures of modern Britain - even in an age of contagion, when people might be in the mood for a bit of religion.

In the churchyard afterwards, the congregants offered their condolences, but the vicar kept his distance.

"You took that awfully well," whispered Wendy. "I'm old enough to remember when the C of E was all gas and gaiters, not all gays and greenhouse gases."

In fact, I'd enjoyed most of the service. The Book of Common Prayer was rather good, and the choir wasn't bad. My mum was the serious Catholic in the family, and she kept up the churchgoing until the dementia made her too belligerent and impatient for Mass. I've never gone in for much contemplation of the Divine – on purpose, now I think about it. Having been deprived of the opportunity to be king, I was inclined to treat the King of Kings the way my subjects had treated me. Religion and monarchy aren't dissimilar, I would say. It helps to have a transcendent meaning to life. For individuals, that's God. For states, that's monarchy.

Or *was*, for both God and me in the new Europe.

As the funeral cortège made its way down the long gravel path from the church, it seemed to me a bucolic resting place: mossy gravestones, cattle grazing across the ancient stone wall. As Michael was lowered into the ground under the shade of an ancient yew tree, I wondered where Roger Severn was keeping the surviving Rassendyll brother.

Between Sir Roger and the protection officers, Wendy and I were not alone until we retired for the night. But she had been fluttery and tactile with me all day – looping her arm through mine at the church, brushing my hair, kissing my cheek – so I knew what was expected of me. It was a sad, damp bedroom of dingy furniture and third-rate paintings. I wondered how long it had been since she and Robert had stayed here. In the bathroom, the cold tap didn't work, and the hot yielded only a cold brown trickle; the toothbrush was stiff and discoloured. I was vividly aware of the man I'd supplanted: there were thin reddish snips of hair between the blades of his razor, and longer strands in the teeth of his comb.

"Unhook me, darling," commanded Wendy, so I did. She leaned down and from the heavy, ugly dresser pulled a thick woollen nightgown and slipped it over her shoulders. She climbed into the faintly musty four-poster, and from another dresser I located a pair of Black Watch plaid pyjamas.

"Change and decay in all around I see," sighed Wendy, sniffing the damp. "Why do we only get the decay and never the change?" She contemplated a hideous Welsh dresser. "Maybe Kissy-Kissy or Sir Brillo would like to make us an offer for the place."

I leaned down to the bed, and kissed her forehead.

"Katrine's so young," she said. "I assumed she and Michael would have had children. Now it's all down to that third cousin of yours in Brisbane. As far as the northern hemisphere is concerned, you're the last of the Rassendylls."

The last of the Rassendylls... It was something about the way she said it. A tear rolled down my cheek, and then another.

"Darling, what is it?"

I fumbled for the lamp on the night stand. It was old, and the switch was halfway down a frayed cord at the back of the table. But I found it and put the light on.

"Wendy, there's something I have to tell you..."

I left the bedroom two hours later, and walked down the corridor. Sanjay was dozing in a heavy oak settle at the top of the stairs, but very quickly came to and followed me down. I walked into a small parlour, ostentatiously closed the door in his face, and curled up in a window seat, my finger occasionally caressing the slight cut on my cheek: She had slapped me hard once she had grasped what I was telling her – and who could blame her? And then I stared at a moonlit lawn until about 5am, when I became aware that I was no longer alone. She was in silhouette, standing at the next window, lit only by a pair of sconces behind her. I rose and joined her, standing awkwardly alongside, with head bowed. Her hair gleamed from the light, but her face was pale. Her hands hung by her sides, and so did mine. We neither moved nor spoke. I wanted to say something, but I'm a ham actor and no one had written me my lines.

She trembled a little, and looked at me. "Mr Elphberg... Rudolf – is that it?" She pressed herself against me and I put an arm around her shoulder, clumsily. "I know you, and I don't know you. I don't even know what to call you."

I felt ashamed of myself. "God forgive me the wrong I've done you!"

"I knew," she said quickly; and then modified it, raising her head and looking in my eyes: "No, I didn't. But I knew something. I don't know what. It's not that I knew you weren't the real Robert, but that I knew you were real. And Robert wasn't. Not these last few years."

"I meant to tell you. I wanted to at the ball, and after the Cenotaph. But…"

"I know, I know! What are we to do now …Rudolf?" The name sounded odd on her tongue, strange and unEnglish.

I put my arm around her. "Your husband wants me to stay, so Sir Roger won't let me go."

"I won't let you go," she sobbed softly. "My husband!" She repeated the words as a sneer. "You should have let them chop his head off. *Five Guys Named Mo – The Director's Cut.* I thought I'd found my lost love, and instead I'm a widow whose husband doesn't even have the good manners to die." A thought occurred to her. "Oh, my Lord. If he had died, they'd have made me a widow forever: The People's Relict would be given a peerage and do good works from the House of Lords. A living memorial to Robert Rassendyll. An eternally burning suttee."

"I can't stay," I said. "I'm not Robert."

"I could come with you!" she whispered very low, and then turned away. "I know… I don't mean it. There's no place but England for people like me. When it dies, we die." She fell on me, and my shirt was wet with tears.

"I did love him. I did. Nobody believes that now. Everybody thinks it was a deal, like all the other deals he did – the deal with Rupert, with the Lib Dems, with the DUP, with the Taliban, with the WHO, with Bill Gates. And they all assume mine was the original deal, with the perfect political armpiece. But I loved him."

She shuddered, wrapping her arms around herself, and then smoothing them out on her robe. "Public figures become their own caricatures," said Wendy, bitterly. "Even minor ones, like the wife of the Prime Minister. Robert became the creature of minders and spinners and a walking anthology of half-a-dozen stupid telly jokes about him. And that's all anybody wants until they get bored with you, and look for next season's running joke." She pressed her fingertips to the window. "But I remember a boy I saw on the other side of the room at a party a long time ago, with silly teenage hair and a striped blazer with a purple T-shirt that he thought was a cool look. And the next day we went to a pub on the river, and had a 'Ploughman's Lunch' and made jokes about it. And I was so in love. The love that aches inside you when you're apart." She shivered.

"But he loved politics. So we were apart a lot. And then we were apart even when we were together." She fiddled with a button. "And years later, just when you think there is no Robert, that he has ceased to exist, someone real turns up again one morning." She moved her hand from the window to the sill, and steadied herself. "But he doesn't exist either."

For Fritz and Roger, it was all about "honour". Very Ruritanian, very English, but not very me. Play with a straight bat? Is that what they say? I was false to all that I should have held by. Not cricket. Her wondering eyes turned back to me, and I grew ashamed. She drew herself away from me and stood against the wall, while I sat on the edge of the sofa, trembling in every limb, knowing what I had done – and loathing it.

"I can't remember the last time Robert and I danced together. But I remember the last time *we* danced together…" Her face was away from me, but I saw the tears roll down and fall from her cheek. I turned away and clutched the sofa with my hand.

For a long time, neither of us spoke.

"Can't we stay together?" she whispered.

I hung my head. "I can't pretend to be someone else for the rest of my life."

"You don't have to," she said. "That was the genius of it. You took Robert's hollow shell and filled it up with you, and people loved it."

"I can't…"

"Then I'll come with you. We'll go to Ruritania and live in a flat. But don't leave me here." She looked empty, as if she were now the shell.

"We would be living in madness," I said.

She stood up and pointed at a sixth or seventh earl above the fireplace. "It's like a family legend Robert told me on my first visit

THE PRISONER OF WINDSOR

here, walking through the long gallery looking at the portraits. A cousin or brother of his great-great-whatever. A dashing adventurer and the princess whose heart he won. But it's not my story, is it?"

She came near me and reached out her hand.

"Honour binds a woman too, doesn't it? So my honour lies in keeping faith with my country and with what you've done for it," she said. "I can endure it. I can endure anything." She pulled away, and slumped down on the sofa. "I wonder what life we might have had had I seen you across the room at that party in Oxford."

"You would have loathed me at eighteen."

"Leave me," she said. "Free yourself."

"I can't. You saw Sanjay outside. I'm a prisoner."

"I know a way. I'll help you. And, when you're gone, there'll be only one Rassendyll left. So Robert will have to drop all this Disney-voiceover cock-and-bull and get back on the job."

The door opened, and there was Sanjay. "Sir Roger wondered whether there was a problem, sir?"

"No, no problem," said Wendy. "Let's go upstairs, Robert."

When we reached the bedroom door, she said, "Stay." And then added: "I don't mean…"

"I know," I said, softly.

She got back into bed, and I held her as she sobbed softly and stroked her hair until at last she was asleep. And then I extricated myself and kissed her gently and went to the couch. I put a cushion under my head and stared at the ceiling and its odd elusive shadows until I fell into a fitful doze.

Chapter Fifty-Three
The last secret passageway

WE SPENT SUNDAY at Chequers, pottering. Wendy said no more about her plan of escape, but Sir Roger came by, and was relieved to find me giving a quickie radio interview to LBC about my forthcoming bill on vaccine compensation. We discussed a further cabinet reshuffle, and I asked him whether he wanted to be Deputy Prime Minister, with a peerage perhaps. He left unsuspecting.

By dusk, I was wondering what Wendy's plan was, but she remained silent and we had a quiet dinner in front of a big telly retrospective on Coronation Week. At the end of the show, she rose, stretched and yawned for the benefit of Mrs Delancey. "What a week!" she said. "What a month! Methinks an early night is called for." We trudged up the stairs to find two protection officers waiting in the corridor. Safely in the prime ministerial bedroom, Wendy turned the key.

"Fancy a nightcap?" she brayed, and then, sotto voce, "One for the road." I still had no idea what she had planned. I was both anxious to go and desperate to stay, and I spilled the cognac as I poured. Neither of us knew what to say, so we busied ourselves raising tumblers and adjusting hair. "I do love you," Wendy said, softly. "No, I don't. How could I? I don't know you, do I? But I love how you made me feel." She stood up. "Thank you for that. Maybe I'll stand for the leadership."

She opened the door to the Prime Minister's dressing-room. Inside hung a long shapeless coat and a countryman's hat that I remembered her packing at Burlesdon. "These will do," she said. "You've met Peter Borrodaile, haven't you?"

I said I had.

"Awful man. But he does love to show off. He was here one weekend shortly after Robert became PM, and started telling a story from his dictator-flack days. Arafat was meeting with Tony Blair, and Peter had to smuggle in two Romanian rent boys to get Yasser through the weekend. He got a little over-excited with one of them. Poor lad had to be discreetly evacuated. Robert asked how he got Arafat's Romanian twink off the premises, and Peter put a finger to his lips and took us in here." She pulled away Rassendyll's suits to reveal the back wall of the dressing room, and then methodically ran her hand over every panel of the wainscoting. "I'm rather amazed this has survived EU building code regulations," she muttered. At the ninth panel, she stopped, gave a gentle push, and, with an almighty creak, a section of wall swung back and a clammy rush of cold air swept into the room. The opening revealed a narrow set of stairs.

Of course. The only possible escape: my last secret tunnel.

"A predecessor of yours," said Wendy, "knew this way well."

She went back to the bedroom and returned with a candlestick from the armoire, which she presented to me, along with some terse instructions.

"I won't come any further," she said. "Better to stay here and bang around a bit to throw them off the scent."

I hugged her, awkwardly, and kissed her cheek. "Wendy..."

"Oh, Robert," she sighed.

And so Rudy Elphberg never even got his big farewell scene.

I squeezed through the opening, down the steep stairs, and into a dank passageway beyond, descending further into the depths, as its clammy walls closed in, and icy droplets plopped on my hat. I walked two hundred metres through that grim tunnel before I was stopped by a partial cave-in. I held the candlestick high, and decided I could move enough stones to get through.

On the other side, it was even colder. To warm my spirits, I thought of her. Beyond the tunnel, I had no great plan to execute, except a vague scheme to head for the East Coast and return home via a freighter for Rotterdam, or Hamburg. If, that is, trading ships still plied the seas after the Europocalypse I had rained down on the Continent.

As Wendy had promised, the tunnel ended in a short flight of stone steps worn down by centuries of English intrigue. At the top of the steps was a stout oak door. I held my candle up above the header, ran a hand through the grime, and found a rusted key. It was stiff but it worked. On the other side of the door, a few more steps climbed up to a rusted grate and a rotted wooden bulkhead. I pushed it open and found myself in the cool summer air of the English countryside. The bulkhead had a thatched exterior covered in moss. When you closed it, it blended perfectly into the undergrowth. I snuffed the candle, and with it my brief prime ministership of the United Kingdom.

I was on a country lane. About a quarter mile ahead were the first twinkling lights of a village. As I got nearer, I could hear voices. A Coronation "street party". They were in the middle of a beery singalong of that song I'd heard a few nights ago:

We'll meet again
Don't know where
Don't know when...

But I knew Wendy and I would never met again. From the party came shouts and whoops and then more singing:

There'll always be an England
And England shall be free
If England means as much to you
As England means to...

But people didn't seem to know the words, and the song petered out, and the next thing you know everyone was bellowing something about a postman called Pat with his black-and-white cat.

Because of the singing, and the rustle in the trees, I didn't hear her at first. It must have been the second or third cry:

"Rudy!"

I knew who it was – even though she'd never called me that before.

"Rudy!" she said again.

What lay on the road ahead, beyond the village? Some voiceover work in Modenstein?

What lay behind me?

She was closer now. "Rudy..." Softly this time.

I started to turn...

THE END

Anthony Hope's Ruritania

The Prisoner of Zenda (1894)
The Heart of Princess Osra (1896)
Rupert of Hentzau (1898)

~

STAGE ADAPTATIONS

The Prisoner of Zenda (play by Edward Rose, 1895)
Rupert of Hentzau (play by Anthony Hope and Edward Rose, 1899)
Princess Flavia (operetta by Sigmund Romberg and Harry B Smith, 1925)
Zenda (musical by Vernon Duke, Martin Charnin et al, 1963)

~

FILM ADAPTATIONS

The Prisoner of Zenda (starring James K Hackett, 1913)
The Prisoner of Zenda (starring Henry Ainley, 1915)
Rupert of Hentzau (starring Gerald Ames, 1915)
The Prisoner of Zenda (starring Lewis Stone, 1922)
Rupert of Hentzau (starring Lew Cody, 1923)
The Prisoner of Zenda (starring Ronald Colman, 1937)
The Prisoner of Zenda (starring Stewart Granger, 1952)
The Prisoner of Zenda (starring Peter Sellers, 1979)
The Prisoner of Zenda (animated version, 1988)

Coming soon

Rupert of Henley
by Mark Steyn

MARK STEYN RETURNS...

......*with a brand new* Tale for Our Time *every month at* SteynOnline.com/tfot